THE KAT SEVERN CHRONICLES

DEBUTANTE WARRIOR

PAUL E MASON

The Kat Severn Chronicles
DEBUTANTE WARRIOR

Published by Fast-Print Publishing

PRINTING HISTORY

Mass-market, paperback format, evaluation copy, limited run
September 2010
Mass-market, paperback format, January 2013

Cover design by Packard-Stevens Photography & Paul E Mason
Cover photography by Packard Stevens Photography, London
Interior layout by Paul E Mason.

ISBN: 978 – 1 -78035 - 2619

Printed by
Printondemand-Worldwide,
Peterborough, Cambridgeshire PE2 6XD

PRINTED IN THE UNITED KINGDOM

PART ONE

THE KAT SEVERN CHRONICLES

PART I

DEBUTANTE WARRIOR

DEBUTANTE:

"A young woman who is being introduced into 'polite society' by appearing at a formal social event for the first time, or to show or perform publicly for the first time."

WARRIOR:

"A person experienced in, or capable of engaging in combat or warfare."

By the beginning of the twenty-second century the world had changed. Climates, nations, politics, all were in a state of upheaval. Much of the Earth, devastated from years of nuclear conflict, was still a contaminated wilderness.

From this decay rose a new order. Those who had survived the conflict and their descendants now built a new life, crowding into a few gigantic cities.

For the vast majority, just existing day-to-day was hard enough; but a twisted few, some living in highly privileged circumstances, plotted to over-turn the new order and fragile peace, and return to a state of global conflict. Their reasoning defying any sane mind.

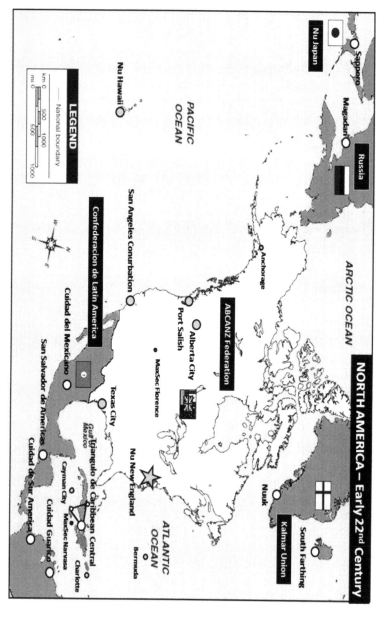

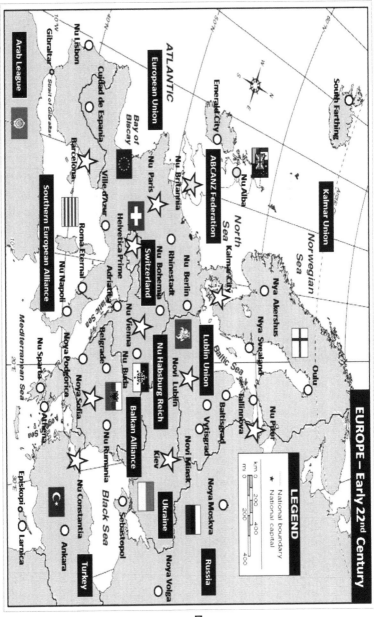

ONE : ONE

"There's a terrified child up there."

Commander Ellis's deep voice reverberated off the metal walls of the *Berserker's* launch bay. Troopers that a few moments earlier had been intent on checking their armoured suits, their weapons, even their souls, for this rescue mission, now hung on his every word. Ensign Kat Severn divided her attention; part of her stood back, studying the impact of his words on the men and women she would soon lead. In her short twenty-two year life, she'd heard a lot of fancy oratory. The other part of her listened to the Commander's words, felt them roll over her, into her. It has been a long time since mere words had raised the hairs on the back of her neck, had motivated her to want to inflict some serious pain on the bad guys.

"The local Law Enforcement Officers have tried to get her back," he paused. "They failed, so now they've called for the dogs."

The Land Force troopers around Kat growled for their skipper. She had only worked with them for three days; only since the *Berserker* had left its home base in Bermuda at two hours notice, short of around fifteen percent of the crew and without a Land Forces Lieutenant to command this rescue mission. And so a newly commissioned Fleet Ensign named Katarina Severn found herself surrounded by Land Force troopers, all with two to ten years service in the military, all champing at the bit to do something defined and dangerous.

"You've trained, you've sweated," the Commander's words had the rhythm of a machine gun. "You've trained for this moment since you joined up. You could rescue that little girl with your eyes closed."

In the red light of the launch bay, eyes gleamed with inner fire. Jaws tensed, hands closed in fists. Kat glanced down; so were hers. Yes, these troopers were ready, all except one new

Ensign. *Dear God, don't let me screw this up,* Kat prayed silently.

"Now go, kick some terrorist butt, and put that child back in her mother's arms where she belongs."

"Ooh-rah," came back from ten very hyped-up men and women as the Commander slowly walked for the exit. *Well, nine hyped Land Force troopers and one very scared Fleet Ensign.* Kat put the same angry confidence into her shout as she heard from the others. Here there was none of the calm of her father's political speeches. This was why Kat had joined the Fleet. Here was something real; something she could get her hands on, her teeth into, something real and something she could make happen. No more endless talk with nothing being done. She grinned. *If you could see me now, Father. You said the Fleet was a waste of time, Mother. Well, not today!* Kat took a deep breath as her squad turned back to their preparations. The smell of armoured suits, ammunition, gun oil and honest human sweat gave her a rush. This was her mission, her squad, and she would see that the little girl got home, safe and sound. This child would live.

As the memory of another child rose to fill her mind's eye, Kat stomped on the thought. She dared not go there, not now.

Commander Ellis paused right in front of her. Eye to eye, he leaned into her face. "Keep it together, Ensign," he growled in a whisper. "Trust your instincts, trust your people and trust Sergeant Jones. These people are good. The Squadron Commander thinks you have what it takes, even if you are one of those damn Severns. So show me what you've got. Take those bastards down, and take them down hard. If you don't think you can pull this off, let Sergeant Jones know before you screw it all up, and he'll complete the mission, and I'll drop you back home to your mother in time for the next debutante ball."

Kat stared back at him, her face frozen, her gut a throbbing knot. He'd been giving her a hard time ever since she first came aboard, never happy with her, always picking at her, never satisfied. She would show him. "Yes, sir," she shouted back in his face.

Around her the troopers grinned, assuming the Commander had a few choice words for the newly commissioned Ensign, none knowing just how choice. He scowled, all she'd ever seen on his face since coming aboard.

It wasn't her fault her father had been the Prime Minister of the ABCANZ Federation for the past eight years. She had nothing to do with her grandfather splashing the family name through all the history files. Let the Commander try growing up in shadows like those. He'd be as desperate as Kat was to make *her* own name, find *her* own place. That was why she'd joined the Fleet.

With a shiver Kat tried to shake off the fear of failure. She turned to face the bulkhead and began wriggling into the top half of the standard-issue, one-piece, chameleon-armoured battle suit. At one-point-eight-three metres tall she'd always had her civilian wet-suits tailor-made, making sure there was always enough room and flexibility for her personal self-learning computer, or HI, to conform around her neck and right shoulder. But civilian suits weren't made from a semi-rigid Kevlar, carbon-fibre and titanium mesh composite over a centimetre thick.

The HI manufactures retailed their top model, client-tailored and bespoke-built , as the 'sAPPHIre,' or: s-Advanced-Personal-Processing-Heuristic-Intellect-re. To Kat she was just 'Safi' and was probably worth more than all the computers on the *Berserker* combined and was certainly fifty times more capable. Land Force personnel were expected to be lean as well as mean, nothing extra was allowed, anywhere, but as Kat's armoured suit was sized for a man of one-point-eight-three metres, it gave her just enough space in the chest area to reposition and secure Safi. Sealing herself into the tight suit, she rotated her shoulders, bent and stooped. Yes, that worked. She put on her helmet, dropped the visor, checked the breather. It was all a bit warm, but she'd been warm, if not hot, before.

> *"Kitty-Kat, can I have an ice-cream?" Louis whined. It was a hot summer day in Nu New England, and they'd run to the park, leaving Tallulah, or Lula, their nanny cum au-pair, well behind them.*
>
> *Kat fumbled in her pocket. She was the big sister; she was expected to plan ahead now, just like big brother Edward had done for her when she*

was just a little kid. Kat had enough coins for two ice-creams. But Father insisted that planning ahead included making things last. "Not now," Kat insisted, "Let's see if the ducks are back."

"But I want an ice-cream now," he whined, with all the dramatics a six-year-old could muster.

"Come on, Lula's almost here. Race you to the duck pond." Which got Louis's feet moving even before Kat had finished the challenge. She beat him, of course, but only by as much as a ten-year-old big sister should beat her six-year-old kid brother.

"Look, the ducks are back," Kat pointed at the dozen or so birds. So they walked along the pond edge, not too far behind the old man with the bread who always fed the ducks. Kat was careful to keep Louis from getting too near the edge. She must have done a good job because when Lula finally caught up with them, she didn't give Kat the usual lecture about how deep the pond was.

"I want my ice-cream," Louis demanded again with the single-mindedness of his few years.

"I don't have any money," Lula insisted.

"I do," Kat said proudly. She had planned ahead, just like Father said smart people should.

"Then you go and buy the ice-cream." Lula grumbled.

Kat skipped off, so sure she would be seeing them again, she never looked back.

There was a tap on her shoulder. With another shiver, she turned to see a familiar face and raised her helmet's visor.

"Need any help?" he asked.

The launch bay was busy and noisy, and her second shiver went unnoticed. She managed a cheery, "No, I'm good, thank you," in reply. Ensign Jack Byrne was from the European Union. Born in Ireland's Emerald City to a mother of dual nationality, enabling Jack to commission into the armed forces of the ABCANZ Federation, the title by which the federal alliance between America, Britain, Canada, Australia and New Zealand was better known. Rather than hang around in Ireland, he'd joined the ABCANZ Fleet to see the world and, more importantly, get his student loans from university paid off, and thereby greatly disappoint his family, especially his grandmother, if not all of his relatives.

At Officer Training Academy (Fleet) he and Kat had passed the time swapping stories about how their parents had stormed and ranted against their career choice. Kat was surprised by how fast they became friends, with one coming from the super-sophisticated, high society of Nu New England, the other from the ultra traditional Irish working classes. Friends yes, but more than friends? No. It had never even occurred to Kat that their relationship would, could or should develop into anything more. Just friends, nothing more.

Jack waved his universal suit tester in Kat's direction. She raised her right arm for Jack to plug his black box into her issued battle-suit. While he ran the required checks, Kat dropped her visor back down and worked with Safi, running her personal computer through interface tests with the command net. Her Aunty Dee, now retired from her civil service job as head of the ABCANZ's combined Security Services, had helped Kat with Safi's interface, as she'd done with most of Kat's maths and IT homework for as long as Kat could remember. Safi lit up her helmet's head-up-display, showing every report screen authorised to a newly commissioned Ensign on a rescue mission . . . and a few it was probably better the skipper did not know she had access to. Kat and Safi finished about the same time that Jack detached his tester. She flipped up her visor again.

"The chameleon circuit is about point-five of a second below optimum, but it's within standards," Jack grumbled. The Fleet rarely met his expectations for perfection. "Your climate-control system isn't too good, either; it's not going to cool you down very well."

"I'm more worried about it heating me up. That's one cold ocean out there."

"And there's a bad gasket in there somewhere." They had been over that one before; one of her battle-suits' articulated seals had a slow leak, but every suit aboard had at least one bad seal. It was a bitter joke among the troops; good seals went to the civilian market, weak ones went to lowest-bid government contracts.

"We're not working at extreme depths, Jack, and I won't be wearing this suit for more than a few hours." Kat gave the standard reply the procurement people undoubtedly gave her father. The Prime Minister of ABCANZ Federation always accepted it. But then he didn't do sub-surface insertion missions. Today, his daughter was. "Hopefully I'll only be in here for twelve hours or so."

She turned to the 'Scuba Craft Insertion – Fast' or SCIF, an enclosed hybrid of scuba-vehicle, jet-bike and bobsleigh. The smallest sub-surface vehicle in the Fleet's inventory, and capable of transporting her and her section ashore undetected. Kat had raced the very similar, but smaller, civilian 'skiffs' for much of her high-school and university years, even winning competitions. "All checked out?" she asked, indicating the craft.

"I've tested every system four times, and it's passed four times. It will get you there." Which only left Kat struggling not to say something flippant. The Fleet trusted its people to put their butt's on the line, but not with the 'car keys.' It would be the responsibility of the helmsman on the *Berserker* to remote pilot both her and Sergeant Jones's craft to the insertion point. During this time, Kat and her nine troopers were supposed to just sit back, dumb and bored. And that wasn't the only part of the plan she would have liked to change, but newly commissioned Ensigns weren't supposed to even contemplate changing plans that their ship's skipper and Land Force sergeant had already approved.

"Help me on with the rest of my kit, Jack" she said.

Along the bay, the squad members paired up, checking each other's suits, loading them up with weapons and equipment. Lance Corporal Kaplin went down Sergeant Jones's section, Corporal Torres checked Kat's three troopers. Sergeant Jones would double check them all; Kat would then check them yet again.

Kat's kit was a slightly lighter than her colleagues, since Safi weighed-in at a third of the standard Fleet issue personal computer, while still holding all the command, control, communication and intelligence routines any officer could ever ask for. However, hanging from her armour or carefully secured within her small pack were multiple reloads for the squad grenade launcher in assorted flavours; six spare forty-round magazines for her own M37 assault rifle; as well as water, medical kit and rations. Land Force troopers never left home unless fully equipped for any eventuality.

Once loaded up, Kat rotated her shoulders, twisted her hips, checking that all was secure if not desperately comfortable, and that there were no problems. She'd carried more weight when back-packing through the Appalachian Mountains during vacations from university. Those carefree weeks of living outside were one of the reasons she was here.

Jack eyed her as she did a deep knee squat, then bounced back up. "Are you good for this?"

"Everything is in place. Not too heavy."

"No, are *you* good for this? Rescuing an abducted kid?" His grin was gone; Jack looked serious.

"I'm up for it, Jack. Land Force personnel aside, I have the best small-arms scores on this ship, and I've got the best fitness rating, too. The Commander's right, I am the best person for this mission, and Jack, I want it. I need it."

"Ensign Byrne to the bridge," came over the ship's comm-system, ending any further conversation. Jack slapped her on the shoulder, "May the luck of the little people and God go with you," he said and headed for the hatch.

"No spare seats for either of them in a SCIF," Kat called back to him, but she was already following Sergeant Jones, rechecking her squads' equipment.

Sergeant Jones then went over her kit, and she went over his. He tightened one of her straps and growled, "You'll do ma'am." She found nothing to modify on him; and hadn't expected to. The Sergeant had practiced for this moment for over ten years. *Practiced.* This was his first 'real' mission in all that time, yet that didn't seem to bother him or Commander Ellis.

"Let's do it!" Kat called to her loaned squad.

With a shout of "Ooh-rah" the two sections turned in unison to face opposite bulkheads and began boarding the two craft. Kat went down the line of her section one more time, checking their restraints and the securing of their stowed equipment as they settled into their positions aboard the SCIF. All readouts showed green. She still gave each restraint a good hard tug. That webbing strap was the only thing holding them in. Satisfied, she settled her own body into the command position of the tiny craft and stretched out her legs, carefully avoiding the control pedals. The legs of Corporal Torres, seated behind her, now surrounded her. Kat had once tried a bobsleigh. Mother had refused in horror when Kat had asked to take a run downhill. That bobsleigh now seemed spacious compared to this craft.

She rechecked to make sure her harness was firmly attached to the craft's composite hull, checked again to make sure none of her gear was out of place, then released the canopy, locking it into place. Like most other parts of a SCIF, the canopy was paper thin, but it added stealth and improved the aquadynamics of the craft when submerged. Only their suits would protect them from the pressure and coldness of the water.

The controls began to move around Kat's body. That would be the *Berserker's* helm running final tests. The sensation brought back some good memories of the times she'd had in her civilian skiff. She wiggled in her seat and felt the craft respond to her movements. This was much bigger than a single-seated racing skiff, but had the potential to be just as much fun.

Kat quickly banished her reminiscing by replaying the insertion plan in her mind as she waited. These kidnapping low-life had a simple plan. They'd snapped up the daughter of Cayman City's Governor during a school outing, then dragged the poor child off to Cayman Brac, a small island one hundred and thirty kilometres to the east of the city before anyone knew what was really happening. All approaches to the building being used by the kidnappers were exposed, booby-trapped too. So far, these bad-guys had outsmarted and killed too many good people.

Kat ground her teeth; how had punks like these got their hands on some of the most sophisticated traps and countermeasures currently available? She could understand the traps; men had always had a desire to hunt wild animals. Although she had never hunted big game herself, what really annoyed her was the legal crap used by speciality retailers to explain their sale of counter-measures and devices that were about to make her job damn dangerous. Normal, honest people didn't need electro-cardiogram jammers. Why would any good citizen need a decoy device to simulate a human heat signature?

Her suit was starting to warm up and she could already feel the sweat running down her back.

The day was so hot, the ice-cream melted even as Kat trotted back towards the duck pond. She paused just long enough to give both cones a quick lick, then felt guilty; "Louis, I've got your ice-cream," she called as she hurried on. She hurried so much that she was down the slope and halfway across the open grass to the pond before the wrongness of the situation got through to her. Kat came to a slow halt.

Louis wasn't there!

The man with the bread had fallen, half in the water. The ducks gathered around him, pecking at the fallen loaf.

Two bundles of clothes dotted the open grass. Kat recognised them as the two agents who had been with her for years, then her eyes saw Lula. She had fallen down. Her arms and legs splayed out like a rag doll. Even at ten, Kat knew that was all wrong for a real person.

She dropped the ice-creams and began to scream. Somewhere behind her, a voice shouted into his comm-link. "Agents down, Agents down. Snapdragon is nowhere in sight. I repeat Snapdragon is missing. I have visual on Tigerlily."

A flashing red light grabbed Kat's attention, yanking her back into reality. Around her the launch bay had been evacuated and was beginning to flood. Kat and her troopers now breathed only what the SCIF's limited internal tanks provided. Kat checked her readouts. Her suit was good, well as good as Fleet issue ever got. So was all her section. "All green, good to launch," she confirmed.

Once the launch bay was fully flooded and the pressure equalised, the bay doors opened and the SCIFs moved silently into the black space outside the *Berserker*'s hull. The helm let them drift for a few seconds. Kat managed to get a brief look at the submerged *Berserker* as her eyes adjusted to the darkness.

Then the SCIF came alive, the controls moved remotely as the helm began piloting both craft towards the insertion point on Cayman Brac.

As the helm was currently doing all the work, Kat decided to use the time to check the ground situation once more. "Safi, get me a satellite up-link, then display a real time feed of the target location," she said.

The building being used by the kidnappers filled her head-up-display. Several dozen human signatures showed up on the infrared scan. Six, no . . . eight, moved around the building . . . all in pairs. As per the guarantee provided with every human heat decoy sold, there was no way Kat was supposed to know that there were actually only six 'real' humans in and around the house. Thankfully, the manufacturers had so far stuck to their pledge of silence that the government had insisted from them. For ten years, no bad-guys had tumbled to the fact that thirty-seven degrees was only the average human temperature. This late in the evening most people's body heat was slipping down to thirty-six, even thirty-five-point-five.

In the upstairs rooms of the building the heat signatures of six little girls lay chained to multiple beds. Two gunmen sat at opposite ends of the landing, ready at the first sign of a rescue to run into the room that held the abducted girl and execute her. Thanks to the satellite sensors and filtering from Safi, Kat knew there was only one gunman on the landing, and which room really held the terrified girl.

Terrified. Kat ground her teeth, then looked out of the SCIF's canopy to try and make out the other craft and their surroundings. She tried hard to do anything but touch the raw nerve that took her again to her little brother's grave. At least these kidnappers hadn't deliberately concealed their victim, under a tonne of farmyard manure, with a damaged breather - the only lifeline to the world for a bound six-year-old child. Louis's abductors hadn't used technology to the degree that these kidnappers were, but the manure smell had effectively deceived the sniffer dogs, and the heat it gave off has made thermal detection ineffectual.

At school, Kat had overheard the other children talking, saying that Louis was dead hours before her parents paid the ransom. She didn't know the truth of that. There were some reports she just couldn't read, even now. Some media coverage she had never been able to sit through.

What could never be ignored were the 'what-ifs.' What if Kat hadn't gone for the ice-creams? What if the bad guys had taken down Lula, and Louis, and *Kat*? What impact would a ten-year-old girl have had on their plans?

Kat shook her head, willing away the images. Stay there too long, and tears always came.

She focused hard on the mission again. A covert night insertion inevitably worked better in stormy conditions. The darkness would hide their approach, and the rain helped to make the guards inattentive and want to stay undercover. Met-data had confirmed that there was a sixty-three percent chance of such weather conditions this evening. That was the positive side to a stormy night. The negative was the impact it had on the sea. Whilst still submerged the SCIF could usually just about accommodate such conditions, but once they broke the surface, the wind and rain could have a hugely undesirable influence on the stability of their final approach.

Kat smiled. Remembering the competitions she'd taken part in, the fast skiff racing beneath her. But her smile quickly slid into a scowl as the memories she'd been struggling to hold at bay came flooding back to her.

> *Father vanished from Kat's life the day after Louis's funeral. Off to the office before she awoke, rarely home before her bedtime.*
>
> *Mother was something else. "You've been a little savage for too long. It's time to make a proper lady out of you." That didn't get Kat off the hook for winning hockey matches for Father or showing up for his political events. But Kat had quickly discovered 'proper young ladies' not only went to ballet classes, but also accompanied Mother to afternoon teas. As the youngest at any tea party by more than twenty years, Kat was generally bored quite silly. Until she noticed that some women's teas smelled funny. It wasn't long before she got a chance to taste them. They tasted funny too . . . but they made her feel better, made the tea parties go*

much faster. It wasn't long before Kat found what was being added to the tea . . . and how to raid her parent's spirit or wine store when she got back home.

Somehow, the drinking made the days endurable. Kat didn't care when her school grades plummeted. It didn't matter; Mother and Father only frowned. By High School she was aware that other kids did fun things, like skiff riding; Kat had her bottle. Her bottle, and the pills Mother's doctor was prescribing to help her to be more 'ladylike.' Her hockey ability suffered too, with the coach sidelining her as much as possible. Monty, her chauffeur who took her to all the matches just seemed sad.

But Monty was grinning one Friday afternoon when he picked Kat up from school. "Your Grandpa James is back at the house. He's back in Nu New England for a few weeks, got meetings in The Capital." Monty added before she asked. Kat spent the drive home wondering what she'd say to a legend, straight out of history.

Mother was in such a flap she would soon make orbit, overseeing dinner preparations personally and grumbling that legends should stay back in history where they belonged. Kat was sent into the library to do her homework, but she positioned herself so she could read the screen with one eye and watch the entrance hall with the other. She wasn't at all sure what to expect. Probably someone ancient, like old Miss Greenwood who taught history and seemed so dry and wrinkled to have lived it. All of it!

Then her Grandpa Jim walked through the front doors of Bagshot. Tall and trim, gleaming in his Number Two Dress uniform, he looked like he could destroy any enemy just by scowling at them. Only he wasn't scowling. The grin on his face was infectious; Mother was right, he was totally inappropriate for a 'legend.' And at dinner, the stories he told had Kat totally enthralled. After dinner, she couldn't remember a single one of them, at least not in their entirety, but during dinner they were all funny, even those that should have been horrifying. Somehow, no matter how bad the odds were or how impossible the situation had been, her Grandpa Jim made it all sound terribly funny. Even Mother laughed, despite herself. And when dinner was over, Kat had managed to evade Mother until she'd excused herself for her weekly bridge club. Kat wanted to hang around this wondrous apparition forever. And when they were alone and he turned his full attention to Kat, she knew why kittens curled up contentedly in the morning sunshine.

"Your dad tells me you play hockey? He said, settling into a chair.

"Yes," Kat answered, seating herself most ladylike across from her grandpa and feeling very grown up.

"Your mum says you're very good at ballet."

"Yes." Even at twelve, Kat knew she wasn't holding up her end of the conversation. But what could she say to someone like her grandpa?

"I like offshore skiff riding. Have you ever been in a skiff?"

"No, some of the kids at school do it." Kat tasted excitement. Then she remembered herself. "But Mother says it's much too dangerous, and not suitable for a proper young lady."

"That's very interesting," Grandpa Jim said, leaning back in his chair and steepling his hands. "As a girl won the junior championship in San Angeles just last month. She was only a couple of years older than you."

"Really," Kat started, wide-eyed. Even from Grandpa Jim, she couldn't believe that.

"I've rented a skiff for tomorrow morning. Want to take a few runs with me?"

Kat fidgeted in her chair. "Mother would

never let me."

Grandpa sat up and leant forward, his nose only inches from Kat's. "Monty tells me your mum usually sleeps late on Saturdays. We're leaving at zero-six-hundred sharp," he whispered. Later, Kat would realise that Grandpa Jim and the family chauffeur were in collusion on this. But she had been too excited by the offer at that exact moment to make any connection.

"Could we?" Kat yelped. She couldn't remember the last time she'd been up that early on her own. She also couldn't remember the last time she hadn't done anything that wasn't on Mother's or Father's 'To-Do' List. She couldn't remember because to do that would be to remember what life was like with Louis. "I'd love to," she said.

"One thing," Grandpa Jim said, reaching across the table to take her small, soft hands in his tanned, calloused ones. His touch was almost electrifying. His eyes looked into hers, finding the true little girl, not the fake that most people saw. "Your mother is right. Skiff riding can be dangerous. So I only take people with me who are stone-cold sober. That won't be a problem for you, will it?"

Kat swallowed hard. She'd been laughing so hard at Grandpa Jim's stories that she hadn't stolen a drink at dinner. She hadn't had one since lunch time at school. Could she get through the night? "It won't be a problem," Kat assured him.

And somehow she made it. It wasn't easy; she'd woken up twice crying for Louis. But she thought about Grandpa and all the stories she had overheard from the kids at school as to how much fun skiff riding could be, and somehow Kat hadn't tiptoed downstairs to her father's bar.

She made it through the night, to stand at the top of the stairs and look down at Grandpa Jim, still magnificent, despite being out of uniform, waiting *for her on the black and white tiles of the entrance hall. With all the elegance and poise she'd learned in ballet classes, Kat went down the stairs, showing Grandpa Jim just how sober she was. His smile was a small, tight thing, not at all like the open-faced one Father flashed at all his sycophantic political cronies. Grandpa's genuine tight little smile meant more to Kat than anything she'd ever gotten from her mother or father.*

Three hours later, she was in a hired wet-suit and helmet and strapped into the front seat of a two-seater skiff when Grandpa Jim started his first run in and pulled away from the tug that had pulled them offshore. Oh, what a ride! The initial dive into the depths, the tight spiralling turns that cut across the breaking waves. The temptation came to her to pop her harness and float away in the foaming water, to drown and make whatever amends she could to dead little Louis. But she couldn't do that to Grandpa Jim, not after all the trouble he'd gone to just get her here. And the beauty of the ocean grabbed Kat, enveloping her in a cold, silent hug. The pure, clean lines of the skiff, the beautiful way it sliced through the water. She'd lost her heart . . . and maybe some of her survivors' self-loathing and guilt.

Mother was pacing the entrance hall when they returned late that evening. "And just where exactly have you been?" *was more of an accusation than a question.*

"Skiff riding," *Grandpa Jim answered as evenly as he told jokes.*

"Skiff riding!" *Mother shrieked.*

"Honey," *Grandpa Jim said softly to Kat,* "I think you'd better go to your room."

"Grandpa?" *Kat started, but Monty had taken her elbow.*

"And don't you come down before I send for

you," Mother enforced Grandpa's suggestion.

"And just what did you think you were doing with my daughter, General Severn?" Mother said coldly, turning on Grandpa.

But Grandpa Jim was already heading towards the library. "Olivia, I think it's best we have this conversation where little ears aren't listening, don't you," he said with all the calm Mother lacked.

"Monty, I don't want to go to my room," Kat argued as she and the chauffeur went up the stairs.

"It's best you do, believe me, it's best that you do," he said. "Your mother's been distraught today. There's nothing to be gained by pushing her even further."

Kat never saw Grandpa Jim again.

But a week later her sessions with the psychotherapist started.

"I don't need a head shrink," Kat told the woman on their first meeting.

"So why did you deliberately underperform in that hockey match last week?" The psychotherapist shot back.

"I didn't," Kat mumbled.

"Your coach thinks you did. Your dad thinks so too."

"How would he know?" Kat asked with all the sarcasm a twelve-year-old could muster.

"Because your chauffeur recorded the entire match," the psychotherapist replied.

"Oh."

So they talked and Kat discovered that the 'head-shrink' could be an ally, if not an actual friend or true confidant. Kat shared the fact that she wanted to do more skiff riding, but thought that Mother would never allow it. Instead of agreeing with Mother, the psychotherapist agreed that perhaps her mother should be challenged once in a while. Kat came to realise that what Mother wanted wasn't always best, and that a twelve-year-

old could have her own way, albeit very occasionally. Kat went on to win Nu New England's junior skiff riding championship eighteen months later, much to the Prime Minister's delight and her mother's abject horror.

Kat's stomach almost emptied into her throat as the SCIF flipped upside down, and began rapidly gaining speed and veering to the left, away from the insertion point.

"Hey, what's going on? Who's driving this bus?" resounded in her ears as Kat grabbed at the wildly gyrating controls. Behind her, Corporal Torres restored discipline with "Cut the chatter."

The controls fought Kat, refusing to obey. She hit the comm-link to the *Berserker*. "*Berserker*, this is Insertion Craft One, what the hell is going on, over?" Her words echoed empty inside her helmet; the data-link was dead, as she and her crew would be if she didn't do something, and fast.

Punching the manual override, Kat took command of her craft. With hardly any thought, her hands and feet went through the motions required to reduce their speed and pitch and regain control. The SCIF was heavier, slower to respond than a civilian skiff, but she fought it . . . and it eventually obeyed.

"That's better," came from the grateful troopers behind her and she turned the craft the right way up. But, unless she reduced their speed and figured out where they were, this momentary 'better' would just mean they were marginally more comfortable when fuel, air or both inevitably ran out.

"Safi, I need the navigation reconfigured into a civilian skiff's format, and I need it now." In a blink, the more familiar routines took shape within her head-up-display. "Interrogate GPS. Where are we?" The craft became a green dot in her display, vector lines then extended, followed by depth references and coast lines. Still their speed was increasing, despite Kat's efforts to slow them down.

"Corporal, try and get me a visual on Sergeant Jones's craft."

"I've been trying, ma'am, but I don't know where he is."

Her HI could probably tell Kat where the Sergeant was in

respect to them, but Safi was busy trying to plot a course that would win Kat another championship.

They didn't hand out skiff riding trophies just for hitting the beach at the right spot. They expected winners to do it in style, be on the dot, use less fuel, less air and take less time. Kat gulped as her head-up-display filled with the extreme challenge ahead. Their SCIF was out of position and lower on fuel and air than any skiff she'd ever raced during a competition. It would take every gram of skill Kat had to land her section anywhere near dry land, let alone in the vicinity of one terrified little girl.

Kat had ridden for many trophies. Tightening her grip on the controls, she began a race for a little girl's life.

ONE : TWO

Acting more on trained instinct than rational thought, hands and feet firmly operating the controls, Kat managed to finally stabilize the craft. That done, she then used Safi to work out a way of getting herself and her troops safely ashore. Thankfully she'd kept Safi and refused the Fleet's standard-issue computer with its long list of limitations. "Safi, based on our present location, and using the building the kidnappers are located in as the target, give me a low-risk insertion plan." Safi did so in under a second; Kat could get them in safely, but they'd be down by the island's small airstrip and more than fifteen kilometres from the target.

Even as Kat adjusted their course to conform to that proposal, she snapped, "That's no good. Assume I can reduce twenty percent of this velocity by increasing hydrodynamic friction. How much breathable air will that leave us?" She also had to have a Manoeuvring-Safety-Zone (MSZ). Sergeant Jones's craft was hopefully somewhere off to her right, probably no more than a kilometre away, with a bit of luck much less. Two hundred metres was the normal acceptable safety zone if the helm of the *Berserker* had been remote piloting both of them in to their insertion point as originally intended, but not now, not with Kat's craft careering about all over the place, outside of helm control.

"Safi, add in the assumption that I need a three hundred metre MSZ from Sergeant's Jones's craft." In a fraction of a second Safi modified the plan, but the result flashed red. Even assuming Kat was eventually able to cut their speed back to almost nothing there was no way she could dissipate it quickly enough. She'd still overshoot the target by a good ten klicks if not more, and then wouldn't have enough fuel or breathable air to make it ashore.

"Bring up my alternative insertion plan. Assume a three

hundred metre displacement from the other SCIF," Kat ordered. A spiralling, braking role to reduce their speed would be needed and would have to be away from Jones's craft and back out into deeper water. Safi quickly generated the requested alternative insertion plan, then over-laid Kat's updated parameters. Kat reviewed the data, thinking it quickly through: yes, she could make this work. An amber button on her head-up-display flashed a warning at this new proposal. Their air reserve would be below the emergency safety level required for competitive standards; she would be disqualified.

With a rueful shrug for the computer's concern, Kat said, "Let's do it, Safi," and settled in for the ride of her life.

Very early on, Kat had quickly learned that every computer-generated course could be improved upon by a human, how else had she won the trophies scattered around her bedroom back home.

"Sir, I mean ma'am, I think I see the sergeant's craft," Corporal Torres voice was a series of nervous squeaks and cracks.

Kat was rooted to the machine. Her hands had merged with the controls; her body becoming one with the hull. Kat's eyes might as well have been the displays indicating attitude, depth, external hull pressure and speed. To break concentration would be agony. "Where, Corporal?"

"Off to starboard, one, no, two o'clock, ma'am slightly ahead of us. I think that's him, ma'am," said Torres, using the 'clock face' method of target identification, with 'twelve' being straight ahead.

Kat risked a quick glance. Yes, there was a SCIF, a bit ahead, matching their course. "Try to get comms with them," she ordered and went back to piloting a miracle.

"All I'm getting is broken up with static, ma'am, it's unworkable."

It was time to seriously reduce their speed and get this show back on the road. She turned the craft, pointing its nose away from the shore, then ordered them all to hang on. Torres made several more attempts to contact Sergeant Jones, but still got only static. Kat told him to stop trying.

Now came the hard part. Diving down, Kat plunged her craft even deeper. Then she put the craft into a gentle - maybe not so gentle - spiralling role, increasing the hydrodynamic friction, in an attempt to bleed off some of the excess energy. Only the craft's thin hull and canopy was between the ocean and their very vulnerable bodies. If you cut a spiralling role too tight or too fast, the water turbulence it generated could take the craft apart, and the crew with it. Cut it too loose and she could potentially lose control and overshoot by several kilometres, or worse, impact with the seabed. Kat had learned these moves when it had been just a fun past-time, then a competitive sport, while riding the best skiff money-could-buy back in Nu New England. Now Kat twisted her craft over on one side, then the other - a craft she knew nothing about.

Kat had checked over the craft. No rider would ever put their body into a skiff without first giving it a thorough check over, but she had never actually ridden it before! She recognised the manufacturer's name emblazoned on the dashboard interior. They had a good reputation, however military adaptations of civilian craft usually went from one extreme to the other. Either they were enhanced way beyond any civilian specification, or the military procured the cheapest, no-frills, bargain-basement model available and usually at a hugely inflated price. Kat had no way of knowing which this was. Her stomach twisted into knots as tight as her grip on the controls. Was this craft one of their top-end models or the low-spec, low-tech version? Was there a fundamental flaw somewhere in the hull or in the hydroplane roots? If Kat pulled too many g's, risked too much hull pressure, would she break its back - send them all tumbling to a watery death?

She forced herself to complete calm: much better to feel every groan, every moan from the craft's tortured structure, as she pushed it to its limits. Behind her a trooper broke into an unfamiliar prayer, appealing to his creator. "Someday we'll all laugh about this," Kat muttered on an open mike. *If we live*, she added only to herself.

The interior of the craft was now cold. Despite limited insulation, Kat could feel the cold passing through the hull, then her suit, rising up to chill, then freeze into her body. The temperature gauge confirmed this; it was well into the manufacturer's warning zone. Out of the corner of her eyes, Kat measured the extra flex in the short wing-like hydroplanes, the growing vibration along their trailing edges.

Still, Kat demanded more. Stopping the roll, she flipped the craft over and brought it round in a tight arc, under the theoretical line above them where she'd started this manoeuvre. Their position was still wrong, and still way too fast to achieve the optimal inbound approach vector. Kat turned the craft back over, then dropped even further into the depths.

Having now re-positioned them onto a better approach vector, although still a long way from an optimal one, she still had to address their speed. She muscled the craft into another spiralling and braking roll. As tight as she had ever dared in a civilian skiff, and managed to bleed-off a bit more of their speed. Kat fidgeted in her position as her skin got colder and colder. The temperature readout confirmed the complaints of her own flesh, as it passed deeper to the danger red zone, or was it the 'extremity blue zone.' She knew she was pushing it, but not too far, providing there were no unwelcome surprises hidden in the structure of the craft surrounding them.

"Er, excuse me, ma'am," Corporal Torres whispered softly into her earpiece, "my check-back says your suit temperature is bordering hypothermia onset, it's dangerously cold. You really must switch its heater unit on, ma'am."

Kat came back to herself just long enough to action the Corporal's advice. Damn it, her civilian suit back home would have done that automatically, maintained an ideal body-temperature. But military suits were intentionally dumb. A Staff Sergeant at OTA(F) had explained, "You don't want them doing anything without your permission, especially when unfriendly folks are shooting and all hell's broken loose around you."

"Can you still see Sergeant Jones?" Kat asked Torres.

"I think he's still out there ma'am, but it's hard to maintain visual when we're in a roll and this deep down."

"Anyone seeing Sergeant Jones, give me a holler," Kat ordered, concentrating on the controls.

"Yes, ma'am," came back in a several part harmony.

It seemed like forever before the temperature gauge started to edge up. Safi tried to get a GPS update, but they were too deep to get the multiple satellite fixing signals required. The craft's internal guidance system insisted they were where they wanted to be, and Safi agreed. With a deep breath, Kat arched her back, tried to unknot every muscle in her body, and discovered it was actually a real kick riding this thing.

"I see him." Then, "There he is," chorused from behind her. "We have visual, ma'am," the Corporal confirmed.

A quick glance showed the Sergeant's craft off to their right, maybe three hundred metres away, if Kat could trust her own judgement. With the second craft within visual range, Kat let out a sigh of relief and put the controls over to manoeuvre them closer. Although still running fast, they were now at more manageable speed, just, and about fifteen minutes out from the beach. She had enough fuel and air remaining, even had a minute or two of each spare if she needed it, but with a congratulatory grin, she knew she wouldn't. A moment later, Kat spared enough attention away from her craft's controls to try calling the other SCIF.

"Insertion Craft Two, re-bro to the *Berserker* that Insertion Craft One has successfully regained control, over." Kat waited a slow count for a reply, then began to repeat her message.

"Roger, Insertion Craft One. I have visual on you. Report your status, over," was Sergeant Jones's response.

"I've lost my data-link to the *Berserker*. Can you re-broadcast me back to Commander Ellis, over?"

"I'd better, the ship's been screaming for you, over."

Kat gritted her teeth and prepared for another 'nice little chat' with her least favourite military person. She didn't have to wait very long. "So glad you could fit us into your busy social schedule," Commander Ellis's voice was full of ice. "Send sit-rep Insertion Craft One, over."

"We've lost our data-link sir. Lowest bidder, I presume." That was the skipper's perpetual moan, that and budget cuts. "Insertion Craft Two is re-broadcasting comm-signal only, back to you. We are in position to continue with hostage rescue using alternative insertion plan, over."

There was a long pause. Kat could imagine Commander Ellis reviewing the reports pouring into the *Berserker*'s bridge, weighing each one up carefully to see what would make a certain Ensign Severn's life the most miserable.

"I see that you are, Ensign," there was a shorter pause. "Ensign Byrne, can you re-establish the data-link with Insertion

Craft One?"

"Negative, sir," came back quickly. "Our data-link to that vehicle is toast, I cannot regain control."

"Then we proceed with your alternative option," the Commander said tersely.

And Kat broke into a grin.

Kat had showed up at the first planning session with Commander Ellis and Sergeant Jones loaded with questions to find the skipper grinning from ear to ear. "I knew those under-funded local LEOs would eventually call for the dogs. I pulled just about every favour I'm owed with the Squadron Commander to make sure we were the ship that got this call. Now let's make sure we do the job right."

"No problem, sir, we'll show the Fleet and those terrorists that the Berserker is the best," Sergeant Jones was grinning too.

Kat had nothing but contempt for people that abducted children. She'd attended the trial of her brother's murderers. Add up the IQ of all four of them, and you still had a negative number. However: "Sir, these terrorists have plenty of specialist gear," Kat pointed out. "They've taken out three rescue attempts."

"They were civilian teams. Now they face the ABCANZ Military." Sergeant Jones's voice was deadly cold, deadly serious.

"A bunch of scruffy, unshaven terrorist can't stand against what the Berserker is about to bring to this party," Commander Ellis said with confidence, then laid out his plan. A fast, stealth night insertion would enable the Land Force troops to get right into the kidnappers backyard. The troopers could then go straight to work. Kat swallowed hard and pointed out that a similar approach had been used in the last hostage rescue. She hoped that would lead their thought process to the obvious question, "Do we dare try the same on a group with this much tech support, shouldn't we perhaps consider an alternative?" She

might as well have saved her breath.

"It worked, didn't it?" Sergeant Jones snapped. "Ten dollars says we can beat the time, from hitting the beach to the last shot being fired, for that hostage rescue in Nu Hawaii last year that the crew of the corvette Maori *pulled off."*

"I've already bet the Maoris' *skipper a case of champagne that we do," Ellis grinned. Faced with that kind of confidence, Kat swallowed her own reservations. The three of them did a thorough review of all the intel available. It showed no problems for a fast, close-in insertion followed by a direct assault; the skipper approved of Sergeant Jones's tactics. And Kat said, "Aye aye, sir," like a good, newly commissioned Ensign should . . . then went looking for Jack.*

But if Kat now used the Commander's original plan, at their current speed, she would almost certainly plough a very noisy furrow up the beach and wake the sleeping beauties atop the nearby bluff. Kat had half expected orders to just keep piloting the craft and let Sergeant Jones take over the actual insertion. But apparently the High Command was truly averse to having heavily armed Land Force troopers wandering around without an officer present.

"Alternative insertion plan it is, sir," Sergeant Jones replied over the net. Kat acknowledged him too, all grin out of her voice.

Commander Ellis cleared his throat. "One last thing before we cut this link. I am required to remind you all that this is not a classic 'find-fix-strike' mission. We have been 'invited' by Cayman City to assist their Justice Department. As such, you will operate under local law enforcement procedures and protocols. I expect you to take prisoners, not come back with a body-count. Ellis out."

Kat keyed her mike. "You heard the Commander. These low-life scum have the right to face a jury of their peers. The people of Cayman City will decide their fate, not you." Kat had done a search; Cayman City still had the option of capital punishment on its statute books. Kat's father had almost lost his chance at the Prime Minister's job because of the tactics he used to delay Nu New England's abolition of the death penalty, just long enough for Louis's murderers to hang. Strange, Kat could never think of little Louis suffocating, but she had no trouble with his murderers dangling at the end of a rope.

Done with the talk, Kat slightly reduced the depth of her craft. A moment later the satellite data-feed lit up as 'active' in her visor's display. The tasked satellite was still on-call, and showed her the target location. Its sensors reported everything was still quiet. "Insertion Craft Two, can Ensign Byrne get a fix on me with any of the *Berserker's* sensors, over?"

After a short pause, whilst Sergeant Jones consulted with the ship, he responded. "Yes, ma'am, he confirms his sensors have you, over."

"Tell him to instruct the remote Helm; tuck you in behind me, as close as the MSZ programming permits. I'm heading for the alternate insertion point, six klicks west of the target building, over."

The pause was short. "Ensign Byrne confirms Insertion Craft Two will conform to your movements, out."

That would take some serious concentration if not ability from whoever was remote piloting the other craft.

The met-data had forecast a stormy night, and Kat's immediate objective was to get them ashore, across the beach and road and into the scrub forest as quickly as possible. The last weather update before launch had advised that two, maybe three nasty-looking storm fronts were moving their way. "Safi, see if you can connect to a weather satellite," *Interesting, the SCIF's data-link to the Berserker is apparently fried, but my own, civilian-spec up-link is working fine, even at this depth.*

The latest met-data imagery was inconclusive, but showed that most of the stormy weather would now miss them, although some rain, likely to be heavy, would almost certainly catch them at some point during the night. From behind her, troopers provided a chorus of groans, grumbles and in general, a wish that if bad weather was on-route they wanted to get out of this tin-can and onto dry land without undue delay, as a SCIF on the surface was no place to be in inclement weather.

At one kilometre out from the beach they silently re-surfaced and began their final run in. Still moving much faster than Kat would have ideally liked, the craft was cutting through the waves rolling towards the beach. Rather than letting the waves do most of the work to propel them towards the shore, their speed meant this was unlikely to be the stealth insertion desired, but their options had become somewhat limited. Corporal Torres reported the second craft was still right behind them.

The craft hit the sand hard with a noisy thud, but no one said anything as their training took over. The canopy retracted and the Land Force troopers exited fast, two from each side, dropping clear of the hull into the waves breaking over the pale sand. Under the Corporal's direction the troopers quickly secured the landing site.

Once she received the nod from Torres, Kat hit her restraint release. Still in the position required to pilot the craft she moved over the side and into the water, the last to leave the SCIF.

She then stood, and ran up the wet sand to join the Corporal in the tree-line. Wow, she felt good, a higher adrenaline rush beyond any race. She lifted her visor and drew a deep breath of air, laden with the smells of the sea, the Caribbean, the night. If felt wonderful to be alive.

Once Torres had cracked a cyalume stick to give Sergeant Jones a landing reference, he and two troopers began hauling the SCIF up the beach and into the tree line, with the third trooper and Kat, keeping them covered as they worked. She studied her squad as they stamped their feet, still trying to restore circulation and get warm, then re-checking their weapons and associated systems, bringing them back on-line.

"Okay, we're alive and back on dry land. I know a little girl who could use a big hug about now, and some low-life who need a good kicking. Let's move out."

The four Land Force personnel returned grim, determined nods.

I'm coming Louis, I'm coming.

Unlike Kat's craft, Sergeant Jones's slid to a silent stop on the sandy beach sixty metres from her. As he and his section disembarked, Kat ran over to them, stepping over driftwood and the half-eaten remains of several large stingray. She had Safi transmit her alternate overland approach route across to the Sergeant. Despite the darkness, the overcast sky and the supposed 'chameleon' circuit within their suits, their bodies still stood out in stark contrast against the light sand.

Long before the call came for the *Berserker* to drop everything and leave for the Caymans, Kat had already been following the kidnapping. It had been the number-one media event for the last few weeks right across the Federation. The betting on Bermuda had been two-to-one that they would shout for the military after the second attempt went pear-shaped. Kat had put these bets down more to hope than expectation. Then, when the third attempt by local LEOs to storm the location where the hostage was being held had also ended in failure, Kat knew the situation couldn't go on and the military would have to be called in. The third attempt had ended when two of the best local trackers had fallen from the limestone cliffs after being deceived by an impressive series of counter-detection devices. They had been over a kilometre away from the true target location, but it was still the nearest any of the local LEOs had ever got. Although she had speculated that the military would inevitably get the call to assist, Kat had never considered that it would be the *Berserker* that would answer it, or that she would actually be leading the rescue mission. But as a Senior NCO Instructor at OFA(F) had growled, "Ours is not to reason why, ours is but to do or die, or fill out the paperwork."

So Kat had spent every waking moment for the last three days either preparing her squad or planning the mission. Sergeant Jones and Commander Ellis had opted for shock tactics, a fast insertion followed by a direct assault. So Kat duly prepared for a fast insertion and a direct assault. But, one of her father's rules was to always have a contingency plan up your sleeve. With little spare time on her hands, she had drafted in Jack to help identify any alternative options.

> "That scrub forest looks heavy going," Jack said, studying the satellite feed of the area they were intending to insert into.
> "It's summer-time. Sub-tropical scrub forest is always hard going at any time of year, but especially

in the summer. The computer says it's well within standards. You don't trust the computer's standards?" Kat asked with a smile and a nudge in Jack's ribs.

"Nope," Jack answered without looking up. "If someone other than me has fed the computer with the data on which it bases its 'standards,' then why would I believe what it tells me?"

"So you'd place your trust with the little people, but not with computers."

"And didn't my ma tell me just that?" he answered without as much as a blink.

"Find me an alternate place to insert," Kat said.

"You could insert on this beach, and then tab in from there," Jack pointed out.

Kat had already been studying the beaches along the island's southern shoreline and the ground between them and the target location: a building about a kilometre east of the lighthouse on the south-eastern cliff-top. This section of ironwood and cactus scrub has the same electronic signature as the places where the local LEOs had got themselves killed. She had analysed the three locations where the Cayman City Justice Department teams had died in-detail. Their bodies were still there: no one would risk bringing them out.

Kat pursed her lips, continuing to study the satellite imagery, looking for something that perhaps the local Law Enforcement Officers had missed. Unlike some city kids, Kat had no illusions about 'Mother Nature' in the raw. She'd spent her last summer at university, when not running her brother Edward's election campaign, hiking in the mountains on the western boundary, or city-limits of Nu New England.

"There," said Jack, pointing at the screen. There was a suitable natural egress from the beach, across a single-track road then into the tree-line. It was then a hard, but achievable, six kilometre cross-country approach through the scrub forest to the

*target building. It then took Kat another thirty
minutes to input all the finer details of this
alternative plan into Safi's memory.*

Kat explained her intended alternate route to Sergeant Jones.
He nodded. "Far from easy going, but none of us joined up for
easy," he commented.

Kat signalled her corporal over. "Corporal Torres, locate
the start-point for the route I've just fed into your visor head-
up." It was nearly twenty-two hundred and the overcast sky was
already a deep black as Kat's two sections finished concealing
the craft in the tree-line and headed off into the scrub forest.
The going was painfully slow. Despite this, the chameleon
circuits on their armoured suits still struggled to match the
constantly changing topography. One trooper's suit completely
gave up, and no matter what he tried, he remained perfectly
undetectable, if only he had been in a desert. Their suits kept
any moisture out, but provided virtually no insulation, and the
wearer soon became chilled if sufficient body activity wasn't
maintained, although this did help reduce the heat-signature
they inevitably gave off. The suit's integral heater function was
deliberately disabled for this kind of covert insertion. To make
matters even worse, the local mosquito population developed a
taste for them. Kat lowered her visor and fitted her breather,
with the others soon following her example. Breathing became
slow as they sucked against filters designed for things a lot
smaller and a lot nastier than biting insects.

By twenty-three hundred Kat's tiny command had
started to climb the 'Brac' itself, the limestone bluff that
dominated the eastern end of the island. Kat signalled a break
while she, Sergeant Jones and Trooper Chang examined the
ground ahead. Evergreen ironwood trees interspersed with huge
cactus and the occasional palm over a rocky limestone
landscape.

While the others rested, Trooper Chang did a scan for
any sign of human life, booby traps or anything that might
impede their already slow progress. Despite the thick cloud
cover, the tasked satellite continued to provide them with useful
thermal imagery. "There's nothing big out there," Chang
confirmed, transmitting his hand-held sensor data across to

Kat's head-up display to complement the satellite feed.

"Anything else?" she asked.

"Plenty of small to medium reptilian stuff, some similar sized feathered and furry, and some big rats, 'agouti' I think they're called, that's about it."

Kat curtailed his report with a "Thanks, that's enough for now."

The break seemed to have refreshed her team. Kat's own legs had gone from screaming to just hurting. *I've got to spend more time in the gym if I'm going to hang about with Land Force types.*

No star or moon light penetrated the storm clouds as Kat and the troops moved off again. Chang kept his sensors active, to alert them if they detected any human presence, but it was nature that got them. It started to pour with rain, heavy tropical rain, making just about everything slippery. Twice a trooper went down. One was just embarrassed by her fall; the other ended up having to activate the pressure bandage in his suit's ankle. He continued with a limp, teeth gritted against the pain.

An hour later, just as the rain intensified even further, Kat signalled another halt. They were about two hundred metres back from where the scrub had been cleared and a more formal, lawned area had been laid out. Their target building lay a further three hundred metres beyond the lawns.

While her troops rested again, Kat, Sergeant Jones and Trooper Chang moved carefully forward to get an up-close and personal look at the very doors they had come to kick in.

The building was a modest two story timber structure, with a central door flanked on both sides by large, sliding picture windows that opened onto a veranda, then down a couple of steps to the lawn. To the rear, another veranda and a parking area with a dirt track. The track led back about five hundred metres to another, much larger track that ran along the entire length of the island. An infra-red scan by Sergeant Jones showed six large human-sized heat-sources scattered between front and back, however night-vision scopes showed only two of the six guards to have a real human body to go with their supposed heat. Both were sheltering under the verandas from the heavy rain.

Kat accessed the satellite feed again. Two real gunmen identified outside, one front, one back, but she also wanted a solid fix on the inside target locations too. Four in-house heat targets showed the correct temperature variations. Kat keyed her mike and whispered, "Six targets."

Sergeant Jones nodded in acknowledgment.

For another twenty minutes he and Kat studied the six as they slept. Only one, the gunman on the back veranda generated any activity, and that was only to go inside to visit the bathroom. In the house, two seemed pretty solidly asleep on beds upstairs with a third on the sofa in the main room on the ground floor. Another sat on the upstairs landing, the appointed executioner if any effort was made to rescue the girl, but he never moved from his chair. The gunman who sat on the front veranda also appeared to be fast asleep, despite the downpour.

"Pretty unprofessional," Kat observed. The negotiations had dragged on during the last week; the main sticking point was an aircraft to take them to wherever they wanted to go. No pilot wanted anything to do with them.

"If we'd followed my plan, my squad would have taken these punks down before they even knew we were here," Sergeant Jones growled.

With a shrug for what might have been, Kat waved Chang forward to examine the three hundred metres of cleared ground circling all around the building. The satellite feed continued to identify nothing interesting about this piece of open ground. However, up this close, Chang's scanner soon began to pick up the signature of several low-power energy sources.

"What are they powering?" Sergeant Jones demanded.

"I'm working on that." It took a few more minutes of fiddling with his scanner before Chang let out a low whistle. "Hyper low-powered lasers," he whispered. A moment later he had the frequencies. Kat adjusted her helmet's visor to match the frequency and found herself looking at a cat's-cradle of beams, criss-crossing the lawn, but only rising two or three metres. Nothing on the satellite would have spotted this mess. *These guys were way too over-equipped. Who the hell was funding them for the up-front costs of this job and who was behind it all, calling the shots, telling them what to do?*

Then again, Cayman City was a rich Federation Dependency, and its Governor had a wide portfolio of investments. Kat wondered who he would be meeting with tomorrow to borrow the inevitable millions demanded in ransom for his young daughter's life. Kat, raised the daughter of a cynical politician, expected there would be many persons offering help . . . for 'minor considerations.' Kat frowned; she'd never considered that point before, *so who'd offered to loan the money for Louis's ransom? And what collateral or concessions had been demanded in return?* Interesting thoughts . . . for later.

Trooper Chang was still busy; he grinned when one of his sensors started blinking in several multicoloured sequences. "I've picked up some out-gassing of plastic explosives," he whispered.

"Let me see that," Sergeant Jones snapped softly and grabbed the instrument from Chang's hand. He frowned at the gadget, tapped it on the side several times, wiped the rain from the display then studied it some more. Finally he glared at the cleared space. "I don't see any digging out there. Didn't see any on the satellite imagery. Don't see any now."

"M49 land mines. Integrated chameleon circuit like our suits?" Kat suggested as the Sergeant handed the sensor back to Trooper Chang.

"They're not on issue yet, not even to us," Sergeant Jones snapped. "They only went into full production a month or two back!" His words slowed as he fought with what he knew was possible, against what he actually saw. "Damn. If these bastards have that kind of influence?" He left the rest unsaid.

"There *are* mines out there," Chang said with certainty as he reassessed the instruments data.

"Rigged to the lasers or just pressure?" Kat asked.

"Your guess is as good as mine, ma'am; but I suggest we assume both."

Kat took a good look at the cleared area of lawn again. Removing her breather and lifting her visor, she rubbed her eyes and looked up at night sky. The rain had eased slightly; the cloud-cover was beginning to thin too, enabling the limited moonlight to briefly shine through. Thankfully there was no hint of it starting to lighten out to the east, dawn was still many hours away. True, these punks had a tendency to sleep until after the sun was up, but that was understandable, as it got light early at this time of year. But, the guards were bound to become more restless as black transitioned into grey, as the dawn inevitably approached. A single noise could easily change a sleeping guard into a shooting one and with enough daylight to see what he was actually shooting at. Kat needed to get herself and her team across the last three hundred metres and get them across fast.

She backed away, to rejoin the rest of the troopers where they had stopped to rest. "Whose laser-viewing function within their visor is not working?" she asked. A few seconds later, four very embarrassed troopers acknowledged that the very gear they had so carefully nursed into operation back in the *Berserker*'s launch bay was now just dead weight. Kat's one piece of luck was that both the limper and the one with the faulty suit camouflage were also among the laser blind; she'd only have to leave four behind.

"You four are now my fire support section. Two things you need to remember. Firstly, you will only open-fire upon the direct orders of either myself or Sergeant Jones," she told them softly, then decided it was time to make her own pre-assault statement. "And secondly, remember, we are here in a civil law-enforcement capacity. These kidnappers have the right to be tried by a jury of their peers. I believe Cayman City still has the death penalty. We will apprehend them only; the local authorities can shoot, hang, or do whatever they do here. No kill shots, if at all possible, from us."

With a contented growl, the troopers prepared to move out. Sergeant Jones's section led off, reduced to just him, Lance Corporal Kaplan and Trooper Barnard. Kat led her depleted section consisting of herself, Corporal Torres and Trooper Chang.

Lance Corporal Kaplan went first, using a hand-held sensor like Chang's to confirm when to step high to avoid laser-beams and to move left or right to avoid the land mines, in addition to everyone using the displays within their helmet visors. Kat eyed one of the indicated mines as she passed it. Its surface was a perfect match for the surrounding terrain. A shallow dish, about fifteen centimetres across and rising maybe one centimetre high, it left no shadow. It had no heat signature either, despite being baked all day in the Caribbean sunshine. Sensors and heat-exchangers within it matched the mine's external temperature to that of the land around it. Only the tiny amount of ammonia out-gassing as the explosive slowly degraded, gave away their location. Taking a data-feed from Kaplin's and Chang's sensors and with a bit of enhanced data manipulation from Safi, Kat could now see the ammonia gas plumes, along with the laser web through her visor. And now that she could clearly see them, she noted that six, no seven, were in very close proximity to her team. No footprints or digging, though. That was what they had looked for using the satellite; footprints or digging on the lawns. These mines must have been dropped from a helicopter. Again, even more expense. *So who was footing the bill for all this?*

Kat badly felt the need for a shower, some coffee, and someone to talk over what had been thrown her in the last few hours. There were patterns emerging here, patterns that needed answers, answers that were so far eluding her.

Louis doesn't need patterns solved, Louis needs rescuing.

Shaking away her thoughts, she tried hard to focus on the matter at hand. Hunched down and moving as fast as the lasers and mines would permit, she discovered a whole new meaning for 'naked' and 'vulnerable.' She watched where she stepped, she checked the satellite feed for activity in the house, she watched the sleeping guard for any hint of him waking up. Occasionally, she also remembered to breath.

Their beach insertion had taken what had seemed like a year, but Kat felt she had aged a hundred years crossing the lawn in front of the house. When finally they were close, Kat silently signalled Sergeant Jones to take his section around to the other side of the building.

From here on, she had a direct run at the central staircase and the gunman located on the landing once the door was down. Kat wanted her armour over that terrified child's body ten minutes ago. Whatever happened in the house, the only harm that would then come to this little girl would be through Kat's dead body.

Their luck ran out just ten metres from the edge of the veranda. The 'sleeping beauty' who had been on the sofa roused himself for a visit to the bathroom. He wandered in front of one of the large sliding picture windows.

"We have movement in the house," Kat whispered into her helmet-mike as a heavy-set gunman stopped in front of the window to yawn, stretch, then scratch his groin.

"Sergeant Jones, you take down the gunman on the back veranda and neutralise any targets on the ground floor. My section will concentrate on the upstairs targets." She paused, in case there were any last minute questions, just as the gunman in the picture window yanked up his weapon and went fully automatic at them, his rounds shattering the glass. "Fire support; take out guard on the veranda before he fully wakes up. Corporal Torres, you return fire on the one who's just opened up. Chang get me in there."

"Doing it," Chang whispered, inserting a grenade trailing a length of det-cord into his under-slung launcher and taking aim at the door.

Behind Kat, Corporal Torres took rounds full in the chest. The force of impact threw him back a good metre or two, and onto a mine.

"Fire in the hole," Chang shouted. His grenade launcher went off with a whoosh, lobbing a round into the door and trailing the line of explosive behind it. The door blew in, then the line-charge detonated, causing two nearby mines to blow. Waiting just long enough for the explosive to do its thing, Kat dashed for the door, went through its smoking remains and into the main downstairs room.

The stairs were ahead of her. She could not see the upstairs gunman. Off to her right the guard on the veranda was already down, but the heavy-set gunman who had originally opened fire was now taking cover behind the sofa he had slept on.

Kat wanted the upstairs gunman, not this one. The nice thing about keeping company with Land Forces troopers was that one of them was always watching your tail, always providing backup. Ignoring the gunman behind the sofa, Kat raced up the stairs, rifle ready in her shoulder.

Halfway up, the seated gunman came into view. The

racket of his colleague opening fire down stairs, and the grenade taking out the door had woken him. He stood, his eyes wide open as he saw Kat's rifle aimed right at his head. His hands came up, maybe he was going for his weapon, maybe he was just trying to fend off what he knew was coming next. It didn't matter. Kat fired.

Rounds stitched into the man's right shoulder, knocking him backwards over the chair. Kat reached the top of the stairs, stepped around the fallen gunman and chair, and headed for the far bedroom. Scream after scream came from the room; there was no doubt which one the hostage was in.

Kat hit the door and bounced off.

Chang was right behind her. He slid to his knees at the door, jammed a wad of explosive into the lock, covered it with a square of armoured cloth, and ducked his head away.

The door blew open.

Kat was moving a second after the explosion. She flew in with the door, did a quick scan with her rifle to the right and left, then dashed for a tiny figure in jeans and a filthy pink t-shirt. The girl was sitting up on the bed, yanking at the restraints and screaming at the top of her six-year-old lungs. All Kat wanted to do was hug the child to her chest, but there were procedures to follow in a situation like this. She dropped to the floor. Something small and nasty-looking was attached by wires to the underside of the bed. "Chang, we've got a bomb in here."

While Trooper Chang assessed the bomb, Kat did a further inspection of the room. What looked like the child's back-pack had been repacked with clothes and other junk. Kat decided that could be ignored for the moment. Otherwise the room was bare. Bare walls, bare floor, no furniture except the bed in the middle of the room. She turned back to the still screaming child, just as Chang finished his examination of the 'monster' under the bed.

Gunfire suddenly ripped across the landing outside the room as the two sleeping gunmen, woken by all the commotion, decided to join the party. Trooper Barnard, coming up the stairs at the same time, made short work of neutralising both of them, one fatally.

As the firing stopped, Chang reported "Bomb, rigged to the restraints on the kid. If I cut them, it goes 'boom.'"

"Then disarm it," came from Corporal Torres as he entered the room, much dirtier but apparently no worse-for-wear following his encounter with live rounds and a mine.

"You okay?" Kat asked the Corporal.

"Shaken, not stirred," he said with a grin. "Landed on the mine flat on my back. If I'd stepped on it, it would have blown my foot off; as it was, it just tossed me around."

"Remind me to inform Land Command that their new mines are crap," Kat grinned back.

"But our body-armour's excellent," he countered.

"I'm ready to cut the wires on this thing," Chang said, bringing them back to a child who still hadn't quit screaming. "If this doesn't go well, it would be nice to have some armour between the kid and the bomb."

Nothing would harm this child. Encouraged by Corporal Torres ringing endorsement of the suits they wore, Kat gauged how much the little girl was bouncing around, but still restrained, then slid herself onto the bed, getting behind, and then between the mattress and the girl. As Kat wrapped her arms around the little girl, she stopped crying, though her breath came in short, choked gasps. "Nobody's going to hurt you now," Kat whispered over the little girl's shoulder.

"Nobody?" said the girl with a hiccup.

"Nobody," Chang assured her. "Corporal Torres, back out on the landing, if you please, just in case." Once the Corporal was gone, Chang sighed. "I think I've got this right." He pulled down his visor and slid back under the bed.

For a long moment, nothing happened. Kat waited. Still nothing happened. Then Chang was getting back to his feet, raising his visor, and grinning like the man who just hit the jackpot in the casino. "Don't just stand there," Kat snapped, "cut her loose."

"Yes, ma'am," Chang said, still grinning.

Torres was back in, forming a barrier between the outside world and their little girl. Kat raised her visor. "The good guys are here. You're safe. Nobody's going to hurt you." The girl took it all in, her face ashen and frozen, her eyes darting from Torres to Chang. As Chang freed the child's arms and legs, the tension in her tiny muscles began to loosen under Kat's hug as she tried, really tried, to believe what this stranger said.

Finally released, the girl rolled over a wrapped herself around Kat, burying her face in the hard battle armour, giving in to deep, body-racking sobs. Ensign Severn held her, protected her, and mingled in some tears of her own. Tears from a Fleet Ensign who'd saved a stranger's child. Tears from a ten-year-old girl who'd failed to save her own brother.

Above Kat, Torres and Chang kept guard, weapons ready, grinning proudly.

"Oo-rah," Corporal Torres whispered.

"Oo-rah," Chang echoed and nodded in agreement.

"Building secure," Sergeant Jones reported over the net. "One gunman dead, the other five are cuffed, three unconscious, one needs urgent medical attention."

Kat sniffed, then managed to stand without losing a square millimetre of body contact with the girl. "Roger that, Sergeant Jones."

She switched her comm-link to the local net. "This is Ensign Severn. The hostage is safe. I say again, the hostage is safe and unharmed. Five hostiles in custody, some injured and requiring emergency medical treatment. Be advised, the ground around the target is mined. Do not approach until we have disarmed them." Kat received acknowledgements from the local Justice Department liaison team and from the *Berserker*.

She looked down into the red-rimmed eyes looking up at her, and hugged the little girl tight. *You are so wrong, Mother. The Fleet is not a waste of time. Some days are worth more than anyone could ever pay.*

ONE : THREE

If this had been a computer game, Kat would have clicked the 'Game Over' function about now and gone out for a pizza. But, in the real world, it's not over until it's over, and this mission was far from over.

The girl, so fragile and light in Kat's arms, mumbled "Erin," when asked her name. Right, that had been somewhere in Kat's briefing notes. From the way Erin clung to her, you'd have thought they shared a heart, and for the moment, Kat wouldn't deny her that.

Trooper Barnard was coming down the stairs with the last of the 'upstairs kidnappers' over her shoulder. Corporal Torres and Trooper Chang kept close to Kat and Erin as they too worked their way down the stairs. No one wanted to lose the girl to some surprise now. Barnard dropped the unconscious gunman down in the main room next to the others. All were alive, all showed blood from where the rounds had hit them; two bled, but not enough to endanger their lives. One shivered in apparent shock. The two conscious prisoners huddled on the sofa, hands secured behind them. A long, dark smear of blood across the tiled floor showed the passage of the dead gunman that had been brought down the stairs and then dumped unceremoniously out the back.

"Who's in charge?" Kat asked.

The two conscious ones glanced around as if only noticing their surroundings for the first time.

"Enzo," one muttered. The other pointed at the shivering body. Sergeant Jones quickly searched him, retrieving a wallet. Enzo Bouchard had a European Union driving licence and IDent, a resident of Nu Paris. A continental European. What was a European doing out here? This situation was way past strange.

But Kat had more pressing housekeeping problems.

"Listen up," she told her captives, "there are land mines out there. I want them turned off. Who has the access codes?" They just stared blankly at Kat. She had Safi repeat her demand in perfect French and German, but still, no response was forthcoming.

"Get me all of their IDents. I want to know who we've got. Lance Corporal Kaplan, do what you can to wake up our sleeping beauties."

Kaplan stepped over to the supine bodies, gave each a shot of adrenaline based stimulant, then started rocking the first one with his boot, a pistol aimed at his face. "Wake up, man. Welcome to my world of pain." Kaplan smiled down cheerfully. His subject came awake with a cough, opened his eyes, took in the pistol aimed at this head, and did his best to roll away. That only put him hard up against another kidnapper's back. The Lance Corporal then squatted down, placing his pistol hard against the side of the man's head. "Who controls the mines?"

"Enzo. He has the codes," he answered in broken English, eager to please. Efforts to then wake 'Enzo' only sent the heavy-set man into a deeper state of unconsciousness. "This one has a bad heart," Kaplan said glancing at his hand-held medical data-pad. "He needs proper medical attention real soon, or we're gonna lose him."

Sergeant Jones stooped to go face-to-face with the other recently awakened sleeper, the one Kat had shot in the shoulder on the landing. "Where does Enzo have the access codes for the mines?" the big Australian sergeant asked.

"In his palm-top, I swear, they're in his computer," came the heavily accented response.

Kaplan searched Enzo again more thoroughly and this time located a battered palm-top computer, smothered with blood. The Lance Corporal tried to wipe it clean on his body-armour, but their armour was designed to keep blood in if they got hit, and did nothing to clean the small unit up. He reached over and wiped it on the sofa before trying to turn it on. Dead, nothing lit.

"He was accessing it when I took him down," Sergeant Jones commented.

"I think he's wiped it," Kaplan concluded. Kat had

learned long ago that nothing in data storage was ever quite gone, not if the right people went after it. She took the palm-top and secured it into a pouch on her suit as she studied the garden through the shattered picture-window. Four of her people were still out there on the other side of a very-live minefield. Kat would risk no one now that Erin was safe. In theory, her team could clear a route through, but mines had no friends, and Kat was not about to see any of her people hurt, even if Erin's parents were in the air and on-route.

"This is Ensign Severn. I have no way of turning off the land-mines. Does anyone have any assets for clearing them?" she asked over the net. The Liaison Officer from Cayman City's Justice Department came straight back with an initial negative, but advised they'd get working on it, see if any civilian expertise was available for hire. As Kat mulled over several unacceptable options, the net boomed back into life.

"This is Commander Ellis, Commander of the ABCANZ Federation's Corvette *Berserker*. We are inbound. Stand by for thermo-baric bombardment to neutralise mines. Confirm grid of target centre-of-mass for incoming salvo."

Kat contemplated trying to suggest that there had to be a better option than this, but realised it was futile with Ellis. With a sigh, she complied with his request and provided the grid reference.

"Roger that," he said, repeating it back to her. "I suggest you all get under cover. Three round salvo, first impact in eighty seconds."

The troops around Kat exchanged puzzled glances. Kaplan shook his head. "The skipper isn't really doing this. Please, someone tell me this isn't happening."

"Sixty-five seconds out. I think he's already done it." Sergeant Jones advised.

Kat shook her head. "He wouldn't. He can't have."

"I think he has, ma'am," Corporal Torres grinned.

"Let's heed the skipper's advice," Sergeant Jones growled, "it's gonna get real messy around here in a few seconds."

While her team moved their prisoners into the back room, Kat contacted her other fire-team and ordered them back . . . way back. She eyed the early morning sky through the shattered window. Thermo-baric weapons had long been used to clear mine-fields, although it was never their primary purpose. They induced sufficient over-pressure to cause most mines to cook-off, and hence why they were used, particularly if time was against you. Except your own people weren't ever meant to have front-row seats! Kat and her team would be on the receiving end too.

The rain had stopped, the sky was clearing. She quickly spotted a white contrail against the dark grey of the pre-dawn sky heading their way. Kat wondered just how you made a house safe when a fuel-air-weapon was about to detonate in such close proximity. Confined spaces would magnify the effects, but it was surely preferable to being caught out in the open. This was not an evolution covered in any lessons at OTA(F). "Sergeant Jones, open as many doors and windows as you can, smash the glass out if they won't open."

"Yes, ma'am."

While her team moved rapidly through the house, Kat took several blankets from the sofa and wrapped Erin in them. "There's going to be a big noise, but don't worry. I've got you. Nothing can hurt you now." The child looked up at Kat with wide, accepting eyes; then, if it were at all possible, seemed to snuggle even closer.

Kat positioned herself next to one of the large, and now completely un-glazed, picture windows to keep an eye on things, both inside and out.

The explosion, and the accompanying roar, despite being over a hundred metres away from the house, went from loud to painful. Kat dropped the visor on her helmet against the intense heat and light, but it still made her turn away. Within seconds of the initial impact the first mine blew. Any noise it made went unnoticed in the racket, but Kat spotted the small secondary explosion. Then another, and another, as mines added their demise to the overall display. Anything and everything within a seventy-five metre radius of the round's impact was consumed in an encompassing ball of fire and extreme heat. "Everyone down."

Reluctantly her troops obeyed. The second and third rounds were still incoming. With her back hard against the wall,

all Kat could think of was the mess the explosions were making to the island. Such a beautiful place, this was probably the first time ever that the harsh reality of industrial, mechanised warfare, twenty-second century style or otherwise, had ever visited Cayman Brac. She sincerely hoped the Cayman City authorities wouldn't take issue. If someone got stuck doing the after-action-review's environmental impact and mitigation statement, Kat knew exactly who would be top of Commander Ellis' list for that duty!

Outside, Kat could just make out the incoming vapour trail of the third thermo-baric round through the heat distortion and roaring fireballs the first two impacts had created; she waited for it to hit home and unleash its carnage before risking a quick glance. Despite the overnight rain, the ground was charred beyond recognition, smoke curling up from it. Justice Department helicopters would soon be on-route and wanting to land. Kat turned to her team. "Sergeant Jones, have our people secure-the-area. If there are any mines remaining let's get them dealt with. Start with the area nearest the house."

There was only one qualified explosives technician amongst Kat's team. Trooper Chang picked up his back-pack of demolition-kit and moved outside. Sergeant Jones tasked Trooper Barnard to assist.

"There's one."

"Another over there," came back before either of them had taken two paces out of the door.

"Team," Kat waved in the general direction of the mines, "the rest of us will stay back in the kitchen until Chang gives us the all-clear."

"Yes, ma'am," Corporal Torres grinned. Having all survived a 'close-up' thermo-baric experience it would now be totally unacceptable to lose anyone to an unexploded mine.

"Where's my mummy?" Erin asked.

"She's coming. Just a few more minutes," Kat said, lifting Erin onto the work-surface in the kitchen, as Sergeant Jones began moving the prisoners into the dining area. Kat dug out her ration pack and rummaged through it for the chocolate bar. Located, she gave it to Erin.

The girl studied it, her mouth twisting in reflection of her internal conflict. "My mummy told me never to take candy from strangers."

"Good advice, Erin, the best," Kat laughed. "But, I'm not a stranger. We're the good guys sent by your daddy."

"Oo-rah!" Corporal Torres agreed.

Erin must have agreed too. She attacked the chocolate with zeal. Kat pulled out the rest of the ration pack from its pouch and started hunting for anything else a small child might like. Not much. Her searching was regularly punctuated by more booms as exposed mines were set off by demolition charges. Kat took several messages from the Justice Department helicopters asking when a landing site might be available. The fifty-six strong complement of Fleet personnel aboard the *Berserker* unsurprisingly had no additional explosive-techs to assist the single Land Force trooper, much to Commander Ellis's abject annoyance. So everyone waited while Kat's team of Chang and Barnard worked as quickly, but as safely as they possibly could.

As the booms got further from the house, Kat took Erin back into the main room. From the window they watched the pair at work. After recalibrating their scanners they started locating the minimal out-gassing of the explosives in the mines that remained, not easy in the swirling mist of smoke still emanating from the scorched earth. Chang would toss a cartridge of explosive at the exposed mine, back off, then detonate the charge. That was usually enough to explode the mine as well. A few didn't respond to this treatment, so were marked and left for later handling by a real EOD team. This informal, yet effective approach to mine clearance finally provided a large enough space that Kat ordered the pair to fall back to the house so a transponder could be set-up for the first helicopter.

Ten minutes later three helicopters had made the short hop from the neighbouring island of Little Cayman and were orbiting the scorched clearing. A small chopper swooped in quickly to deposit a two man team of hastily contracted civilian explosive 'experts' before lifting off again. The civilian contractors immediately began assisting Kat's pair as they resumed their mine clearing activity. As soon as a larger area was declared mine free, the second helicopter swooped in, without asking permission.

There was no question as to who was in it. A woman and a man jumped down from the open door and ran to clear the rotor downwind. Erin let out a cry of joy, and Kat almost lost her. She held on, trying not to fight, and was amazed at just how strong the six-year-old was when she wanted to be. The woman, Erin's scream identified as "Mummy, mummy," raced across the still smoking former lawns, slipping and sliding until she was covered in streaks of ash and mud. She dashed up the steps and onto the veranda, the man was no more than two paces behind her. The child that before had seemed bolted to Kat's hip now flowed into her mother's arms. There were tears and hugs and all kinds of blubbering as the three of them lost themselves in each other.

Kat had cried her tears; she turned back into the building, and found the prisoners being moved from the dining area back into the main room under Sergeant Jones's less-than-gentle care. When Kat next stepped outside onto the veranda, the rejoined family were exactly where she had left them. A large Justice Department transport helicopter now occupied the make-shift landing site. Twin rotors still turning, it disgorged a dozen men whose uniforms immediately identified them as Cayman City Law-Enforcement-Officers. Kat politely moved the family to the far end of the veranda, then brought the prisoners out under the watchful eye of Sergeant Jones, Corporal Torres and Lance Corporal Kaplin. Erin and her parents, still locked in a hug, spared no attention for the kidnappers. The senior officer of the LEO's took in the cable-tied walking four and the half carried fifth with a hard glare, as if he was already measuring them for their coffins.

"There's a dead one out the back. Do we need to exchange any paperwork?" Kat asked. "Or do I just turn them over to you?"

"I'll take them off your hands. If you want paperwork, I'm sure I can find some, but no real need," he said, not taking his eyes from the prisoners as they were escorted away. "I understand one of them needs medical attention."

"The wobbly one," said Kat, pointing him out.

"He'll make it," the senior LEO growled.

"The others say he's the boss," Kat said with a nod towards the other prisoners. "I'd certainly like to hear what he has to say."

"He'll be talking real soon, they all will," the LEO grinned. "In a few hours they'll be desperate to talk to us."

That left Kat wondering if any other parts of the ABCANZ Federation's Human Rights Legislation were going to be conveniently overlooked by Cayman City's Justice Department. But Kat had other, more pressing problems. "Sergeant Jones, have our people police the area for our equipment, but try not to disturb the crime scene." As she said it, she realised what an absurd statement it was. The whole area had just been subject to a thermo-baric bombardment, so it wasn't likely they'd be much for the forensic people to work with. "Just make sure we don't leave anything behind."

"Yes, ma'am," he saluted.

Kat turned to Corporal Torres. "Our section will retrieve the SCIFs. I want to personally do the breakdown on our craft's data-link. Nobody touches it before me. Got it?"

"Roger that, ma'am. No tech is going to get away with sloppy work that nearly drowns me and mine." It was always good when the management took a 'personal interest' in their people's work.

Kat did a slow look around, and found everything under someone else's control.

It took her a while to locate the other section that had provided fire-support from the lawn-edge; they'd managed a considerable distance before the mine-popping salvo had struck. With them in tow, she headed down through the forest towards the shoreline, towards a location very close to intended insertion point of Sergeant Jones's original plan.

After a good twenty minutes of brisk walking they reached the beach. Anchored off-shore was the *Berserker*. On the beach at the edge of the lapping waves, a Rigid-Inflatable-Boat and a medic were waiting to take over responsibility for the 'limper.' Standing right next to the medic and the RIB was Commander Ellis himself, grinning like some fictional Caribbean pirate as he watched Kat and her team break from the cover of the tree-line and trek across the sand.

"Damn good, even if I do say so myself."

"Yes, sir," Kat agreed, coming to a halt and saluting. "I

need to pick up the two insertion craft. Can I use the other RIB, sir?"

"Ensign, are your people too lazy for another walk across this beautiful island?"

"No, sir. It's just that I thought you might want everyone back onboard before the sun gets too high," she answered. If she had gone straight to the SCIFs, he'd be damning her for wasting time. Kat was getting used to being damned if she did, and damned if she didn't.

"Take the second RIB, and make it quick," Ellis ordered, then added as an afterthought, "Well done, Ensign."

Kat saluted again, and used the RIB on the beach to get her people and the medic back onto the *Berserker*. As they pulled up alongside, the 'limper' was quickly helped away and Kat and the rest of her team located the second RIB and got it prepared.

Working as a team, less than fifteen minutes after coming aboard Kat and Corporal Torres had checked over the second inflatable craft, secured their M37's and most of their other now un-required mission related equipment within the *Berserker*, and launched the other RIB. The Corporal operated the boat, with Kat seated next to him. The troopers let out whoops and shouts as the RIB shot away from the rear of the corvette.

As Torres increased their speed and jumped and bounced the boat over the waves, their celebrations got louder. He leaned towards Kat. "Thanks for getting us in safe, ma'am. I thought we were all going to die. I don't know any other officers who could have done what you did. Getting us ashore was about all I was hoping for; but getting us ashore where we could still complete the mission and help that little kid - Well, ma'am, you may not be Land Forces, but I'd follow you any day."

"Thanks," was all Kat could manage. *Father, you are so wrong. A won election isn't the greatest feeling in the world.* Kat doubted she'd ever feel more pride that she felt at this moment from her subordinate's praise. Better than medals any day.

The two SCIFs were where they'd left them at the edge of the beach, concealed in the tree-line. Three troopers moved

Sergeant Jones's across the sand and into the water, before securing a line between it and the RIB. Kat and Corporal Torres gave their own craft a 'once-over.' The data-link was still very dead. "Go easy," Kat said as the troopers hauled it back into the sea and secured a line to it.

"Yes, ma'am, it'd be a real shame to knock whatever went wrong with it back into working again," one trooper commented. Kat smiled; just because they were troopers it didn't mean they were stupid, just, well soldiers, with their own unique black humour.

The trip back to the ship was much slower. By the time they reached the *Berserker*, the launch bay at the stern of the ship was fully open to enable them to drive right in, before hauling the two towed craft up the launch ramp. Jack was waiting, test kit in hand.

"Ready to tear this piece of crap apart?" Kat asked as she climbed from the RIB.

"Nope," he said leaning against the bulkhead, "just thought I'd get some fresh air." He waved his tester towards the two craft. "Which one was yours?"

Kat had the troopers move it into position, then she dismissed them so they could go and get cleaned up. Jack began his analysis straight away, and with nothing to do for a few minutes Kat also went and found her cabin. She would have loved a shower, but that would have to wait. The ship had been reconfigured in her absence, from sub-surface to surface configuration, and it was always her cabin that seemed to come off badly during the process. Ignoring the chaos, Kat wriggled out of the tight armoured suit, returned Safi to her normal position and donned yesterday's ship-suit from where she'd discarded it on her bunk the previous afternoon. As soon as she'd finished changing she swiftly went back to the launch bay. Jack waved her over to gaze with him at the exposed innards of her craft's controls. "What can you tell me about my faulty data-link?" she asked.

"That my heart stopped beating when the link dropped out," he replied.

Kat wasn't sure if that was just pure Irish blarney, the genuine concern of a friend or Jack's feeble attempting to flirt with her. She dodged the issue by ignoring him.

He went on, "There's a recall out on these data-links. The manufacturer obtained of a batch of non-standard parts, but they initially passed inspection, both ours and his . . . or so the paperwork implies. Let me check this one."

With the cover now off, the inner workings of the control panel stood bare. Kat didn't need Jack's technical toys to locate the problem; the circuit board he pulled showed scorched plastic. "Is there any way to know if this was just bad luck or if someone has deliberately tinkered with it?" Kat asked, giving full reign to the paranoia she'd learned at her father's knee.

Jack looked up at her, "Who'd tinker with it? This requires depot-level maintenance."

Kat sighed and leaned back against the bulkhead. She reviewed the parts laid out before her, trying to make sense of what she was looking at. Had a random distribution of sub-standard parts almost killed her and her team?

"What are you thinking?" Jack asked.

"That I ought to debrief my team," she said to no one in particular. "Didn't one of the instructors at OTA(F) say something about an 'after-action-review.' That talking it through will soften any post-traumatic issues if anything stressful had happened? Do you think almost drowning, and rescuing a hostage under fire qualifies as stressful?"

"I know my ma would probably agree with you," offered Jack.

"The thing is, I'm feeling a little stressed myself. I need to talk with my father about the quality of Fleet procurements." Then something hit her. "If that part is on recall, why hasn't this one been replaced?"

"Because we didn't have a replacement. The Squadron's Supply Officer promised me a replacement in three days, but we drew this mission and left base on the second."

"Luck? Right. You know, Jack, I think I need to do something to change my luck. Any suggestions?"

"Have you tried leaving a wee drop of poteen out for the little people?"

"Right now, I'd rather drink it myself," she muttered. "They'll just have to make do with any I spill."

"Fine by me," Jack grinned up at her.

Before Kat could say any more, both their comm-links

went off. They both hit them at the same time, so were treated to the same message, in stereo.

"Cayman City's Governor requests the presence of all ship's officers at a reception being given at his residence at nineteen-thirty local time this evening. The *Berserker* will depart this location one hour from now and be in Cayman City by fifteen-hundred. Dress for this engagement will be full Ceremonial, less leather and metal, but with waist sash and miniatures."

Kat's cabin was located directly beneath the bank of hydraulic rams required to raise and lower the outer hull engine nacelles when the hull was re-configured. As usual, it never managed to survive any reconfiguration intact. Hopefully she and Chief Martinez would get an opportunity to get in there and sort things out properly. As expected, almost all of Kat's uniforms had vibrated off their hangers and sat in a heap at the bottom of her locker. "Our presser unit seems to be screwed too, you'll have to use the one in the girls' mess area," the Chief said as Kat pulled out a jumble of heavily creased kit.

Chief Martinez's locker on the other bulkhead had fared only slightly better. Their cabin was the first of the female crew spaces. The 'sentry-post' you had to pass to gain access into the 'Temple.' The space where the Fleet accommodated its 'vestal virgins.' This was someone's bright idea of how to keep men out of the enlisted women's sleeping quarters. Kat assumed it worked; she'd never bothered to catch any males making a run in or out of the spaces the enlisted women shared four to a room, or more often three, thanks to the *Berserker* being crewed at her peace-time establishment. As it was currently within work hours, Kat didn't feel the need to have the obligatory 'coughing fit' before entering the enlisted women's mess area. Their presser unit was easy to locate and despite theatrical levels of shock and dismay among her fellow cadets at OTA(F) that a Severn would, or could, press her own uniforms, Kat had quickly got the hang of how it operated.

ONE : FOUR

At eighteen-thirty, Kat joined the eight other ship's officers on the dockside next to the tied-up *Berserker* as a small convoy of vehicles arrived to take them to the Governor's reception. Commander Ellis and the XO shared the Governor's own limo; Kat and the other Junior Officers piled into a pair of reasonably clean all-terrain rigs supplied by the Fleet's limited support facility in the city.

Upon arrival at the official residency of the city's Governor, the officers arranged themselves in rank seniority before entering a crowded reception hall lit by several crystal chandeliers that would have been right at home in Nu New England or Nu Britannia, but somehow seemed quite out-of-place on a Caribbean island. Commander Ellis, like all his officers, wore Ceremonial Dress uniform, modified for social occasions, with miniature medals rather than full size ones, and the wide black leather belt being replaced with a crimson waist sash. No sword, or scabbard, or any headdress was worn for such occasions. He led his officers towards a formal reception line comprising of civilian men in dinner jackets and bow-ties, their women in floor-length couture from last season, if not the year before. As the most junior of the officers in the *Berserker*'s crew, Kat and Jack made sure no one was behind them. That didn't last very long.

   "Kat . . . Kat Severn? That *was* you in that skiff last night!" Kat looked around for the voice; she didn't recognise it. A young man in tux, a drink in both hands headed towards her. He looked vaguely familiar.

   "You don't recognise me?" he beamed.

   Raised on politics where everyone was your best friend, at least until the door closed behind them, Kat had plenty of experience watching Mother or Father fake eternal friendship.

"Long time, no see," she said smiling, and taking the offered drink.

"Hey, Lucy, Frank, you have to meet this girl. Come on over. This has to be the woman Erin says saved her." The receiving line disintegrated, just as Commander Ellis extended his hand to the City's Governor.

Leaving the skipper's hand waving in empty air, the man and the woman at the front of the line headed for Kat, with everyone else only a step behind.

"Are you the woman who rescued my Erin?" Behind the dark blue velvet dress and expensive hair-do, Kat saw the woman who had climbed from the helicopter earlier that morning.

"I led the ground insertion team, ma'am" Kat answered, trying to avoid letting her small area of responsibility impinge in any way on Commander Ellis's overall command.

"I told you it had to be Kat Severn piloting that skiff, didn't I?" Kat's unidentified friend went on. "She beat me three years running at university. I'd recognise those moves anywhere. Ought to, I spent nearly every night studying them. Can't tell you how glad I am to see you again."

Erin's mother then introduced herself as Lucy Bodden, wife of Frank Bodden, the City Governor and older sister to the tux attired former skiff rider. A member of their household staff was dispatched to wake Erin, who had gone to bed early under protest at not being allowed to come to the dinner. Through all this, Commander Ellis stood ignored at Governor Bodden's elbow. Watching the red rise on her skipper's neck, Kat did what she knew she had to do, and save the entire crew from a week of hell, if not a year. "Governor Bodden, sir, may I present to you the Commander of the ship that saved your daughter, Commander Ellis."

Frank Bodden turned to shake the Commander's offered hand. "I want you to know that as the appointed Governor of this ABCANZ Dependency, I have recommended this Ensign for the Distinguished Service Medal. I may not be the aficionado of skiff riding that my wife's brother Tim here is, but I want you to know that I've never seen an ability the likes of when she was piloting that craft last night." Kat started backing up, looking for a convenient place to hide. Governor Bodden sounded like one of those politicians who knew just enough about the military to make it really miserable for anyone he took an interest in. "We were watching on the secure feed you provided to my Justice Department, Commander. I was hardly breathing when your people started their run in. Then this young lady's skiff takes off, starts doing all sorts of strange things, and even I could tell it was using up too much fuel and too much air. Did she have any of either when they finally came ashore?"

"I will have my Executive Officer find out what the fuel and air situation was on Ensign Severn's *Scuba Craft*," the Commander said, emphasizing that it was not a civilian skiff that Kat had piloted last evening.

"Despite all that, she still went on to lead the team ashore that saved my dear daughter, Erin," the City Governor continued.

"The steadfastness Ensign Severn has displayed," Ellis replied with a nod in Kat's direction, "is undeniably in the highest traditions of the ABCANZ Military. However, Governor Bodden, the DSM is out of the question. It is a combat medal, sir."

"And those kidnappers weren't more heavily armed and better equipped than anything the Fleet has come up against in recent years?" Frank Bodden observed dryly.

"So it would seem, sir, but we are here in support of Cayman City's Justice Department, and so it is therefore a civil matter, and *cannot* be considered a combat mission."

Even Kat, just getting used to being subordinate, could read the Commander's cut-off as clearly as a brick wall. However, Kat had witnessed several of her father's failed conversations with military types. This had all the potential to be such a conversation.

"I should think, Commander Ellis, that as commander of the ABCANZ Federation's Fast-Attack Corvette *Berserker*, you would be happy to have one of your crew recommended for a bravery award by the governor of a Federation city?"

Oh, boy, here we go. Kat glanced around for a place to hide. As the daughter of the Prime Minister, this might be fun to watch. As a very junior officer at the centre of all this attention, she'd gladly forgo the honour.

"Is that her? It that the soldier that came for me?"

The developing situation was diffused as a tiny form in a pale yellow nightdress with matching ribbons dashed into the room; teddy-bear tucked under one arm. Kat found herself gazing down into familiar wide blue eyes, and this time, there was no red rim from tears. The face had been washed and was about as angelic as a six-year-old ever got. Her mum bent to pick Erin up, but the girl made a beeline for Kat.

Handing her untouched drink to Jack, Kat stooped awkwardly down in her tight breeches and tunic to pick up the child. Erin gave Kat a hug that had to be worth all the medals the Fleet had ever given out. "You have a beautiful little girl," Kat said to the mother and father. "It was my pleasure to return her safe and well to you. I know I speak for all the Land Force personnel who accompanied me, and for the entire Fleet crew of the *Berserker*, when I say it is an honour and a joy to see her reunited to you both."

That drew a round of applause.

Made unsure by all the noise, Erin decided she wanted her mother's arms around her. As Lucy took her daughter, Kat muttered, "If only all horrible things ended so happily." The Governor's wife blanched. "You're Kat . . . Katarina Severn. You lost your . . . Oh, no. I'm so sorry; I didn't make the connection, I . . ."

The breath went out of Kat like she had been punched in the stomach. It was easy to handle thoughtless people and their clueless comments. Thanks to Father, she had plenty of experience of that. But considerate, educated people; people who thought they knew the pain she'd been through, that was something far more daunting. Steeling herself to put on the required face, Kat nodded. "Yes, ma'am. I'm that Katarina Severn. And I am very glad that your family's ordeal has ended differently from mine."

Lucy Bodden seemed at a loss for words; her husband stepped in. "I think they're about ready to begin serving. If Erin is ready, I think she can go back up to bed and we can talk further over dinner."

Erin left with backward waves for all. Kat excused herself, claiming she needed a visit to the loo. There was an exit just past the ladies' room; Kat took it.

Outside, the evening air was warm, but a breeze helped cool the extensive gardens of the Governors' residence. Hands stiff by her sides, Kat fought to organise the emotions ripping through her mind. What was it that her psychotherapist had said? Know the monsters coming at you out of the darkness. Name them if you must, but get familiar with each and every one of them. Some were easy. The Commander she knew.

He needed his ship and the authority it gave him. He needed control of his domain. If he hadn't chosen the Fleet, he'd be a senior manager by now, perhaps running his own business. But he'd chosen the Fleet because it did important things that mattered!

Kat understood Governor Bodden as well. He was building things, a city! People looked up to him for what he did. Someday, they'd put a statue of him up in some tree-lined square or park.

The Commander and the City Governor were important people, and Kat had watched her father take the likes of them apart, leaving them bleeding career-wise and begging for his help. Yes, Kat knew big men like these could be made to feel very small indeed.

So why was she in the Fleet where Ellis could order her to risk her life using second-rate equipment to rescue Bodden's daughter because he hadn't funded his own Justice Department well enough to do the job themselves?

Because today I did what I couldn't do when I was ten. Today I saved Erin. If only I had been there to save Louis. There it was. Still the survivor's guilt. No matter what she did, she'd always be alive and the little boy she was supposed to take care of would always be dead.

The door she had used to access the gardens opened and yanked Kat out of this all too-familiar round of psychological self-punishment; Jack stuck his head out. "Thought I might find you out here. You need to come back in. We're about to go in for dinner, and I don't think you want to make another grand entrance."

"Thanks, I've already made one today, I'll try and save any more for tomorrow."

"Even the little people would consider you've done enough for today and should start saving for tomorrow, if not tomorrow's tomorrow."

Kat gave Jack a grin at the mixed up world of his 'little people' and slipped back inside and into the dining room before the movement at the tables had subsided sufficiently to make her absence or arrival noticeable. The guests were seated in a rank seniority. This put Kat well away from the head of the table, although Tim, the Governor's brother-in-law, had somehow managed to seat himself next to her. That settled the evening's conversation on skiff riding. Kat found that if she played it right, she did very little of the talking.

Late in the meal, a Land Forces Lance Corporal brought a signal for Commander Ellis. The officers grew silent at something so important that it required the old formality of the Commander reading a piece of paper. Talk among the civilians continued undiminished. Ellis signed the receipt, then folded the message and placed it on the table. The *Berserker's* officers would learn about it only when their Commander was ready.

Dining complete, Governor Bodden stood to lay more profuse praise upon them. Commander Ellis then asked if he might say a few words. As the skipper rose, he picked up the message from the table. "The *Berserker* has been ordered back to Bermuda, effective immediately," he said glancing around the room. "There is a funding issue, and all eight ships of 1st Fleet's Fast-Attack Squadron are to stand down for four weeks as a cost-saving measure. We will be leaving Cayman City at zero-six-hundred tomorrow." That said, the Commander sat down.

"That's impossible," Governor Bodden spurted. "The Senate and the Prime Minister agreed in principle to full Fleet funding. Or so I've been advised."

The Commander did not stand, but his command voice carried to the farthest corners of the room. "You are correct, sir. However, full Fleet funding required a slight increase in taxation, and it was at that point that the Senate vetoed it. All Fleet ships and shore based establishments, right across the Federation, are being stood down a month at a time on a rolling program spanning the next six months." Ellis paused for a moment before adding. "Be glad your daughter was abducted this month. Next month there might not be ships available to respond."

The Commander wasn't completely correct.

Supplemental appropriations were always available for emergency activity. Indeed this entire mission could be debited to that account, leaving more funding to cover routine Fleet operations, but Kat was not about to correct her Commander. Conversation in the room limped on. An hour later, Ellis requested their host's kind permission to withdraw, and he and his ship's officers collectively left. As the doors closed behind them the civilians' conversation took off like thunder. Kat could easily imagine the topic.

The Executive Officer was waiting for Kat as she climbed onto the hull of the *Berserker*. "Ensign, a moment."

Kat stayed with him as the other officers passed through the hatchway into the ship. He said nothing until they were alone. "Commander Ellis has forwarded a recommendation to Fleet Command that you receive the Meritorious Service Medal for your efforts today. Governor Bodden will forward a copy of his report to support this." Kat nodded, but the XO wasn't finished. He stared off across the port to the lights of Cayman City. "I hear this Dependency is trying to get Nu New England to finance some new light industrial complexes along the eastern side of the island. Got to look good, him putting the daughter of the Prime Minister in for a damn medal," he spat.

Stunned at the pure venom in the XO's voice, "Yes, sir," was all Kat managed to sputter. *I risked my life today to save a small child's life, not for some stupid medal. All anyone can ever see is that I'm one of those damn Severns!* she though angrily. Dismissed, she stumbled through the familiar passages to her cabin, slamming the door behind her.

"Is there a problem ma'am?" a quiet voice asked from the darkness.

Kat turned quickly around, the dark room showed nothing. "Lights-dim," she ordered, trying to keep the emotions strangling her throat from turning her voice into a series of squeaks. The overhead lighting came to life, casting low light around the room.

"I'm sorry Chief. I thought you might be ashore with the other Seniors having a beer or two. I'll be quieter. Lights-out," Kat ordered to hide herself.

"Lights-full," the Chief said as she threw back the covers and swung her legs over the side of the bunk. Worn pyjamas, the two top buttons missing and the trousers cut off above the knees, revealed more of Chief Martinez's flesh than Kat really wanted to see at this, or any hour.

"Ma'am, you look like you've had a hard time, dinner not good?" asked the small woman of Hispanic origin. The question really was, *do you want to talk to me, and get off your chest whatever it is that's eating you up*. As far as Kat was concerned, the answer was a definite *no*.

Kat turned to her locker and begun to remove her tunic.

"The Fleet has its stories, and old Chiefs like me do love passing them on to the new enlistments. Like today. It'll make quite a tale; new Ensign goes out, saves her section of troopers with some fancy SCIF piloting, then saves the whole damn squad when she gets them through the minefield their Sergeant and the Skipper were enthusiastically planning on inserting them into. Great story. So tell me, why do you look like the kid who lost her candy?"

"XO just told me that the skipper is putting me in for the Meritorious Service Medal."

"Ma'am, everyone of the ship knows that. Skipper had it entered into FDO about ten hundred this morning."

"He's not doing it because the Cayman City Governor wanted to put me in for a medal?"

"No, ma'am."

"Then why did the XO . . ." Kat started to form the question, then stopped. 'Never ask a question you already know the answer to' was another of the Prime Minister's rules.

"I expect the XO is pushing you hard. Like the Skipper is, maybe was. Wants to know what you're made of."

Kat removed the remainder of her uniform and turned to the sink, toothbrush in hand. The Chief was still watching her. "Why are you here? If you don't mind me asking, ma'am?"

"I wanted to do some good," Kat said squeezing paste onto the brush. "I think I did today," she said, jamming the brush in her mouth to cut off further discussion.

The Chief shook her head. "My sister wanted to do good. She joined the Salvation Army. In case you didn't notice, the good you did for that little girl means some very bad things for the people that grabbed her."

"They're getting what they deserve," Kat spat through a mouthful of foam.

"Right, you're one of those Severn's. But trust me; the bad guys aren't always going to be so deserving or so obvious. The Fleet shoots what it's aimed at, no questions asked, no answers sought. Politicians like your dad point us. Are you sure you want to be out on the tip of the spear?"

"I joined," Kat said, rinsing out her mouth.

"So did every mother's daughter sleeping down here. Some joined to get away from that very mother's house, or father's. Some joined to dodge the law, some to get their university loans paid-off. Everyone of those girls knows why she joined, so why did you?"

"Like I said, Chief, I joined to do some good," Kat snapped.

"And?" Chief Martinez wasn't going to let her get off that easily.

"Would you believe I wanted to get away from home too?"

"Maybe," she said with a raised eyebrow.

"No. I'm not some poor little rich kid who joined the Fleet to get her parents' attention. I had the Prime Minister and the First Lady's attention. Dear God, did I have their attention. So much of it that there wasn't any room for me. That's why I joined the Fleet. To find space for me. To find a little air of my own to breathe. Is that a good enough reason to join your precious Fleet?"

"Maybe," the Chief said again, replacing the covers and stretching out beneath them. "Good enough reason to join. Not a good enough reason to stay. Let me know when you work out why to want to be in the Fleet."

"Why are you in the Fleet?" Kat snapped, as she got into her bunk.

"So I can have these fun, late-night talks with Junior Officers and still get a good night's sleep. Lights-out."

In the dark, Kat could hear the Chief rolling over, and in only a moment, she was snoring, leaving Kat to sort out a single day that was fuller than most months back home. She tried to organise all that had hit her in the past thirty-six hours but quickly found that all her mind wanted to do was spin, the precise details of the day just a blur. Kat measured her breath, slowed it and in a moment, exhausted sleep found her.

The *Berserker* left Cayman City's limited Fleet Support Facility exactly to schedule at zero-six-hundred. At zero-seven-hundred, with most of the crew at breakfast, the XO converted the ship from its 'surface' configuration into 'sub-surface' mode. The *Berserker* then dived to a depth of fifty meters and entered a Safe-Transit-Routing via the ABCANZ Dependency of Charlotte in the Virgin Islands before routing back to 1st Fleet's Fast-Attack Squadron's offshore base in Bermuda. Kat reached the Bridge just as the reports of the success, or lack-there-of, following the latest hull reconfiguration began to come in.

Whilst a *Warrior* class fast-attack corvette was not a submarine in the traditional sense, it had the capability to operate sub-surface to shallow depths. Intended for stealth attack runs and covert insertions, and officially designated as a 'wave piercer,' the hull could withstand depths of up to sixty-five meters. Despite not being a submarine in the purest form, she still made use of many of the latest technological advances used in true submarine design. Acoustic tiles to absorb sonar and reduce detection, with aluminium-vanadium-titanium alloys, enhanced with carbon-fibre and Kevlar composites for the hull construction. Fibre optics ensured the bridge wasn't too claustrophobic, and officers and senior ranks only shared a cabin with one other person and the junior ranks were accommodated in fours.

The XO had followed the documented procedure on how to change from one mode to the other. Painful as it was for him to admit, the reconfiguration hadn't quite worked out as the manual promised.

Kat got the job of figuring out what the manual missed. As Warfare Systems Officer, it wasn't normally part of her job to raise or lower the engine nacelles in the outer hulls as part of the reconfiguration process. It now meant Kat was going to become the resident expert among the *Berserker*'s nine officers, forty-seven enlisted Fleet crew members, and nine Land Force personnel, becoming intimately acquainted with how it all worked. She spent most of the three day trip back to Bermuda trying to get the *Berserker's* internals back to how they were supposed to be. Ninety-seven percent of everything had worked just like the shipyard specifications said it would. Nevertheless, Kat still worked two sixteen hour days trying to resolve that remaining three percent.

It had its compensations. There was a new respect in the crew's eyes as they questioned her about this and that. Quite a few put in a good word about the rescue. Finally, with Bermuda in sight, the *Berserker* seemed to tremble with a quiet sign of relief and a cheer when Kat finally finished. "Hope we don't do that again anytime soon," Kat muttered to herself and the rest of the bridge crew.

Commander Ellis raised an eyebrow to the Exec.

"I followed the steps exactly as per the manual," the Executive Officer defended himself. "And you were looking over my shoulder, sir."

"Yes, I was." The Commander chuckled, then turned to Kat and actually let the smile stay on his face. "Right, Ensign, we will avoid that drill if at all possible in the future. Before you stand-down, write me an Evaluation Report, addressed to the Squadron Commander, Captain Duvall, for his review, entertainment and subsequent referral to the shipyard for an explanation." The bridge team all shared a laugh, and Kat stowed away the skipper's smile. It looked like she'd finally made it; she was a Fleet Ensign, just one of the crew.

At a steady twenty-five knots all the way, they arrived back at their home base during the afternoon of the third day, and within hours went into stand-down mode. All crew members now had four weeks leave. 'Just provide a number,' so the Fleet could contact you in case of an emergency recall.

That evening Kat found Jack in his cabin, head in his data-pad, searching on-line through the various sea-freight companies, looking for a low-cost passage back home to the Emerald City. "We Irish have always known that we're a little island off a slightly larger, little island, but with these connections . . . I can get from here to the Canaries, leaving tomorrow, but then have to wait two days for a connecting ship to get to Gibraltar, assuming it's not delayed, I'll get home just in time to start coming back."

"Why don't you fly home?" Kat asked him.

"It's three flights from here. Bermuda to Nu New England, from there to Nu Britannia and then a third to the Emerald City. I simply can't afford it on Ensign's pay."

"There's a flight leaving for Nu New England tomorrow morning. We could be there in two hours."

"I know, but then what? What would I do in Nu New England?"

"Keep me company. Tell my mother there was nothing dangerous about how I won the medal my father is going to pin on me in a couple of days time. You know, provide some moral support?"

Jack laughed. "Like your ma's going to believe me?"

"More than she ever will me."

So it was settled. Kat had Safi arrange two tickets for the flight from Bermuda to Nu New England the following morning. She then spent that evening packing her kit, followed by a long shower and an early night.

At breakfast the next morning, she found herself in the line behind Captain Duvall, the overall commander of the eight corvettes in 1st Fleet's Fast-Attack Squadron. He had come aboard the *Berserker* to discuss something with Commander Ellis over breakfast. He eyed her like she was something really hideous that he had just trodden in. Kat was getting used to senior officers giving junior officers that treatment. Despite being out of uniform, she braced up and said, "Good morning, sir."

"Ensign Severn, isn't it?" the tall officer rumbled.

"Yes, sir." Kat confirmed.

"Interesting report on hull reconfiguration. I'm sure the Lennox Group's shipyards will find it informative."

"Yes, sir," she repeated, then headed for the other end of the mess area where the other junior officers were seated. For the next hour, until it was time to go to the airport, she did her very best to be wherever a more senior officer wasn't.

Once Safi notified them that the Speedbird Imperial flight had landed at Bermuda, Kat and Jack made the short journey over to the airport. Kat had Safi take charge of seeing that their limited luggage was tagged and secured onboard using the fast-drop baggage service. Despite travelling light, she wanted her hands free as she moved about the airport, hurrying through the departure area. It couldn't possibly be that she was excited about going home?

Safi's assistance was further required to upgrade their tickets when Kat discovered that the aircraft was one of the new Boeing 838's. It had a glazed nose section, not unlike the bombers of World War Two vintage, giving passengers with seats in the 'observation lounge' an unimpeded view of the world below them. Safi obtained the last two available tickets.

There were multiple oooh's and aaah's at the view as the aircraft lifted off from Wade International and gained altitude over the black waters of the Atlantic. They quickly reached an altitude of around ten thousand metres and levelled off. Kat found tears forming in her eyes. Just a few months ago she would have been glad never to have seen Nu New England again. But today it was the most beautiful place on Earth, as the white clouds spread across inky dark waters of the ocean, as if lining their route home.

A direct route it certainly was, with little change in their initial course for the entire two hour flight. After ninety minutes the aircraft began to lose altitude and reduce speed and Kat started to pick out the prominent landmarks of the city. Long Island to their right, Jersey to the left. "That's the Peconic over there; we used to have a sailboat. Edward, my older brother, Louis and I would go sailing whenever we could. We would have sailed all summer if they'd let us. You ever been sailing?" There, she'd said Louis's name. She hadn't choked on it. Her heart hadn't bled. She'd saved Erin; maybe now she could face Louis.

"The pool at OTA(F) was the first time I've ever had water over my head," Jack reminded her.

Now only a thousand metres up, the city stretched for as far as the eye could see in all directions. Kat noted how much the city had developed in her Father's eight years as Prime Minister. Prosperous years, good for Nu New England. Good for the Federation, Good for his re-election campaign.

The Hudson River cut through the urban sprawl, reaching far back into the city and enjoying a renaissance as a means of moving both people and goods around the central areas of the city, beating the road traffic congestion. The Statue of Liberty, recovered, fallen and twisted from the waters of the bay, had been lovingly repaired and was standing tall and proud once again.

"What's that needle?" Jack asked.

"Lennox Tower, my Grandpa George's doing," Kat answered. "Most of Lennox Group's facilities are in the industrial complexes far away from this part of the city, but we still own the tip of Manhattan, south of the old Warren Street line. He's turning it into one huge office, apartment and leisure complex, decontaminating the land and landscaping it into parkland. He bragged you'd be able to see its centre piece from space - you probably can."

"You own all that?"

"My mother's family does," Kat corrected, not relishing the awe in Jack's voice. "It's quite a big family. I don't own all that much, only three-point-seven percent."

"Yeah, right." Jack didn't sound all that persuaded. Kat suppressed a sigh; right about now she usually lost a lot of friends.

The nose-canopy suddenly darkened to become completely opaque, as they began their final approach. Despite providing spectacular views, the clear canopy had been found to be more than a little disconcerting when coming into land. Although there was no actual danger, the sudden up-rush of the runway was just too much for some passengers.

The aircraft shuddered as the brakes were applied upon landing at Union Airport, then the plane slowed to a crawl, and finally to a stop as air-bridges connecting it to the terminal were attached. As soon as the aircraft stopped, passengers were unhitching their seat-belts and reaching under chairs for their carry-on bags, even before the flight attendant had announced such activity was safe. Kat was in no hurry. Even though Safi had messaged ahead, she doubted there would be anyone here to meet them.

As she and Jack waited for their luggage, Kat got a surprise tap on her shoulder. She turned and yelped with glee.

"Monty." She threw her arms around the old family chauffer, giving him a hug and a kiss on his scarred cheek. It took considerable effort to believe that he'd actually been younger than she was now when his one and only battle had shattered his right leg had qualified him for a disability pension, and had resulted in employment by her Grandpa Jim. To Kat, he'd always been old Monty, and he'd always taken her to hockey matches, the school plays, ballet classes and all the other places little girls had to go. And he'd stayed there to cheer her on, buy an ice-cream to celebrate victory or take the edge off defeat. They'd been through Louis together. Monty was the one person she'd shared her "*If only I had . . .*" horror with. And by sharing, she'd discovered she wasn't alone with thoughts of what might have been.

"Where's Mother and Father?" she asked.

"Now, you know they're real busy, or they wouldn't be the important people that they are," he said, as their luggage finally arrived. "You're travelling light, only one bag? I haven't seen you manage that since you were shorter than my knee, and the real one at that!" he said, tapping his prosthetic leg.

"I'm an officer now, and you always said you travelled light in the Land Forces, well the same goes for the Fleet."

"And who's this other poor sailor hanging around, looking eager for a ride?"

"Monty, this is Ensign Jack Byrne, the only real friend I've made in the last year. We're both on leave. He's from the Emerald City, but he'll be spending his leave with me. I thought we might have a room for him for a few weeks."

"Not at The Residency, they've just hired two new specialist assistants. Damned if I can tell what's so special about them? Anyway, there are no spare bedrooms anymore, so it'll have to be at Bagshot," Monty said, reaching for Jack's bag.

The young Ensign swung it out of the chauffer's reach, "My da would tan by hide if I let an old fella like your good self lug my kit about."

They exchanged grins. "Come on then, you two, the car's only a short walk away. Let's get moving."

The waiting limousine brought back more happy times. Lucas was with it. A two-meter plus, linebacker or rugby prop type, Lucas had been Kat's security detail at hockey matches and restaurants and whatever for at least the last ten years, if not longer.

"What's Mother's schedule like?" Kat asked as she settled into the backseat of the dark grey armoured car. "I was hoping for a quiet dinner tonight."

"And it will be for you. Both your parents are at a State Reception this evening," Lucas said. "We've got a visiting delegation from the Latin American Confederation. You know, usual format with the LatCons'. Lots of talk, not much of anything else. A quiet dinner is scheduled for tomorrow evening, right after the medal presentation, just you, your parents, your brother and about twelve others."

"Tell Mother I'll have Ensign Byrne with me." She immediately silenced Jack's protestations with a wave. "If you aren't there, the Prime Minister will have me paired off with some old, or even some young lecher whose vote he's chasing. With you, at least we can 'talk shop' to pass the time." That settled, Kat eyed the city around her. Everywhere she looked, something was being built from glass, stone or both. The grey concrete of post-war 'temporary' structures were finally being torn down and replaced. Yes, times were good, traffic was still bad, and Father was at no risk of losing any election he called. Eighteen months ago, before OTA(F), that was all she supposedly needed to be happy. How a few months had changed all that.

ONE : FIVE

After two hours of steady driving they approached Bagshot, almost at the tip of Long Island. Monty began regaling Jack with the tale of its growth. "James Severn Senior started with that two-story block on the right, when he came over from Nu Britannia. That's where me and the wife live now. Then he added that three-story wing when the grandchildren started coming. Then, when his son, the General, began bringing in all kinds of people, not just the likes of me, he added the new kitchen and dining room, a ballroom, a couple of dozen guest suites, and then remodelled the front with the columned portico. The library was the General's late wife, Lizzy's idea." He paused. "They say old James Severn Senior was building till the day he died. Apparently you can hear his ghost walking the halls at night."

"I've never heard him." Kat frowned.

"That's because you were never quiet long enough to hear him, or anyone else." Monty shot back.

Lucas smiled, in silent agreement with the chauffer.

Now, Lucas - he was someone quiet enough to hear a ghost. Kat was just about to ask him; but, before she got a word out, the main gates came into view. It was guarded by a squad of Land Force troopers in full chameleon battle armour and assault rifles.

"I thought you said Father was at The Residency?"

"He is, this is for some other visitors your Grandpa James is hosting."

"What's going on?" Jack asked.

The driver and security guard exchanged glances. "Need-to-know only, son," Monty answered.

Kat and Jack had to produce their Fleet IDents and undergo retina scans to prove who they were. As the car came to a final rest before the front steps, Kat realised that between university, then OTA(F), and then her first Fleet posting, it had been a good while since she had climbed these steps. The doors at the top opened automatically as she approached; Safi had done her job and answered the doors silent challenge. The entrance hall was almost deserted, but it was the floor that caught her eye.

Laid out like a gigantic chess board, the large black and white squares dominated the room. As a child Kat and Louis had played on it, her on the blacks, Louis on the whites. It had been a while since she'd walked on it. The Ensign who'd saved Erin Bodden wondered what it would feel like to walk upon it now.

The library, off to the left, had more armed troops at the door. These were without body armour, but still had their assault rifles to hand. They eyed Kat as she crossed the cold marble squares. It was quite clear she wasn't to venture any closer. Kat frowned. She was no expert, but their uniforms didn't look familiar, and the flag on their upper arm certainly wasn't that of the Federation.

Both she and Jack headed directly for the thick carpeted central stairs. Kat got her old second-floor room back, and Monty duly apologised for putting Jack so far down the hall. "All the rooms in between are already occupied."

"Who's in them?" Kat asked. "Can they be moved?"

"Admiral, admiral, general, commodore, brigadier, brigadier, colonel," Monty said, pointing at each door.

"I guess we don't move them," she agreed.

"Would you happen to have a small corner, maybe up in the attic, where I could unroll a sleeping bag?" Jack asked, his voice cracking.

"Jack, what's to be afraid of?" Kat asked.

"You're a girl. You don't have to worry about meeting one of them when you're halfway through a shower, or sitting on the loo. I'll be standing there at attention, myself 'hanging in the wind.' Kat, this is not what I bargained for."

Monty turned to rest a hand on the young Ensign's shoulder. "I know how you feel, son. I was fresh out of the Land Force, but had 'military' etched into my soul. Being around a general and those that ended up around him, it was a shock to the old system. But son, they get up, just like you and me, every morning. And it seems the higher up they go, the more they know that. Not all, but trust me, any around General James are the good ones. If they weren't, they wouldn't have the sense to come and ask the General how to get out of this mess. Anyway, all the rooms are en-suite, so they'll be no 'hanging in the wind.'"

"Get out of what mess?" Kat asked.

"Not for the likes of you to know, girl, but if I was a betting man, I wouldn't bet a single dollar that NATO still exists by the end of the year."

"Disbandment," both Kat and Jack whispered the word. "Is it really that close?" Kat finished.

"Maybe even sooner, could be weeks rather than months. Ask the Prime Minister. Better yet, ask your Grandpa James."

Kat wasn't too sure she wanted to meet with her Grandpa Jim right now, and besides; she had details to work through about her last mission that still didn't add up. "Monty, can I borrow a car? I'd like to go and see my Aunty Dee about some computer stuff."

"Dee will enjoy that, I'm sure," Monty agreed, "but why borrow a car? Isn't my driving good enough for you anymore?"

"Yes, of course it is, but aren't you busy?"

"Hang around this place too long and they'll have me baby-sitting the chef's kids or even looking after my own grandchildren. Nice as all these kids are, if I don't keep busy, the women here will have me changing diapers. I'd rather be driving."

Within thirty minutes Kat and Jack were in the back of a much smaller, far less conspicuous car.

"Of course I have time, my dear. I'll make some lemonade." Aunty Dee had replied when Kat had Safi call ahead to check Dee was available to see them. As Monty drove them back through the city traffic, Kat explained to Jack how Dee had helped her through sixth grade elementary algebra and even given Kat her first personal computer. A further ninety minutes and they arrived at Dee's Upper Manhattan apartment; it hadn't changed a bit, though a shiny new complex of glass and stone was going up next door.

"I thought you said she was a retired civil servant?" Jack said.

"She is. She bought this place when she won the city lottery about fifteen years ago."

Jack gave Kat a raised eyebrow, but didn't say a word. Kat didn't miss it, and commented on what wasn't said. "Aunty Dee would never cheat. If she could win the lottery every week, why doesn't she." Kat said to no one in particular.

"Because she's a smart woman who knows not to push a good thing too far." Monty winked.

"Anyway, despite being a five-point-five percent shareholder in the Lennox Group, that win gave her financial independence, assets that couldn't be influenced by her father, my Grandpa George."

In the elevator up to the penthouse apartment Kat reflected about just how much of what she had accepted without question as a child was in dire need of a second look now she was a grown woman.

When Dee opened the door, Kat got lost in a hug of huge proportions. Mother never touched, and Father never even came close to Kat, but Aunty Dee hugged. Kat let the breath go out of her as she had so many times before.

Dee broke the hug and ushered them into her living room with its spectacular views over the city. With almost all of the heavy industry in specially designed environmentally controlled complexes, far away from the city centres, it was a beautiful vista of parks, wide tree-lined boulevards and towering city blocks in glass and stone. Dee had heard of Kat's activity in the Caymans . . . it seemed most of the ABCANZ Federation had. There was even officially released footage of her SCIF ride, so that was not something she could avoid when she eventually caught up with her mother, although with a bit of luck Mother would have absolutely no idea as to what she was actually looking at. Dee briefly recalled the one or two occasions when she too had ended up working with Land Force troopers, dodging bullets while trying to find the right algorithm to enable them to hack into or gain access to somewhere or other.

Dee excused herself to get tea and lemonade for her guests. That was one of Dee's rules; no talk before some good, healthy refreshments. Even in Kat's 'bottle days,' a dose of Aunty Dee's homemade lemonade had been better than any hard spirit. Kat rummaged in her back-pack and produced the computer she had removed from the crime scene on Cayman Brac. When Dee returned with a tray, it was sitting innocently on the coffee table.

"A little present for your Aunty?" Dee said, putting down the tray.

"It's a bit old and beaten up to be a present," Kat said. "More of a puzzle. You do still like puzzles?"

"Umm," Dee said, giving the computer a quick once-over while the others served themselves. The computer was an old palm-top unit, fairly thick, quite heavy. Old fashioned display, no jack for eyeglasses. Dee tried and failed to activate it. "Wiped at a pretty low level," she observed.

"Can you access it?" Kat asked.

"Probably," Dee muttered, eyeing the empty tray. "I thought I had some cookies, but I seem to be out."

"I can bake some," Kat said, jumping up. Dee had been the one who had taught Kat all she knew about kitchens and cooking. Which wasn't much. However, Dee could knock up a great batch of chocolate-chip cookies, and Kat had learned from the master.

"You've talked me into it," Dee smiled, her eyes still concentrating on the unit. So, while Dee turned her coffee table into cracker-hacker dreamland, Kat led Jack in an assault on Dee's immaculate kitchen. As they had for many years, the pans and baking trays waited for Kat in the drawer beneath the halogen hob. The flour was concealed within the bank of floor-to-ceiling larders that filled one wall. A bag of Lindt & Sprüngli bittersweet chocolate chips was similarly hidden. So much in Kat's world had changed, but Aunty Dee's kitchen was a constant she could count on.

There was something to be said for the spiritual power of turning a little girl loose in a kitchen to bake cookies . . . or a big girl for that matter. As the wondrous smells collected around them, she and Jack licked the spoon, and ate bits of uncooked dough, until Dee looked up and announced loudly her fear that there would be nothing left to actually cook. Monty curled up in the corner with his data-pad, checking the oddities in the latest news feeds and sharing the stranger ones with anyone listening. Dee tinkered with the computer, its front and rear covers now removed, its innards revealed like entrails for the ancient soothsayer to interpret.

"This piece of artificial intelligence is part of an abduction investigation, still ongoing in Cayman City, isn't it?" Dee asked, attaching parts of the offending unit into an analyser she'd built herself.

"Yes," Kat admitted, closing the oven door. "But the local LEO's didn't seem all that interested in it. At least, no one asked where it went. I figured you'd have a much better chance than anyone in Cayman City of getting anything from it. And besides, I came near to being killed in that minefield; brand new M49 mines that aren't even on issue to our Land Forces, let alone low-life kidnappers. I want to know where all their tech came from." Kat paused, "And the up-front money to fund it."

"And what are the perpetrators telling us?" Dee asked absent-mindedly.

"Their interrogation, you mean," Monty put it. "All four are singing nicely, like drunks in an over-stocked bar apparently."

"Four? We captured five."

"One had a fatal heart attack the day after you bagged him." Monty said without looking up from his data-pad.

Kat had a pretty good idea which of the kidnappers had gone to meet his maker, almost certainly Enzo, their leader, but before she could ask Monty to confirm this, "Hmm," Dee muttered. "I'm in, but it looks like it's all encrypted. It's a standard package, I should be able to cut-through to the interesting stuff in a minute or two. Who are these abductors?" Dee asked aloud.

"They claim to be just small time crooks," Monty said, scrolling down his data-pad.

"And where are they from?"

Monty scrolled back up. "Europe. Two from Nu Paris, another from Ville d'Azur, two from Rhinestadt and one from Nu Bohemia." That covered a sizable chunk of western and central Europe. Five of the six came from the European Union. Six petty criminals from continental Europe had snatched the child of the City Governor of an ABCANZ Federation Dependant

Territory. *Why, for what purpose?* thought Kat.

Monty's summary got a raised eyebrow from Dee. "It doesn't sound like an established gang. Suggests they were brought together specifically for this abduction, if you ask me" she said.

Monty snorted. "Damn Euro-trash gets fed and clothed by their government's over-burdened social welfare, for which they do absolutely nothing in return. Small-time thugs must have figured they could make it big, hitting on some hardworking Federation official, then retire to perpetual fun and luxury back home."

Kat hid her surprise at Monty's attitude. She knew a lot of ABCANZ Federation citizens didn't think much of the millions of people in Europe that wouldn't work and wouldn't relocate to where workers were desperately needed, just expected the welfare state to finance their existence. Kat had even studied the phenomenon at university. It wasn't that the European states wanted to be continually handing out welfare assistance; their teeming millions were as fully employed as you'd expect for any mature post-war economy. What they were was egocentric, maybe a bit self-important, and perhaps a little bit decadent. It wasn't a mixture that appealed to many citizens in Europe, and certainly not those of the ABCANZ Federation. Add an incident like this, which only served to solidify misconceptions like Monty's, and things had the potential to get volatile. "That's the way some people might perceive it," said Kat, skirting confrontation with her old friend.

"Perception is everything," Dee muttered. "And reality . . . may be subject to change," Dee finished with a smile and sat back in the chair. "There, that didn't take too long to sort. Let me copy this across to Max. He can organise the data while we try a few of those cookies," Dee said, then mumbled softly to her own HI to get it working on the tasks required.

"They need to cool," Kat said, taking them from the oven. So much had changed in Kat's life, but Aunty Dee's cookies had not.

The first dozen cookies were gone, a second batch were already in the oven, when Dee grew distracted by her own HI's report. She slipped in an ear-piece, muttered a few things under her breath, and passed on the second batch of cookies when Kat offered the plate around a few minutes later. Dee leaned back, eyes closed as she listened to Max's findings, a frown growing on her face. "Seems to be a perfect match for the news reports," she finally said. "Too perfect."

Kat set down the plate of cookies and took a closer look at the dismembered palm-top unit. It looked old, battered, pretty much the standard type of unit that anyone could have purchased for a couple of hundred dollars at any point during the last fifty years. Kat stood and turned the unit in the natural light from the panoramic windows. The inside of the unit was a mess. "What's all this crud in here?" she asked.

Monty looked up from his data-pad, squinting. "Looks like the muck that gets in your watch wristband."

"Yeah, but it's inside the unit, and it was sealed until Dee just took the back off," said Kat, thinking out-loud.

"He must have sweated a lot and never cleaned it. Either that or the back's been off before? Surprised it's still working," Monty shook his head.

"Let me see that. Oh, you silly old woman." Dee said shaking her head ruefully. She left the room, returning a few moments later with a black box that Jack was immediately transfixed by. Dee placed it next to the computer, then began muttering instructions to her HI. Two tiny mechanical tentacles sprouted from the box then weaved their way, almost organically, to the unit under study. The tiny strands glistened in the light as they wandered over the surface of the palm-top's exposed rear. Then they attached themselves to something. More strands telescoped out and attached.

"Input and output located." Max advised.

Kat frowned. "Input and output of what?"

"The real computer this bastard was carrying. Your poor old Aunty has been wasting her time looking at the wooden horse they put there to distract her. Now we'll get to the real stuff. This may take a while," Dee said.

While Kat cleaned up the kitchen, Dee and Jack leaned over the palm-top unit, studying it with new respect. "What's a low-life punk doing with that kind of technology?" Monty asked.

"They've been surprising us with their technology all along," Kat called over her shoulder from the kitchen area. Wiping her hands she came to stand with her two favourite elders. "What kind of computer is that? I've never seen anything like it."

"And you won't, at least not for a few more years," Dee assured her. "Self-organising circuitry will revolutionise wearable computers like my Max and your Safi, but the current cost is astronomical. Some of my 'old acquaintances' are using them for covert operations."

"Like this one?" Jack asked.

Dee leaned back in her chair, eyeing the objects lying on her coffee table as if seeing them for the first time. "Yes, like this one," she nodded. A long silence followed. Only broken when Dee ordered, "Make sure the oven is off, and grab your coat, we're going visiting."

"Where exactly?" Monty asked.

"Back to Bagshot. Kat urgently needs to talk to her Grandpa Jim."

"We can't bother *him*!" Kat shouted, gulping hard.

"You can't," Monty said bluntly, pocketing his data-pad.

"Her grandfather needs to fill Kat in on a bit of Severn family history," Dee said, placing the computer parts carefully into a stasis box she had produced from a drawer within the coffee table. "He is at Bagshot, so we are going to Bagshot, simple as that."

"But he's doing important stuff," Kat pleaded. "We can't bother him."

"More important than your life?"

Monty cut in before Kat could figure out what kind of response that deserved. "Dee, *you* won't get in at Bagshot. They've got Land Force troopers crawling all over the place. They're applying the mark-one eyeball to all visitors and their credentials. You and all your computer wizardry will not get you past the first eager trooper with an M37."

"Doing it the old-fashioned way, are they?" Dee sighed, closing the stasis box.

"The *very* old fashioned way," Monty said.

"Then we'll just have to go elsewhere. Monty, take us to the Prime Minister's residence."

"No," Kat squeaked, but her chauffeur was already moving toward the door, Dee right behind him. "We can't bother the Prime Minister. He's got a full schedule, there's a

State Reception in a few hours. You can't just barge in on the man who's running the Federation." *Boy, did Kat know that.*

"He will find time in his busy schedule," Dee paused, her mouth moving in whispered communications with her HI again. "Oh, he already has, and so has your mother."

Kat hurried after Dee, with Jack following behind. "My *mother.* Oh, no. She's got a social schedule that's booked solid into next year. Besides, you *never* want to talk to my mother. Why do we need to talk to either of them?"

Dee and Monty were at the elevator. Kat and Jack hurried to squeeze in as the doors closed. A woman with a large coiffured Persian cat, on a lead, joined them on the next floor. The ride down was silent.

"What is so important that you have to talk to Mother and Father about it right now?" Kat asked as she hurried to keep up with Monty's pace in the cool shade of the underground parking garage.

"Your life," Dee snapped, settling into the front seat beside the chauffer, leaving the back seats for Kat and Jack.

Belting in, Kat still tried to stop the impending trip. "So the mission could have gone badly. That's part of the risk you take when you put on uniform. Yes, I do want to talk to the Prime Minister about the equipment currently in service with the Fleet, but I was planning on getting him alone, and when he's in a good mood, perhaps when he pins that medal on me. There's no rush," she insisted. "You don't just barge in on my father, and most definitely not my mother." *No way. You check with their personal secretaries first. Check their moods. Then you make an appointment to slip in. There are a few basic protocols you learn when your parents run a federation of five nations!*

"Kat, you are wrong. There are things evolving here that you are not aware of." Dee turned to Monty. "Please hurry, I don't want to reschedule this meeting. People might notice what I've done." Dee smiled as she turned to Kat. "People are so confident anything a computer tells them is true. It won't do to undermine their illusions." Satisfied that she'd said all she intended, Dee faced front and began to mumble to Max. Kat had seen Dee deep in conversation with her HI many times before and knew better than to interrupt.

Accepting the inevitable, Kat leaned back in her seat. Outside, heavy torrential rain lashed into the car as it moved through the city traffic. Jack nudged her. "Are we really going to meet William Severn, the Prime Minister of the ABCANZ Federation?"

"We certainly are," Kat shrugged. "That's my father."

"I think I'll stay in the car."

If Jack thought he was scared, Kat wanted to find a deep, deep hole to crawl into. She knew only too well what they were in for. She weighed several options, including leaping from the speeding car, and decided that if she couldn't wait in the car, Jack couldn't either. "You're with me. I need some backup. You were on the mission too. You can tell Mother it wasn't that dangerous."

"But it was."

"No, it wasn't. I had everything under control."

"If you say so."

"I do. I need you to back me up on this, Jack."

Jack looked none too sure about that. For several seconds he eyed Kat, his mouth half open as though he was going to speak, but then chose to remain silent.

Kat kept quiet for the remainder of the journey to The Capital, reminding herself that she was a grown woman, had commanded a rescue insertion, and she was not going to let her mother or father bully or intimidate her.

The rain outside the car got even heavier. Lightening forked across the darkening sky, emulating the feelings raging within Kat. Conflicting thoughts continued to tumble through her mind until they stopped in a 'reserved' space in the basement of The Residency. They rode up in the 'reserved' elevator, then walked down the cold marble hallways, marked 'No Admittance.' Automatic doors opened as they approached, despite the prohibiting signage. "Safi, remind me to ask Dee how she does that."

"Yes," Safi responded into Kat's ear-piece, "I would very much like to have that application."

Then, without going by his personal assistant's desk, they were in the Prime Minister's cluttered private office, and William Severn, 'Bill' to his cronies, was rising from his paper-covered work desk. "So glad you could make it on such short notice," he said not looking up, but extending his hand. "It's critical we discuss . . ." then trailed off as his HI failed to fill in the expected words. As Dee shook his hand, his smile changed into as much of a frown at the professional politician could ever allow himself. "Dee, you've done it to me again, haven't you?"

"I'm afraid so, William."

"Who else have you invited?"

"Just your wife," Dee smiled, teeth showing.

Before the Prime Minister could react, the door to his front office opened, and Olivia Lennox-Severn sailed in, regaled in the dress she was wearing to the state dinner in less than an hour. "I hope I'm not too late. I must talk to my secretary. We went over today's schedule, and she didn't say a word about meeting with you, Diana. If I hadn't glanced at my watch, I might have missed it entirely. I know I'm overdressed for this, but I won't have time to change again before dinner. Do let me catch my breath."

"Olivia darling, you look divine," Dee said, kissing the air adjacent to her younger sister's left, then right cheek. "Your breathless dash has got you here before we could begin." From their private talks, Kat knew just what Aunty Dee really thought of Mother: a relic from another age. How a woman born in the late twenty-first century could carry on the way Mother did was a wonder to everyone who met her. Except Kat, who knew several other women of wealth that could easily be clones of her mother. *No way am I going to ever be like you,* Kat vowed.

It was no real surprise when Mother threw Kat nothing more than a curt nod by way of greeting.

Never one for informal chit-chat, Dee folded her hands and began. "As you know, Kat recently drew a rescue mission."

"Yes," Father nodded.

"No," Mother breathed in shock. "It wasn't dangerous was it, darling? After all we've been through with . . ." The sentence petered out like they always did where Louis's name might be mentioned.

"Mother, of course not," Kat immediately filled in the vacancy left by the sudden hush, trying to put the right spin on the words to take them beyond reasonable doubt.

"I think we should all be seated," the Prime Minister suggested, pointing to a report-laden low table surrounded by worn sofas and chairs where he met with his closest staff. William Severn took the single-seat armchair at the head of the table. His wife took a similar one at the opposite end, leaving the two sofas in between for Dee, Kat and Jack. Kat hated it when her mother did that. It left her swivelling her head, trying to keep track of how each of them was reacting to whatever the other was saying.

"What about this rescue mission?" Mother insisted. "If it wasn't dangerous, why was the Fleet ordered to do it?"

"Honey, the Fleet would never put our only daughter at risk." Father assured her. "I followed the entire thing on-line." He told them all about the 'family addendum' he'd implemented several years ago on his news searching software after his father-in-law, George Lennox did something with Lennox Group that had caused him a lot of political fallout, especially when George had demanded that his son-in-law give up his seat in Parliament too. Not only had Father not left politics, he'd wrangled all his party connections into making him the next Prime Minister. The two hadn't shared a good word since.

"You knew all about it and you didn't tell me!"

Kat tuned-out to what followed; she'd heard it too many times before. While Mother and Father did their individual theatrics, Dee cleared a space for the captured computer and attached its working parts to the table's docking station.

"Unfortunately, I must disagree with you, Mr Prime Minister," Dee said softly into a break in Mother and Father's battle of clichés.

"No!" came from both of them. Now Dee had everyone's attention.

"Before I begin, may I point out what we are dealing with here," Dee said, pointing at the computer components arranged on the table. "Outward appearance of a very old, very cheap and very battered palm-top personal computer . . . all totally deceptive. Concealed on the inside of this case is the very latest in self-organising computer hardware. The cost of this alone is several times the ransom demand." Dee raised an eyebrow to the Prime Minister but did not state the obvious. "Money was not the object of this crime."

Kat's father sat back in his chair, his hand coming up to his chin, but he said nothing.

"You must be wrong," Mother said, filling the silence. "No one with money would behave like that." That was Kat's mother's inevitable answer to money. Born into it, and now through successful marriage, she was the high-priestess of lucre in Nu New England, if not the entire ABCANZ Federation. And since those with money had servants to do their work, they, of course, could never do anything nasty.

"I've cracked two of the longer messages in its rather sparse collection of mail," Dee said. "Here's one."

"They've taken the bait. Fleet being called in. Deploy greetings," appeared on the wall screen.

"What kind of greeting?" the Prime Minister asked, leaning forward. Kat had a strong suspicion that 'greetings' almost certainly involved the minefield.

"Here's the other message," Dee said. "We got the ship we wanted. Activate greetings. Assume Plan B," scrolled onto the screen.

"What kind of greetings, and what do they mean, the right ship? I hate it when people don't say what they actually really mean," Mother snapped in a voice that had made Kat jump when she was eight or nine. Now she hated it.

Dee, for her part, leaned back into the sofa and folded her arms. As so many times before when teaching Kat, Dee had laid out the problem; just like now, then left Kat to work it out. Kat had learned to hate that, too. Where was a good role model when a young woman needed one? What was it about Lennox women that managed to infuriate Kat quite so much?

Kat leaned forward, looking at the two messages. *Assuming the* Berserker *was the 'right ship,' then these greetings were . . .*

"The kidnappers," Kat began slowly, "had a field of M49 land mines scattered around their hideout. If we had inserted as initially intended, we would have all been killed." Kat had intended to corner her father about the poor equipment. *But the faulty data-link back to the ship forced me to pilot my SCIF in, and thereby spoiled the best laid plans of the bad guys. Poor equipment, on this occasion, actually saved our lives. Makes bitching about it a little difficult right now!*

The Prime Minister mumbled to his HI. "M49 mines have not been issued yet," his computer advised.

"Yes, Father. Neither the Fleet, nor our Land Forces have any. And a field of them cost a hell of a lot more than their supposed ransom demand."

"Katarina, a lady does not use such language," was all Mother could contribute to the conversation.

"Between the traps that wiped out the first three rescue attempts, the mines, and this computer," Dee pointed out, "this was a losing financial proposition."

The Prime Minister rubbed his chin some more, raised an eyebrow to Dee, but said nothing.

"But who could do this?" Jack blurted out.

Mother shot a freezing stare at Jack for interrupting, then an even colder one at Kat for dragging a complete stranger into something that was clearly a family matter. *Well it wasn't a family matter when I came in here*, Kat shot back wordlessly, then remembered she was a serving Fleet officer, not just Mother's 'little darling.' Leaning back, she gazed up at the ceiling.

"I'm staying at Bagshot," she said to no one in particular. "The place is crawling with troops. Grandpa Jim wouldn't happen to be home?" she asked the ceiling, wanting official confirmation to the bits of speculation that Monty had given her.

"Yes," Mother spat. He obviously remained her least favourite person. She blamed James Severn for Kat's decision to join the Fleet. Grandpa Jim normally stayed away from Bagshot. His current job as Commandant of the ABCANZ Federation's Land Forces Command and Staff College, the post he'd taken after finishing as Chief of the ABCANZ Defence Staff, was also located within Nu New England, but was too far away from Bagshot for a sensible commute each day.

"I'm somewhat new to the military, but some of the troops at Bagshot are not in Federation uniform. Some look decidedly European to me." Kat found the hint of a grin starting to form as she turned to eye her father.

"Who my father is meeting with is on a need-to-know basis, young lady. Need I remind you, you're a serving officer in the ABCANZ Fleet, and I can, and will have you posted to some frozen-over backside-of-beyond if this gets leaked," the Prime Minister snapped. "And, darling, you should not have confirmed that he is currently at Bagshot," he added tersely to his wife.

"Why ever not, you've invited him to the ceremony tomorrow evening?" Mother pouted. "It can't be that secret."

"By then they should be finished," the Prime Minister answered, a tinge of sadness creeping into his voice. "Until then, we don't want it plastered all over the media."

"So NATO is being disbanded," Kat said, surprised she could get her mouth around the words.

Father blanched; if he had any faith, it was in the NATO Alliance, the absolute belief that it had kept the peace for the last thirty plus years and shouldn't be broken up for purely economic reasons. The ABCANZ Federation had always been a stalwart of the Alliance, even before the Federation had even existed, with the United States, Britain and Canada being amongst the twelve founding nations, over a hundred and fifty years before. "It is my policy," Father said, hand going dramatically to his heart, "and the policy of every previous Prime Minister of the ABCANZ Federation, that the North Atlantic Treaty Organisation has, if not actually prevented war, given us the platform to defend our nation and its allies, and set the conditions for an acceptable peace, if not out-right victory." Father repeated the words Kat had heard hundreds of times before. Missing today was the vigour and confidence that this policy would remain.

Kat shivered and was startled by her own reaction. In her mind's-eyes she saw the blue and white flag of NATO come down the flagpole, as it did every evening at sunset. The thought that at some sunrise soon, it would not be going back up brought a chill to her. How many times had she and her university class-mates debated a new, more appropriate role for the Alliance? Now their hypothetical sessions were fast becoming a reality.

"What would the domestic reaction be, if not only had a little girl been abducted by low-life European thugs, but then the 'Severn' trying to rescue her had been killed too?" The words came ice-cold from the logical part of Kat's brain. They were out of her mouth before she remembered Mother was on the other side of Jack. Mother turned a stony stare at Kat, who ignored it. "Mr Prime Minister," Kat said to show that she had not been intimidated.

The hand that had been over his heart now took a worried swipe of his forehead. "There would be public uproar against Europe," he said slowly. "It would certainly make my job much harder."

"And strengthen several of the anti ABCANZ Federation coalitions in Europe, would it not?" Dee asked.

"Yes."

"Especially the European Union, and more specifically the von Welf's in Rhinestadt?" Dee said.

"Oh, the von Welf's are such a nice family. Ernst dated me in university, proposed to me on a beautiful moonlit night."

"Yes, Mother, we know," Kat snapped, without taking her eyes off her father. "Mr Prime Minister," Kat repeated, wanting to hear what was going on in her father's 'political' mind.

"No," he shook his head. "No member of any democratically elected government would dare do that. No policy is worth that much risk. If it ever got traced back to a sitting government, it would crush it. They'd never get elected again," said the head of a democratically elected government.

"He has a son about your age, Katarina, you really ought to meet him," Mother added.

"I know, Mother, you've only mentioned him about a million times before."

"Have you told Kat about the von Welf's and the Severn's?" Dee put in softly.

"I have told her many times," Mother insisted.

"No," Father answered. Mother cocked a questioning eye his way, but his eyes were locked on Dee. "It has never been proven the von Welf's had anything to do with either the war or the drug trade. And just because Rhinestadt almost always takes the opposite side of any major international issue to the Federation is no reason to ascribe personal motives to them."

Dee shook her head. "Someone was manipulating the European Union's bureaucrats through the 'back door' before the war. You've read the reports. There was far too much corruption at senior levels. Hardly a cent ever reached the people. That's one of, if not the principal reason, it eventually fragmented. In the numerous post war clean-up operations, the Federation military closed down the hub of the central Asian drug trafficking network in Uzbekistan and almost overnight the von Welf's fortune vanished, and the family located back to continental Europe. A certain Brigadier James Severn forced them to either give up or deny their 'investments' in Samarkand. You would no doubt agree William, that the Severn's have undoubtedly cost the von Welf's a lot of money."

"Yes." The Prime Minister was out of his chair and pacing around the room, his feet stomping into the carpet. "But that proves nothing. There's not a single piece of evidence, not now, not back then, that will stand up in a court of law." He turned on Dee, "And, I'm a man who must operate within the law."

Dee looked at the screen, then recited from it. "We got the ship we wanted. That ship was the *Berserker*, your daughter's ship. It was one of five ships within that squadron that didn't have a Land Forces' officer aboard. Normally, I would have thought that would have been a very good reason to pick an alternative ship, one that had a Land Forces' lieutenant, or perhaps even their captain aboard, given what they were about to undertake."

"The skipper really wanted that mission," Jack put in. "The word around Bermuda was that he was calling in all his favours with Captain Duvall to get it."

"Understandable for a warrior," Dee agreed. "Still, I imagine it was also common knowledge that Kat was on that ship and that Ellis was pushing her pretty hard."

"How'd you know that?" Kat said.

"Just because I used to head up Military Intelligence doesn't mean I spent all my time with computers and gadgets. I've known plenty of 'hands-on' warrior types who like the whiff of cordite . . . and who'd want to know if you were a 'warrior' too, or just some politician's daughter who'd run away from home. If he was a 'politician' he'd have treated you with tact and sensitivity. If he was a 'warrior' he'd push you; see what you're made of."

"Oh, he certainly pushed me," Kat grumbled.

Dee turned to the Prime Minster. "If I can put those pieces together, so can anyone. The death of a little girl and a Severn in a botched abduction would get the entire Federation up in arms against continental Europe. NATO would fragment in all but name, well further and faster than it already has."

"Who said anything about the little girl dying?" Kat tried to slow Dee down. What she was saying took Kat's breath away.

"Oh, sorry. I forgot. You haven't seen Plan B." Dee muttered to herself, and the screen on the wall changed. "No surprise, I found no reference to a Plan B in this computer. No Plan A, either. However, the Justice Department inventory of the hideout had two interesting items. One, hidden in the bottom of the girl's back-pack, stuffed under spare clothes, two kilos of high explosive, along with a radio receiver cum detonator. Two, found concealed on their leader, a tight beam radio transmitter, set to the same frequency as the detonator. As I recall, they were negotiating for a helicopter to take them to the airport and then an aircraft to take them to wherever they wanted to go."

"If their leader could somehow manage not to be on the helicopter, perhaps due to a chemically induced heart attack at the right moment, he'd then be in the right position to blow up the helicopter as it was taking off or landing elsewhere," Kat concluded slowly.

"That's certainly the right gear for it," Jack agreed. "Or maybe blow it up as it was overflying the city to the airport, have pieces of helicopter raining down on Cayman City."

"All that is just supposition," the Prime Minister snapped.

"All this means nothing," Mother said, cold and distant.

It meant something to someone. Someone wanted Kat and a little girl very dead. Who would profit from such a losing proposition? Kat didn't know about the recent events in Cayman City, but she did want to know about the one twelve years before. "Father, who offered to help you get the money to pay Louis's ransom?" Kat asked in the growing silence.

"Katarina," mother snapped.

"That's enough, young lady."

"Mr Prime Minister, the State Reception with the delegation from the Latin American Confederation will be starting in forty minutes and you still need to change" his personal HI informed him.

"I know, I know. This meeting is over," the Prime

Minister snapped. Mother rushed for the private exit, searching through her clutch-bag for her pills. Two, no three, blue ones were quickly swallowed. Kat shook her head; Mother would probably not remember anything from this meeting. Dee collected the computer parts and Jack stood. When the door closed behind Kat's mother, Father put his face only a few centimetres from Dee's nose. "Diana, you have crossed the line, gone too far this time. I really do not need you setting my own family on me. I'll be doing well if I get a single word from your sister this evening," he said glancing at the door his wife had just left by. He turned to face Kat, his face cold rage. "You, young lady, are staying here at The Residency tonight. I don't want you anywhere near this reckless individual," he said pointing at Dee.

"Father," Kat cut in, "there aren't any spare bedrooms, remember. You just converted the last ones into extra offices for additional assistants."

The Prime Minister muttered to his HI, scowled at the response the computer gave him, then turned on Kat. "How did you get in here?"

"Monty drove us."

"Monty will take you two back to Bagshot," he said, indicating Kat and Jack. "You can do whatever Fleet types do when on leave, but you will not talk to Dee under any circumstances. I can, and will get you posted to the frozen-over backside-of-beyond if you ever bring this up again," he said. Turning back to his sister-in-law, "Dee, my chauffeur will take you home."

"This doesn't solve anything, William," Dee said. "You can't run away from the reality."

"This will solve it as well as anything can," the Prime Minister said, turning his back on them. Dee strode for the door her sister had used only a minute or two earlier, just as the Prime Minister's personal driver poked his head around it.

Kat, eager to beat a quick retreat, used the door she had come in through, Jack was close on her heels. Halfway to the door, Kat stopped, causing Jack to almost bump into her. "Father, I really need to know how you arranged for Louis's ransom money."

He had already taken off his jacket and was removing

his tie, putting on his formal face as he turned to the main entrance to his office. "Since you persist, I will tell you. I went to my father-in-law, your Grandpa George, for the money. Now get out."

ONE : SIX

"Is your da always like that?" Jack asked.

The drive back from The Capital had been full of poisoned silence. Kat was grateful for any break, even if there was no answer to his question. Kat had had a lifetime to get used to her family. Jack had been thrown in at the deep end . . . and if she was totally honest . . . he *had* asked to be left out of the entire thing. "Just what *exactly*, regarding my father's way of doing things are you curious about, Jack?"

He shrugged. "I don't know. Is he always so legalistic? I mean, if I told my parents someone was out to kill me, they wouldn't ask me if I had proof that would stand up in court."

"Oh, my father would," Kat answered easily.

"Then your da really would get you posted to the frozen-over backside-of-beyond."

"Oh yes," she answered without a second of hesitation or reflection.

"His own daughter. You're joking, surely not?"

"I need a drink," Kat announced, glancing out of the car window and actually seeing her surroundings for the first time since leaving The Capital. The rain had stopped and they were cutting through the city district of Mercer, not far from her old university. "Monty, let's stop at the Common Room."

Monty didn't touch the car's controls. "Miss Severn, I don't think that would be wise."

"And what have I done so far today that was? Will you tell the car to head for the Common Room, or shall I have Safi override you?"

"I've had this vehicle's security upgraded since you graduated from university." Monty advised.

"I've had Safi upgraded too. Want to see who brought the better upgrade?"

Monty gave the car new instructions. Even though the

traffic in Mercer at that time of the evening was its usual manic scramble, the city computer found them a parking slot less than half a block from the Common Room; there were advantages to having a car registered to the Prime Minister's household.

The Common Room hadn't changed in the eighteen months or so since Kat had graduated. A new crop of first year students had taken over the tables near the door. There was the inevitable bullshit session going on at the years-three-and-four-only table; Kat overheard 'disbandment' and was tempted to join in. But she wasn't a senior any more. And besides, it was one thing to argue for or against Europe or China and the remit of NATO when it was just hypothetical, a game, but now it was for real, and she was a serving officer. A serving officer who would have to face the hard consequences that disbandment would inevitably bring. Somehow the fun was gone.

Kat settled for a table in the 'professors' section.' Relaxing back in her chair, she tried to see the place as she had for the three years of her university education. The diffused lighting showed every crack and flaw in the interior decoration. Despite the aroma of beer and pizza, the overriding smell was of students; sweat, computers and hormones, more like a library than a bar or diner. The thick wooden tables were disfigured by student carved graffiti. Across the room was the table Kat and her entire Twenty-Second Century Modern Political History class had carved their initials in on the last Saturday night they met here; old Professor Barrett had refused to talk about the problems of the world without a beer in his hand, so they shunned the classroom and lecture theatres and met here every Wednesday for a term. That table was occupied; a dozen students had it covered with data-pads, readers and keypads. Some were actually concentrating on their work, while several couples amongst them were definitely much more focused on each other. Kat smiled at the familiar scene.

"What do you want?" a waiter, who was also a student obviously earning some extra cash, demanded with the usual lack of concern typical of the service at the Common Room.

Jack passed the question to Kat with a glance. Monty sat in his chair, back ramrod-straight, his face a study in disapproval. She knew that face only too well. He'd driven Kat to school enough times, twelve years-old and hung-over. Now he eyed Kat with all the silent disapproval that any Senior NCO had ever put into a blank face.

That answered the question of why Kat took so easily to the Chief Petty Officers and Staff Sergeants at OTA(F). She'd effectively grown up with one at her elbow. Of course she knew what they were thinking, behind those blank, formal faces they wore when they addressed the officers of the future.

"I'll have a carbonated water, with ice and a twist of lime, please." Kat said. Monty relaxed just a little, and that was all the approval he would ever give her. And it was all she ever needed.

"I'll have a Coke-Zero," said Jack.

"Same for me," Monty said.

"Right, Fleet," the waiter said, and added as he turned back to the bar. "I'm sure you military types are banned from drinking in here?"

Kat blinked twice at the snide remark. Despite being in civilian clothes, was it that obvious? Jack and Monty both sported the standard short-back-and-sides of the uniformed services, and Kat's hair was considerably shorter and a lot more organised that it had been when she'd sat at Professor Barrett's elbow arguing for this or against that. She almost stood and called the kid back, to give him a dressing down. That was what Ensign's did to insubordinate junior ranks.

But the waiter was no sailor, and as Kat took in the Common Room with opening eyes, she realised it *was* out-of-bounds to her kind. This room was full of cloud dreamers who had no idea of the cost or implications of their wild plans; or the consequences or budgetary reality required to pay for them. Now that Kat had put her life on the line for a plan of her own making, this place seemed rather cheap, unreal, a waste of time and space. She almost got to her feet and marched out.

Jack had asked a question, and he still hadn't really got an answer. "Yes, if I crossed my father, he would have me posted to the frozen-over backside-of-beyond, in fact, I'd probably spend the rest of my Fleet career there."

Jack looked blank for a moment, then connected her statement to the question he'd asked twenty minutes before. "I can't believe that."

Kat noted that Monty said nothing. Again, that silence

was all the verification she needed. She was reading her old man correctly. "My father is a politician," she told Jack. "I once heard him say that a good politician is one who stays loyal. Loyalty is about the only virtue I've ever heard him praise. If you're loyal to him, he'll move heaven and earth for you. Break that faith, and he'll damn you to hell without even a backwards glance. You haven't seen the way he locked up when an ally of over twenty years changed sides. He didn't even blink, but that ex-friend never got the time of day from Bill Severn ever again."

Kat leaned back in her chair, took a deep breath, then let it out slowly. "The pressures on my father must be unbelievable." A quick glance in Monty's direction showed the merest hint of a nod. "This threat is real, but it doesn't matter. I really don't want to add to the burden he's already carrying."

Jack pulled out his own data-pad and began searching. "Maybe I can get a boat back to the Emerald City from here? I really appreciate you asking me to stay, Kat, but I'm beginning to think that knowing you could be a career-ending relationship."

"If not life-ending," Monty growled.

Kat reached over and flipped his data-pad closed. "Get ready to march," she ordered as the waiter approached with their drinks. As the kid slapped them down, slopping carbonated fluid on the table, Kat stood. Jack and Monty were on their feet with her. Scared he was about to be stiffed for the drinks, the waiter opened his mouth in protest, but Kat slapped down a twenty dollar bill that was easily twice the cost of the three drinks. That silenced him.

"I led the squad of our Land Force troopers that rescued a six-year-old girl from terrorists a few days ago," she said in a voice she'd learned at her father's knee that carried right across the room. "But apparently, people who work for a living aren't good enough for this place." As the tables fell silent, she glared at the one she'd sat at just eighteen months before. "You might add that to your problems of the twenty-second century."

Everything worth saying said, she marched for the door. Jack and Monty fell in beside her. In step, they quickly covered the distance to the exit. A couple of students were just coming in. They took one look at the phalanx bearing down on them and took two steps back, holding the doors wide as Kat led her tiny detachment out into the damp night air, then they rapidly scurried inside and pulled the doors closed behind them.

"That was fun," Jack grinned.

Kat squinted up at the evening sky. The rain clouds were clearing away, a few stars already shining back. "It's going to be hot tomorrow; we need to get Jack some sun-screen and sun-glasses."

"Why?" Jack asked.

"You're in my city now, Jack," Kat said, turning for the car. "We need to protect those blue eyes and your lily-white skin."

"And just why might I be needing to do that?"

"Monty, do my parents still have the *Rubicon* on the Peconic?"

"Yes, and the marina staff at Shinnecock still check her over each week to make sure there are no problems, but the Prime Minister and his good lady haven't been aboard her in four, maybe five years."

"Their loss." Kat grabbed Jack by the arm. "Jack, tomorrow you will discover how great it feels to have the wind in your hair, the sun on your face and a tall ship beneath your feet, perhaps even a good star to guide her by, even if it is only as far as Gardiners Island," she said with a grin.

"A real-live sailing ship!" Jack enthused with underwhelming excitement. "Any chance I could get Commander Ellis to let me hide out on the *Berserker* for the next four weeks? My bunk back there is looking better and better."

"Come now, Jack, you've travelled the oceans, haven't you ever wanted to do it under sail, like they used to do?"

"No. I never wanted to swim either."

"Have no fear; we'll hitch you up to a life jacket. That'll keep you safe should you encounter more water that you can drink."

"Just what I've always wanted. A bit of plastic and compressed air between me and drowning."

"What about when you go outside the hull on the *Berserker?*" Kat laughed.

"That's something I'm a bit more familiar with."

"Monty, home if you please."

As the car slipped into the evening traffic, Kat took a moment to commune with Safi. "Do a global search on Severn, Lennox and von Welf, every contact that they or their businesses have had in the last fifty years. Before you get too consumed, check with Aunty Dee's HI; see if Max has anything on this."

"Dee's HI has very good security," Safi advised.

"Yes, but be open, ask, I'm sure there will be a file or two in the less-secure areas of Max. Father told me not to talk to Aunty Dee, but I'm assuming that you and Max are not covered by that."

"Beginning search."

Kat relaxed back into the car's leather seat. Even if someone did want her more than the usual 'dead' she'd learned to live with as the Prime Minister's daughter, here in Nu New England she'd hopefully be as safe as she always had been, and that would just have to do. She had four weeks to analyse if a certain new Ensign had more than the usual problems of a fledgling Fleet career to worry about. That was plenty of time. Growing up with a politician in the house, there was one thing Kat had quickly learned. Time could change everything.

The next evening, slightly sunburned, but happy as Kat could only be after a day of sailing, the cobwebs blown from her mind by a tacking wind, she and Jack were attired in their Ceremonial Dress uniforms once again. Monty manoeuvred them onto the driveway in front of the Jefferson Building, back in The Capital. The former Great Hall and the Main Reading Room had been drafted as the venue to what Monty grumbled was going to be one of those mutual back-slapping affairs. "May it break their sycophantic arms," was the old trooper's fond hope. Jack had again done his best to duck out, but once more Kat had dragged him, protesting all the way.

"What's there to worry about? No one's ever been hurt at one of these things," Kat assured her friend.

"There's always a first time," said Jack, "and given my luck . . ."

"Not possible. There is absolutely no way anything can go wrong," Kat said with a confidence that evaporated as Monty brought them to the bottom of the entrance steps. Several limos were already parked up nearby, including one identical to Kat's, except for the red and white paint dripping down its shiny, dark-grey exterior.

"Whose is that?" Jack asked.

Lucas, riding shotgun once again, pointed his data-pad at the paint-speckled limo and thumbed an application. "One of ours, number eight. It's has been assigned to Admiral Lefebvre, visiting from the European Union. I thought we had the anti-European demonstrators far enough back."

"I didn't see any demonstrators," Kat said.

"So I guess we had them far enough away from you," Monty chuckled as he came to a halt next to a huge white limo. So huge it needed twin front axles to support itself.

"Who owns that monster?" Jack asked.

Again Lucas aimed a query at the vehicle license plate, then smiled. "Thought I recognised it. Not too many like that one about. Ernst August von Welf, the Seventh's private battleship," Kat's security guard announced.

Jack raised an eyebrow as he opened the door. "Did you just say that no one ever got killed at these events?"

"And didn't you suggest that there's always a first time," Kat shot back, as she assessed the mammoth vehicle. Carbon-fibre and Kevlar composites were light, so it had to be the titanium or steel plates that necessitated a six wheel configuration.

"What am I going to say to my ancestors when I come before them with no descendants to carry on the good Byrne family name?" Jack said as he stepped gingerly out and held the door for Kat.

"I'm sure your blarney-spewing Irish tongue will come up with a fine story to regale them with," Kat answered, dismounted, and squared her shoulders. While it was true that no real blood was ever spilt at these affairs, the political equivalent of the red stuff could run knee deep. Before, she'd just been Father's darling daughter, Mother's eligible debutante. But today, she was Kat Severn, Ensign, serving officer and medal recipient. Maybe she should rethink this.

With a shrug, Kat joined the line of people moving up the stone steps of the former Library of Congress and into the Great Hall. A five metre tall statue of Thomas Jefferson, one of the Founding Fathers and the third President of the United States, stood as guardian atop the stairs.

The part-glazed, high ceiling of the Great Hall was resplendent, supported by pairs of white marble pillars, streaked with pale grey. The vast expanse of red carpet in stark contrast made the immensely beautiful room even more overbearing. A splendid venue for this month's great and good to celebrate their moment of glory.

Kat took in the human company and found it rather pathetic compared to the surroundings. Most of the men were ignorable in white tie and tails. Mother had set the women's fashion this season, and wore a floor length black dress. Although the skirt was acceptably modest, the top ended far too soon for Kat's tastes in a tight, gleaming black corset that forced up everything a woman had for all the world to see. Except that all the women were wearing them, and the men all seemed far too busy 'being seen' to notice all the exposed flesh around them. All the men that is except Jack.

When Kat had first put on her ceremonial uniform's dark grey tunic with its high collar, she'd figured it for a torture device. Trust Mother to usurp her with something even worse. Kat now found she was quite content in her tunic, most thankful that she too wasn't 'all pushed up' into a corset.

Her mother 'held court' on the far north corner of the hall with most of the 'celebrity' females, parliamentary wives and alike. Father, for his own reasons, circled through most of the men of parliament and business in the southern corner. Kat's elder brother Edward, still in his first term in parliament, was at her father's right elbow. He was learning the family trade from the best; Kat wished him well.

The western corner was occupied by a gaggle of Admirals and Generals. Commanders and Majors formed an outlying picket line that seemed to shelter the top brass from all but the most insistent civilians. Kat considered taking refuge amongst their ranks, but at the heart of it was her Grandpa Jim. She had no idea how to handle meeting him for the first time in several years, and in public too. Does an Ensign throw her arms around an old General and give him a hug, or stand stiff at attention and throw out a brisk "Good evening, sir?"

General Hanna, the Chief of the ABCANZ Defence Staff,

stood elbow to elbow with Admiral Lefebvre, Commander of the combined European Fleet. Around them was an unusually large contingent of senior officers from other European nations. Somehow Kat doubted she had the security clearance for even their small-talk.

Resigning herself to the inevitable, Kat turned for the Prime Minister's contingent to see what official duties had been assigned to her. Before Kat reached her father, Edward Severn detached himself from the Prime Minister's elbow and moved to intercept her. Following in his wake was a new face. Judging from the dress, build and hair-cut, he had to be a security agent. *Ruggedly handsome, but not pretty, a good body,* Kat thought, as she smiled a greeting. The agent actually nodded in her direction, whereas Edward immediately launched into the business at hand.

"Little sister, you really have the old man in a flap. It's even worse than when you ran off to join the Fleet."

"I do seem to have that effect."

"Listen, I've got him calmed down for this evening, but can we please not risk you two having another little chat?"

"I could just circulate and smile and say a few nice words."

"Very *few*, very *nice* words," Edward emphasized with that irksome way he had of making out he'd won you over when actually you'd already surrendered.

Kat came to an exaggerated attention. "Yes, sir. No questions asked, sir."

"Somehow, I doubt even the Fleet can get you to do that, my dear little sister." Edward smiled. "And, Kat, I really do appreciate what you did for my campaign. Even Father says so, in his calmer moments, that it was you who pulled it back from the abyss."

Kat leaned over and gave her big brother, who was a good five centimetres shorter than her, a peck on each cheek. "Keep up the good work, Edward. Make Father happy."

"I will, now shoo. The more Severns circulating the more hands get shaken." He quoted Father's perennial demand, then glanced at each of the corners of the room not under family domination. "Say something nice to that officer clique over there or to those veterans; you and I both know Father could use all the help he can get on the right wing, and what with your medal and all, it can only help."

It was nice to know that risking her life was so valued by her father. "On my way," Kat said dutifully, turning away.

"Is that the way it is?" Jack asked once Edward was gone.

"You mean politics first, everything else not even a close second?"

"I guess so."

"Isn't it business first in your family?"

"Perhaps, but we have fun too."

"Jack," Kat said, glancing around, keeping her smile firmly pasted on her face, "in the political world, this is a target rich environment. It's at times like these that my family does its business."

"Do you think Monty could take me back to Bagshot?"

"Just smile and listen, and nothing can go wrong," Kat said, giving Jack the minimum survival advice her father had offered when she was about six.

Opposite the active military was a collection of old veterans, identified by their senior years and the rows of medals proudly worn on the lapels or necklines. Since they included no family that Kat could recognise, she headed towards them, but her progress was slow.

"Kat, I hardly recognised you in that outfit," one of Mother's socialite cronies called loudly. "Girl, that grey is so not your colour." Kat sighed and paused as a matron and her daughter ambushed her and Jack. The mother bulged the latest fashion in all the wrong places, especially for a more mature woman. Her daughter however, was enough to make Jack's eyes bulge out even more, if that were at all possible. Her breasts were obviously cosmetically enhanced, and her corset was cut in such a way to reveal more flesh than even Kat's mother displayed, the material not entirely covering her nipples.

"I was so hoping you would organise our summer fashion show the way you did last year," the woman gushed. "You have such a way with schedules and checklists and that kind of thing."

"Mother," the daughter said, rolling her eyes at the ceiling, "even you can see Kat has other things to organise. Or are they not letting you do that much of anything?" she said, looking Kat up and down. "You're starting at the bottom aren't you, a pennant or flag or whatever it's called."

"Ensign," Kat provided. Behind her a far more interesting conversation was going on.

"There'll be no limit on the profit potential," assured a high-pitched voice, "but we must get the Overseas Investment and Development Directive revoked. We're being forced to invest in barely profitable opportunities, just because they're considered of low international risk. We need to be making bolder, higher stakes investments, before the Chinese clean up and leave us with nothing. Again!"

"Now, I know that sweetie General Hanna," the matron went on. "Maybe if I ask him nicely he will loan you to me for this year's fashion show."

Kat muttered something like "Good luck," and turned away at the same time. She found herself face-to-face with a rotund businessman who went as red as the waistcoat he was wearing beneath his jacket when he realised his last comment had been made in the presence of the granddaughter of the man, a certain George Lennox, who whilst Prime Minister of the ABCANZ Federation had made the expansion of Overseas Investment and Development Directive his last achievement, just before standing down, over ten years ago.

Kat smiled, offered her hand, and he took it reflexively. "Don't you think expanding the Federation's economic boundary twice in the last thirty years has shown a lot of courage on the part of those who actually fought in the war?" Kat said, her heart not missing a beat.

He spluttered something in reply, and Kat passed on.

"How do you do that?" Jack asked.

"Do what?"

"Keep track of all the conversations and switch from one person to the next like some kind of HI," he said.

"Well, for one thing, Jack, I don't forget my name every time a pair of breasts come bouncing towards me."

"It must be great having your own nice pair to look at every time you take a shower," Jack grinned shamelessly.

"I have no idea what you're talking about."

"I'd be happy to offer an opinion," Jack said solicitously,

then swallowed a laugh. "Can you imagine the look on Commander Ellis's face when he gets notification that you're on a Temporary Detachment to run a society fashion show?"

"Don't even go there," Kat said, trying not to visibly cringe. All she'd done, worked so hard for, to be a Commissioned Officer in the Fleet, would vanish if General Hanna gave in to that awful woman.

"Kat, what are you doing in the Fleet? I thought you were going into politics?" came from Kat's left. She paused to give a young woman, who was actually quite conservatively dressed, time to catch up with her. It wasn't enough time, however for Kat to recall her name. Kat smiled and offered a hand.

"I bet you don't remember me," the woman started. "I'm Jan Nickels, from Port Salish. You spent a week putting our campaign headquarters in shape for your dad's last re-election."

"Of course, Jan," Kat lied. "How are things in Salish?"

"Wet, it hasn't stopped raining for weeks. I still can't get over how quickly you took over that chaos and turned it into something effective."

"Well, I have a bit of experience in that sort of thing."

"I bet you do," Jan grinned.

"And I didn't know any of you, so I just started sorting things out, and you were all kind enough to go along with me."

"When is Bill Severn finally going to admit we need to raise import duties to protect our industries from the cheap crap China spews out from its ever growing slums?" Kat heard from behind her. A quick glance showed two older men in concentrated talk. "And look at all these women, corseted up like Olivia Lennox-Severn. They look like eastern European whores. Maybe after that debacle in the Caymans, Bill will impose tighter entry restrictions on non-ABCANZ citizens. In a few minutes we're going to pin a medal on the Severn girl for saving one of our kids from a bunch of low-life scum from continental Europe. Tighter immigration would have kept that trash where it belongs."

"If a Severn pulled it off," his associate assured the speaker, "it couldn't have been too difficult. After all the kidnappers were just small-time petty criminals."

Jan blanched.

Kat shrugged, smiled and went on her way.

"Why didn't you say something back there?" Jack asked.

"Ever tried to teach a pig to sing opera?" she answered.

"I guess that would be a waste of time. So tell me, how did you turn the Port Salish election office around so fast that you left such a lasting impression on Jan?"

"Just about anything is easy, Jack, if you don't care how successful you are, or the people you're leading are 'so honoured' to have you. I learned that the second time I got dumped in a far away city with orders to make a bunch of strangers work together, and fast, to help get Father votes." *And joined the Fleet so he couldn't keep sending me off to wherever his butt needed saving. The military stays out of politics, so now, Ensign Katarina Severn, so shall you.* "Of course," she finished, "whatever you do, smile while you're doing it."

"Smile, huh?"

"Yes, and keep smiling. I know these two."

"European industry is robbing me blind because they refuse to recognise our patent period," Doctor Coney, Research Professor of Microbiology moaned. "Just about the time we get one of my ideas into production within the Federation, those thieves in Europe or the Far-East declare my patent expired and start spitting product out for themselves. We are doing all the research and development and they're not paying us a single euro or yuan for it."

"We need a global patent law, Drew, and the Federation has been actively trying to lengthen patent durations for many years," Professor Barrett, Kat's old Political History lecturer, pointed out.

"And the last time our Senate passed it, the European Union's President confirmed it had no validity across the Atlantic, closely followed by the Chinese. As far as I'm concerned, we're better off on our own. Close the borders, cease all non-Federation trade. They need us far more that we need them."

"That may be true, but they are also our largest markets," Professor Barrett pointed out, taking a sip from his drink.

"And they have the largest military," Kat said, joining the conversation on cue. "During the war, the nations that are now the ABCANZ Federation would never have survived without our European allies, it was their extra resources that helped turn it around."

"Hello Kat, I see you've done well," Professor Barrett beamed.

"Just doing my job," Kat answered.

"Who cares about what happened thirty plus years ago," Doctor Coney growled. "The Chinese dragon has gone back to sleep and nobody now has the military capability to seriously oppose us."

"Thanks to the non-provocative limitations of the Overseas Investment and Development Directive," Professor Barrett pointed out. "It's a small planet and we all need to live side by side, and in peace, if at all possible."

"You sound like some limp European socialist." Coney spat.

Kat nodded to Professor Barrett and moved on, leaving him to the old familiar arguments. She was in a contest to shake as many hands as possible. A bar wasn't far ahead. Kat paused just long enough to get a carbonated water; Jack finally got a beer.

Close to her left were the veterans she'd been working her way towards. Easily recognised by the war medals that adorned their lapels, these older women were the only ones in the room who had collectively stayed with the more traditional and modest attire of jackets, blouses and skirts of an older era. Then again, Kat couldn't think of anywhere to pin medal ribbons onto a corset. The thought of mother trying to find a suitable location for such decorations anywhere on her attire made Kat truly smile. Several of the veterans returned her smile and Kat easily gravitated towards them. As the Prime Minister's daughter she had spent little time with these people, but as a serving officer, they welcomed her. They did not, however, let her arrival interrupt the inner circle's ongoing topic of conversation.

"What these kids need is a good war."

"Too soft, the lot of them. Too soft by a long shot, I tell you."

"A good war would give them some backbone."

"Look at those women, all done up like a bunch of

street-corner hookers."

"Oxygen thieves, the whole lot of them. Corrupt politicians, all scratching each other's backs, you know, providing mutual support to their own kind, helping to maintain the lifestyle to which they've all become accustomed, and at the tax payers' expense no doubt."

"A good war would teach them to be independent."

"And look who's leading them. That damn Bill Severn and all his sycophants. Bastard never served a single day in uniform."

"A couple of hours with a good Drill Instructor, and then maybe that man would know which direction to lead us in."

"A good Drill Instructor might help him grow a backbone."

"Is that after he'd ripped him a new arse?" got chuckles all around.

A few of the insiders of the circle noted Kat's presence; it was hard not to notice her, the contrast of her sober, dark grey tunic against some of the garish colours circulating around the room. Gentle nudges were followed by glances her way, but there was no slowdown in the grumbling about her father. Jack seemed ready to withdraw, but Kat just ignored it, let it roll over her. Once you've been up close and personal with cold steel, a minor thing like a politician's daughter could hardly make you change your mind, let alone your favourite topic of conversation.

It was nothing new to Kat; she'd heard it all before. Even some senior officers, Commander Ellis included, felt that kids today were only out to make their first million, and damn the impact on society. It was everyman for himself. Duty and honour were lost on this generation and the politicians supposedly leading them. In some corners there were even darker rumblings. Some considered that the wrong people were running the show and a good war would restore the natural order, survival of the fittest, or the biggest bastard with the biggest gun would rise to dominance, eliminating any who opposed the new order.

Eye contact made and a smile exchanged with everyone, Kat turned away. "You know, I can begin to understand why these vets think they way they do, they've been there, done it" she told Jack, "but I'm not sure I understand how someone who's not actually been through what they have, could have the same opinions."

"Could it be that you're too close, if not actually one of, those that have it so good?" Jack asked.

"Are you suggesting I'm part of the problem?"

"No. Just that maybe you're too close to one side to see the other impartially."

"You're not in favour of war surely?"

"Hey, Kat, I'm Irish. We've stayed neutral in every conflict since the early 1920's. Even when the European Union entered the last war, we still managed to maintain our non-aligned status. Well sort of, anyway."

"As I understood it, you supported the stance taken by the rest of the European Union, but didn't provide direct military support." Kat had studied this as part of her political history studies at university. "A bit of a cop-out if you ask me. You're either in or out. Only politicians think sitting-on-the-fence is a viable third option. And I should know. Some people see it one way, others see it differently, but going to war is a very different matter. We all have to live on this planet. We've nearly destroyed it once already. You'd have thought people would have learnt from that, wouldn't you? There's no alternative option. Okay, we have fledgling colonies on the Moon and Mars, but how many people actually live there? A few hundred on each, certainly no more than a thousand. Another war isn't the answer."

Kat studied the room. Mother and her cronies were to her left. The military was ahead of her. Kat started across the room to see what she could do there.

And ran straight into Captain Duvall and . . . "Katarina Severn, I bet you don't remember me." A slightly grey, middle-aged and impeccably dressed man said, holding out his hand. Behind him, four, no five security types gave Kat an immediate visual assessment to confirm she was no threat to their primary, then went back to scanning the crowd. These five weren't making any assumption that no blood would be spilled here this evening.

"Hello, Mr von Welf," Kat said, making sure her smile

didn't falter. "What brings you to Nu New England?"

"Oh, there is so much happening here at the moment. Right now, this is where the action is, where the power is focused. And so I go where action and power go. Once I convince your father to revoke your outdated Overseas Investment and Development Directive, there's a whole world of opportunity out there, but we Europeans don't want to act unilaterally. We want the consent, if not outright endorsement from your Federation."

"The last time we tried that we woke up a very angry, and very powerful fire-breathing dragon as I recall," came from behind Kat. She turned to find her Grandpa Jim, also attired in ceremonial dress uniform, but with the dark green tunic of the Land Forces, giving von Welf a rigidly neutral face.

"The Chinese have been quiet for the last thirty-two years," Captain Duvall pointed out.

"Some might say dormant," General Jim countered, taking a sip from his champagne.

"But we must expand our trade opportunities," von Welf said. "Nothing should restrict us, I can't believe you want to restrict yourselves?"

And that was the essence of the 'expansionist' position. Trade was everything, capitalism reigned supreme, above all other considerations. Whereas the non-provocative, restricted expansion policy pursued by the ABCANZ Federation had preserved the peace and not woken the slumbering dragon.

"Yes," Grandpa Jim nodded. "Expansion is necessary, I wouldn't disagree, but it must be managed, negotiated, so there are no unpleasant surprises. As well you know, the United Nations was disbanded at the end of the war because it couldn't prevent a global nuclear conflict, and was therefore deemed ineffectual by almost everybody. NATO has filled the gap and has kept the peace since then. Do you want another 'toothless tiger,' or just an 'everyman-for-himself' policy, bugger the consequences, letting profit and avarice dictate foreign policy?"

"What do you think, Miss Severn?" von Welf turned his smile on Kat. She tried to measure the sincerity behind it and on a scale of five, got both a plus ten and a minus ten.

"The World's an interesting place, but I'm only just starting to find my way around it," Kat dodged as she'd been taught. Father was not going to see any sound bites from Kat on this evenings opposition media update.

"You sound like a most careful young woman," von Welf's smile got even blander, if that were physically possible.

"Not a bad way to sound," Grandpa Jim nodded.

"Well, my son is with your mother's entourage. I hope you'll join me there later. I don't believe you've met my son."

"No, I haven't had the pleasure."

"Well, maybe later this evening."

"Perhaps." Kat stayed put, while von Welf made his way, smiling and glad-handing all the way, towards Mother's side of the room. Without a single word, Captain Duvall turned his back on General Severn and joined another group of officers. Kat took a moment to catch her breath and check her smile.

"I hear good things about you, young lady," Grandpa Jim said, slipping his thumb into the top of his crimson waist sash and taking another sip from his glass.

"I got everyone that mattered out in one piece, sir."

"You're not going to start 'sir'ing' your old grandpa are you?"

"When we are both in uniform and in public, I think I am, sir."

"Damn right," he said.

"How bad is this mess?" she asked him.

That made the old soldier pause. He studied the bubbles in his champagne for a moment, then shook his head and glanced briefly at Jack. "Not quite bad enough that I wish you weren't wearing that uniform. I think us old farts who still remember what a real war is like should be able to keep the forgetful and ill-informed from doing anything too stupid." He sipped his drink again. "I hope. So, what are you drinking?"

"Water, Grandpa, just water."

"I still think those pills your mother was pumping into you when you were a teenager to make you into a 'nice girl' were a big mistake. I doubt you were ever a true alcoholic."

"There are some things in life I don't need to know," Kat smiled at how gently he passed over what occasionally still woke her in the middle of the night.

The announcement of "Ladies and Gentlemen, if I may have your attention, please . . ." caused only a slight reduction in the ambient noise of the room. "You want to join us?" Grandpa Jim offered, "seeing as you *are* dressed for it?"

"If you don't mind, I think I'll stay right here," Kat said with a grin, Jack nodding in rapid agreement beside her.

"Afraid of a few old Generals and Admirals?"

"You've got more than a few senior officers over there,"

"It's your world too, kid. Someday you'll probably be amongst them."

"Grandpa, we're serving Ensigns. We are not even cleared to listen to your idle chit-chat."

"You're chicken? You've faced bombs and bullets. You can't be afraid of a few old men and women. Or is it just me you're afraid of? God knows, with your family, you've a right to steer clear of all relatives."

"Not you, Grandpa, never you."

He took her arm; reluctantly she let him guide her from the Great Hall into the former Main Reading Room, its domed roof resplendent after many years of repair and restoration. Jack followed with all the enthusiasm of a ship being towed to the breakers. They passed through the outlying pickets without any difficulty. Father was already presenting the first award to an artist, next would be the civil servants. Grandpa Jim asked a Brigadier to relinquish his seat so that Kat could sit at his side. At her other elbow sat Admiral Lefebvre from the European Union. Kat stamped a smile on her face and took the vacated seat between them as Jack took the opportunity to head for a safe, quiet corner.

"Admiral Lefebvre, may I present my granddaughter, Ensign Katarina Severn." While Kat struggled to remember she was the Prime Minister's daughter and had survived situations much worse than this, she rapidly went through the protocol requirements. *He's not wearing headdress, nor am I. Do not salute. Wouldn't anyway; this is a social occasion. Like hell it is.*

Kat returned his formal nod.

"I understand you've apprehended some miscreants from my side of the pond," the Admiral said in good English.

"I did what any junior officer would have done in a similar situation, Admiral."

"And don't you forget that," said Grandpa Jim to Kat,

"being a damn Severn, well that might not be so easy."

Help, screamed through her brain. She was still trying to work out how to operate as an Ensign amongst all these senior officers, but now she had to do the dysfunctional family thing as well!

"If you survive, you might learn a thing or two along the way," Grandpa Jim chuckled.

The Prime Minister was going down the list and getting more long-winded as the recipients became more politically important to his party. However, the attitude of the ABCANZ military around Kat saved her from further reaction. They had been invited by their political masters, so like good disciplined military types, they followed orders and attended. As a collective mass, they sat, arms folded across their chests. Silently, they faced out towards a society that did not understand them, rarely needed them, and pretty much ignored them.

As Father reached the end of an unmercifully long list, he announced that the last award would not be given by him, but by General Hanna, the Chief of the ABCANZs Defence Staff. True, Kat was serving in the Fleet, but it was the Land Force's turn to hold the top job, so it was a General rather than an Admiral, but he was still the top military man in the Federation.

General Hanna raised his eyebrows a centimetre or two in surprise, and the disapproving creases around his eyes and mouth got deeper. He made his way to the podium without hesitation. The Master-of-Ceremonies handed the General the folder with Kat's citation, then passed the medal to her father. Kat had spent the last couple of days praying to every bureaucratic god that her family would leave this to the military, who knew how to do such things, but to no avail. Mother was making her way forward. This was rapidly becoming a three-ringed circus. General Hanna did not suffer political circuses, three ringed or otherwise. "Ensign Severn, front and centre," he growled.

The other award recipients had glad-handed their way onto the stage, laughing, talking to Father, or even shouting at people in the audience. Kat marched, shoulders back, head up; her Drill Instructor would have been proud of her.

General Hanna read the citation in his clear, gruff voice.

"The Meritorious Service Medal is awarded to any members of the ABCANZ Armed Forces who distinguish themselves with outstanding meritorious achievement, in a non-combat environment." This preamble was to enlighten the non-military types in the audience, and put Kat's achievement into some kind of context. He continued with a brief account of the events on Cayman Brac, before concluding "Your actions, in the face of criminal acts and hostile fire, reflect credit on yourself and the ABCANZ Fleet in which you serve."

Kat blinked; in the past, such citations always concluded "and the wider traditions of our allied nations." General Hanna offered her the citation folder. Behind her the high ranking officers shuffled their feet, a virtual scream of opposition to what was missing. Kat sneaked a peak at the citation. The traditional phrase was there in black and white. General Hanna had deliberately omitted it. Was this his way of telling his fellow officers that the blue and white flag of NATO was coming down?

The civilians completely missed the bit of drama playing out in front of them. They were on their feet applauding as Mother and Father surrounded Kat. Mother, of course pinned on the medal.

"Well, dear, now that you've got your bauble, are you ready to come home?" she whispered as she managed to put the pin into Kat's left breast. "The miniature of it would make a lovely pendant. I know a great jeweller who could enhance it with a cluster of diamonds and make it truly divine."

"Mother," Kat whispered back, "you don't just walk away from the Fleet. They call it desertion."

"Oh come now, your father was only telling me this morning that the Fleet is over-budget and it's going to have to make cuts somewhere."

"Yes Mother, but I am an officer. They can't make me redundant. It doesn't work like that."

"Well it seems to me that . . ."

"Ladies, smile for the cameras," Father ordered through a clenched-toothed smile of his own. Kat and Mother obeyed.

The ceremony self-destructed after that, as everyone went their own way. Mother and Father had people to meet, but said they'd see her later that evening for dinner at The

Residency. General Hanna had a number of 'raised eyebrows' to answer amongst the military and needed Grandpa Jim's support. Kat went looking for an out-of-the-way chair where she could recover her normal disposition and staunch the desire to order a real drink.

She had expected there to be a least a few well-wishers, but she found herself alone with Jack and free to observe. The chasm between the civilian and military parts of the ceremony was as glaring as the differences between what they had done to get here. The civilians had built, discovered, made things happen, all for the greater glory of the Federation, if not humanity itself, and probably lined their own pockets in the process. Whereas Kat had very nearly got herself killed so a little girl might live.

Kat shook her head. "General Hanna muttered something under his breath as he left the stage. Something about them being so far out of the stadium they didn't even know what sport was being played," she said to no one. "I didn't ask him who he was referring to, the politicians or the military."

Jack looked around. "It would certainly fit both."

Kat watched as her Grandpa Jim circulated, trying to manage an endgame for NATO, striving to resolve the tension between the two factions; one with almost religious faith that the western world had to remain united and not act independently, in order to preserve World peace. The other, diametrically opposed, insisting everyone had a right to do whatever they wanted, regardless of the wider consequences. Even after the split between them got resolved, there would still be two groups in each of the new factions, one playing for profit, power, and the glory that brought with it, the other for self-sacrifice. Games within games. How much 'game playing' would the moral fabric of society tolerate?

Kat came alert, Grandpa Jim was heading her way. At the same time Mother, with a young man in tow, was heading her way from the opposite direction. Kat hoped Mother would turn away. Grandpa Jim remained Mother's least favourite person on the entire planet. No such luck. Kat resigned herself to more dysfunctional family antics.

"Kat, I want you to meet Ernst-August von Welf the Eighth. You two really should get to know each other. I've invited him to join us for dinner this evening. You have so much in common." *Right*, Kat thought, *and if I marry him, my future father-in-law will stop trying to kill me?* The hard look on Grandpa Jim's face as he took in the young man left no doubt to that question.

Ernest-August von Welf the Eighth smiled warmly, showing perfect white teeth, then held out a hand. About Kat's age and height, he had the beautifully sculptured look that parents with too much money and ego gave children in these days of genetically manipulated offspring. *Very handsome, hope he's not gay*, though Kat as he took the offered hand, but before she could say a word, both her and Jack's comm-link went off in duet. A quick flick of the wrist informed her; "Recall. All leave is cancelled. Emergency situation in Elmendorf, you are recalled to duty immediately."

How's that for a reprieve! But Kat still managed a frown. "Elmendorf, where's that?"

Before Safi could answer, Grandpa Jim chuckled. "Oh, that one. You keep drawing all the ace cards, kid. Anchorage, Alaska. They had a volcano blow on the other side of the inlet."

"Lucky for them," Kat replied.

"Hardly. Massive eruption, tossed enough ash into the air that the region missed its summer. Total crop failure. Then the warm Alaska Current in the ocean went missing, and they had several months of acid rain that then turned to snow, and hasn't gone away. Looks like you'll have your work cut out for you, young lady. Starvation, flood, and oh, yes, a complete breakdown of civil authority. Bands of heavily armed and desperate types roving across a frozen landscape, fighting over what's left. Yup, looks like you drew another ace. Kind of reminds me of the good old days," Grandpa Jim said with a smile, a genuine one.

Mother frowned, probably not comprehending what was happening. Young von Welf shrugged indifferently, and Kat despite the bad news, felt like a huge weight had been lifted from her shoulders and she and Jack promptly excused themselves.

They needed to get back to Bagshot, get changed and packed. As they climbed into the car, Jack asked "Is this the frozen-over, backside-of-beyond, your da promised us?"

ONE : SEVEN

A senior instructor at OTA(F) had warned the Officer Cadets "Being in transit on a contracted civilian aircraft is the closest thing to being a civilian you can get whilst still wearing uniform. And don't you smile at me. It's hell, and if you happen to be the Senior Officer Present, it's worse than hell!" Kat had only been on a civilian transport in uniform once before. Her first posting, when she'd initially joined 1st Fleet's Fast-Attack Squadron on Bermuda. A Commander had been the Senior Officer Present on that occasion and he'd spent most of the two hour flight at the bar in the Business Class passengers' section that became unofficially known as the 'Officers' Mess.' Kat had buried her nose in anything Safi could dig up on the *Warrior*-class of ship and hadn't unsealed her 'privacy pod' until just before the flight touched down. Now she wished she'd taken better notes, as on this flight, Kat was duly designated 'Senior Officer Present.'

Not that there was a lot of officers to choose from, at first two, then four newly commissioned Ensigns. But Kat had passed out a term ahead of Jack, and the other two who boarded in San Angeles were 'brand new' and eight months junior to her. Kat found that out from their Personnel Files because the two of them came aboard, went straight to their allocated seats and sealed themselves into their privacy pods and never came out, except for meals.

"I doubt the comm-link between their pods goes inactive too often." Jack mumbled to himself. The link between Kat's and his pod remained decidedly inactive . . . except when Kat needed help on official duties, like going over all the vaccination records of *her* personnel. Kat signed for all the Fleet personnel that came onboard, then had to verify everyone was up to date on their existing shots, and identify any who needed additional vaccinations when they landed. Unfortunately, those requirements were subject to change as conditions at Anchorage were rapidly deteriorating. Not only was the settlement incubating all kinds of new bugs, others that healthy humans normally kept under control were turning epidemic.

"Typhus," Jack exclaimed, "I thought we'd eradicated that fifty odd years ago!"

"So did I, but there must have been a carrier, as people are getting infected." That particular problem left Kat pacing the runway at San Angeles, waiting for a hastily ordered shipment of the antibiotic vaccine as the *Amy Johnson* prepared to depart. The vials arrived minutes after the second deadline imposed the aircraft's purser had expired, and so remained firmly on the tarmac as the aircraft took off. Kat was none too sure if she would have minded being left behind too.

Kat also doubted that the *Amy J*, a hastily chartered low-budget, 'no-frills' civilian aircraft, had ever had maintenance to the level a military aircraft would receive and although none of the crew advised them, Kat quickly learned to keep herself strapped in at all times and to keep her equipment secured. It seemed that the *Amy J*'s four engines had trouble maintaining a steady output. The aircraft's climbs and descents were subject to wild excursions without the benefit of warning. The civilian flight attendants' smiles and winks to each other left the passengers feeling more like zoo exhibits than military personnel on their way to administer emergency assistance to a civilian community.

Her initial glance through their military 'P Files' enlightened Kat why the rest of her colleagues were taking so long to adapt to the *Amy J*'s wild ways. For most, this was their first posting. The vast majority of them were new enlistments, fresh from various ABCANZ Federation training establishments. After a more thorough look into the files at her disposal, she began shaking her head and finally accessed the comm-unit of Jack's pod.

Putting down his data-pad, he unsealed his pod.

"Have you seen our troops?" she asked.

"Yes. Unfortunately I have."

"No, I mean their records. We've got no senior ranks, only two Master Crewmen and four Leading Crewmen, all the rest are straight from training, almost all have never deployed before."

"Kind of makes you suspect that a posting to Anchorage is the Fleet's way of telling all involved to shape-up or get out," Jack said, picking up his data-pad again. "Maybe just get out."

Kat did not ask him what that said about the two of them. Was her father trying another approach to getting her back where he wanted her? *No way, Mr Prime Minister.*

"Did you know that Alaska provided around twenty percent of United States crude oil before the war, and that the airport in Anchorage was one of the North America's busiest when it came to transiting cargo, handling millions of tonnes per year?" Jack asked as the pause lengthened.

"No," she said, glancing over at his data-pad. It showed Anchorage and the surrounding region.

"Although they once exported significant amounts of oil, coal, metal ores and fish, it appears that almost everything else they needed to survive had to be shipped in."

"That still doesn't explain why our government is sending the dregs of the Fleet here. This settlement can't, and perhaps never could, really support itself." Kat frowned. "Safi, what's the organisation on the ground for this mission?"

Safi took longer than normal to begin projecting an organisational chart. "My apologies for the delay," her HI advised, "but, the daily reports do not balance, they change from day-to-day with no explanation."

Jack raised an eyebrow at that. Even as newly commissioned Ensigns, they'd learned that the Fleet took daily reports, actually any reports, very seriously.

"Who's running the show?"

"Colonel John G Hepburn, ABCANZ Federation Land Forces," Safi advised.

"Him," Jack breathed.

"There must be two of them," Kat assured him, but she didn't have Safi check that out. There were some things better seen first. Instead, she studied the organisational diagram. A MACC tasking like this one did not have to follow any definitive structure; commanders had a lot of latitude to improvise on the ground as the circumstances dictated. However, they usually followed the structure of a battalion or regiment, depending on the size and scope of the task. Elmendorf Base wasn't anything close to battalion strength, only two hundred strong, plus or minus the thirty or so the daily reports couldn't agree on. But the 'wiring diagram' didn't seem complete, something wasn't quite right.

"Communications, Medical, Intelligence, Logistics and Military Police," Jack said, "are all reporting direct to the Officer Commanding, and then there's this huge Administration section with the majority of the personnel."

"Notice what's missing?" Kat said.

Jack studied the projected information, then rolled his eyes. "The tail's wagging the dog."

"Right, all tail, no dog. Therefore no hands actually delivering the handouts."

"Perhaps it's all within Administration?" Jack suggested.

"We wait and see," Kat sighed. Father might be right; today's troubles were enough to keep her busy. Maybe tomorrow's troubles would solve themselves before they got to her. *Maybe Father really is an optimist!*

Five hours passed slowly, but eventually Anchorage dominated the view from the aircraft windows, as Kat took her first look at desolation appearing below them. The snow laden clouds parted as they began their somewhat erratic decent towards Elmendorf's single still-active runway, enabling her to glimpse the ruins of the original pre-war city. The rain, and now the snows' high acid content, had taken a heavy toll on everything it came into contact with it, both infrastructure and individual. Despite this brief pause in the snowfall, she could see another storm already blowing in from the Arctic to add even more to a ground already frozen with several metres of snow and ice.

"Are you the woman in charge of the reprobates wrecking my aircraft?" Kat turned to find the captain of the *Amy Johnson* approaching her, data-pad in his hand.

"I believe I am the Senior Officer Present," Kat confirmed.

"Sign here."

"And this says. . ."

"I'm delivering ninety-six enlisted and four officers to Anchorage to contribute to this MACC tasking, as per the contract."

"Safi, do we have ninety-six enlisted personnel?" Kat had studied their files, but had not actually done a physical count.

"Yes."

"Kat, all personnel are ready to disembark" Jack reported.

"Do you have ninety-six enlisted personnel?"

"I don't know"

"Get them to number off."

Jack disappeared for a couple of minutes, then returned with a crisp "Ninety-six enlisted personnel present. Myself and the other two ensigns are awaiting your disposal, ma'am."

"Thank you, I'll be with you shortly." Kat said and signed the data-pad with the offered stylus. "I want a copy," she said, her attention returning to the aircraft's captain.

The captain pressed a button on the pad and a signed copy scrolled out from one end. He tore it off and passed it to her. "Thank you, Captain. With luck, we won't be sharing a ride again anytime soon," Kat commented tersely.

The aircraft's final approach was bad, made even worse as one after another of the new enlistments lost his or her lunch. Despite being in a lull between the almost continuous snow storms, the landing at what had once been Elmendorf Air Base was a whole new experience.

Combats were the dress for today, tonight, and probably next week for this operation. The Sergeant Major back in Nu New England who briefed them had taken great delight in pointing out that new Ensigns were permitted to get their hands dirty on this tour. From the looks of things, there would be plenty of opportunity.

Upon disembarkation, Kat found a rutted runway dotted with potholes.

"Don't these people have any pride?" a trooper snorted. "Back in Texas City, we'd never let a runway get this bad."

"Your city might not look so sweet after a year of endless acid rain and snow," a civilian unloading the aircraft's cargo bay snapped back.

"Natives appear to lack a sense of humour," Jack noted.

"I think it washed off with most of those buildings' paint."

Between large rusting streaks, the former Arrivals Processing structure showed patches of its original paint, once there might have been whites and blues, but all were now dull.

Vehicle headlights pierced through the dwindling late afternoon light as a pair of civilian buses, modified for arctic conditions, rolled up alongside the aircraft. Their doors stayed closed while Kat's troops collected in the snow at the foot of the steps. Only when the last one had reached the icy tarmac, did the bus doors open. Several dozen troops then made a dash for the aircraft. There was no order, no structure to their mad stampede for the 'freedom flight.' Few had any attention for their replacements other than the occasional obscene shout or gesture. Jack watched them, then gave Kat a shrug.

With the buses now empty, the other two Ensigns grabbed the front seats in the nearest one. "Are these two deliberately avoiding me or just being damn ignorant?" Kat muttered, standing in the snow as she oversaw the boarding of her ninety-six enlisted personnel.

"Maybe they've heard that things can get 'interesting' around you," Jack said, a lopsided grin only taking part of the sting out of his words.

"And you?" she shot back.

"I have the luck of the little people," he assured her.

"Then you and your little people take charge of that bus. I'll handle this one and our two prima donnas. Didn't anyone ever tell them that seniors and officers enter the vehicle last?"

Jack glanced up, blinking into newly falling snow. "Whoever made the rule didn't spend any time at Elmendorf," he said, and headed for his bus. Kat took the other and found herself stuck standing, the fiftieth person aboard a bus intended for forty-eight. An adolescent crewman, his face heavy with acne offered her his seat. Mother or Father would have taken it without a second thought; Kat couldn't picture Grandpa Jim doing the same. She stood for the fifteen minute ride.

The ride was as dismal as the former airbase. The roads were more potholes than tarmac; all the buildings showed the effects of constant assault from acid rain and snow. A few troops plodded along, heads down, shoulders hunched against the cold. The personnel on Kat's bus grew quiet as the signs of desolation and despair accumulated.

Before the war, Elmendorf Airbase and the adjacent Camp Richardson had been home to around five thousand service personnel. Although not directly targeted like the missile defence system to the northeast at Fort Greely, Camp Richardson had been abandoned once the peace was signed. Elmendorf however had been retained as an early warning facility, and had limited staging capacity to provide MACC support should a need like the current situation arise, but the events of last year had taken its toll. As quickly as anything was repaired, the acidic environment would negate any improvement within a few months. The consensus now seemed to be to wait until the habitat had stabilised before any concerted effort should be made to return the base to its former operational status.

The buses pulled into a large, approximately triangular shaped compound surrounded by a high wall topped with rusting razor wire. Ahead, along the far edge was the base headquarters. A large, but tattered ABCANZ Federation flag, flapped resolutely from a centre flagstaff in front of the building. To the left a three storied accommodation block and across the other side, forming the third side of the triangle was another larger accommodation block, this one of six floors. Despite the area between the buildings being regularly cleared and salted, the incessant snowfall ensured it was covered in several centimetres of slush.

The civilian driver demanded that Kat hurry her charges off his bus; he had 'other places to go, other fares to earn.' Kat doubted that, but the buses were civilian, and the Fleet always kept its people moving. Unfortunately, that just meant her troops hurried off the warm bus to stand in foot-freezing slush and falling snow. The civilian truck that had followed the buses with their kit then pulled up. Its two civilian operators climbed from its cab into the cargo area and began tossing kit bags down into the slush of the compound.

"Okay troops; let's form a line, single file," Kat ordered, "let's find our kit. You, you, and you," she pointed at the biggest men in the assembled ranks, "help those civilians unload the truck. See that the baggage lands on snow rather than in puddles if at all possible." That helped; the kit bags started landing on their bottoms, and Kat could read the names on them. She re-thought having the troops file by. Calling out names might work better.

"Is anyone in charge here?" Jack whispered to her.

Kat's curt answer died in her throat as she caught movement out of the corner of her eye. The Headquarters building's double-doors slid open. A tall Land Forces officer in combats strode out, back ramrod-straight, with the standard ruggedized military personal computer, officially called a 'Tactical Data Tablet' or TDT, but universally known as a 'battle-board' tucked under his left arm. There was no question who was in charge. From the scowl on his face as he took in this new addition to his command, there was also no doubt about his opinion of them.

"Atten-shun," Kat ordered.

"Who's in charge here?" came from the officer, more a challenge than a question.

"I am, sir," Kat fired back, not hesitating for a moment to take on her responsibility.

"And who might you be?"

"Fleet Ensign Severn, sir."

"Right." He eyed her for a moment, didn't seem to care much for what he saw, then turned his back. "Form your personnel into two detachments, Ensign."

An easy command, but one there was no way Kat could obey properly. By all that was good, holy, and Fleet, Kat should turn to a Senior NCO and ordered him or her to form the troops into two detachments. Anything else would be considered most inappropriate behaviour for an officer. But all Kat had was a pair of master crewmen, probably in technical trades, as they'd shown no initiative in transit or since arriving. No, the chain-of-command here consisted of her and maybe Jack.

What had Grandpa Jim said the morning he picked her up from her first skiff ride. . . . without clearing it with either of her parents? *"If you're going to be damned if you do and damned if you don't, then do it, and do it with style!"* She turned to Jack. "Ensign Byrne, form a detachment of your bus's occupants."

He saluted. "Yes, ma'am," did a snappy about-turn, and stepped into a deep slush filled pothole. Still, he kept his balance as he marched away.

Kat turned to face the milling group of freezing Fleet and Land Force personnel. "My bus, form on me. Master and Leading crewmen will form three ranks to my left." As a suggestion, she pointed to where she wanted them to stand. They took the hint and did so. Kat had one Master Crewman and two Leading; that gave her enough for the other ranks to form-up from. "Dressing, Right dress." It caught on. Twenty metres to Kat's right, Jack's bus went through the same drill. In a surprisingly short time, the gaggle transformed itself into two detachments, each of three ranks. They were cold and growing more miserable, but at least they now looked military.

The other two Ensigns watched all this from under a dry overhang as if it was all for their entertainment. Kat followed the Colonel's lead and completely ignored them as she did her own about-turn, saluted, and reported "Detachments are formed, sir. All new arrivals are present."

The Colonel turned, a scowl still occupying most of his face. "You have a nominal role, Ensign?"

Kat pulled it from her pocket. She could just as easily have had Safi transmit it into his battle-board, but he was doing this the old-fashioned way and he had the rank.

The Colonel took the paperwork, pocketing it without even a glance.

"Welcome to Elmendorf Base," he began, addressing the assembled formations. "I am Colonel Hepburn, the Base Commander. Mine is the only welcome and thanks you can expect to get here. For those of you who joined up to 'do good,' look around? This is as 'good' as it gets. All personnel below the rank of petty officer or sergeant will draw body armour, webbing and an M37 assault rifle. Carry them with you at all times, even if off duty, on the base, or both. Seniors and Officers," his scowl got worse, if that was possible. "You will also draw body armour, webbing and a pistol. If you are smart, you will draw an assault rifle too. If you can't remember how to use one, learn." He paused briefly. "So far I've only shipped three of you ladies home. All were medi-vac cases, and none were in body bags" he growled at the assembled formations. "One may even get to keep his arm. We are officially on a MACC tasking, so we cannot appear hostile in any way to the local population, despite the extreme hostility many of these people have towards us. We have managed to return fire on just one occasion, and that was from a young female crewman who managed to shoot a local with his own gun. She claims it was in self-defence. He survived, and naturally has witnesses to the contrary. It is being treated as a civil matter and *she* will be tried by a jury of *his* peers, since this incident occurred off base and in her own, off-duty time. My advice to you boys and girls is to stay on base and consider all your time, my time. Do that, and you might just make it home to your mothers."

He turned to Kat. "Ensign Severn, is it? Are you one of those Severns?"

Kat turned her head just enough to look him in the eye. "Yes, sir." She didn't add, *General James Severn sends his compliments*, despite the temptation. Grandpa Jim would not send any kind of compliment to Colonel Hepburn. Not this Hepburn anyway.

The Colonel scowled again. "Well, Ensign, get your people processed by Administration, then draw their body armour and webbing before checking into the accommodation. If they hurry, they might get a meal before the mess hall closes down for the evening. Admin will see they get issued work assignments." The Colonel turned back towards the troop formations. "I advise all of you to turn in any cash you're carrying as well as credit cards and any other valuables. The locals are desperate and will kill for them." He redirected his scowl from the troop formation to the other two Ensigns, then to Jack, before finally to Kat. "You officers, report to me when you've been processed."

"Yes, sir," Kat saluted. The wave she got in return might have been at an annoying insect.

Kat turned back to her troops. They looked as stunned as she felt. The snow was coming down even more intensely, and Kat appeared to be the only officer around that had any concern for them.

"Master Crewmen, fall out and call the names on those kit bags," she ordered. On that bit of guidance, the troops got organised. Kat set up a smooth flow as they collected their kit, lugged it across to the Headquarters building and got processed by the Administration Branch that occupied the right side of the ground floor. From there they moved to the Quartermaster's

Department for body-armour and webbing, and then on to the armoury to draw a weapon. With no bunching up, her new arrivals proceeded fairly smoothly on to find their assigned accommodation and from there to the mess hall. Of course, the last to have their name called would be frozen to the bone.

As luck would have it, the other two Ensigns' names were called very quickly. They took their kit and headed inside. Kat's bag was also called early. She made a note of where it lay in the snow and stayed with her shrinking command, taking over from the Master Crewman calling the names when he found his own bag. With a pained expression, Jack took the place of his detachment's caller when she located her kit. When the last person's name was called, Jack and Kat followed the sopping-wet, freezing-cold crewman into the Headquarters building. Their own, supposedly 'waterproof,' boots squishing and adding a litre or two to the pools of water flooding the tiled floor.

"Did we have to do that?" Jack asked.

"Grandpa Jim would have tanned my hide if I'd left them out there alone in the snow."

"No one in my family would have complained. What do you say next time we flip a coin? Heads we follow my family traditions, tails we do it your way."

"You two are late. I finished with those other officers an hour ago," a huge Chief Petty Officer complained. "You're making me late for dinner."

"You would have to wait for all these," Kat indicated the rest of the crewmen still checking in.

"No, I just had to wait for the officers. The Colonel told me to make sure you got your accommodation and standing orders. Then I'm done for the day."

"I thought the Colonel suggested we work dawn to dusk. Apparently it's safer?" Jack said.

"Who wants to live safe? Listen, there are a lot of obliging women out there, you'd be amazed what a little hard cash can get you." The Chief glanced at the papers he was handing Kat. "Oh, right, you're a Severn, so you can buy just about anything anyway, whatever the circumstances."

Kat signed for her accommodation and her orders, but kept her money and valuables to herself. "Where's the Fleet

Chief or Sergeant Major? Where's the armoury and the mess hall?"

"You're looking at the closest thing we've got to a Fleet Chief, ma'am. Like you, us 'enlisted filth' did not volunteer for this mission. Nobody gets posted here unless they've pissed off somebody, somewhere, big time."

"And you?" Kat asked.

He ignored the question. "The armoury is out the door at the end of the corridor," he said indicating the double-doors behind him. "The mess hall is on the ground floor of the tall accommodation block. You Officers eat with the Senior NCOs as there aren't enough of you to have your own Mess. Officers and Seniors on one side, Junior Ranks the other, just different sides of the same kitchen. It closes in thirty minutes, so I'd get over there quick if you want something."

"Thanks for the advice, Chief." Kat looked at her orders. "I'm reporting direct to Colonel Hepburn?"

"The Colonel hasn't been sent enough officers to have a normal chain-of-command. You'll see soon enough. Now, I'm finished and out of here." He turned for the main entrance. "Turn off the lights when you're done."

Jack stuffed his orders into the side pocket of this combats. "It's so nice to be working amongst such happy people. Do you think it'll get any better?"

Kat stowed her paperwork, then picked up her kit. "I have absolutely no idea Jack, but I think I'll draw an assault rifle and a pistol first, then maybe risk eating!"

She drew body armour and webbing, then an assault rifle and a standard issue pistol, before dropping off her kit bag in her assigned room and locking her rifle into the concealed weapon bay within the room's floor. She then raced into the Mess Hall five minutes before it closed down for the evening. What they slopped onto her plate would win no awards, except from maybe a pigswill purchaser, but it filled an empty stomach. She and Jack were just getting the first mouthfuls when their comm-links went off. Kat waved Jack to keep eating.

"Ensigns Severn and Byrne here. What can I do for you, Colonel?"

"What the hell's keeping you two?" Colonel Hepburn growled.

"Just enjoying a delicious, nutritious meal in the Mess Hall. Exactly what a growing girl needs, sir."

"I told you to report to me as soon as you were done." Jack started to get up. Kat waved him back to his seat.

"Yes Colonel, I planned to do that, sir. We saw that the new arrivals were processed properly, got our standing orders and work assignments, drew our body armour and webbing, and then our weapons. Found our accommodation, secured our rifles and are just enjoying the first mouthful of this wonderful meal they're serving in your mess hall. We should be with you in about 30 minutes, Colonel."

"What are you going to do, take a walk in the moonlight?"

"Unlikely, sir. I doubt it's stopped snowing sufficiently to make the moon visible." Jack's eyes were bulging out. Kat just smiled.

"Severn, you have fifteen minutes to get your butt over here. Do I make myself clear?"

"Understood, Colonel. See you in fifteen minutes." she replied and ended the transmission, then reached for her second mouthful of dinner.

"We can be there in five." Jack gulped.

"And add indigestion to our problems? No, I'm eating it nice and carefully."

"Like a true Severn?"

Kat studied her plate as she chewed unidentifiable and probably indigestible food. "I don't know," she shrugged. "Maybe Jack, maybe. I really don't know, but when you get hell for a billet like we have, you can either run with the demons or confront them, head-on."

Kat knocked on Colonel Hepburn's door exactly fifteen minutes after she had ended the call. He was seated, feet up on his desk, face in a data-pad. She and Jack marched in and came to a halt in front of his boots and saluted. He glanced up, took in the clock on the wall, then went back to his data-pad. "You took long enough."

"Yes, sir." Kat answered.

"The warehouse complex is a shambles," the Colonel said, not looking up. "Sort it out. For some reason, we're only issuing rice and beans to the people of Anchorage. There has got to be a better diet in those warehouses. Find it."

"Yes, sir." Kat said again. Waited. Nothing further happened. She saluted the Colonel's boots again; Jack joined her. Colonel Hepburn threw her another wave. She led Jack in an about-turn, and they marched from his office.

"What was all that about?" asked Jack.

"A game." Kat said.

"Do you know the score?"

"We're ahead on points, I think," she replied. "Where is the warehouse complex?" Safi had no answer to that question, so Kat went looking for the Operations Room.

Down the hall from the Colonel's office they found two crewmen sleeping in their chairs. "Where's the warehouse complex?" Kat asked. Twice.

One woke up, looked around, saw Kat, reached for a sheet of paper, and passed it to her. Kat eyed it; it did indeed show a plan of the entire base and surrounding neighbourhood. She rotated it slowly trying to orientate it to the layout she had seen on the drive in. The map worked best if you held the paper at about a forty-five degree angle. "Looks like it's about two klicks away," Kat concluded.

"You're going there tonight?" the barely awake crewman asked, before getting comfortable again in his chair.

"Planning to," Kat answered.

"Wear your body armour and take your pistol, ma'am," he advised.

Kat and Jack left the two in the Ops Room to their dreams.

"A sloppy bunch. Do you think we should have woken them up?" Jack asked as they walked away.

"If they feel safe being asleep with Colonel Hepburn just down the hall, do you think a couple of lowly Ensigns are going to get them excited?"

"What kind of operation is this?"

"I thought you'd recognise it, Ensign Byrne. This is the Fleet your family and friends warned you about. This is the ABCANZ Federation's finest!"

ONE : EIGHT

Kat and Jack returned to their accommodation to collect their body-armour, webbing and assault rifles. She had to remind Jack how to load and 'make ready' his weapon.

Together, rifles slung 'muzzle down' over their shoulders to keep the snow out, they walked the two kilometres through knee deep snow to a complex of several warehouses, all surrounded by razor wire. A civilian guard stood at the gate, his rifle also muzzle down against the ever falling snow.

"Who are you?" greeted them.

"Ensigns Severn and Byrne. I'm in charge of the Elmendorf Base warehouse complex. I've come to inspect them."

"You can't. It's dark."

"So I noticed," Kat said, taking in the warehouses. The area was bathed in light; several civilian trucks were backed up to the loading bays. "Looks well enough lit to me."

"Listen, I don't know who you are or what you think you're doing here, but you don't belong here. Get lost while you can, or I'll. . ." The rifle started coming Kat's way.

Kat knew she couldn't out-run a bullet, but at that exact moment, the rifle looked within reach. Without thought, she grabbed for the muzzle. Her hand wrapped around the cold gun metal, sending a shock through her. *You're crazy woman.* The guard looked just as shocked to see her hand on his weapon as she was. He struggled for a brief second, but she yanked the rifle from his grasp and brought the butt up under his chin.

"Looks like we need to have a little talk," Kat growled. Up close, under the lights, she got her first good look at the guard. A kid of maybe thirteen or fourteen, he stared through wide, round eyes at his rifle in her hands.

"What's going on here?" Kat demanded. When running

her brother Edward's political campaign office she'd walked into some real messes, although most of Edward's crowd didn't routinely carry guns and looked significantly less hungry. For an answer, the kid started babbling out names. Kat brought the butt up hard on the former guard's jaw, just like they did in the movies, and to her surprise, his eyes rolled back in his head and he collapsed noisily into the fence, then pitched forward into a slush filled puddle. Heads then began appearing out of trucks and loading bays. Kat had the attention of a good twenty or thirty people. Time for a campaign speech.

"You are trespassing on ABCANZ Government property," she shouted, then ducked as someone took a shot at her. The round was high, but Kat felt a distinct lack of cover. Dropping to one knee, she brought her M37 up into her shoulder and snapped off a three round burst, likewise over the target's heads. People swarmed from the warehouses into the trucks. Engines came to life.

"Is there any other way out of this compound?" Jack called from his improvised fighting position in the bottom of the largest snow filled pothole available.

"I don't think so."

"Then they'll be leaving right over the top of us," he squeaked.

"Oh, crap," Kat breathed. She need not have worried. The trucks turned away from her, a few more un-aimed shots came in their general direction, then the lead vehicle smashed a hole in the fence opposite the formally agreed upon exit. Kat stood only after the last truck was long gone. She glanced at the kid, still prone in the snow.

"What you gonna do lady?" the terrified adolescent whispered.

"Send a message," Kat said, using the muzzle of her M37 to signal to the boy to slowly stand. He looked painfully thin. His clothes needed patching. "Who hired you?"

"I'm not tellin' you nothin'."

"What's your pay for this?"

"A sack of rice. My mom, my brothers, sisters, we're all real hungry."

"Come back here tomorrow. Work for me and I'll see your family get fed. And tell the people you were working for that if they come back tomorrow, I'll see what jobs I can find for them too. If they come back tomorrow night there will be armed troops patrolling this perimeter. They can either change and eat, or do it the old way and starve."

The kid's face changed as she spoke. Terror drained out. Dismay and shock were there for a while, along with a large measure of doubt. But he was nodding his head as she finished. He started backing away, slowly, carefully. Kat watched until he disappeared into the darkness.

"What do we do now?" Jack asked.

"Well, unless you want to spend the rest of tonight patrolling the fence-line, I say we go back to the main base and get some sleep. I strongly suspect that tomorrow is going to be a bitch of a day."

"But the fence is wide open."

"I had noticed. And it's going to stay that way until we can get it fixed tomorrow. Kind of inviting to anyone who wants to walk in. Hungry women, kids, anyone really, but then we are here to feed these people, are we not?"

"We are that," he agreed.

"Well, if a few good people want to help me in the distribution of the food, that's fine by me."

"Then why did you shoot at those trucks?"

"Because they had guns. How much of that food do you think they were planning on sharing?"

"Right," Jack snorted. "Trust a politician to care more about how they do it, rather than what they actually do."

Kat thought she was just being practical. With a shrug, she turned and started back towards the main base, now shouldering two rifles.

At the main base's compound, Kat paused in the snow. The Colonel's first floor office window was still lit, the only light showing in the Headquarters building. "What is it with him?" Jack asked, shaking his head.

"There was trouble on New Zealand's South Island." Kat said. "Terra-Formers and Agri-Farmers didn't think they were getting a fair rate for their efforts to decontaminate the land and start getting a useable harvest from it. It happens every once in a while. They trashed Nu Canterbury and were moving on Cook

Straits. Hepburn led an experienced infantry battalion, the 74th, I think it was, to restore law and order to the South Island. Standard crowd-control procedures didn't seem to be working, when someone opened fire on his troops, who naturally returned fire. There were lots of recriminations. Hepburn was subjected to court-martial for the incident, but found Not Guilty."

"So he is *that* Hepburn. We even heard about it the Emerald City. Media had a field day. How could that man not be found guilty when a hundred or so terra-formers and agri-farmers were gunned down?"

"Do you know many farmers or formers in the Emerald City?" Kat asked.

"No, a few maybe."

"I know a few Generals. They felt Hepburn had done his job. He prevented a bunch of anarchists from murdering, raping and looting the streets of Cook Straits like they'd just done in Nu Canterbury."

"You agree with them?"

"No, but I understand them. I also wonder if the High Command had sent two or three battalions to the South Island instead of just the one, the mob would have seen the wisdom in standing down before anything got out of hand. But the mob was on a high after Nu Canterbury, and clashed with Hepburn's troops. It was a recipe for disaster from the outset, and the High Command, in hind-sight, knew it. Anyway, Hepburn was exonerated of all charges by the court, but you can see what sort of assignments he's subsequently drawn."

"I'm not sure I really understand."

"The military won't give him up, purely because the civilian authorities want him, and he won't get a fair trial. But, the military also don't want any other officer thinking that they could get away with a similar incident. Since Hepburn didn't do the honourable thing and resign, he's here having his nose rubbed in the fact that he's now considered a failure, despite an illustrious war-time record as a junior officer."

Jack glanced around the Base. "It certainly does look a mess."

"And I suspect it will only get worse. When I was at university, I read an essay on leadership by my Grandpa Jim.

He had a lot to say, but he also had a notion that stuck with me. He suggested that an element of leadership depended on belief, perhaps even illusion."

"Belief? Illusion?" Jack didn't like the sound of what she was saying."

"As a commander, you have to believe that you are the best person to lead. That you can achieve the mission with fewer casualties, less grief, and better than anyone else. And your troops have to believe the same, even if it isn't really so. Actions speak louder than words, we all know that, but if you don't have a track record or a reputation that precedes you, then an illusion of confidence that you are competent and capable is required."

Jack shook his head "The troops here aren't under any such illusions!"

"Right," Kat agreed. "And that, more than any amount of acid rain or snow, is what is making this place hell."

"What are we going to do?"

"I don't know," Kat said slowly. "Well, yes, I do. We are going to see that these people don't starve. Beyond that, we'll have to wait and see."

"Why do I find 'wait and see' from a certain Ensign Severn a very frightening concept?"

"Oh, you haven't seen frightening yet, Jack. Right now, what do you say we get out of this snow?"

Back in her room, Kat removed her snow encrusted jacket, secured the two rifles and her pistol and did a quick survey. Standard junior officer accommodation: bathroom with shower, large walk-in closet, easy chair, desk and bed. As long as the building's self-contained energy, water and sanitation continued to work, she could take care of the rest. Her kit bag sat in a puddle of water-logged carpet. She dragged it into the bathroom; most of its contents were soaked. For a moment she considered leaving it for mess staff to sort out, however, a glance at the mould on the shower tiles suggested that there might not be any 'mess staff' waiting on her slightest whim, no matter how large the tip might be.

With a wry smile, Kat fed her various uniforms through the ageing washer, dryer and presser units in the bathroom. Whilst she worked, there were other things to do. Having to ask for a map to find her own warehouses was ridiculous. "Safi, did Max pass you any new software routines before we left?"

"Several."

"Can you get access into the local military network?"

"I have several applications that should enable that."

"Can you do it from here?"

"Searching." Safi responded obediently and maybe just a little bit too enthusiastically. By the time Kat had her Number One Dress (Ceremonial & Mess) and Number Two Dress (Parade & Barrack) uniforms ready to hang up she was wondering why she hadn't taken the Sergeant Major's advice and left them both at home. The presser unit was starting to overheat and was scorching her fingers when Safi chose to respond. "I now have access."

"Can you turn off the warehouse compound lights?"

"Yes."

Kat thought for a second. "At zero two hundred local, turn the warehouse compound lights out." That should give any of the locals in true-need enough time. "Can you lock down the warehouses?" Kat took that moment to pull off the remainder of her still damp uniform and hang it in the shower, including her soaked-through boots. She turned the room's humidity down to its minimum setting. Taking Safi off, Kat placed the HI carefully on the desk.

"That information is not on the military network." There was a short pause, "but I can access it on the warehouse system."

"The warehouse has its own system?"

"Yes ma'am."

"Then lock them all down at zero three hundred." Kat ordered pulling the bed covers over herself. Her feet were still cold, but hopefully that wouldn't last too long. "What time is reveille?"

"The Administration branch handout welcoming you to Elmendorf Base details reveille as zero six hundred."

"Wake me at zero five thirty."

Kat awoke to a skull-splitting headache and a dry mouth. "Safi, lights. What's the humidity in here?"

"One moment while I connect to the building's

network," was not what she wanted to hear, but it told her that another system had not been merged into an overall base network. Kat was no computer guru like Dee, but this was poor systems management.

"Humidity is currently at six percent within this room, and your climate control unit is fast approaching mechanical failure."

"Turn it up," Kat ordered as she glanced around at the disarray of part-dried uniforms and the stink of fast-dried boots. She headed for the shower, then went back into the room, made her bed, before dumping everything that had dried out overnight in the bathroom onto it. Only then did she take pain-killers and step into the shower.

Feeling almost human again, she dried, attached Safi and dressed. Laced on her spare boots, pulled on her temperature adjusting, moisture retardant over-jacket and at zero six hundred met Jack in the ground floor lobby of their accommodation block.

Half way across the open space between the buildings, snow already beginning to settle onto them, Kat stopped. The mess hall was in complete darkness. Likewise, not a single light showed in the windows of either of the accommodation blocks above them.

"What's up?" Jack asked.

"One place I want to check before I do something I'm probably going to regret," Kat said, before leading Jack across the snow concealed part-frozen slush to the Headquarters building. As she expected, the lights were dim; the Ops Room slept at their desks. A light still burned in the Colonel's office. Kat walked quietly to his door. The man slept, head thrown back, snoring. Jack frowned her a question. Kat motioned him back down the hall.

"So," Jack said, "if that's the way it is, there's nothing we can do."

"I'm hungry, and I intend to eat," Kat said as she marched purposefully through the snow towards the mess hall. "Safi, give all personnel's rooms a wake-up call. Lights on everywhere. Locate the chefs. Tell them I want them down here now."

"Yes, Kat."

"Can your computer do that?"

"Dee gave Safi a couple of new routines. Why?"

"It's just, well, I'm not sure I like the idea of someone else's computer waking me up." Jack's frown deepened. "And, Kat, are us four Ensigns the only other officers assigned here?"

"Oh no!" Kat gasped. "Safi, are there any other officers on base?"

"Affirmative. In addition to four Ensigns and the Colonel, there is Commander Deane, the XO, Commander Goodhew, who is the MO, and a Lieutenant Harper."

"Did we wake them up?" Kat asked.

"I hear no noise except snoring from both Deane's and Goodhew's rooms."

"Turn off their lights," Kat and Jack both shouted.

"Done."

"Lieutenant Harper's room?" Kat asked.

"She is showering."

"Two out of three isn't bad," Kat sighed.

"*Senior* Ensign Severn, are we going about this in the correct manner?" Jack asked, very respectfully.

"Doesn't look like it," Kat acknowledged, as Safi opened the doors to the Mess Hall without bothering to ask. Kat reviewed her problem for an extended minute or two. Strong-arming the workers in her brother's political campaign office was one thing, but how would fellow officers react to her actions? Some might consider what she was doing as a good show of initiative, but others would fall back on works like *insubordination*. Upon further reflection, Kat decided on a new approach. "Safi, locate yesterday's new arrivals. Inform them that they are wanted in the mess hall in fifteen minutes, and show me a list of all those assigned to the warehouse complex."

Thirty seconds later, Kat knew that a significant number of those she'd brought in yesterday had been allocated to her department. Good. If she was going to play power games, it would be best if she started with a crew she'd already had some responsibility for. She eyed the Mess Hall around her and scowled at her first impression. Upon further review, her scowl got deeper. The floors of both restaurants were dirty, and the tables needed wiping down. She headed for the kitchen; that definitely needed a good clean.

"Show me the personnel files on the chefs." Safi did; Kat was not impressed. Two leading crewmen appeared to alternate being in-charge . . . at irregular intervals. And one seemed to have an unproven allegation of diverting potatoes to an, as yet, un-located illegal hooch still. Had this operation drawn the arse-end of everything? *Well, you're here aren't you?*

"Safi, do any of our other personnel have any catering experience?"

"Master Crewman Cowell graduated from Alberta City's central catering college. Her father is a celebrity chef with several restaurants and a TV show in the same city. Master Crewman Jayne Cowell has been posted in from the Electrical and Mechanical Engineering branch's Technical Trades School at Fort Lee and is a Weapons Tech by trade."

Kat and Jack exchanged looks. "Another kid trying to avoid the family curse," Kat laughed.

"She's a Master Crewman too, so she out-ranks the two Leading Chefs," Jack chuckled.

"Safi, inform Miss Cowell her presence is required in the Mess Hall immediately, if not sooner. And where are our chefs?"

"Still sleeping."

"Safi, do you have the traditional reveille bugle call amongst your files?"

"Yes."

"Full volume into all catering staff's rooms if you please."

Even in the restaurant on the ground floor of the enlisted personnel's accommodation block, Kat could hear the bugles sounding on the floors above.

A few minutes later, Master Crewman Cowell appeared and saluted.

"You wanted to see me, ma'am?" she said sourly.

"Did you eat in here yesterday?"

"Yes, I did, and no, I didn't like it much, but no, I'm not interested in cleaning up this mess."

"What's your price?" Kat added.

"My price?"

"Yes, everyone has one. Right now, I need you. In case you haven't noticed, this unit isn't going to hell, because it is already firmly established there. Food can change a lot, and we certainly need to change things!"

Cowell scowled at the praise. "You're a Severn?"

"Yes, and I don't much like having what my father does thrown in my face, so I suspect you don't, either."

"How many chefs do they have?" Cowell said, glancing around.

"Two Leading Crewmen that like to drink the potatoes, and three Crewmen with only basic catering training." Cowell wrinkled her nose at that. Slowly she paced her way to the kitchen. That drew a disgusted grunt.

"No wonder the food's so bad." She turned to Kat, "I'll name my price later, and it won't be cheap. But for now, the challenge has hooked me. And I'm hungry. I want six volunteers to start cleaning this kitchen right now. If that's alright with you ma'am."

Kat volunteered the first six from her warehouse team that came through the door.

When the chefs finally wandered aimlessly into the kitchen, Cowell took one look at them and declared them unsanitary and unsafe. Kat detailed off a further six of her crew with a leading crewman in charge with orders to get the five chefs clean, even if they had to use wire brushes. After last night's meal, Kat had to turn down volunteers to undertake that duty.

Lieutenant Harper showed up as the chefs were being marched away to the showers. "When is breakfast?" she asked. The voice was high, the handshake limp, and the dark roots showing in the blond thatch left Kat wondering, *is anything about this woman authentic or genuine.*

"Give me half an hour," Cowell shouted from the kitchen.

Harper didn't hide her disappointment. As the Lieutenant glanced around the mess hall, Kat could hear her grinding her teeth. "I guess I'll be at my desk. I'm still trying to define the correct policy for who we help. There are so many in need, but so many of them are armed. What this place needs is a tightening up of the gun ownership laws. Ensign, have someone bring over some coffee, toast and some fruit when it's ready. I'll just start the day at my desk early." Her exit, however, was slow, as if she expected Kat to stop her, do the proper junior officer thing of asking the wise senior to tell her all she needed to know.

Kat didn't have time for that; she headed for the kitchen and its scrub teams. That got Harper moving in the opposite direction. "Safi, what is Harper's job?"

"She commands the Administration branch."

"Last night's sleeping watch-keepers." Jack remarked.

"Looks like it. Can you imagine her and Hepburn in an Orders Group?"

"Why do I suspect we won't be having many Orders Groups?" Jack grinned at the prospect. "Did I hear right? She's developing our policies?"

"And probably will be for the next ten years!" Kat knew people like Harper, from civilian voluntary work and on political campaigns. They were usually too fixated on the minutiae to get in Kat's way. "We'll get everybody fed, with or without her policies."

Cowell came and stood by the kitchen door, hands on hips. "Scrambled eggs and bacon is the fastest thing I can get out this morning. Any of you smiling faces ever flipped burgers in that fine Scottish restaurant or done some industrial-strength cooking in your sordid little lives before you joined up?" Kat cringed at Cowell's choice of words; the woman grinned unrepentantly. Several hands went up among the gathering troops. The new head chef waved them into her kitchen with a proprietary grin and a "Scrub your hands and get an apron on."

While the place took on the smell of a kitchen in use, Kat circulated. Safi gave her a summary of who had what assignments and how long they'd been at Elmendorf. With Safi coaching, Kat asked a question here, made a neutral observation there, and managed to get most talking about their jobs.

Then Kat listened. There was a lot of resentment, some at the locals of Anchorage, a significant amount directed at Fleet Command, but most of it was just frustration, pure and simple. Anchorage was a lousy place to be, and they were just sitting on their butts while it got progressively worse.

"Who's in charge of the warehouse complex?" she asked the first person who admitted to working there.

"I don't know, ma'am. I think we come under the

Admin Branch, rather than Logistics. There's a Petty Officer that shows up sometimes, but most days we just sit about until a shipment comes in, then we unload it and stack it in the designated warehouse."

"Who built the perimeter fence?"

"A local contractor. Why, ma'am?"

"Because there's a large hole in it that needs fixing."

"It wasn't there yesterday when we knocked off ma'am," a leading crewman assured her.

"No, but a truck drove through it last night when I started shooting at it."

"You went there at night!"

"You shot at them!" The young women beside him added.

"It seemed like the thing to do. They were shooting at me. Do you know anything about the nightly shipments from the warehouse?"

The two looked at each other, obviously uncomfortable. The female crewman answered. "We know things are missing most mornings, but we were told to ignore it."

"Well, not anymore," Kat said.

As they walked away from those two, Jack shook his head. "I'm starting to think the smartest move I ever made was to tear the ligaments in my ankle during training and get back-squaded a term. I can't tell you how glad I am that you graduated from the Academy ahead of me."

"And all this time I thought it was because you had to re-sit the final exam on Mess etiquette," Kat said, elbowing him in the ribs.

The chefs returned from the showers to impromptu applause and started work under Cowell's ever-watchful eyes. Two of the kitchen volunteers asked to stay on. Kat started making a list of things she was going to need forgiveness for. She definitely wasn't going to ask permission first. Father always said it was a lot easier to get Parliament to forgive what was working, than to get those prima-donnas to approve something which may or may not fail. Everything she'd seen in the last few months convinced her that, at least in one respect, her father's way of doing things and the Fleet's way were not that different.

Breakfast finished, Kat went through the line again and took a couple of trays and coffee across to the Headquarters. Harper was bent over her workstation, moving a paragraph from one part of the page to another. Hepburn was still asleep in his chair. Kat placed the tray and mug on his desk and turned to go.

There was a snort behind her as the snoring stopped, then the sound of boots hitting the floor. She turned. The Colonel looked at her through red-rimmed eyes for a long moment, then reached for the mug. A long swallow later, he put it down. "What are you looking at, Ensign?" he growled as he attacked the plate.

Kat mentally flipped a coin. As William Severn's only daughter she'd got away with a lot. As an Ensign, it might be a good idea to at least let the Colonel know what direction she was heading off in. "Nothing, sir. I was wondering if I might ask for some guidance, or whether I should wait for an Orders Group."

"There is no way I'm going to. . ." The Colonel decided not to finish that sentence. "Okay, Severn, what do you want?"

"Am I in charge of the warehouses, sir?"

"Yes."

"I report directly to you?"

"Yes, I told you all this yesterday."

"There's a hole in the warehouse fence where a truck drove through it last night. Who do I talk to, to get it fixed?"

"Harper," he bellowed. "Get in here."

The Lieutenant did not rush to her Commanding Officer's call. Adjusting her uniform, she came to a halt beside Kat, just inside the Colonel's doorway. Her "Yes, sir" came out with a mixture of pain and disdain.

"The Ensign here wants the warehouse fence mended."

"I'll have to inspect it, sir. The warehouse is under my jurisdiction."

"Not anymore. This Ensign has it all to herself, with Ensign Byrne as backup."

"But, sir!" Harper didn't quite squeal. Kat had heard enough similar bureaucratic shrieks when her father had taken away a small part of someone's empire. She waited to see who had the upper hand.

"Ensign Severn has the warehouse; I gave you the other

two Ensigns. Maybe the three of you can finish your policies." The Colonel eyed the eggs, took another mouthful, then took a piece of bacon. "This breakfast in good. New chef?"

"Yes sir," Kat cut in. "Master Crewman Cowell had some catering experience before she joined up. She's willing to oversee the kitchen." Kat turned to Harper. "With the Lieutenant's permission."

"My toast tasted the same as it always does," Harper sniffed.

"Well my eggs are the best I've had in a very long time. Ensign, you want the mess hall assigned to you too?"

"Not if you and the Lieutenant don't want it to be, sir" Even a Prime Minister's daughter had learnt a little bit about tact.

"I want it to be. Also, see if you can't do something about the accommodation. It's filthy. Lieutenant, transfer the catering and accommodation budgets over to Severn, and let her run with it."

"If you say so, sir"

"I think I just did. Now, if you two ladies will please get out of my office. I need to get cleaned up."

Kat saluted, about-turned and marched from the Colonel's office, closely followed by Harper, who stopped her outside in the corridor. "Just remember, Severn, I'll be the one auditing those budgets, and people can end up doing time in Florence for misappropriating government funds, no matter what their name is."

"Yes ma'am. I understand completely," Kat said and marched down the stairs and out of the Headquarters building. "Safi," Kat whispered, "is there anyone assigned to me with any accountancy training?"

"No."

"Does anyone have an accountant in their family?" Another crewman or trooper was going to hate her for dragging them into a profession they'd learned to loathe at their parents knee. "That's just life, kid," she'd soon be whispering to whomever her next victim was.

Kat had Safi inform her warehouse personnel to parade, with weapons, at zero eight hundred. Uniform for the day was Number Eight Dress (Combats) with over-jacket and body armour. She passed on the temptation to put her five Land Force troopers into fully armoured chameleon suits. Somehow, she doubted that kind of equipment had even been brought with them, this being a MACC tasking. Kat delegated the Mess Hall and accommodation to Jack, which left her just enough time to interview a pair of leading crewmen who both had very similar opinions of the accounting profession and of their rarely home accountant parents. Jack and her flipped to see who got which. To loud protests of "I didn't join the Fleet to count beans, ma'am," Kat informed Leading Crewman Leonard he'd being doing exactly that for her in the warehouse.

At zero eight hundred, Leonard formed the troops up and marched them to the warehouse complex. If he had ever learned drill commands he'd completely forgotten them. However, he made up some fairly convincing replacements and managed to get the formation moving; the troops got the message, even if they couldn't keep in step. "Call the step," Kat shouted.

The first "Left" was pretty weak, but by the third "Right" and a lot of 'skipping' it was getting better, with even the worst offenders eventually managing to get their feet into step with the others.

"Look up, dig those heels," came from the rear ranks where the Land Force personnel marched, tall and proud.

Despite the weather, as they marched down the pitted and pot-holed *Arctic Warrior Drive* from the main base to the warehouse complex, a significant number of civilians were out and about, hunched in upon themselves against the cold and ever falling snow. As Leonard called out the step again, the civilians raised their heads too, some with mouths agape, others curious. A few took a good look, then took off running, carrying what message and to whom, Kat had no idea. But anyone spreading the word that a new day was dawning at the warehouse complex was fine by her.

There were shouts from the crowd already gathered at the warehouse fence as they approached; people milled around the gate and the new hole. Others raced to join them from *inside* the warehouse yard. Apparently the building lockdown had been successful; the runners came empty handed. Only as the troop formation came to a halt did Kat have Safi unlock the four warehouses.

She turned to face her first real command. Some knew her; she'd done her best to get them out of the snow as fast as was humanly possible last night. Others were old hands, stationed here for up to six weeks . . . a long time to serve in hell. As soon as they stopped the incessant snow began to settle onto them. Kat re-ran some of the pep talks she'd given in political campaign offices, did a quick edit, then began.

"I don't know how some of you feel about the work you've been doing. Maybe you're happy about it. Maybe you're not. That doesn't matter. Today, here and now, we start the relief mission to the civilian community of Anchorage. There are hungry people out there. We've got food. We're going to see they get fed. Those of you who have been working on this for a while, help the new faces. I'll be circulating for most of the day. If you have a problem, see me. If you have a solution, see me too. Many of you are new to the Fleet or Land Forces. If you had been posted to a ship duty, then right now, you would probably be dry and warm." That drew a few laughs. "You would also be a small cog in a very big wheel, doing what you were told to do. Here, you are critical to saving people's lives," She paused. "We are all in this together. I need ideas. You come up with a good one, you'll find I'm a good listener. Any questions?" Kat spoke the inevitable end to these kinds of talks. Just as inevitably, there were none. "Leading Crewman, fall out the detachment to their duties. See those needing specific assignments get them."

Oh, that sounded so easy. Maybe with a good petty officer it would have worked. Her leading crewman was just as out of his depth as she was. Still, she left him to it, and did the first of her many walk-abouts in the slush and snow.

The warehouse complex's eastern side opened out onto a large loading and unloading area. A huge un-manned drop-pod lay like a beached whale, ramps down, half empty in the centre. A young crewman led a group who started hauling twenty kilo bags of rice or beans onto waiting shoulders and lugging them into the adjacent warehouses. Back-breaking labour. That couldn't be the way it was usually done.

At the hole in the fence, people just stood in the falling snow. They needed food and work. She needed labourers to help distribute the food. "Safi, can I hire local workers?"

"No. There are no funds available to this MACC tasking for hiring local employees." *Of course, Fleet all the way.* The less charged to an emergency operation the more left for the rest of the Fleet. Kat had heard rumours that some commands even managed to keep an extra ship in commission, gambling that enough funding could be found through budgets provisionally allocated for emergency relief operations.

"Excuse me, ma'am," a quiet voice called to Kat as she walked towards the damaged fence line. Kat turned to face a thin woman in a long oilskin coat, with an oversized scarf over her white hair. "Are you the new person in charge?"

"Yes," Kat said; then when the woman seemed unable to respond, Kat softened. "How can I help you?"

The woman was surprisingly well spoken. "My name is Ellen Tutt. My church runs a soup kitchen. Most of men lost their jobs when the crops failed. Families are going hungry. We're seeing that they get one hot meal a day."

"That's very good of you," Kat offered the women when she seemed uncertain how to go on. None too sure how to help, Kat could at least give the woman a listening ear.

"We're out of food." Kat knew what was coming; she nodded. The woman's words stumbled on. "We've been buying food from this Fleet man, but we're out of money."

"A Petty Officer?" Kat asked, remembering what she'd heard about the warehouse leadership. The women shrugged; military ranks were a mystery to most civilians. Kat wondered if she could arrange a line-up but suspected the culprit would be long gone, even if he hadn't managed to ship out on the *Amy J* yesterday. No, Kat's problem was how to go forward, not look backward. She brushed the settling snow from her face and she thought through the problem. She was here to feed people, but see couldn't just hand out food. Obviously someone had been, for a price. *But I'm a Severn.* Oh, joy!

"Safi, who can hire local civilians on a MACC tasking like this?"

"Non-Governmental Organisations are the usual employers of the local labour forces." The women listened, being slowly smothered by falling snow, as Kat continued the conversation with her assisting HI.

"Do we have any NGO's in Anchorage."

"No."

Not a surprise. This place really was at the frozen-over backside-of-beyond. "Safi, what does it take to set up an NGO?"

"I have almost completed the paperwork required to set one up. Before I send it for registration and processing, what should I name it?"

"Safi, you're wonderful," Kat grinned, and the women across from her almost cracked a smile. "Make it the Alexandra Langdon-Lennox Fund for Displaced Farmers," Kat said. Now that would make her grandmother's day.

"I went to school with a girl named Alexandra Langdon," the woman muttered, "a long, long time ago, back in London, just before the war. We had fun in those days."

"I hear Grandma Alex still is having fun. She was from London, although a long time before I was born. Safi, is that application processed?"

"Nearly done. How large do I endow this fund?"

"What would I have to pay you to do what you're already doing?" Kat asked Ellen.

"If you feel you must pay me, I'm willing to work for ten dollars a week," the woman answered. Kat tried not to show any reaction to that. With just a week's interest from her trust fund she could probably hire everyone in Anchorage for an entire year at that rate. Safi's last upgrade had taken two months interest.

"I can get volunteers to work for free," the women went on, mistaking Kat's silence for disapproval. "If you arrange the release of food to the soup kitchens, a lot of men will work for you. Not just my church's kitchen. There are many others in town."

"I think we have a deal. Kat said quickly to reassure the woman. Then she whispered to Safi, "Put a hundred thousand dollars in it for starters." To the woman, Kat continued. "I need to run this past my boss." Kat accessed her comm-link. "Operations, this is Ensign Severn, I need to talk with the Colonel."

"Hepburn," came from Kat's comm-link a moment later.

"Colonel, Ensign Severn here. I need some more

advice."

"And you expect good advice from me?"

Kat ignored the question and quickly ran down what she'd done.

"This displaced farmer fund is a legitimate NGO?" he asked as she finished.

"I have it on the best legal advice," she said, grinning at Ellen. The old women did actually smile this time.

"Yes, we can release food to soup kitchens, food banks and alike, just so long as we've got an NGO vouching for their legitimacy. You may have noted the distinct lack of any media coverage or mainstream NGO support, as this gig isn't the most popular show on the planet. If you've got one, do it." He terminated the call.

Kat pulled a single ABCANZ dollar coin from her pocket and handed it to Ellen. "I guess that makes you the fund's first employee. Do you know anyone else who might help me?"

Ellen glanced around; a man stepped forward. His boots had holes in them, as did his jacket.

"I'm Oscar Krejik. Oz to most. I was a foreman at the docks before the winter snows didn't melt and most sensible folks high-tailed it out of here. I see your people lugging bags of beans around. I know people who used to work here as civilian contractors. They'll know where the lifters and loaders are, although they don't work too good in all this acidic snow. It screws them real bad, plays hell with the rubber of the hydraulics, or so the boss said before he got out."

"You're hired," Kat said and fished in her pocket for another coin. Like the Prime Minister, Kat always carried a couple of dollar coins. You could never tell when you'd want a soda and the net would be down. As she hired her second employee, she asked, "Do either of you know anyone who used to work in the accommodation blocks in the main base?"

"Amelia Boggart was the manager of the Senior NCOs' Mess." Ellen said. "But when large numbers of troops stopped being sent to Elmendorf, the staff were reduced. Then folks started leaving town and were never replaced by the base, and hence no staff."

"Sounds like a lot of people left?"

"All that could."

"Well, for those still left here, this is the drill." Kat rushed out her words before anyone could change their mind. "The pay is ten dollars a week." Kat handed her third and last dollar to Ellen. "Please give this one to Amelia. The rest will have to wait a while for pay. Also, they'll get all that they and their families can eat at the nearest soup kitchen. That sound like a fair deal?"

Ellen and Oz glanced around at the others standing further back in the snow. A head nodded a bit, a finger twitched, a hand raised a little. They came forward when Oz motioned them through the hole in the fence. Under Ellen and Oz's direction they began unloading the drop-pod's remaining contents. A check of the three military trucks parked in the yard revealed only one actually still worked.

Kat tapped her comm-link. "Jack, how's the main base coming along."

"Crap. Kat, I can't keep my own room tidy in an environmentally and humidity controlled facility. How am I supposed to clean up this place?"

"I think our local Non-Governmental Organisation just hired someone to take over the accommodation for you."

"I didn't know there were any NGO's here."

"There wasn't this morning, but there is one now."

"Why do I not want to know how that happened?"

"Just pray to Saint Patrick or whatever it is that you do, that Colonel Hepburn is also content to not get bogged-down with the finer-details either. Now I've got three trucks out here, and only one will turn over. Apparently I've got lifters and loaders too, but all are damaged by the acid in the snow. You got any ideas about how to get them fixed?"

"The trucks could have damage to their solar panels," he paused, thinking through a solution. "But I think it's more likely to be no stored power left in their battery packs. Given that they're not about to get anything solar anytime soon around here to charge them back up, they're going to need replacing. I might be able to stimulate a chemical re-charge in the existing ones with my nano-techs, but at the moment they're busy shining the metal-work on my uniforms."

"You're using nano-techs to clean your uniforms?"

"Of course, doesn't everyone?" came back in pure

astonishment. Kat rolled her eyes back at the sky . . . and got snow in them for her dramatics. Blinking, she turned back to her comm-link.

"Tomorrow morning Jack, you turn the accommodation over to someone who knows how to get it sorted out, then you get your butt over here. And bring your nano-leprechauns or munchkins, or whatever they are with you, to work on my broken equipment."

As Kat finished the discussion with Jack the working truck was being loaded with food. She found a crewman with the appropriate licence, then detailed two armed crewmen to guard the cargo while it was dropped off at the kitchens Ellen had marked onto Kat's map. Ellen also promised to get all the guards back unharmed before it got dark. The crewmen might be the ones carrying the M37s, but they still looked relieved at the woman's assurance of their safety. With all her pocket change gone, Kat had Safi do a search for any kind of local bank or facility that she could physically draw funds from. She finished the day feeling pretty good.

ONE : NINE

The next morning started bad and got progressively worse. First, for Amelia Boggart to take over managing the accommodation buildings, Lieutenant Harper demanded a meeting with Colonel Hepburn. The Colonel immediately went on record as not caring who did it as long at the accommodation got sorted out. Harper insisted on a signed contract and only withdrew her long list of objections when it became clear that this service was being provided under the Federation's 'Apprentice Training Volunteer Program' and so it wasn't actually costing the Fleet anything. Safi's fast law search found that bit of legal fiction while Kat stalled. The Colonel seemed to be enjoying himself immensely as Kat danced around Harper's opposition to almost everything proposed.

Once free of Headquarter red-tape, Kat got Jack doing a full inventory of what had once been vehicles or mechanical handling equipment and what work was required to convert them from cold and rusting junk back into something more useful. She assigned herself the miserable job of getting a full, complete and honest inventory of supplies in the warehouse complex, separating Fleet issue from relief provisions. Kat had barely touched the surface that afternoon when a breathless runner skidded to a halt beside her. Armed thugs had held up a soup kitchen, cleared out the food, and beaten up Ellen Tutt for reasons that completely escaped Kat.

Kat stopped herself two paces into running down to Ellen's kitchen. That would do no good. In this snow nothing would leave tracks for more than a few minutes, and if things followed the usual pattern, no one would have seen anything anyway. While Kat struggled with lousy options, Oz took over the inventory. Free, she stepped outside and let the incessant snowfall cool her rage down.

Rushing across town would achieve nothing; the boy

said Ellen was already being treated by the best doctor available. It was so tempting to take her five Land Force troopers and chase the culprits down. Fat chance she'd have. That then left her with the no lesser problem of working out how she'd prevent it from ever happening again. She spent a good hour pacing up and down in the snow, thinking through her limited options.

That evening at supper, she set her plate across from Colonel Hepburn and settled into the chair.

"I need your advice, sir."

"Why am I starting to get concerned every time you utter those words, Ensign?"

Kat updated him on the warehouse. He nodded, satisfied, as he buttered his bread roll. She then hit him with the problem of food being ripped off by thugs who beat up old ladies. His bread went down uneaten and he looked at her. "And you expect me to do something about that?"

"Sir?" Kat left the question hanging there.

He leaned back. "I don't doubt you are fully aware that I am not the most popular field-ranked officer in the ABCANZ Land Forces, and was charged with using heavy weapons for crowd control, amongst other things."

"I am aware of that, Colonel."

"You are also no-doubt aware of the quality of the personnel we've got here, Ensign Severn."

"Not really, sir, but . . ." she lied.

"But what?" he interrupted her. "Let me give you a little history lesson. As long ago as the Romans, enterprising civilian industry and services have set themselves up, outside the wire, or wall, of military camps. There to service both the needs of the garrison and the individual soldiers. Not much has changed in a couple of thousand years. After the war the High Command decided to keep Elmendorf Base open. These people, or their parents came here of their own accord. We didn't ask them to support the military, they just arrived. What they refer to as Anchorage is mostly the old married quarters from the original Elmendorf base. The community outside the wire got bigger as more and more people came, then settlers arrived, trying to scratch a new life in this hell hole. Many of them aren't even

ABCANZ citizens. In addition, this was mutant territory. Nothing like as many as the Badlands between Nu New England and San Angeles, but mutant country nonetheless. Therefore the settlers agreed that every home was entitled to weapons, preferably automatic. No more mutants, but a population that's seriously armed, and now very desperate and very dangerous. And I'll be damned if I'll put personnel under my command out there for anybody who has the inclination to start taking pot-shots at them." He looked hard at Kat, then went on more softly.

"They said those terra-formers and agri-farmers were only throwing rocks on South Island. I swear to God they used automatic weapons. But we didn't find the guns in the wreckage, and no one believes Land Force grunts. Except other Land Force grunts. But I'm still in this hell-hole, and I'll be damned if I'll put anyone else in a worse spot." He screwed up his napkin, threw it on his half-eaten supper, scowled at it, then looked at Kat.

"So, Ensign Severn, what are *you* going to do about thugs that steal food from soup kitchens and beat up old ladies?"

"I intend to post a constant guard on the warehouses."

"Putting our people out patrolling in the slush and snow? Makes them easy targets, too."

"No, sir. One warehouse has a small office tower, four stories high. Its roof is flat and should give those on duty clear fields of vision all along the perimeter fence." *And clear fields of fire.* "I've recycled empty rice bags into sandbags and built an emplacement up there. That should give our personnel some protection. I'll need a searchlight."

"I can get you one of those."

"I'm also asking the locals, councillors, officials, small business types, teachers – to share the night watches."

"So they can give the order to fire?"

"No, sir. To serve at witnesses in any local court, if one of our people does give the order to open-fire."

The Colonel eyed Kat for a long moment. "Not bad, Ensign. You know they're starving out on the farmsteads."

"Yes, sir. We're expecting a dozen trucks to arrive by sea sometime this week. Once we have them we'll start spreading our footprint."

"First convoy is bound to get shot at, maybe even raided."

"I'll be leading that one, Colonel. Unless of course, you want to?"

He snorted. "Sorry young lady, I've been in that predicament. Once you've been hung out to dry by the High Command, you learn to take what minor privileges the power of delegation offers you."

"Thank you, sir," seemed the only answer to that. Hepburn stood, abandoning his unfinished meal. "One more thing, Colonel," Kat added quickly. "That NGO that's helping me, I hear it's hiring locals with guns to guard the kitchens."

That got her a long, measured stare. "What the locals do to each other is their own damn business," he said slowly. "Just don't go spending too much time on it."

"Of course not, sir," she replied as the Colonel turned away.

First thing next morning, Kat checked in at the warehouse. Oz and a dozen of his team had worked through most of the night. They expected to complete a full inventory by noon; she left them to it. Jack showed up a few minutes later. Amelia had arrived at the accommodation block earlier that morning with seven or eight ex-employees, Jack advised. "We can handle things from here, sir. We should have everything sorted out by this evening, sir."

He had several ideas how to get the trucks and loaders operating again, so Kat left him to get on with it and concentrated on what she wanted to do.

Much to Kat's surprise, Safi had managed to locate a bank that was still operational within Anchorage. She paid it a visit on-route to Ellen's kitchen. Eventually given access into a fortress-like structure by highly officious staff, she withdrew several hundred ABCANZ dollars.

Despite what had happened the previous afternoon, Ellen was back, hard at work. Her soup kitchen was a well-run operation. Undeniably it needed a good coat of paint on the outside, but so did the rest of Anchorage, yet inside it was homely and warm. The woman sported a bandaged head but didn't let that slow her down at all.

Kat placed three hundred dollars in low denomination notes onto the counter in front of Ellen. "How long will it take to get armed guards on each kitchen?"

"They're already here," Ellen answered. Two younger women smiled and produced machine pistols from under the counter. "My daughters," Ellen explained. "Their husbands are out front."

"And at the other kitchens?"

"All have guards today. No man wants his wife or daughter put through this," she said with a wave to her head.

Kat pointed at the bank notes. "See that everyone gets his or her pay. And Ellen, it will be a problem for me if my Colonel is embarrassed by something done by our guards. Could you please make sure they understand that while they're taking our pay and eating our food, they are. . .?"

"On best behaviour," Ellen smiled. "Yes, I will let them know that Grandma Ellen expects only the best from her men."

Not really the response Kat wanted, and it certainly wasn't how a Land Force's Colonel would express his expectations for discipline within the ranks. However, it was probably the best assurance this lash-up was ever going to provide. Kat walked back through the snow to the warehouse complex.

Somehow word had gotten out that Jack needed mechanics; the warehouse fence was already lined with men and women with automotive skills, all seeking employment. For a repair workshop, Jack identified a large building on the other side of 9th Street that could easily be included within a revised perimeter fence. One of the locals Jack hired was also the owner of a failing small-scale delivery company on the other side of the settlement. He was most eager to sell his vans for just thirty-three percent of their value. Kat was uncomfortable at the idea until the man confessed that his San Angeles based bank had called in the administrators and was trying to sell him off for even less. If Kat would buy him out, he could pay off his debts and be in a position to buy his business back from the NGO when this relief operation was over. Under those conditions, the Displaced Farmers Fund happily made a payment and got the oversized delivery vans moved inside the fence.

While the actual transaction was quickly concluded with the shake of a hand, the paperwork required Kat to coordinate with Logistics, Finance and Administration. Kat quickly discovered why Logistics and Finance wanted nothing to do with Admin. Of the three departments, Logistics was by far the easiest to deal with. As a separate Branch-of-Service, the Petty Officer in charge turned out to be professional and accommodating and wanted to keep Lieutenant Harper as far away from him and his department as was practically possible. Finance was significantly more complicated, as although the Petty Officer shared the philosophy of his colleague in Logistics, Finance was not a separate branch and came under the direct control of Administration, and therefore Harper. Finally, the actual Administration branch itself: although Kat thought she detected a desire to cooperate from many of the people she spoke with, none wanted to show any initiative or act independently from Lieutenant Harper and provoke her fury, or malevolence. Getting Harper to sign off or approve anything turned into a most formidable task.

"Why do we need all this stuff?" the Lieutenant sniffed.

"If it's broken, we need to fix it." Kat had to go to the Colonel to get that answer declared acceptable. Still, five times the Admin Branch's Petty Officer returned Kat's paperwork for minor corrections, and five times Kat resubmitted it.

"Why are you putting up with this crap?" Jack asked.

"I wouldn't, if we had some proper sized vehicles to make our deliveries with, but they're all still 'on-route' and could be another week." Kat sighed and went along with the Lieutenant's little games. When the twelve trucks did finally arrive, Kat was most grateful for the preparation she and her team had already undertaken. Land Command had kindly back-loaded a dozen vehicles that were all due for the breaker's yard. The newest rig had a hundred thousand klicks on it, and the oldest was fast approaching two. The local mechanics took one look at them, shook their heads, then got on with totally rebuilding them, cannibalising two trucks for parts in an attempt to make the other ten road-worthy. All would need their IVeNS (Integrated Vehicle Navigation System) working at one-hundred-percent efficiency for the terrain they would be moving through. IVeNS used a clever combination of historic mapping, satellite updates - when available, GPS and ground penetrating radar to ensure the vehicle didn't leave the road, even if the road wasn't visible. Most Land Force vehicles had this function disabled, as being 'off-road' was usually desirable, but in these conditions it would need to be on; on and fully functioning, or the vehicle would not be leaving the base complex.

Kat didn't let Harper and her people use up all her time. Most mornings she quickly covered-off her Fleet duties to enable her afternoons to be devoted to the Alexandra Langdon-Lennox Fund. If she failed to hitch a ride with a supply van, she walked, visiting each of the soup kitchens, checking how everything was going. Despite there being no more robberies, and no more beatings, the snow still came down non-stop as Kat travelled the freezing streets of Anchorage. The people were still hunched over against the weather as they moved through the slush and snow covered streets, but now, just maybe, they seemed slightly less beaten by it all.

Whether she hitched a ride or walked, she wound up chilled to the bone by the time darkness fell, from the top of her head to the tips of her toes. The only thing between Kat and utter misery was the climate control in the accommodation block, and when Amelia reported that the entire unit was about to fail, Kat paid extra to hire the only man in Anchorage apparently able to repair the failing system. A dry, warm room each night was a necessity, regardless of the price.

Harper was still developing her policies when the mechanics whipped the oil from their hands and advised that six of the trucks were now as road-worthy as they were ever going to be. Kat didn't intend to wait any longer for 'policy.' The farmsteads were starving. She collected together the people she'd met on her visits and put the question to them: "Where do we start?"

"I think the Mat-Su Valley to the north is having it hardest," a former tractor salesman advised. "Across the west side of the Inlet the land is all mountains and gullies. Those gullies will take a lot of the snow, and not many folk live out there anyway, only the mine employees, but in the Mat-Su and along the Parks Highway it's a bit flatter. The water doesn't have anywhere to run to except into the rivers and lakes and they're all solid ice too. The land's frozen solid, it physically can't absorb any more."

Across the table from her, a priest and a teacher nodded their heads in agreement. "That's what we hear too," said the priest. "But, young lady, the armed gangs are also worse along the highway towards Talkeentna. A lot of gunmen are operating in those parts, and with the land being so snow-bound, there's no way anyone can effectively pursue them."

"We've got some pretty smart gear, Padre," Kat answered.

"I know you do, but I haven't seen any of it flying around here," the red faced priest answered back. "Is it only my imagination or is this whole effort being done on the cheap?"

"Father!" Ellen Tutt slapped his hand. "My mother taught me to say 'thank you' when someone offered a helping hand, not to count the fingers."

"Sorry."

"Nothing I haven't thought myself, Father." Kat acknowledged. "Tomorrow, I'll take all six trucks along the highway. See how far we can get in a day. Thanks for your advice."

"Do you want a few of our armed men to go with you?" Ellen asked.

Kat had been thinking a lot about that. Armed civilians riding shotgun for the Fleet just wasn't right. A few witnesses? No. "This is a Fleet operation, Ellen. So, we'll do it the Fleet way."

All the trucks were eight wheelers with a load capacity of ten tonnes. Each wheel was supposed to be good for both drive and steering; Kat was just happy they turned. The cabs had a pair of seats in the front, either side of the engine block, and a bench seat behind. Above the centre position on the bench was a roof hatch where a heavy calibre machine gun could be externally mounted, but Kat had no such weapons and Colonel Hepburn certainly wasn't going to authorise them even if they had been available. She assigned three 'gunners' to the bench seat of each truck. That left room for a driver and a commander in the front. Kat would command the first truck. She initially assigned Jack to command the last truck, but he asked to be her driver; there might be an advantage to having both officers up front. With her pair of leading crewmen, that only put a 'commander' in three of the six vehicles. Her accountant insisted on commanding one truck. "I get out of the office, or the auditors are going to find really weird things," was a threat Kat respected.

Unfortunately, when you give into one threat, you only get more. "Burnt toast if I don't get a truck," Cowell smiled. So she got a day away from the Mess Hall.

The sixth vehicle had an 'all Land Forces crew'.

With her convoy now on the move, Kat found herself with time on her hands and a puzzle that would not go away. Everyone here was supposed to be armed to the teeth; those in Anchorage certainly were. So, how come the farmsteads were off-line with rumours they'd been attacked by armed gangs. Archived satellite imagery showed that almost all of the farmsteads were no more than six hundred metres from the Parks Highway; clear lanes of fire as far as their weapons could be lethal. Anybody trying to rob a farmstead should have been very dead three or four hundred metres out, if not further. Perhaps someone could sneak in up to one or two hundred, but Kat had planned to stop at four hundred. Four hundred! Something was wrong here.

To the three young crewman riding in the back, there was definitely something wrong, but nothing of the magnitude that worried Kat. "I didn't join up to be a delivery boy," one young lad said, not caring if Kat heard.

"Hell," the next one agreed, "if I'd wanted to do deliveries, I could have stayed at home and worked in my dad's shop. At least there, after you put in eight hours, your evenings are your own. No offence, ma'am. It's not your fault we have to do a guard duty once a week."

"None taken," Kat assured him, knowing full well that all the troops knew she was the reason for the extra night duty.

"Wouldn't do you any good to have spare time," the third crewman, a woman, chimed in. "No place to go, and even if you did, it's snowing, snowing, snowing. Join the Fleet and see the snow!"

The first one was ready to come back in. "I joined up to be a weapons operator. I got the maximum score with the

127mm gun at Whale Island."

"But we're not at war anymore." Kat pointed out. "Getting food to starving people is a bit more pressing than getting ready for a hypothetical conflict."

"Yes, I know. But you're an officer ma'am, and you have to think like that. But me, just give me a 127mm and a formation of incoming enemy ships, and you'd see what I can do. This stuff, it's just making the do-gooders in their overstuffed sofas back in civilisation think they did something worthwhile when they paid their taxes. They ought to come out here and work every day in this freezing hell-hole like we do."

Kat didn't confide in him that one of the reasons she joined the Fleet was to get away from those very same 'do-gooders.'

ONE : TEN

The first farmstead on their list, some sixty kilometres north-east out of Elmendorf Base, was large and situated on the south side of the pre-war township of Palmer. All ABCANZ citizens, the owners, their children, wives, grandchildren and unrelated farm workers, filled several dozen family size houses. Add in the barns, silos and equipment sheds, and the farmstead tagged as 'Thomas 840' was not an insignificant site. A number of families from smaller farmsteads further up the highway had also taken refuge there. Before going off-line they had reported groups of truck-mounted bandits roaming the area. Kat shook her head; they ought to have been able to man a continuous watch. They ought not to have gone off-line. This just didn't make any sense.

Approaching the first farmstead, Kat matched the map Safi had provided on her helmet's head-up-display with the actual reality outside the vehicle. The driveway had been recently cleared of snow and salted, and was just about wide enough to permit two-way traffic, but it was also heavily pot-holed and in need of repair; Jack slipped and slid from side to side looking for the shallower holes as they began their approach. The fields on either side of the driveway were covered in at least a metre, if not considerably more, of snow. The crops no longer grew and the snow never stopped falling. Kat had an unhindered line of sight across the snow to the raging Matanuska River that had burst its banks and swallowed hundreds of metres of land with flood waters. The flooded areas were now frozen solid. An abandoned combine harvester was up to its cab in floodwater turned ice. *The ice would have channelled any attack; the raiders had to have hit them from the road. They should have been mowed down.*

What were Kat and her tiny convoy driving into?

"Make ready." Kat ordered as they came within three hundred metres of the farmstead. Jack left his assault rifle in the retaining brackets alongside his seat.

"Can't use it and drive."

Once, this farm had obviously been successful, if the five large barns said anything about its pre-eruption wealth. A big house held pride of place facing a central courtyard. Other out-buildings and houses turned this farmstead into a small village. There was nobody in sight.

Kat ordered the other trucks to halt and go on over-watch, then had to explain that 'over-watch' meant loaded rifles, watching in every direction, while she had Jack drove slowly in. Maybe she spotted movement behind a window. Maybe the barrel of a gun protruding out of a door. With a fatalistic grimace, Kat ordered Jack to stop at the gates. She dismounted, then started to walk the final sixty metres.

Activating her mike, Kat announced, "I am Ensign Severn of the ABCANZ Fleet," when she was less than thirty metres from the nearest building. Her voice boomed from the truck's loudspeaker, echoing off the buildings. "My vehicles have food. You went off-line over a month ago. Do you require assistance?"

A barn door opened; three men slipped out before closing it, then started walking slowly towards the centre of the courtyard. At the big house, several women appeared at the front door, two with babes-in-arms. They also started walking towards the centre. Kat followed their lead and walked forward too.

They met in the middle. A tall, balding man held out his hand to Kat. "I'm Henry Thomas. My father started this farm not long after the war." He waved at a thin, greying lady leading the other women. "This is my wife, Maria."

Kat shook his hand, then the woman's when she joined the group. "I have food packages for you. I was hoping to leave about a month's supply. How many people do you have here?"

The man shook his head. "A hundred or so, but a month's worth of food is far too much. They'll just come back and take it," he said bitterly.

"We could hide some, Henry," his wife said.

"They'd make us tell. Someone would talk, they'd *make* us."

The wife looked away but nodded in agreement.

"I guess we can come out here once a week," Kat offered, not really wanting the extra workload. Others now came from the barns, houses and outbuildings; the numbers kept growing. Kat had expected to see guns. There weren't any.

She slung her own weapon, removed her pilot-like helmet and partially unzipped her body-armour in an attempt to present a less aggressive posture to this obviously frightened and starving community. "Before I can leave any food, I'll need every person's ABCANZ IDent card to verify the delivery."

"We don't have our IDents anymore. They took them." Henry dropped the words like lumps of hot iron.

"Does that mean you can't help us?" Maria asked. The two silent women beside her clutched their children.

"I didn't drive all this way to tell hungry people I can't feed them because they don't have the correct paperwork. Don't worry, we can initially process you the same way as we would non-ABCANZ citizens." Kat said. *And Lieutenant Harper can finish her policies in hell.*

She activated her comm-link. "Jack, bring them in."

Nevertheless, losing IDent cards was no minor matter. For the last month, these people could have had their bank accounts emptied, their identities misused on the net. Anything could have happened to them while they were off-line and unable to say a word in their defence. This did not sound like the work of local hooligans. "With no IDents I'm going to need photographs of everyone," Kat said, then ordered Jack to break out the camera as soon as he arrived.

"Henry, if they've got a live up-link, I could check the bank account," one of the men suggested.

"You do that, Joe."

At that moment Jack's vehicle drew up beside Kat in the courtyard.

"Jack, see that this man gets access to the net." Jack took the flood of orders with a grin. "Yes ma'am."

"Can you get everyone out here to be photographed and processed?" Kat asked.

"My mother is sick, in bed," Henry said, "but, I guess we could bring here down here."

"I'll go and see her. I'm just trying to keep the damn auditors from flaying me too badly when this is all over."

"I understand. We're in business . . ." Henry stopped, glanced around, ended up staring at the snow covered yard. "We were."

"We will be again," his wife said, offering a hand that he flinched away from.

Kat entered the house and took the stairs slowly to the upper floor. The house was made of wood, finely polished by work and constant use. In a bedroom hung with a huge tapestry, made with the needlework of many hands for many years, lay an old woman, alone in an oversize bed. She moaned in pain. With three quick strides, Kat knelt by the bed, lifting the covers briefly from the old women. Her weathered, leather-like skin showed the purple and yellow discoloration of a several-week-old beating.

"I have a medic in the convoy. Can I have her take a look at your mother?"

"We've done what we could for her," the man said, his eyes flinching away.

"Do you have any painkillers? They took ours," his wife said.

"Jack, send up the medic. Have her home-in on my signal."

"Yes ma'am."

Kat turned from where she knelt, and looked up at the couple. "Are you going to tell me what happened here? Everybody told me when I got posted to Elmendorf to 'watch your back, everyone carries a gun.' Our Colonel doesn't want us on the streets at night, too many guns. And yet, I haven't seen a single weapon in this compound." Kat pointed at a gun rack hanging on the wall beside a window – empty. "Where are your weapons?"

"Gone," the man said. "They're just gone. Leave it at that, Fleet girl, please!"

"My husband went to the fields," the woman began softly.

The man turned on his wife, his eyes begging for her silence. She met his eyes with her own; level, unflinching. When she didn't turn away, he walked to the far window and stared out.

"A farm isn't something that you take care of when you

feel like it, not if you're like Henry and his family. His father built this farm up from nothing just after the war had ended. It was nothing when he came here, just mutant infested ruins. Radiation mutated wolves, bears, all sorts of ugly and angry critters, even the odd human. Anyway, they eradicated the mutated creatures, rebuilt, then decontaminated the land. The radiation detectors still have to be monitored. We can't sell what we grow if the levels become too high. Some of the detectors are close to the river bank."

"There were five of us," Henry said to the triple glazed window. "All armed. We knew that those" – he failed to find the word – "those men were out there. We figured we'd see them coming." Henry turned and looked at Kat. "We're good shots. My father had us practice every week, there's still the occasional mutant creature out there." He paused briefly, before turning back to the window. "They came out of the snowline, right on the river's edge. They must have had breathers or something. Had the drop on us before we even knew they were there. If we'd gone for our guns, they'd have slaughtered us." The man looked at his wife. His voiced choked. "Honey, I wish to hell we'd fought back."

The women went to her husband's side, gave him a shoulder as he sobbed. Kat had rarely seen men cry. On the bed, the old woman struggled to find a more comfortable position and let out an agonised groan. Kat stood, her hand going to the butt of her pistol. There were things she'd joined the Fleet to take care of. At the moment the local bad-guys were winning two points to nil, and she didn't like the score.

As the man wept, his wife continued the story, her voice a low monotone that screamed, *Wrong*, by its very softness. "Their trucks stopped about two hundred metres out. About ten, maybe twelve got out. Anyone that we didn't recognise we had in our sights. Then someone shouted, 'Woman, I got a pistol at your husband's head. If you and your people drop your weapons, then everyone's gonna come out of this alive. You people start shooting, and your husband dies first.'"

"I told you to shoot." The man's voice was begging for understanding, for forgiveness. "I shouted at you, screamed for you to shoot."

Kat wondered what she would have done, as a wife, as a

husband.

"More men then got out of the trucks," the woman continued, "spreading out on either side before hiding in the snow. There must have been thirty or forty of them. We have children," she looked up at Kat, pleading for understanding. Kat nodded, tried to give the woman what she wanted. The wife shook her head and went on. "Some of the men were for fighting it out, let the devil take the last one standing."

The woman looked Kat hard in the eye. "We have our children here. We women voted to put the guns down." The women glanced at her husband. "Maybe if we had known what was coming next, we'd have fought them. Some of us say we wish we had. Most of us don't."

Kat almost told the woman she didn't have to finish the story; she already knew the ending. But the wife had come this far; the rest tumbled from her mouth. "They took our guns first, then our food, IDent cards, medical supplies, gasoline, anything that seemed important or that they wanted. They had the men tie each other's hands. Then, in the snow, in front of our husbands and children, they raped us. That seemed to add something to it for them. Henry's father, her husband," she nodded at the old woman in the bed. "He fought them, tied up, he still fought them."

"Why didn't I? Why didn't I, too?" Henry moaned.

"Because I told you not to. Because if you had, they'd have killed you like they did your pa. Probably beaten me like they did your mother." A large sigh racked the woman. "We're alive. Over at the Wilson place they're all dead. They slaughtered the kids like pigs because they tried to fight them off. We are alive, Henry," she took her husband's face in her hands. "We are alive. We will come through this."

"But we'll never get even with those bastards," Henry whispered.

"Who knows? It's all in God's hands," his wife said tenderly.

The medic arrived; Kat left the wife to assist, as Leading Crewman Tremblay began unpacking her equipment. Kat headed back downstairs. Outside, she paused; her mission plan called for the delivery of food. Their rules of engagement were quite clear, 'Weapons Hold.' They could only return fire if they were fired upon, in order to defend themselves.

"Come on you sons-of-bitches," she whispered to nobody. "I've got thirty trigger pullers and no kids in this convoy. You know we're here. I know you want what we've got. Come and get it. *Please.*" She put her helmet back on and plugged in the jack-lead that provided its integral head-up display with power.

Zipping her body-armour back up, she marched purposefully across the yard. The man who had asked to check on-line the status of their finances came walking back, shaking his head. "They sold the farm. Right out from under us, they sold it."

Kat stopped him. "I'm recording what I'm saying for a legal deposition," she said to Safi and the man.

"You can do that?"

"That and more." Quickly Kat recounted how she'd found the farmsteads, stripped of IDent cards and any communications. "Any financial and legal actions taken between the time this farmstead went off-line and now are not legal or binding. I, Katarina Sophie Louisa Severn, do testify to that in a court of law," she finished.

"Thank you," the young man said.

"We'll see what else I can do," Kat said, spotted Jack and shouted, "Are we done here?"

"I think so. I've got photographs of everyone. Even Harper should be happy."

"Good. Let's pack up and get moving. We've got a lot more to do today."

"Yes ma'am." Jack stepped close. "Kat, is something wrong? You look like. . . well, like you want somebody dead."

"Nothing wrong with that," she snapped. "We're armed, and there are bad guys out there. Everyone, let's mount-up. We've got things to do, places to go."

The troops began to collect by their respective vehicles. They seemed in no hurry to be moving on. Several of them were holding small children, helping them to stuff their faces.

"Excuse me, ma'am," one of Kat's backseat crewmen said. "The bad guys are just going to come back. Take what we left them. Could we, maybe at least take the kids back into town? They've been starving for the last month. That mother told me the little kids don't have the stomach to digest some of the berries and wild plants that have been keeping the grown-ups alive."

"Next week maybe we will. Not now." Kat cut him off. "When I said move it people, I expect to see you moving, now shift your butts!" she shouted. Fleet and Land Forces got moving. Henry came out of the large house, spotted her, and began a slow jog towards Kat. Despite his emaciated state the man still put one foot in front of the other until he came to stand at Kat's open truck door.

"Listen, those bastards use the ruins for their hideouts. If you keep away from the old settlements, you might avoid them." Kat had Safi project her planned route so she could share it with Henry. He shook his head. "There," he pointed, "about ten kilometres down that road, you're headed into what was Wasilla. You've got to go around."

"Can't," Kat found she was grinning. "Everything south of the lakes is iced over. We're going to cut through Wasilla then up onto the highway."

"They'll be waiting for you."

"I kind of hope they are," Kat said, letting her grin take over her entire face. *Grandpa Jim would be proud.*

"Just so long as you know what you're getting into," Henry said.

Safi terminated the projection as Kat turned around, glancing down the line of trucks. "We have no children, only Fleet and Land Forces. This is what we get paid for."

"Be careful, Lieutenant or Ensign, or whatever you are. I thought we could take on anything that came our way. I was so wrong."

"I may have some photos for you and your wife to identify next time we come through. You may not have to wait until this mess is over before you see a few of them punished." *Damn, I'm starting to like this.*

"Just be careful."

"Not what they pay me for," Kat said, closing the truck's door. She glanced back, out of the open window. All her troops were mounted-up. "Jack, move us out."

"Yes, ma'am."

In her rear-view mirror, Kat watched as Henry went

from group to group, saying something. One of the women fell to her knees in the snow, hands clasped in prayer.

"Say your prayers for the bastards ahead of us. Not for me and mine," Kat whispered through tightly drawn lips.

"Would you mind telling me what the hell is going on here?" Jack asked, his eyes locked straight ahead, hands in a white-knuckle grip of the steering wheel. "I *am* your second-in-command, and I'm *supposed* to take over if anything happens to you."

Kat keyed her mike. "Listen up everyone. You just saw why we're here. Those people are starving because a bunch of thugs stole everything they had. They killed an old man and beat up his wife. They raped most of the women you saw back there."

"Raped" echoed through the backseat like and electric shock. *So, not everyone had gotten full disclosure. Well they had it now.*

"Even the teenage girls," Kat snapped. "Some of you aren't too happy about being glorified delivery boys. Maybe you could have stayed at home and delivered pizza for what we've achieved so far. Well, I'm told that the road ahead is probably going to get a bit dangerous in a few minutes. These bastards like to steal things, and our supplies are the only thing worth stealing today. Make Ready. Payback time is here and now."

Kat turned to Jack; while she talked, he had called up the route on the truck's IVeNS display. Overlaying that with the latest satellite imagery, he stabbed a finger at Wasilla. "There?"

"Looks like it."

Jack studied the map. "We could go north, try and cut through Hatcher Pass?"

"Looks snow-bound to me," Kat cut him off. "We've got food to deliver. If we go wandering all over the place, we'll never make it back to base tonight."

"We could over-night at one of the farmsteads. Those folks were friendly. They'd be glad to have us stay with them."

"We've got other deliveries to make tomorrow. Jack, we are going up this road. I suggest you check your weapon. I've never actually seen you fire one."

"I qualified at OTA(F). I had to, to graduate."

"What did you score?"

"The minimum required," Jack said, not looking at her.

"Jack, you're a Fleet officer! You knew this was part of the job when you took it."

"You may have noticed: I'm driving a truck, delivering food to starving people. Every time there was a bar-room brawl in the Emerald City and someone got sliced-up or shot down, the priests always preached 'Thou shalt not kill,' I joined the Fleet to get my university loans written-off, not to kill people. That's why I'm in the Electrical and Mechanical Engineering branch and not Warfare Systems like you."

"What about men who rape and kill and steal food from starving kids" spat Kat, "does, 'thou shalt not kill' still apply?"

Jack looked out at the snow covered land. "This wasn't what I had in mind."

"But it's what you've got, Jack."

Behind Kat, while she and Jack talked, the backseat got very quiet. *What are they thinking? Does it matter what they're thinking? They had their orders. They will follow my orders. Why am I wasting time even discussing this with Jack?* She had things to do. Again, she keyed her mike.

"This is Ensign Severn. All personnel are to lower their visors immediately. Power down all side windows and retract the front windshield. We do not want flying glass in the cabs when the shooting starts." Kat looked around, examining the front window. She spotted the button and hit it. The front screen retracted and snow immediately blew in, smothering everything inside the cab. For a long moment they rode on in cold silence, swaying from side to side as Jack wrestled to keep the truck where the IVeNS said the road should be.

"Ma'am" came quietly from the back seat.

"Yes." It was the young woman. She been in the middle on the first part of the journey, but was now directly behind Kat.

"Are you sure we can shoot these people?"

"They'll be shooting at us. Yes, we shoot back."

"My mom and the preacher, they always said death belonged to God. That's why the gangs in our city-block were wrong and bad. Now you're saying that it's okay to kill. Are you sure, ma'am?"

Kat had grown up a politician's daughter where you did anything you had to, to win the next election. Grandpa Jim had come in like some knight in shining armour when she was so far down, there could only be up. She'd loved to read the historical data records about what he'd done in the war. He and Grandpa George. Even Grandma Alex and Grandma Lizzy were in some of the files, fighting for what was right. Of course Kat had learned 'Thou shalt not kill.' But for her, it had never been an absolute.

"As I see it," Kat began slowly, hunting for the right words that would release the safety catch on her crewmen's souls, "There's a time to build and a time to destroy. A time to live and a time to die. If these men choose to shoot at us, then it's their time to die. Or they can throw their weapons down and put their hands up. And hang after the courts are done with them."

Kat turned in her seat to study the three young crewmen behind her; despite the cold, they all looked decidedly pale. The crewman in the middle licked his lips nervously. The girl fingered her weapon as if to confirm if it was actually real. The '127mm marksman' glanced at Kat, then went back to staring out of the open window. "What those men did back there took them outside the bounds of humanity. If they shoot at us, we kill them like the wild dogs they've now become. Those are your orders. You will carry them out. If I'm wrong, I'll be the one who stands trial, not you."

"But they'll be just as dead whether a court says you were right or wrong," the middle crewman said.

"Just like the Colonel," the woman agreed.

This conversation was not going the way Kat had wanted. In the historical data records there were no reluctant soldiers. Then again, these were Fleet types, little more than recruits. Maybe Kat ought to have the Land Force personnel pull their truck up closer to the front of the convoy.

Maybe I ought to re-think this whole thing.

Kat swung around in her seat. While she'd talked, the open expanse of snow had given way to ruined buildings. Some structures looked almost untouched, whilst others were little more that piles of bricks on either side of the compressed snow track that weaved between the ruins.

Kat watched both the route ahead of them and what stretched out behind them in the side-mirrors. More snow, compacted snow and ice on the track, a snow-filled track-side ditch, a pile of snow covered bricks, a half-standing house. Should she turn the convoy around? *Couldn't even I wanted to.* Licking her lips, she put that option aside. For better or worse, this convoy went forward.

She had to focus on what lay ahead in the next few minutes. *Have I done everything? What have I forgotten? Wasn't that supposed to be the perpetual question of the commander. What's left undone?* She felt a rising panic. *What have I missed?*

Kat checked her rifle, eyed the ruins getting closer and closer to the track edge, then activated her mike again. "Listen up. We can expect the hostiles to be hiding somewhere amongst these ruins."

Kat swallowed hard as the truck came around a bend in the track. The buildings that had blocked her view ahead now moved past to the right. In front of them, two maybe three hundred metres away, a large tree lay across the road.

Kat assessed the situation quickly. *No root ball on the downed tree, so it's been felled, placed there deliberately.* Kat switched the sights on the rifle to thermal. Yes, three people knelt behind the trunk. Kat quickly scanned the ruins to the left and right. Yes, more thermal images, about twenty. A lot. Kat remembered what Henry had told her, people rising out of the half frozen river shallows. She tried to scan the ditch alongside the track's edge. Some of the snow there did perhaps show slight traces of being warmer than other areas.

Beside her, Jack was slowing. "How close do you want to get, Severn?" he asked through clenched teeth.

Kat went through her options fast. *Drive into the trap and stop, let the bad guys shoot first, then take them. I have more people . . . correction: I have little more than recruits, and these hostiles are desperate killers.* She eyed the ditch ahead; gunmen coming out of the shallows had gotten the drop on the farmers.

"Stop here," she ordered. Jack slowed to a stop in the middle of the snowy track, about a hundred and fifty metres from the tree. For a long minute, Kat watched the makeshift roadblock as nothing happened.

"Throw down your guns and nobody gets hurt," blared

over the ruins, sending a pair of roosting bald eagles squawking and flapping into the snow filled sky and out across the unfrozen Upper Inlet in search of fish.

Kat scowled; she was about to say the very same thing. Well, that settled the question of their intent. Kat sighted her rifle and the far left thermal outline behind the tree trunk. She keyed her mike. "All vehicles, open fire."

Obeying her own command, Kat sent a long burst into the tree, raking the rounds from left to right. Someone tried to get up, run away, and went down from her second burst.

Then she switched target and sent another long burst into the trackside ditch that had appeared slightly warmer in her thermal sights. A snow concealed man wearing a breather-unit stood, rifle in his hands, and took aim at Kat. He fell back as rounds took him in the chest.

Forms were slithering from the ditch and forming up on the track to Kat's right. She opened the door, jumped down from the cab and settled into a squatting position against the front wheel. A quick burst at the nearest gunman left him slumped across his rifle.

She took aim at the next one. He threw down his gun and rolled onto his back, holding his hands up in the air. "Throw down your weapons and you will live," Kat heard her voice boom out across the ruins, amid the clatter of gun-fire. "Keep them, and you're dead."

Five, six people along the track edge were now on their knees, hands up. Kat swept her rifle sights along the line of ruined houses to her right. People were standing, hands waving high in the air.

"You," Kat snapped at the female crewman still in the backseat of the truck. "Put those prisoners under guard."

"Yes, ma'am," the girl's voice was a ragged whisper. She stumbled as she got down from the cab. Kat flinched away from the crewman's rifle, then realised that was the least of her fears. The girl still had the safety-catch applied.

"Take the safety-catch off," Kat whispered. She got a blank look in reply. Kat reached across, flipped the safety across. "Now it will fire."

The crewman glanced down. "Oh," and went back to waving her weapon unsteadily at their prisoners.

"You, in the buildings, walk slowly out to the track," Kat ordered. "No sudden movements. Those of you on the track, lie down in the middle."

Kat glanced up at the cab. Jack was just getting his rifle out of its retaining bracket next to his seat. The '127mm marksman' and the other crewman were frozen in place, eyes and weapons covering the right side, but doing nothing.

"Are you okay?" Kat asked. When they didn't respond, she repeated, "Are you two okay back there?" the '127mm marksman' blinked twice . . . then threw up, violently out of the cab window.

From the back of the convoy, two Land Forces troopers advanced with their weapons at the ready. *At least their training is good, and seems to have included how to take the safety off their weapons!* "Cover this side," She ordered. Without a word, they both acknowledged Kat's instruction with hand-signals.

Moving in front of the cab, she looked down the right side of the convoy to see the three other Land Forces troopers moving forward, keeping their weapons levelled at the slowly moving prisoners. One indicated a body sprawled over a pile of bricks, "I got that one."

Kat quickly cut off any further conversation. "Keep the others covered. I don't want any of them getting away."

One of the prisoners picked that very moment to run for it. Using her thermal sites, Kat searched the ruins but with all the other bodies moving around, the image was too confused to provide any real targets.

"He's getting away." Jack observed as he climbed down from the cab.

Kat scowled. "You prisoners be warned. The next one of you that tries to run, I'll shoot the rest of you too."

"But they're unarmed," the female crewman said.

"They're escaping," Kat pointed out. "And until we check them out, we don't know who is unarmed. You crewmen still in the trucks get out here. I need you to search the prisoners for weapons." The rest of the trucks began to empty. The Fleet crewmen brought their weapons, but about half still had the safety catches applied. Most of their weapons didn't look as though they'd need cleaning. Now Kat realised why the fire-fight had seemed so quiet around her. She and the Land Force troopers had been the only ones firing. Them and the bad guys.

Pairs of Fleet crewmen moved down the slowly forming line of prisoners. While one kept a rifle trained on the prone figure, a second crewman searched the captive, making sure they were no longer armed. "Hey, this one's a girl," a crewman said, taking two steps back from the figure he started to pat down. Her response was far from ladylike.

Kat waved a female crewman over to frisk that prisoner, then paused to look at the growing pile of kit being taken from the captives. No communications equipment, no data-pads, lots of knives and usually one gun each, with very little ammunition. The prisoners, stripped down to their underwear, showed thin and hungry. Not to the starvation levels of the farmstead inhabitants, but even the bad guys had been on short rations. Bad girls, too. Four of the fourteen were women.

"Jack, get this lot photographed, including the dead. We need to start a 'rogue's gallery.'"

Kat then turned from the live ones to check out the less fortunate. Behind the splintered tree trunk two lay in the blood stained snow. She swallowed hard to keep her own stomach where it belonged. One face was contorted in death. Rage, anger, agony. Kat could not tell, and the dead were not likely to answer her question. The one next to him seemed asleep on his side, quietly drawn up like a child. He had the only communication device amongst the group. The third gunman was still alive, despite taking a least two rounds in the back. He was lying face down in a growing pool of his own blood as Tremblay, the medic, did her best to patch him up. He'd be in fine shape for hanging, or whatever they did for capital punishment in these parts.

Kat walked slowly back up the track. Two more bodies lay half-in, half-out of the roadside ditch. "You and you," she pointed at two of the prisoners, young lads, probably only a few years younger than she was. "Pick up those bodies. Hang them up by their feet from those girders," she said, pointing to a nearby ruin that had its rusting internal structure exposed.

Jack was at her side in a moment. "It's not right to disrespect the dead."

"And leaving them down here to be gnawed on by

ravenous wolves and bears is better than hanging them up there as a warning to the rest? I am not taking the time, assuming we even could dig in this frozen ground, to bury them." She glanced up and down the track. "What do you suggest instead then?"

Still, Jack shook his head. "Kat, this is out of bounds."

"You two, start doing what I told you. Trooper, see that these two do what they're ordered." The assigned trooper nudged the two boys to their feet with his rifle. They'd been pale before, now they looked like ghosts. Terrified ghosts.

Kat turned to Jack. "If you've finished photographing the prisoners get them dressed again. Then tape or cable-tie their hands and load them onto the trucks. Once they're loaded, tape or tie their feet to something on the vehicle, I'm not losing any more. Once you've got them secured, leave a sentry, then get everyone else up here to help move that tree out of the way."

"Yes ma'am." Jack snapped to an exaggerated attention, threw a salute and marched off to comply.

An hour later, the convoy moved slowly past Kat's stark message to the residents of the Wasilla ruins. A new team was in town. Get out before you join these.

At least, that was the message Kat wanted them to hear.

ONE : ELEVEN

The next farm on their list, tagged 'Wilson 820,' was empty of life. A few bodies still lay where they'd fallen or been cast aside, and more were undoubtedly buried under the surrounding snow. Decomposition had slowed considerably due to the ambient temperature. "This must be what happened to the farms that fought back," Kat commented to Jack as they slowly drove through the farmyard.

"Maybe she isn't such a bitch" someone muttered on a live channel. Kat chose to ignore it.

The third farm was a repeat of the first. Kat distributed the food quickly, neither asking how they came to be in this fix nor offering to listen to the silent screams behind dry eyes. She had to post a guard on the prisoners to prevent any of the farmers initiating a quick vengeance killing. "They are Fleet prisoners. I will turn them over to the local officials in Anchorage. You can get your justice there," she snapped when the knife wielding wife of the farm owner had to be forcibly removed from one of the trucks.

"Do you seriously think you can get them back there?" her husband asked.

"I captured them, I keep them."

"Good luck. You know that they're not the only group out there?"

"How many?"

"Well over a hundred, possibly nearer two."

"Who are they?" Jack asked. "Why are they doing this?"

"Ask them," the farm owner spat.

Two further farmsteads on, and with the trucks sitting considerably higher on their axles, Kat was no closer to understanding the dynamics of what made someone a killer and another the starving victim. And she didn't like not fully understanding a situation.

She also was getting a bad feeling about their route back to Anchorage.

The last farmstead on her list, 'Duncan 868' was around 190 kilometres from their start point earlier that day, and shown as being one of the smallest, just north of what had once been Talkeentna. At its most prosperous before the war, only around eight hundred people had ever lived in Talkeentna, but it now seemed that almost half that number had taken refuge in this small farmstead, a far larger number than any other location they had visited. It also seemed far less brutalised; at least, there was no attempt made to attack her prisoners. Two women even went from prisoner to prisoner, giving them a drink of water and a taste of the rations, although still under the strict supervision of Fleet personnel.

The owner was a short, middle-aged man. He stood aside and let his people organise themselves to quickly unload the trucks into barns and several small houses. He had a pistol strapped to his right thigh, the first civilian weapon Kat had seen all day. By now Kat's people all knew the drill, so she and Jack joined the farmstead's owner in just watching.

"Greatly appreciate the food. We were down to eating berries and roots."

"You've got an awful lot of people here?" Kat asked, not quite knowing where the question was leading.

"Yes, I didn't let go of my indentured workers when the crops failed. Where would the poor bastards go?"

"Indentured workers?" That was the great thing about being an Ensign, there was so much to learn.

"Do you remember when the Maximum Security Prison on Navassa Island in the Caribbean, the underground one, began to flood about three or four years ago, and had to be evacuated?" he asked. Kat nodded. She remembered it only too well. Her father had nearly been in court over it, sued by the inmates' families, who claimed William Severn's government had not provided sufficient funding for the maintenance of the facility's infrastructure. Only eminent geological scientists had kept it from reaching the High Courts, verifying it was an unpreventable natural occurrence.

"When the inmates had to be relocated, MaxSec Florence in the Rockies didn't have the capacity, and so it was decided that a number of both Navassa's and Florence's low-risk, Category D prisoners, would be 'Released On Temporary Licence' to work in the community, and so several hundred were shipped here to work on the farmsteads."

"They kept that one quiet," said Jack.

"It was never a secret," the man continued, "but, yes, it was introduced without the usual media circus."

"And these prisoners worked for you?" Jack asked.

"No, there's no financial incentive from their employment for me at all. They pay off their debt owed to society, however long that might be, then they're released. A warder from Florence visits every six months to review and authorise any releases that are due." The man squatted down. "Of course, once they're released they have nothing, no money, nowhere to live, nothing. The lucky ones end up working in Anchorage, trying to earn enough to buy a ticket back to wherever they came from. Some stay; maybe get re-hired as paid workers on the farms."

"We must be feeding some of them out of our soup kitchens back in Anchorage."

"I wondered how they were making out," the man said.

Kat did a quick count around the farmyard. Lots of children, lots of old, lots of in-between. "So, you had a lot of firepower when the gunmen came," she said, pointing at his pistol.

"Gunmen didn't come here."

"Smart of them," Kat grinned.

Jack frowned. "Then why did you go off-line?"

"Solar packs failed. No sun, no power. Batteries kept us going for a while," the man shrugged.

"We'll leave you some power packs." Kat nodded. "But why were you the only farmstead not attacked?"

The man looked at Kat like she was a very slow learner. "Lady, you still don't know who the bad guys are, do you?"

"You kept your indentured workers," Kat repeated slowly, then saw where it led. "The other farmsteads didn't."

"The penny drops!"

"The people in the ruins are the indentured workers from the other farmsteads."

Jack blinked rapidly for a long moment as his mouth slowly opened. "So the raping, the stealing, the killing was all done by former indentured workers from the other farmsteads."

The man looked up at Jack. "Maybe, maybe not."

Kat crouched down beside the farmer. He offered her a piece of dried fireweed. She sucked on it; slightly sweet, but not much taste. Probably not much nutritional value either. But, she'd eaten a full ration pack in the truck jostling along between farmsteads. Lack of food was not her problem. People were.

As Jack crouched down too, his eyes wide in puzzlement, Kat shook her head. "Are you telling me that it's a bunch of low-risk Cat D prisoners, most of them serving sentences for non-violent crimes like bankruptcy, public office corruption or embezzlement, who've been doing manual labour out in the fields, that have stolen the IDent Cards, fencing them on the internet, and in some cases selling off entire farmsteads."

"For a Fleet type, you're not too stupid kid," the farmer said, with a grin. "Although most of the inmates were serving sentences for those kinds of crimes, some were guilty of other more serious offences that were not part of their current incarceration. Therefore we did end up with a few punks, thugs, and mafia wannabes. Small time trouble makers the warders undoubtedly wanted rid of. Once they arrived here, we put them to work with all the others. Maybe he works; maybe he sets up a poker game. Somebody always has something to risk. Then he brings in alcohol, maybe some drugs too. No matter how poor people are, they always seem to find funds for that." The man shook his head.

"And when all hell breaks loose," Kat took up the story, "the likes of him can see their ticket out of here."

"Right, collect a few tough henchmen, some guns, go find their former cell mates starving in the ruins of the old settlements, promise them a meal if they'll help you get back at the very people that put them in this predicament. You know the rest of the story."

Jack shook his head. "But the raping."

"Not always just the big men and the henchmen. Some of the indentured workers have a lot of anger too. There are a few women I've taken in from other farmsteads whose brothers or husbands have tried to stop it. They got beaten up, or a bullet for trying."

Kat eyed her prisoners. Somehow they seemed slightly less loathsome, but only slightly. "Do you think I have any of the main players or their henchmen here?"

"I don't know. Some of my people might know who's who. Eva, who was giving your prisoners water, she has a boy-friend out there." Kat frowned at the farmer. He shook his head. "Hal has a job here anytime he wants it, a good lad, hard worker. Sad thing is, he also had a kid brother who thinks being a gunman is what being a man all is about. Hal's out there trying to keep his brother out of trouble until he can get him to see sense."

"What about these?" Jack waved at the prisoners. "What will happen when we hand them over to the authorities in Anchorage?"

"I don't know. Even if they aren't the murderers or rapists, they were running with them. The people that'll be sitting on the juries are going be desperate, scared and angry. That doesn't make for a good combination where justice is concerned. And the Chief Warden at Florence will need to be involved. Most of these people are still technically under his jurisdiction."

"So much for truth and justice." Jack sighed.

Kat nodded, but she was now replaying the events of their little skirmish in Wasilla, thinking out-loud, trying to make sense of it all. "I shot the gunmen behind the felled tree first, including the man with the speaker unit. I got the first ones out of the ditch at the trackside."

"And after that, the rest didn't fight much." Jack nodded. "Most seemed ready to break and run. What's that make our prisoners guilty of? Being as hungry as their victims? But, just looking the other way when the tough guys got their kicks, no way! In the Emerald City no man touches a woman that doesn't want it. A man gets that wrong and anyone within hearing will help him learn that lesson fast." Pain ran across Jack's face as he shook his head. "My priest taught me that a poor man has a right to steal a rich man's bread to feed his starving family. He didn't have much of an answer when I asked about poor stealing from the poor. Damn, Kat, this is a hell of a mess. But nobody touches a woman. Who wouldn't answer a woman's cry for help? Whatever the circumstances might be." He glanced at the trucks, empty of food, now only loaded with prisoners. "What a crock of shit you've gotten me into, Severn."

Kat only half listened to Jack's moaning about who was right and who was guilty. She had a bigger problem. She'd pissed off a lot of bad guys with guns. *Now what do you do, smart girl?*

"How are you getting back to Anchorage?" the man asked.

"Same way we came in," Kat waved absentmindedly. "Back down the Parks Highway."

"Through Willow?"

Kat ordered Safi to project the map again so she could share her intent with the farmstead owner. On the way in they'd stayed to the western side of the ruins to visit a smaller farmstead on her list, but this time they would stay on the highway itself. The farmer pointed. "Waldron Island, that's where they'll be, although it's no island anymore with all this snow and ice. The eastern edge of Lake Nancy runs real close to the highway, that's where they'll attack. From the trees between the lake edge and the highway."

"We'll be without any cargo and travelling as fast as the vehicles will allow, I thought it would be the safest route back."

"There've been a fair few trucks going that way this afternoon. I'm surprised you didn't run in to any on your way in? I think you've kicked over a hornet's nest. If people like you and your food convoy can move around free in these parts un-challenged, it won't be long before the authorities will come looking for the likes of them. Maybe they can buy a ticket out of here, but maybe they don't want to. Maybe some of them think they have enough collateral to buy part of this hell hole. I hear some of them are already moving onto some of the abandoned farmsteads, the ones that got shot up when the owners fought back."

"We didn't see anyone at 'Wilson 820.'" Kat told him, her mouth running while her thinking was still elsewhere. "Joe Thomas went on-line and found that their farmstead had been sold to someone using their stolen IDent Cards."

"Seems the history files are full of this year's bandit being next year's revolutionary and an established politician the year after that," Jack observed dryly.

"Yes, nobody is ever very demanding of a rebel leader's credentials," Kat agreed. But that was next year's problem; right now Kat had to survive today. "How many bad guys would you say are headed for Lake Nancy?"

"At least a hundred, probably more," the farmer said. "Everyone they've got."

"How many of those do you think are the ringleaders and their bully boys?"

"Twenty, twenty-five."

"Problem will be separating the two," Kat muttered.

The snow started to come down heavily again, the last few hours had thankfully been just light flurries. She accessed her comm-link. "Operations, this is Ensign Severn. I need to talk to the Colonel."

"Roger, wait out."

The wait was short. "Let me guess, Ensign, you want some more advice."

"It would seem that way, sir."

"Give me a sit-rep."

Kat reported on her earlier skirmish and what looked to be happening to block their route back. She explained about the indentured workforce, and emphasised the divided nature of the opposing force. She also suggested he contact the Chief Warden at MaxSec Florence.

"I've been hearing stories that some of the worst problems might just be hungry people the local establishment didn't view as deserving poor," the Colonel said. "You came up with some pretty unorthodox strategies here in Anchorage for feeding everyone, no questions asked. The level of violence went down as the number of full stomachs went up. Do you think we can do the same out there?"

"I doubt it, sir. The murder and rapes have peoples' opinions polarised. The damage is done; a lot of them just want payback." *Like me.*

"You've got yourself a tough tactical situation, Ensign," was his crisp reply.

It was nice not to face one of Father's rants about

responding with her emotions rather than thinking with her head. "It doesn't help that I won't know where they are until they start shooting at me," Kat answered, staying on the present problem, and not re-visiting a past that could never be changed. "I'd give my right arm for a 'sky-eye' right now."

"I figured you might be asking my advice at a time like this. Sky-eyes are too fragile for this kind of weather, but a big old MQ-22 Griffin can fly in a near hurricane. I ordered one to be taken out of storage at the Barstow Logistics Base in San Angeles; it's almost a museum piece. It arrived last night. I'll have it over you in an hour or two."

"Thank you, Colonel." Kat breathed, half in prayer.

"Don't thank me until you've got yourself back to base."

"Any suggestions, sir?"

"None that you haven't already thought of. Try not to get any of our people killed. Try not to kill any more bandits than you absolutely have to. You know, the usual crap. Now, if you'll excuse me, I've got a Griffin to launch, and I may be the only one here old enough to remember how to wind up the rubber band! Hepburn, out."

Kat glanced slowly around, reviewing her assets and was far from happy.

Hunching her shoulders against the snow, she stood. "Jack, let's mount up."

Jack got to his feet, shook himself, and glanced around. "I'm so glad this problem is yours," he muttered as he strode towards the trucks and began the usual spiel. "You heard the boss, we're out of here. Vehicle commanders, mount your crews." It didn't take long. The civilians gathered for a celebration. Some of the Fleet personnel looked to have been invited, but when their vehicle commanders hollered, they came running. Jack was beside the lead truck, watching as the others vehicles filled up when Kat joined him. "So, what's it going to be? Are we going to try and go around these bastards, or are we going to kill some more rapists?" he asked matter-of-factly.

"What would you think of another fight?"

Jack blew out a long breath. "There are over a hundred of them. There are only thirty of us, and we've already shown our fighting prowess this morning. Still, my da would whip my butt if I didn't come when a woman hollered for help. But my grandmother will be most disappointed if I don't come back home. Tell me, Ensign Severn, What are we going to do?"

"The only thing we can do. Fight the ones that want to fight, and let the rest run."

"Even if they're rapists? Even if they looked the other way?"

"We need to break the hold of the bad guys, but I also want to get us all back to base safely too. I can't afford to worry about anything else."

"If we wanted to get home safe, we'd take the scenic route, go right around this mess," Jack pointed out.

"We've got to break them, Jack." Kat would not give on that. "It will be easier doing it when they're all together."

Jack shook his head. "They'll massacre us. Half of us didn't even get our safety-catches off. Most of us didn't have the stomach to shoot. At least this morning, it was thirty of us against twenty of them. Now, there are a hundred or more of them!"

"That was this morning. Now we've all been there once, we can go there again."

Jack looked at her like she was crazy.

"Or maybe I've just learned a few tough lessons. Listen, Jack, we have to do this."

Jack looked at her for a moment longer; then with a rattling sigh, he said, "Didn't my da warn me. If you take the King's shilling, he gets your body, your soul, and you do what you're told." Jack turned and went to his side of the truck.

Kat pulled herself up into the cab, brushed as much snow off as she could, and settled into her place with a big smile of encouragement for the three crewmen in the back. They were getting comfortable, preparing for the long ride back to base. The women glanced at Kat, and her eyes grew wide. The friendly chatter that had started in the backseat fell into silence as the other two followed her glance to Kat.

"Oh, shit." The '127mm marksman' snorted.

"Land Forces, I want Truck Six up behind me." Kat spoke softly into her mike.

"Does that mean you're going to have some more targets for us ma'am?"

"We'll be stopping a few klicks down the road to talk

about the current tactical situation," Kat advised everyone on the net. Silence came back to her.

In an open, desolate spot, Kat stopped the convoy. With fields of snow in all directions, it gave Kat a good view of anyone approaching their position. She gathered her people around her by vehicle crews; they came quietly. She waited until they stood about her, then she told them to make themselves comfortable, well as much as they could in the falling snow.

"Between us and Elmendorf are about a hundred bandits," Kat said bluntly, "maybe a few more." There were low whistles and bitter swearing at her announcement.

"The good news is that not all of them are armed and most of them aren't really interested in opposing us. Twenty, maybe twenty-five of them are looking for a fight. The others are just part of the crowd that's hungry and wants to eat. You saw his morning how hard our prisoners fought once their leaders were down." That got Kat several thoughtful nods. Kat quickly filled her teams in on the background of their adversaries.

"So, most of them are non-violent criminals, who were released on a temporary licence to finish their sentences. They're just victims of circumstance and are very, very hungry. When times got hard, the farmsteads couldn't feed their own, let alone the indentured workers so they just turned them out." Master Crewman Cowell said in summary.

"Most, not all. The guys who sold the IDent Cards and the muscle who act as their enforcers, those guys don't want us moving around freely here. If we show everyone that we can, they lose, and civilisation starts to win again in Alaska." Kat paused to let that sink in. Then she took a deep breath.

"I made a mistake this morning. I threw you into the middle of a fire-fight without preparing you for it. Some of you may have heard about the hostage rescue mission I led a few weeks ago." That got nods. "My team had three days to prepare for that op." And most of her Land Forces team had three to ten years service. *No need to mention that.* "I should have given you more time to get ready, to familiarise yourself with your weapons. It's one thing to be issued with an assault rifle. It's another thing to be comfortable with the idea of using it. That is why we have stopped here. I'm assigning a Land Force's trooper to each vehicle of Fleet crewmen. I want each trooper, with your vehicle commander to take you all through your weapon-handling-drills. I know you all did this in training, but how many of you have done it since?" she said. "I don't know about you, but I did some quick revision when I pulled the short straw and found myself with a night insertion and a hostage rescue." That drew nervous laughs.

"Finally, I want each of you to fire off half a magazine of rounds. There's nothing like the feel of a rifle actually kicking back against your shoulder, the sight of bullets hitting what you aimed at. It lets you know you really can do this." Kat paced off two steps, made them move their heads to follow her.

"One last thing. I'm assigning the Land Force troopers and the vehicle commanders the responsibility for putting down the boss men and their bully-boys. The job for the rest of you it to put rounds in the air, in the ground, into the trees. Show anyone willing to cut and run that now would be a very good time to do just that. Put the fear of the Fleet into them. You send the hungry ones running, and the troopers and your vehicle commanders will put down the ones who put up any kind of resistance."

"If we see someone running, can we shoot at them too?"

"Anyone who shows you their back, let them run."

"Where can they run to, ma'am?"

"I think that last farmstead would be glad to take them in."

The crewmen glanced around at their other team members. Some actually had nervous smiles for one another. "We can do that." "Okay, that's not too hard." "If they run, let them run, that's okay."

Kat let that sink in for a moment, then sent each vehicle crew to its own corner of the stationary convoy, with the other team at the gap between the third and forth truck. She then moved between each crew, observing, encouraging. The Land Force troopers, now shared out between the other crews had a good philosophy; weapon drills were skills to be shared by all.

Kat stood beside her '127mm marksman' as he sent rounds into a lone tree about two hundred metres away. "Good shooting," she said.

"Not bad for a coward," he spat into the snow.

"I don't see a coward."

"I locked up this morning. Didn't do a damned thing."

"How long did that shooting last, ten, twelve seconds?"

"I don't know, ma'am. It seemed like forever," the crewman said, staring at his rifle.

"I checked with my computer. Ten point five seconds from first to last shot. Didn't give a hero or a coward much time to react. This time, I'll see that you get more time going in. Then you can tell me which you are, coward or hero."

"You think so?"

"I wouldn't have you wasting my ammunition if I didn't. How many small-arms rounds did you fire in training?"

"The minimum requirement, ma'am."

"Well now you've fired the weapon again. What do you think of it?"

"It's sweet, ma'am."

"Then keep shooting." Kat said and continued her walk. By the time each crewman, including the five troopers had fired off half a clip, there was an air of confidence mixing in with the falling snow.

As the impromptu 'rifle practice' drew to a close, the first Griffin coverage of the problem ahead came in, beamed direct into Kat's helmet head-up-display. It showed a lot of thermal images and human heartbeats. At least this bunch hadn't acquired any hi-tech deception devices! Thankfully the Colonel had thought ahead, arranging for the Griffin. While the last rounds were fired off, Kat and Jack studied the enemy's deployment.

"Sloppy," Kat concluded. "They're expecting us to come right up the highway."

"Yes," Jack agreed. "But, this bunch seem a bit smarter than the last. They haven't used a tree trunk to block the road. They want us to drive into the trap before they start shooting."

Kat shrugged. "So we make their trap into our trap." As she turned back to the vehicles her eyes fell on one of their dejected prisoners, leaning half out the back, trying to catch snow on his tongue.

"Jack, we're going into a fire-fight. P.O.W.s cannot be subjected to hostile fire. Tie them up here. I'll call that last farm, now that they're back on-line, they can come and pick them up. If he wants to offer any of them a job, we'll call it even. Any he wouldn't employ, I'll pick up next week."

Jack eyed the prisoners for a moment, then brought up his hand in a salute. "Yes ma'am."

"Now, let's go and give some pain to these bastards." Kat said, returning the salute.

ONE : TWELVE

Kat halted the convoy about two kilometres before the bend that lead to the stretch of highway running briefly parallel to the frozen shoreline of the lake. From the water's edge the bank rose steeply before levelling off. An old rail track had once ran atop the levelled section before the bank rose steeply again, through a hundred metres of densely packed spruce and birch trees to the highway.

Kat had her battle planned.

The bandits were amongst the trees, between the frozen lake and the snow covered highway across a frontage of about two-hundred metres with a second, much larger formation on the opposite side of the highway. The tree-line that faced directly onto the highway, on both sides, was unoccupied, giving no indication that the bandits were in position. Most of the hostiles were located between five to ten metres back into the trees from the highway's edge. There was little depth to their formation, but why should there be? This uncomplicated tactic had been invented by hill tribes several millennia ago and used again and again for the simple reason that it worked.

It worked if the target didn't know you were waiting for them.

Kat did.

"Jack, take the crews from Trucks Three, Four and Five and form an extended-line at right angles to the highway, form up on both sides. I'll take the Land Forces Troopers and the other two truck crews on a fast walk behind those on the left side of the road. We'll open fire into their rear, driving them forward, across the highway, into their comrades, then down the bank onto the frozen lake."

"We can do that," Jack agreed.

Dismounted, the crews spread out, the snow and wind lashing at their bodies. Cowell's crew, with three from another truck took the left side of the highway. Jack took the right side with the other six crewmen. That left Kat with fifteen, including herself, to begin the flanking manoeuvre. She had them count off by twos to form fire-groups. "Remember whether you're a 'one' or a 'two,' and move when I tell you."

She gave her nervous '127mm marksman' a reassuring thumbs-up as she went down the line and took her place at its front before ordering them to follow her. With luck, she wasn't leaving too many bad guys for Jack to sort out. But then, that was what Custer thought when he left Reno attacking the front and went off searching for an undefended flank and found only oblivion. Kat shook that thought away; she had a Griffin. It showed her where every single one of the bad-guys and not-so-bad guys were. She didn't have to worry about blundering into them before she wanted to. Technology was good.

The feed into her visor's head-up-display suddenly went blank as Kat reached the point where her single-file was going to right-face, turning to become an extended line, then begin advancing through the trees down to the highway, flushing out the former prison inmates. She made the turn, with her nine Fleet crewmen and five Land Forces troopers. She called Headquarters.

"I know, I know, we lost the feed too," the Colonel answered. "It's ancient software, so we're having to manipulate the hardware big-time to get it talking with our net. We're re-booting it now. Give us five minutes. By the way, I like your deployment. Flank them, get then running, good psychology."

"I'm kind of counting on the Griffin to let me know about any surprises."

"You'll know when it's back as soon as I do."

"Thanks, sir. Things are getting a bit busy here."

"Good luck, Ensign."

With her airborne surveillance gone, Kat reverted to the old fashioned method. Two of her troopers she designated as scouts and sent them ahead of her main group. She let them get a good twenty metres ahead before she moved her thin main force forward again. They were supposed to be seventy-five metres behind the enemy's main positions, but it only took someone looking for a secluded place to take a crap, and they were screwed, any surprise would be blown.

*   *   *

The snow fell in great gusts, and the trees shivered in the wind. The forest floor was not completely covered in snow and small patches beneath some of the larger trees were still clear, although they stank of rotting pine needles and animal faeces. Kat could no longer see the two scouts. A herd of elephants could have stampeded past at that very moment, and she wouldn't have heard or seen a thing. Deaf and blind, Kat's formation plodded on through the snow, weaving between the trees. There was no time to waste. Sooner or later, the bad guys would start wondering what was holding up the trucks.

"Griffin's back," was all the Colonel said.

"Roger that," was Kat's own short reply. She tapped the stud on the side of her helmet to power-up her visor's head-up-display. She liked what she saw. She was at the rear of the enemy's position, roughly in the middle of their line. If she hit them from where she was, there was a good chance some of the bandits would run right into Jack's advancing formations. That of course assumed whoever was leading the opposition didn't get his people moving against her. If she did, Kat was susceptible to being encircled on either, if not both flanks.

"Trooper Lillie here."

"Yes," Kat whispered. He was ahead of her and closest to the enemy positions.

"Two bad boys heading your way, no wait, make that a bad boy and a bad girl."

"Take cover," Kat ordered, probably unnecessarily.

She signalled everyone down, then went to ground herself behind a far too thin birch trunk, then she checked the Griffin feed. Located the scout, then found the two more rapidly beating hearts and started looking in that direction. Movement eventually drew her eye. Yes, there was the couple. They made towards a large spruce that had only a little snow beneath it.

From behind her birch trunk Kat was trying to make herself invisible. To her right the rest of the formation did the same, well as much as city raised, Fleet crewmen ever could. Kat concentrated on the pair ahead of her.

After much fumbling with various layers of clothing, and despite the icy wind and general coldness, bad-boy still managed to rise to the occasion. Obviously satisfying their carnal desires was far more important than following the orders of the ringleaders and their bully-boys. How many others amongst their number weren't completely committed to the impending ambush?

The girl was now on her hands and knees, having refused to lie down on the forest floor, as bad-boy entered her from behind. Within a minute or two she was noisily encouraging him to provide even greater acts of sexual prowess.

Kat recalled once reading in a women's magazine that seventy percent of men kept their eyes open and thirty percent closed them during moments like this. She couldn't remember which type was supposed to be the better lovers. She just hoped this guy was one of the 'eyes closed' variety.

The wind suddenly died, and someone along the line from Kat sneezed loudly.

With the freezing temperatures and all the snow, colds were epidemic in Elmendorf. Just about the time they got the right vaccination for one strain of virus, it would mutate into something different. The Medical branch personnel were kept constantly busy creating new vaccines. Everyone had to put up with a cold for a few days each month.

Kat hoped the passionate pair would assume the sneeze had come from one of their own people.

Bad-boy did lose interest, and his first glance was indeed back towards the highway. The girl murmured something, but he shushed her. Still joined, he picked up his rifle, and this time did a scan in Kat's direction. Kat thumbed the safety off her own weapon but didn't dare move. She waited.

The man then shouted something, withdrew from the girl and fired two rounds in a direction Kat had no troops. "Stay down," Kat whispered on the net. "He's firing at shadows. Let's not give him anything real to shoot at."

The girl didn't get up, encouraging him to finish what he'd started. But the man ignored her, although his trousers remained around his ankles. He shuffled a few short paces towards Kat, eyes roving the forest. His head stopped moving, his eyes locking onto Kat. Both his rifle and his ardour were half-up. He brought the weapon up into his shoulder and took aim.

For a second, they just started at each other as Kat brought her rifle up too. She knew he'd beat her, but she had to try.

Then his head exploded in a cloud of red as Trooper Lillie took him down in a short burst of automatic fire.

That brought the girl up onto her knees, one hand trying to pull up her clothes, the other to her mouth. She turned and half ran, half crawled back to the waiting ambush.

With no other choice, Kat sent a single round at the girl. It caught her in her still exposed rump and she collapsed forward into the snow. A glancing shot, no more than a flesh wound, she'd certainly live, but it was enough to take her down.

"Prepare to advance. Fire-Group Two prepare to provide covering fire on my command. Fire-Group One, advance with me. Now!" Kat was up and running as she finished the last word. Her team was a bit slower, but they were up by the time she was down.

"Hold your fire you idiots," a voice bellowed against the wind. "Their trucks aren't here yet. Who's shooting?"

"I think it was Jacob. He and his girl headed out back a few minutes ago," another voice shouted.

"Well, tell him to get his butt back down here now."

Kat took advantage of the confusion to move Fire-Group Two further forward, before advancing Fire-Group One for a second time. A startled bandit loomed up in front of her.

Kat shot him.

"Weapons Free. I repeat, Weapons Free, this in Ensign Severn. If a target presents itself, engage."

Unfortunately, there weren't many targets. Despite moving her people forward, she still wasn't at the main ambush position. Sporadic fire came from beside her and ahead of her, but the only things taking hits were the trees. Ordering Fire-Group Two forward again, Kat fired a few rounds, more to keep the enemy's heads down than hit any target.

"They're behind us, you idiots," the first voice was shouting off to Kat's right. "Turn around, shoot them."

"Scouts, whoever is doing that shouting must be close to your location. Drop him if you can."

Twenty metres to Kat's front, Lillie and another trooper moved from between the trees, bodies low, guns level. "Roger that, we're looking for him ma'am."

It was Fire-Group One's turn to advance again. She signalled them forward. "Leonard, watch our right flank for encirclement, any sign of Cowell yet?"

"Negative ma'am. I've been watching out for her, but we're stretched a bit thin out this way." Leonard responded in her earpiece.

Kat went to ground beside a large spruce trunk. To her front, people were moving towards her. She sent a long burst of fire into a tree, high above their heads, then another burst into a second nearby tree. People anywhere near the splintering trees began dropping into the snow. One man, behind the rest, shouted at them, waved his gun. Kat took aim on him. He went over backwards as three rounds took him in the chest.

Five nearby bandits took one look at his fallen body and ran. Several others hugged the ground, tried to burrow into the knee deep snow. Kat sent another long burst into the trees above them, and another half a dozen took to their heels. Kat ignored them and checked to her right. More movement.

"Fire-Group Two, move forward to reinforce Group One. Let's hold this position."

She waved the second half of her command forward, signalling the two closest to move to her left. Her troops were spread too damn thin. Kat tapped her helmet stud to access the latest Griffin feed. The hostiles seemed disorganised in front of her, some moving forward, others back. She shifted the view to check things out in Jack's location.

The display went blank.

"Colonel," she squealed.

"We're re-booting again."

"It'll all be over by then," Kat snarled.

"I have a lot of movement to my front, heavy firing," Cowell hollered over the net. "Lots of people shooting and moving my way. I think they're trying to outflank me."

"Discourage them," Kat ordered, "Keep trying to push them back."

"I saw a few trying to run. One of their own shot them. I got him, but there's a lot of them, and I'm not sure if I can hold." Cowell's words were punctuated by automatic fire.

"Damn, why can't a plan ever hold together?" Kat

snapped. She glanced over to her left. Her two Land Forces scouts were there, about fifteen metres away, opening up on any targets that presented themselves. The two Fleet crewmen she'd moved to the left were now in position and supporting them too, one was her '127mm marksman.'

"All personnel to my left, you will remain here and hold this flank as we advance. Understood?"

She got four acknowledgments. No shakiness in their voices now.

"Fire-Groups One and Two, we are going to herd these bastards a bit faster than planned. We will advance in fire groups, flushing them onto the highway. Fire-Group One, move now."

Kat was up, shouting, firing at anything that moved. Behind her, half her people fired as well. Ahead of her, the advancing hostiles stopped, apparently startled by the sudden appearance of so many – *or perhaps so few* – assaulting troops. Kat went to ground well away from any trees; she wanted a clear field of fire.

"Group Two, prepare to advance. Advance now!"

They came out of their positions, shouting, shooting. Kat swept her sights over the position to her front. A short burst from her sent four more running, weapons tossed away. A man turned to gun them down, but Kat got him first. Another man was shouting, waving his arms as others fled past him. Kat drew a bead on him, but he too went down as someone else beat her to the trigger. She kept searching.

Two people huddled on either side of a tree trunk. Both were shooting as fast as they could pull the trigger and work the bolt. Kat sent a burst into the trunk, shattering bark and splinters over them. They ducked. One was on his feet in a second, running, his hunting rifle left behind. The other one shouted something, then went back to shooting. She put a burst between his eyes as her magazine clicked empty.

Quickly reloading, Kat shouted, "Fire-Group One," and got back to her feet, "prepare to advance." This next move forward would put them into the enemy's original ambush positions. "Advance now!"

Kat fired a long, high burst as she raced forward, past the line occupied by her other fire-group and into the space beyond. A pair of gunmen in front of her threw up their hands and fell to their knees. Kat had no time to stop and take prisoners. "Run! Damn you, run!" she shouted.

Instead, they fell on their faces in the snow as bullets smashed into the trees nearby. Kat spotted the hostile shooter and sent him sprawling backwards with another long burst.

She slid to the ground behind an all-to-thin tree trunk. "Group Two, prepare to advance. Advance now. Jack, what's the situation on your side?"

"Damned if I know," was the unexpected reply she got back. "We have people all over the place. Some of the bandits are running, others attacking. Kat, I have no idea what is going on."

"Cowell, what's your situation?"

"I've pulled some of my people in so that the flank is better protected. I think more of them are running than fighting. Maybe, if I can . . . wait out." Lots of rapid small-arms fire came over Cowell's live mike. "Yes, more are running."

"Lillie, how's that left flank?"

"Plenty of targets, ma'am. Someone is pushing them at us, but we can't seem to locate their leader. We could certainly use anybody you can spare."

Kat stood up, trying to listen to the sounds of battle around her. Damn, what she'd give for thirty seconds of Griffin feed right now. The wind was back and resumed whipping the falling snow into her lower face as she turned towards their left flank, bringing with it the crackle of small arms fire. She'd robbed Peter to pay Paul, by taking the pressure off Cowell on the right. Now it sounded like the left flank was rapidly going to rat-shit. "Leonard, you take command of this line, hold here until you link up with Master Crewman Cowell's team that should be flushing through from the right at any moment."

"Yes ma'am."

"I'm taking the three people I can see." Kat signalled the only trigger-pullers in sight; one was a Land Force's trooper. "Wherever you other two troopers are, fall-out of line and join me on the left flank."

Two "Yes ma'am," answered her.

Kat dropped back through the trees, collecting her people around her. The sound of weapons fire grew louder. She kept her team moving forward but did not return fire, even though an occasional stray round came their way. This was her last reserve.

Whoever was hitting her left could still roll up her flank; the day was not over. Her only hope was to hit them so suddenly that they broke and ran before they knew what faced them. Snow continued to smack into her visor and lower face, Kat struggled to make out the forms ahead, heat images, movement, weapons fire.

"Ma'am, this is Trooper Franklin, I'm up point. I think I can see one of our guys ahead of me."

"Trooper Lillie, can you see us yet?"

After a pause, "Negative, ma'am."

"Let's go a bit further," Kat ordered.

"This is Franklin, ma'am, that sure looks like Fleet ahead of me. He's firing to my left, and I'm taking a lot of incoming from here."

"I see you now," Trooper Lillie confirmed.

"Okay, everyone load a full magazine." Kat ordered, "then get a second one ready. Anyone out?"

That got no answer.

"On my mark, rapid fire, empty a full clip. Then reload and charge. Any questions?"

None.

Kat loaded her own new magazine. That left her just one more clip of forty rounds and whatever was left in the one she'd just taken out. It was going to be close.

"On my mark. Three, two, one, mark." Around Kat the forest came alive with rapid fire. Each rifle filled the air, trees, flesh, with a continuous sweep of lead. Kat had read about 'mad minutes.' The M37 could empty a full magazine in a lot less than a minute, but the fire from Kat and her five Land Force Troopers and four Fleet Crewmen lasted for a good thirty seconds.

Kat's rifle clicked as the last round left the chamber. She yanked out the empty magazine, rammed a new one in and made ready the first round. "Charge," she shouted, coming to her feet. If they had had bayonets she would have ordered them to be fixed. "Up and at 'em," she screamed. "Go, go, go! Charge." Then, with a half roar, half scream that meant nothing but drove through the insanity that temporarily possessed them, her command was obeyed.

Here and there survivors of the rapid fire hugged the ground, trembling, others tried to raise their hands. A man stood, screaming at others to follow him. Kat got him in her sights, but he was hit from so many different angles that he didn't fall and danced a macabre jig, very dead but not allowed to drop. The bad guys further back were running. Most had already thrown away their weapons. Not all. Kat keyed her mike.

"Those with a weapon will be shot," rang through the woods, overpowering the snow and wind. "Throw down your weapon, and you will not be harmed. Keep it, and you will die."

Most of the runners with guns took only a second to correct their error. A few did not. Maybe they were too confused to notice what was still in their hands. Maybe they were the bully-boys and could not think of facing the world unarmed. There was no time to ask. Kat and her team took them down. A few of the armed runners who were not among the first to die took the hint and more weapons were tossed away. Others still didn't take the hint. More died.

"Griffin feed is back," came quietly in Kat's ear, reminding her that she was supposed to be in command here. Reluctantly, she took the rifle from her shoulder, mastered the blood rage that coursed through her, and fought to regain the control a commander needed. She took two deep breaths as she tapped the helmet stud to access the images. Crouching to get under the low canopy of a nearby spruce tree, she stopped against its trunk.

The Griffin feed confirmed that gunmen were running from her troops all along the line, fleeing back towards the highway, then down the bank to the frozen-over lake. Jack's people could head them off, easily. Then she remembered, this wasn't about the body count. Most, if not all of those running were harmless. "Colonel, can you give me an image that shows if any of those running away are still armed?"

"They're using old fashioned, metal based hunting rifles and automatics? Nothing ceramic?"

Kat glanced around at the two or three dropped weapons nearby. "Looks like it, sir."

"Magnetic mass is very low," the Colonel answered. "My call would be they're down to their belt buckles."

"Thanks, Colonel. I'd rather not pursue." She changed the subject with hardly a moment's thought. "Vehicle commanders, casualty report."

"I have two wounded, one bad." Cowell advised. "Medic is already here."

"Roger that, anyone else?"

"One flesh wound," Jack reported.

"This is Lillie. I've got . . . oh shit, he's dead."

"Where are you?" Kat turned. A crewman to her right was waving and pointing. Dread growing, Kat called up her last reserve of energy to jog to where he was now pointing.

She found a trooper from her final assault team standing over the sprawled body. The woman who had sat behind Kat for most of the day was on her knees, helmet off, tears flowing down her face. Trooper Lillie looked up as Kat joined them. "He was okay. I swear to God, he was okay. I saw him stand up when you ordered the charge. I thought he was right there with us."

Kat stared down at the crewman she had only known as the '127mm marksman.' A round had taken him in the neck. He'd fallen onto his back, his green eyes were open, staring expectantly into the snow filled sky. His ammo pouches were empty; the magazine in his rifle must have been his last. He'd more than made up for this morning's inability to act. *How will I ever explain this to his parents, what he won and lost this day?*

There were a thousand feelings, questions, demands, all tumbling around Kat's brain. But not now. Now she had a battle to clean up. "Jack, get the drivers back to the vehicles and get them moving. Leading Crewman Leonard, get the walking wounded, including any bad-guys, moved onto the highway for pickup. Trooper Franklin, there are a lot of weapons lying around. Form an extended line, get them picked up. I want anything we leave behind rendered inoperable."

"I've got a real problem case on my hands, ma'am. She really does need urgent surgical attention," Cowell urged. "Tremblay can't stop the bleeding."

"I understand, Master Crewman. We will police the area

for weapons until the vehicles arrive and the wounded are loaded. We destroy as much as we can before we leave, but the rest, we'll just leave to rust. Good enough?"

"Yes, ma'am, sorry, ma'am" Cowell whispered.

"You three," Kat indicated the other three Land Force troopers from her assaulting team. "When the trucks arrive get a tarp and wrap him in . . ." She didn't even know his name.

"Joel, ma'am," the woman looked up, "Joel Collins."

Kat left them with Collins's body. She moved with the others through the forest, picking up rifles, stripping out the firing pins. She smashed a shotgun hard against a birch tree. It felt good as the mechanism gave way and the butt came off.

She was smashing her sixth weapon when Jack called her from the road. "Kat, I have all the wounded loaded. We need to get moving."

"Roger that. All crews, mount up," she shouted. Around her, tired personnel finished what they were doing and turned towards the nearby highway.

"Jack, as soon as you can get a driver and four of our people into the cab of the truck with the wounded on, get them out of here."

"You're not staying behind, are you?"

"No, I want everyone out of here as quickly as possible, but the wounded go first and the wounded go fast."

"Yes, ma'am."

Kat was just in sight of the highway when the truck carrying their wounded pulled away into the snow. If she knew Jack, he'd be driving that truck. It would have been interesting to see how much he would go for speed and how much for safety. *Poor Jack*, she thought, he was spending a lot of time being torn between two less than ideal options today.

With Safi's assistance, Kat then sent a brief communication to the last farmstead, 'Duncan 868,' as she waited for her people to trail out of the forest. Yes, the owner had picked up the prisoners from their first fire-fight without incident. Kat terminated the link as the five Land Force Troopers came out of the forest, three carrying a heavy burden; she waved them to the lead truck. They settled the body of Crewman Collins in the back, then refused to ride in the cab, preferring to share the cold truck bed with the 'fallen' as per Land Force's tradition. Kat started to join them, then realised there was no one to keep the driver company. It had been a long day; the drive back would not be easy. Someone had to keep him awake.

Kat climbed into the cab. Leonard was behind the wheel. He had already returned the windscreen to its normal position, closed the side windows and cranked-up the heater. "Move out," she ordered.

After several kilometres in silence, Leonard asked "Do you think we turned a profit today, ma'am?"

"You're the accountant, Leonard, what do you think? Will you be happy keeping to your computer ledgers after today?" she asked him.

"I don't know. It was good, getting out here, seeing the looks on the faces of the kids when we arrived with the first real food they'd had in a long time."

"And the fire-fights?" Kat asked, looking at the forest at the edge of the highway.

"We hurt the bad guys today, didn't we? They won't mess with the Fleet next time we come out, will they?"

Kat thought for a long moment. They'd come out here to feed the starving . . . and they had. They'd had a chance offered to them to make things better . . . and they had. Although the price seemed far too high to Kat at this precise moment. "Yes," she agreed. "They won't mess with the Fleet again."

Kat's truck drove slowly into the main base compound that evening like the hearse that it was. She dismounted and moved to help the Land Force troopers remove the body of her single fatality. Colonel Hepburn, however, was in her way. "How did it go?" he said.

"Not bad, I guess, Colonel," Kat answered, leaning around him to watch as three crewmen from the base helped with the tarpaulin wrapped body.

"Let them take care of that," the Colonel told her.

"Him," Kat corrected. As Hepburn showed no intention of getting out of her way, she turned towards the Headquarters block. "I'd better look in on my wounded."

"They're being taken care of. I want to talk to you in my office."

"I'll be there in a few minutes."

"Like last time?" the Colonel asked with an arched eyebrow.

Kat entered the Headquarters block and turned left for the med-centre. The Colonel's office was up the stairs; he followed her into Medical. Just as she had expected, Jack was applying his limited battlefield casualty training, helping one of the medics while the doctor and other surgically trained staff struggled to keep Cowell's 'bleeder' alive. The bad-girl Kat had shot in the butt was back on her knees, this time receiving treatment for her wound, and glaring defiantly at Kat as she passed her by. Kat paused at each of the wounded military personnel, telling them they'd done well. One picked that exact moment to go into shock. As a medic rushed over to start treatment, the Colonel edged Kat out of Medical and up the stairs to his office, an iron grip on her elbow.

A few minutes later she was seated in his office, a large glass in her hand. Colonel Hepburn then produced a bottle of fine single-malt whisky and removed the stopper. The aroma filled the room even before he started filling her glass, right to the brim. He did the same for himself, raised the amber filled glass in a toast, and said, "You did a very good job out there today."

Kat eyed the glass for a moment. How many times had she almost gotten killed today? Did it matter if she finished it sober or drunk. She took a long sip. It was truly fine whisky, flowing smoothly down to warm her stomach, massaging out the knots. She sighed and relaxed into her chair. "I suppose so."

"No, Ensign Severn, *you* were very good today."

Kat took another sip. If she'd done so good, why did she feel so bad? That was the problem; she didn't know how she felt. Maybe Grandpa Jim would know, but she didn't. All of it was new, too strange, too scary. She did know what Grandpa Jim would say though. "A lot of people did a good job today, Colonel, not just me. How do I write them up for some kind of recognition? Everyone on those trucks deserves something."

The Colonel took a long drink from his glass. "And

they'll all get the Humanitarian Service Medal."

She almost hurled her glass at him. "Sir, with respect, virtually all the personnel deployed on this tasking will get that medal. My people were out in the snow, getting shot at, outnumbered three or four to one, in the finest traditions of the ABCANZ military." She finished her rant with a larger gulp of whisky than she'd intended, fire searing into her belly. At least the pain felt good. After today, she ought to hurt somewhere.

Hepburn took another sip. "I know Katarina, and I don't disagree with you, but was it technically combat?"

"I don't know what else you'd call it, sir. If that was a non-combat situation, someone forgot to tell the bullets!"

He nodded. "I hear you. So, are *you* prepared to declare that those indentured workers were in armed rebellion against the lawful government of Anchorage?"

Kat blinked twice at the sentence, tried to extrapolate its full meaning, and gave up. She retired into a sip of her own drink. "I haven't seen much in the way of lawful government." She made the words bitter. "Does it exist?"

"Around here somewhere," the Colonel waved his glass at something and nothing. "They do have a governing body, and by their constitution, it can only meet for one, one month period every three years. They had the last one just before the volcano blew, so can't have another one for at least another eighteen months or so, unless they hold a new election. You want to try running an election in this mess?"

"There must be something on their statute books that covers a situation like this?" Kat knew her father manipulated and interpreted the laws and legislation back in Nu New England to get what he wanted. That brought her to a quick stop. She eyed the Colonel over her glass.

"The policy here is that you govern best, by governing least," he scowled. "It's the first sentence of their damn constitution, and that's restricted to a hundred pages exactly. Size of page, margins and font size all specified to prevent any modification. The founders of this settlement were only just on the right side of the law, and were quite adamant that they were not going to have any 'big government' here. So, no chief executive, no town mayor, just a governing body that meets tri-annually and a hundred page law book to encompass everything."

"Then who asked the ABCANZ Government for assistance?"

"As I understand it, there's a strip mining operation across the inlet, significant commercial investment. One of the major shareholders probably has influence in The Capital. Suddenly the Senate authorises this mission, and here we are. Could even be one of your relatives!"

"On my mother's side, probably," Kat mumbled and took another sip of her whisky. "Father's family would have thought this through before committing the military." She paused for a few seconds. "So let me see if I've got this right. We are here to help a local authority that for all practical purposes doesn't exist, and these people who are shooting at us, despite being convicted ABCANZ felons, cannot be considered 'rebels' because there isn't enough of a government for them to actually 'rebel' against."

"Now do you understand why I'm falling asleep at my desk, trying to find a way to work through this mess? Trying to find a practical, deliverable solution?"

Kat had never had a senior officer come so close to a blunt admission of failure. To hide her embarrassment, she took a long drink from her glass and changed the subject. "We'll need to get more convoys moving, sir. They're starving out there. Adults are eating berries and roots, but the kids don't have the stomachs for it." There, that was something she could tackle with both hands.

"Already checked. Byrne's mechanics will have another three trucks in a usable state for tomorrow. I figure three small convoys, each with three trucks."

"Which one do you want me to take?" Kat asked, watching the whisky swirl in her glass.

"None of them. I'm restricting you to this base and the warehouse complex, nowhere else."

Kat bristled. "Sir, I only fired when their intentions were beyond doubt. We were engaged by the gunmen, and I did my utmost to keep the casualties to a minimum." Kat didn't know how to count her single fatality. Even one seemed more than this frozen-over, backside-of-beyond was worth. Yet against those odds, how could she have done better? *Why do I feel so bad about it?*

The Colonel waved his drink again to calm her down. "I know. As I told you, you did very well today. Nevertheless, I am ordering you and Ensign Byrne, to limit your movements to this base, and you are only to move to the warehouse complex by vehicle, not on foot. Do I make myself clear?"

"Yes, sir. Can I ask why?"

"You, young lady, have become a very high-value target. You beat the bad guys today, and there will now be a lot of them that will want you dead. I will continue to send out the food convoys, and the message is clear, they now know not to mess with them. But if I send *you* out, and some gunman decides he wants to get himself a reputation as the one who took out Ensign Katarina Severn, well . . . like it or not, *you* are that Katarina Severn, the one who confronted them, and beat them at Lake Nancy." He took another sip before continuing. "The Chief Warden at MaxSec Florence obviously has considerable influence. Within hours of me updating him on the situation regarding his 'indentured workers' the High Command notifies me that they're sending a battalion of infantry here to backup the Apprehension Squads being sent in from Florence. They should all start arriving in a few days. I am therefore sending you and Ensign Byrne back to Nu New England, and I intend to send you back alive."

"You're relieving me, sir!"

"No Ensign, I'm rotating you. You weren't planning on making Elmendorf a career, were you?"

"No, sir, I just didn't expect to be out of here quite so soon."

"It happens on these emergency jobs, Katarina, especially when there are tight budgetary considerations. Nobody stays here for more than six weeks . . . except me!"

Kat tried to think how long it had been. She couldn't. "Safi, how long have I been here?"

"One week, six days, eight hours . . ."

"Enough," the Colonel growled and took another sip. "It's bad enough getting that from the junior enlisted personnel, without getting it from a damn computer!"

Kat took another sip from her almost empty glass. "Who will command tomorrow's convoys, Colonel?"

"Those other two Ensigns have had it easy up to now, and I think I'll take the other one. I've done enough paperwork. I don't know if I dare send Harper. People might refuse the food."

They shared a smile. "Send Harper," Kat said. "She needs to see what the reality is. Might help her with her policies. With their IDent cards stolen there's no way to validate who's getting the food. Can't we just declare everyone in this region starving and call it quits?"

"Can't do that. Because everyone isn't starving." Hepburn replied, shaking his head.

"Okay, so outside of our mess-hall," Kat narrowed it down.

"Apparently there are still some civilians who haven't missed a meal. Some people are still eating pretty well by all accounts. Maybe not quite so well now you've got the Fleet rations properly secured." Again the Colonel raised his glass in salute. Both drained their glasses. "Another?" said Hepburn, offering the bottle.

Kat eyed the swirling liquid. *'The drinker takes the first drink; the second drink takes the drunk,'* or something like that. She remembered how hard it had been to dry out. How humiliated she had been when Monty or one of the household staff had to clean up after her. Did she want the Colonel to see that Kat Severn? "Thank you, Colonel, but no, I think I'll go for a walk, get some air."

The Colonel refilled his glass. "Watch your back, Ensign."

"I will, sir," Kat said.

Kat found herself outside the Headquarters block, standing in the swirling snow. Her uniform was quickly covered, but the whisky kept her warm. She could go for a walk. She'd done a lot of walking recently, seen a few men throwing-up in side-streets, stumbling down back-ally's. With food in Anchorage being so scarce, most of the settlement no longer imbibed of alcohol. Nevertheless there was still hard drink to be found, if you looked hard, if you really needed it, and tonight Kat really needed it. She started walking. "Safi, I don't want to talk to anyone. Take me off-line."

Despite the Colonel's restriction on her movements, Kat was almost at the base gates when the snow began to fall even harder and her conscience finally got a hold of her, and she turned back to her accommodation. Dripping wet, almost frozen solid, she threw herself onto the bed, stared up at the ceiling and tried to get hold of herself. She'd done good. She'd lost a crewman, maybe two. She'd fed some very hungry kids. She'd shot at people whose only issue was hunger. She'd beaten the bad guys. The room spun, instigated by the Colonel's whisky. She remembered the squirrels back in the gardens at Bagshot, chasing each other's tails. There was a mark on her ceiling. She wondered where it came from. She closed her eyes, but she couldn't sleep. She'd done well today. She'd killed and almost got herself killed.

ONE : THIRTEEN

There was a light tap at the door. "Kat, can we talk?" asked Jack.

"I don't want to talk to anyone," Kat shouted.

"Jack would really like to talk to you," Safi said softly.

"So you told him where I was?"

"No, I took you off-line as you requested. However, he interrogated your room's motion detector. I assume he therefore concluded you were in here." Kat scowled. Apparently, her Heuristic Intellect had not exercised its full initiative to protect her privacy.

"Kat, I'd really like to talk to you," Jack repeated.

"And I'd really like for everyone to just go away."

"Do Severn's always get their own way?"

"No, but this Severn is in a lousy mood. I'd go away if I were you."

"Haven't you noticed? I'm not you."

Kat could almost see Jack's lopsided grin. "I've brought a bottle," he added.

That complicated matters. Damn, she wanted another drink. "Open," she growled at the door.

There he was, grin and all. As he stepped through the door he tossed a bottle at her. She caught it, then made a face as she read the label. "Carbonated water."

"Don't knock it. That's probably the only bottle of the stuff in town."

Kat aimed the bottle at Jack's head, but he caught it before it hit home. "Do you mind if I notify the Colonel where you are?"

"Why would he care where I am?" she spat.

"Because I panicked him when he gave me this big glass of whisky and told me he'd just shared one with you. A second later, he discovered just how much Safi there can do. Which, I have to say, did not enhance his opinion of rich girls in the military."

"Do I look like I care, Jack?"

"Can I call him?"

"Make your damn call."

Jack did. The Colonel sounded relieved and cut the call short.

"A minor point, Kat, but as you didn't have any cash on you, how exactly did you intend to pay for any alcohol you just happened to find off-base?"

"Which is why I'm not off-base. You didn't think I'd be stupid enough to flash my credit card, did you?"

"I had an uncle who wasn't too thoughtful once he'd got a sip of the old moonshine inside him. I didn't know what you'd do."

"I came up here to get some cash, then decided it wasn't worth going back out in the snow. There, are you happy now?"

Jack settled into the easy chair next to the bed. Kat rolled over onto her stomach, propping her chin in her hands.

"Shit of a day," Jack said.

Kat was ready to mutter a nice throw away comment, like '*wasn't it,*' but that wasn't what she felt. "How the hell would you know?" she snapped. "You just did what you were told."

Jack eyed her without flinching. "I guess I wasn't much of a backup."

"Didn't feel like much of one out there."

"MO says Maddy, sorry Crewman Maddox will live." Jack said, quickly changing the subject.

"That her name?" Kat snapped.

"Your foreman Oz, he thinks we'll have nine trucks ready for tomorrow's run. But the Colonel says we can't do any more runs. We've got to share the fun with the other Ensigns."

"Yes, I know," she snapped. Now wishing she'd stayed and had some more of the Colonel's whisky.

"So when are you going to share the pain?"

Kat blinked twice. "What pain?"

"I was trying to give Cowell all the support I could." Jack said, eyes locked on Kat, "They ignored me, just followed her, but there was just so many of them and so few of us."

"There certainly was a lot of them," Kat said, eyes seeing

the forest, the snow, the bodies. "How many did we kill?"

"I've no idea."

"Safi, how many did we kill?"

"I do not know, Kat. I have not analyzed the final MQ-22 feed for bodies. Should I do so?"

Kat took a deep breath, then rolled over again, focussing on the mark on the ceiling, she shrugged. "It really doesn't matter, does it Jack? They'll still be dead and I'll still be alive and I'll never know if they did something that deserved being dead or were they just poor bastards who were hungry."

A sigh rattled out of Jack that would have made any Irish mother proud. "No, we'll never know."

"I always end up alive. Someone else always ends up dead."

"Like Louis?" Jack didn't flinch as he used the banned word.

"Like Louis," Kat whispered.

"So you're alive and wondering if you should get drunk, and they're dead and not all the alcohol you can drink will give Louis a moment more of life." Jack lowered his gaze to the floor. "It won't help any of them out there either, they're dead, frozen in the snow."

"My, my, aren't you quite the poet tonight," Kat said.

"It's the truth, Kat. You're alive. I'm alive. They're dead. It happens that way. When a ship gets hit, it kills some, and others live. The guy off duty lives, the girl who went to the heads, she lives. The kid who mans the comms station, he lives. The old Chief in Engineering is caught in the initial explosion . . . he dies. And there's nothing that anyone can do about it. Maybe we raise a glass to them tonight, but we're glad we're alive. That it was them that died and not us. And if it had been the other way around, they'd be raising a glass to us." Jack shrugged and looked her in the eye. "It's always better to be raising the glass than not."

"Is it? Is it better to be alive? What makes you so sure? Have you ever tried dead? I think I will have that drink," Kat said throwing her feet over the side of the bed.

Jack didn't stand, but shook his head. "You've had plenty enough."

"There's no such thing as enough." Kat stared at him.

He didn't tense, didn't give any indication he was getting up. Yet, she knew if she went for the door, he'd be there to stop her. For a moment she wondered if she could take him. Would he really fight to keep her sober tonight? She laid back down again, hands behind her head. "What are you feeling, Jack?"

"I don't know what I'm feeling. I'm wishing I'd stayed back home in Ireland. I'm wishing my mother never had the dual nationality that enabled me to join this organisation. I'm wishing I'd never come to a place where the very same people I've supposedly come to help actually want to shoot at me, and that I had to shoot back at them, and that I actually wanted to shoot back at them! You Severn's, you live in a very confusing world, far too complicated for a simple Irish lad like me."

Now it was Kat's turn to sigh. It was a genteel one, most ladylike. Mother would be proud. "I've read so many of the official war histories, so many data records of this battle, that theatre-of-operations or campaign. Always they told of Grandpa Jim and Grandpa George's valiant exploits. But never . . . never did they reveal what they felt like afterwards."

"So how did they handle it?" Jack asked.

"I don't know. I just don't know." Kat rubbed her eyes, found herself suppressing a yawn. Maybe the drink was finally kicking in. "Now, why don't you go away and let me sleep," she paused, "please."

Without so much as a backwards glance, Jack stood and left the room.

Kat awoke next morning with no memory of dreams and only a slightly unpleasant taste in her mouth; there were advantages to staying sober. Showered, dressed and feeling painfully alive, she made her way to the Mess Hall. Maybe it was just her, but the troops seemed to have a bit more spring in their step, perhaps their heads were held a just little bit higher. The snow kept falling though, no change there.

She went down the serving-line, and with a full breakfast on her tray walked towards the seating area. The Colonel looked up from his breakfast and waved her over to his table.

"Sleep well?" he asked. Kat nodded, "Yes, thank you, Colonel. Very well."

"I've checked on your wounded. All three are recovering well."

"I'll drop by the med-centre when I'm finished here," Kat said, as she found herself decidedly hungry and dug into the food.

The Colonel leaned back. "I hate to tell you, but I've got another difficult mission for you today," he said with a grin.

"It can't be any harder than yesterday, sir."

"Much harder, much safer, but much harder." If possible, his grin got even wider.

"Colonel, has anyone ever complimented you on your wonderful sense of humour?"

He managed a frown for a moment. "No, don't recall any."

"Something you might want to think about," Kat paused for a protracted moment, then added the required "sir."

"Just for that you get no more sympathy from me, Ensign. We've got a visiting do-gooder coming today. He's come a long way, Europe I believe. Wants to see all the nice things we've been doing with his company's donations. I want you to escort him around the place, show him what's going on, while I take a nice drive in the countryside."

It sounded like a thoroughly boring way to waste a day. "Who is this old goat?"

"Not so old. You might find him cute. An Ernst August von Welf, the eighth of that name," the Colonel said, shaking his head.

Kat only just managed to swallow what was in her mouth and to smile. *Oh Mother! All my dodging of 'such a nice young man' that you've been throwing at me, and now I've got to spend the day with him!* The fact that his father was at the top of Aunty Dee's list of people wanting Kat dead really shouldn't complicate the day's proceedings now, should it? *And you thought today would be safe, Colonel.*

Kat supervised the loading of the trucks for the day's convoys, while Jack inspected any last-minute mechanical work, then signed-off on the vehicles road-worthiness. As the three small columns prepared to move out, she kept a smile on her face, despite the prospect of being chained to a desk, while most of those who had been with her yesterday faced more snow, ice covered roads, ruins and potentially more bandits. Kat stretched the humour of offering to trade jobs with anyone just about as far as a lame joke could go.

When the trucks finally headed out she returned to her office. Oz was waiting; they quickly went over the schedule of unmanned drop-pods and remote guided containers due in later that day, the location of their contents once unloaded, and then made plans for continuing the relief convoys tomorrow. Leonard was at his workstation outside her office; one trip out had been enough for the accountant. As an Operations Specialist, he brought order out of the information that would flood in, populating battle-boards and alike. Now he was doing the same for her. He shook his head as she walked by.

"Is something bothering you?" Kat asked.

"It's the junk they're sending us, ma'am. Five year old ration packs are a bit harder to swallow, but half of the medical supplies in Warehouse Three are out of date. Look at this," he waved a printout. "Raw vaccine culture, well past its 'use by' date. Can we still use this stuff?"

"No idea. Check with the med-centre." Kat said, coming to look over his shoulder. Over half of Warehouse Three was potentially out-of-date junk. "It had probably expired when it was donated."

"By what, a week or two, more like a year? Someone is using us for a dumping ground!"

"No, someone is using us for a tax break for their generous donations." Kat spat.

"My old man probably suggested that scam." Leonard growled. "And he wonders why I don't want his job."

Kat scowled at the printout, confirming in her mind that this was the world she'd joined the Fleet to get away from.

"Hey, look what the cat dragged in," Jack cheerfully called out, as he came into view up the flight of stairs.

"I had hoped for a somewhat better introduction than that," said a second voice.

Kat looked up to see Jack grinning and Ernst August von Welf, the Eighth; arms folded standing in front of her. His finely sculptured handsomeness was a lot easier to take without Mother hanging off his elbow. Today he wore 'field dress' or a finely tailored, very expensive, civilian take on a pseudo-military uniform.

"You don't have a visitor's badge. I'll take you over to Headquarters and get you checked in." Kat said, falling back on standard procedures to give her brain a chance to catch up. *Still extremely handsome, but is it just skin deep?*

"You'll need to see Commander Deane. He's in charge today, as Colonel Hepburn is out on a relief run."

"Can't we avoid all that? I can see enough paper-pushing without leaving home," he said with just a hint of a scowl.

"What do you want to see?" Jack asked, giving Kat a sidewise glance that yelled, *Besides a certain Katarina Severn.*

"Anything but my father. What are you doing out here, Kat?" Ernst quickly sidestepped Jack.

"Whatever the Fleet orders me to do, Ernst. Joining the Fleet looked like the best way to give my mother an early heart attack."

"Ah, our dedication to our parents' coronary health," he chuckled. "So, we do have much in common. And call me Gus, as in Aug-Gust. My father has the monopoly on Ernst."

"Sounds good to me. I'm sure Mother will love to hear of it."

"So, your mother is throwing you at me, just like my father is throwing me at you?"

"Oh, you'd better believe it."

"Then I probably owe you an apology." Gus smiled warmly, showing his perfect white teeth.

"Given, taken, and returned," Kat said, offering her hand. He took it; for a moment she thought he might kiss it, but no, he just shook it firmly. *No first impressions*, Kat shouted to herself. She should let this man define himself and not take on their parents' past history, especially Mother's delusions, or even Aunty Dee's suspicions.

"So what can we do for you?" Jack said, bringing the handshake to an early halt.

"I think the plan is for me to do something for you. At least, that was how I sold it to my father. I'm on route to Magadan in eastern Russia. We're part-financing the extension to the port and a new Free Trade Zone. If we're going to get our faces in the media for doing good, then let's do it well, I told him. So, I have a very large ship full of all sorts of things, some of which might well be useful to your work here."

"And after it's been unloaded?" Kat asked.

"Then I go on to Magadan as planned."

"How long do you think it will take to unload?" Jack asked.

"Depends on how long it will take me to figure out what's onboard that you can make use of here?"

"A few hours then," Jack said, as Kat came back with, "Perhaps even a few days." Jack threw her a quizzical glance.

Well, no one said this young man was out to kill me. His father perhaps, but Gus . . . "Leonard, here has just came across some interesting issues this morning." Kat watched Gus's face while her accountant enlightened him in on the scam regarding medical supplies.

When Leonard was finished, the visitor tapped his comm-link. "Hans, do we have any medical supplies in our cargo?"

"Many tonnes, sir."

"Send all data on them to my location, including expiration dates to, what's your name?"

"Leonard, sir."

"I have that address, sir."

"Good, Hans. Make the von Welf's proud." He turned to Kat. "That should handle that. Leonard, please select what you need."

Kat nodded. If there was a scam, that should put an end to it, for today at least. "So, what would you like to see?"

"What your average day is like."

"That could be somewhat messy," Kat smiled.

"Or dangerous," Jack added.

"Yes, I heard about yesterday. A real shoot out."

"Something like that," Kat evaded.

"Why don't I show you where we rebuild the trucks?" Jack suggested.

"Not a bad place to start," Kat agreed. It would give her a chance to get her thoughts in order while Jack and Gus did that male bonding thing. More like male bashing, as Jack did his best to show the rich kid just how little he really knew.

*   *   *

"You've never stripped an engine?" Jack said twenty minutes later, wiping oil from his hands.

"I've never even been this close to one with its covers off before."

"Not even a car engine?"

Gus stared out the garage door at the falling snow. "My chauffeur took care of that kind of thing. Didn't yours, Kat?"

Kat saw the '*help me*' on Gus's face, but wasn't about to throw him a line. "I helped our chauffeur change the oil and tune up our limos all the time." *Well, twice when Mother wasn't looking.*

"This all helps when the trucks that get sent here are really long overdue for the scrap-yard." Jack suggested.

With a huge sigh, Gus tapped his comm-link. "Hans, what's the usage on those trucks we have onboard?"

"Highest is just under fifty kilometres, pre-embarkation positioning only, sir."

Gus tapped off with a satisfied smile. "I have thirty trucks on board, but could certainly spare you ten, and I doubt any of them will see the inside of this place for a while. What else is on my tour of the seedy side of ABCANZ Federation relief work?"

Jack looked sorely distressed at being bested. His grin actually went for a full ten seconds before it popped back onto his face. Kat stepped in before anyone got hurt. "Let me show you the warehouses." That moved the centre of attention away from Jack and gave her a chance to show off what she'd done. As Kat walked Gus around she found him easy to talk to. Well, it was easy talking about what she was proud of, how she'd blended the Fleet personnel she'd inherited, her new arrivals and the civilian volunteers she'd recruited. In her life, she'd straightened up plenty of other people's political campaigns, volunteer programs or charity events that one of Mother's cronies had dreamed up, but then subsequently couldn't organise to save their life. This yard and the people it now fed were all her show.

It also gave her plenty of chances to point things out to Gus. And while he looked, she studied him. There had initially been a wariness about his eyes, in his perfectly sculptured face, but now they were wide and expectant as he took in her work.

The walk round also gave Kat a chance to compare the two men presently in her life; one boyish in his eagerness to make sure the other was no threat, the other self-contained and seemingly oblivious to anything but Kat's words, listening intently, never interrupting, always asking good questions that got her talking again when she ran out of things to say. A guy like this was easy to have around. *No contest really.*

They finished their tour in the loading yard, watching a remote-guided container enter the compound from the dockyard. It braked into a sliding halt, sending snow and slush flying in all directions. A team ran forward, attached handling lines and an IT link and then guided the un-manned container to the unloading area. "That's one of mine," said Gus, pointing at the red and white logo on the side, "Loaded with something called ERB's. Each 100 gram Emergency Ration Bar has a third of a day's recommended proteins, vitamins and minerals. Good thing about them is that with fluid they expand in the stomach to make it feel like you've had a real meal."

"That'll be a nice change from rice and beans." Jack commented.

"What do you do with the empty containers?" Gus asked. "In some locations they get used for emergency accommodation."

That was a question for Kat. "We collapse the actual containers," she pointed to where a number of units were already stacked up. "The power units will eventually get recycled into the local economy, but Anchorage hasn't got any real economy at the moment, so I guess we'll just leave them here until someone comes up with a use for them." She shrugged.

"But you can use the trucks?" he fixed Kat in his gaze for the first time.

"Without a doubt," Kat agreed. "Safi, show us a map with a two hundred and fifty kilometres radius from this location." She partly undid her jacket to enable Safi to project a three dimensional, fully contoured map onto the warehouse floor. Kat concentrated on the map to avoid the intensity of the young man's eyes. She hadn't heard a thing in the last hour that she didn't like. What was there not to like about a generous young man who took the time to come out and see what was actually really needed? She'd joined the Fleet to do just that. From the sounds of the business empire Gus was half heading up with his father, this was probably about the closest he was ever permitted to get to the 'real' world.

"We've got food going out to the soup kitchens in town," Kat said, pointing at the centre of the map and getting Gus's attention, "so no one goes hungry here. But it's the outlying areas that's the current problem. Even with Jack's teams working around the clock, we currently only have nine working trucks. We had to cannibalise two for parts and one has never worked, and with the roads in the condition they're in, not to mention the age of the trucks, it won't be long before we start getting more break-downs," she sighed.

"So, my ten trucks are going to help with that" Gus said, following Kat's gaze to the map. "But across the Inlet it's going to be a very different set of problems. Lots of hills and river valleys, all snow bound. I don't see many bridges."

"There aren't any," Jack confirmed. Kat quickly filled both of them in on what she had learned from the Colonel about the settlement's desire for minimal government. "Unless a local farmstead owner built a bridge himself, or it's left over from before the war, then there simply isn't one." She had Safi overlay a pre volcanic eruption map onto the present situation. There had been a dozen major bridges in that area, most, if not all now looked to be no longer there.

"So, what you need are boats or bridges?" Gus mused. Then his smile widened. "Let me tell you what I have for you," he said, sounding like a salesman preparing to sell sand to a Saharan sheik. "My father has just brought a company that's making boats and bridges out of a magnesium-aluminium-nickel alloy. It's not new technology; in fact, it's a lot like the base metal that your *Warrior* class ships are made from. The components are preformed, and depending on the erection sequence and orientation, can form into a number of different boat formats or an over-bridge, all ready to load up or drive over. The metal composition certainly isn't new, but the superconducting electro-magnetic shoot-bolts that keep it all together are, it's very clever stuff. And, what's more, it's at a price you just won't beat, as for you, I'll let you have six units for free."

"How much do they weigh?" Jack cut in, no smile at von Welf's second-hand car salesman routine. "These roads are either part-cleared frozen slush or hidden beneath a metre plus of compacted snow. Just how do we get the components off the truck and launched into the water or over the gap? Do they walk themselves into position too?"

"No," Gus conceded. "They're heavy. We usually use a crane. The metal is strong and comparatively light, but it's not that light."

Kat did her best to suppress a grin at the testosterone powered battle beside her. "Do any of these trucks you're so kindly donating have a crane fitted to them?" she asked.

"There might be on one or two of them," he said, then changed the subject. "I'm hungry. Will you have lunch with me?"

Now Kat did laugh. "For six mobile bridges, cum boats, yes, I think I can afford to sign your meal chit in the Mess Hall. But I'll warn you now; it's not going to be anything special. Almost all our Mess Hall staff are out on today's relief convoys."

"I was thinking of somewhere a bit more intimate and upmarket," Gus countered. "Apparently there's a restaurant in town that serves the most fantastic steaks."

Jack looked like someone was stealing his toys. "I can't believe it's still in business."

"My sources assure me that it is."

Kat also had her doubts that it was, and she had another dozen or so good reasons to say no, from *'My boss won't let me go outside the base perimeter,'* to *'Should we really be eating steak when everyone else here is starving?'* "Sounds great," was what she actually said. "Do you want to come, Jack?"

"Someone had better hold the fort," he said. Kat had never seen the little leprechaun in such full defeat.

Checking her pistol, Kat let Gus lead her towards the gate. Just inside the compound stood a top-spec civilian all-terrain vehicle, with two men who were almost certainly ex-military, standing by it. "Father won't let me go anywhere without these two. Where's your bodyguard?"

"The Fleet doesn't authorise them to Ensigns, no matter how much of a pain you are, or who your father might be." Kat answered. "Back home, my chauffeur was ex-military, but I always thought of him as a friend rather than anything else. I mean, it's hard to think of the guy who cheers for you at your weekly hockey match to be anything other than a friend."

"You got to play hockey! That must have been amazing."

"Didn't you play anything?"

"No, my father didn't think it was suitable, all those other children out there in an uncontrolled mob. Too risky, he always insisted."

Kat thought she'd had an overprotected childhood, especially after Louis's abduction, never even considering the possibility that her big brother Edward had actually been a barrier against excessive parental concern; she usually thought of him as a pain. "I was the middle child," she said, without letting the thought of the younger one make her flinch.

"I have a little sister, but we're not close. We attended different schools, so I only saw her for a few weeks at home during the holidays." Gus said. Before Kat could comment any further, they reached their destination.

The restaurant was on a side street well away from Kat's normal soup kitchen routes. No sign announced its presence, though Kat spotted a group of armed men loitering across the street from it, with a second group on the roof. If she needed armed guards around her soup kitchens, she could well imagine the protection a really decent place to eat would need.

The door opened before Gus's bodyguard reached it. A portly man in black-tie stood in the foyer, menus in hand. He quickly led Kat and Gus to a quiet corner and a table covered with crystal, silver and linen. Kat had to make a conscious effort to locate where the bodyguards discreetly went to ground, taking over separate tables on opposite sides of the room. Their grey suits somehow merging into the restaurants décor of wood panels, subdued lighting and thick carpeting. There were three other tables occupied with dining couples, but a thoughtful layout made it impossible to make out their faces.

So the Colonel was right; not everyone was starving in Anchorage. Where there was money, there was still fancy food to be eaten. More education for a new Ensign, a Prime

Minister's daughter, and one of the recipients of George Lennox's millions.

The menu promised several delicious cuts of steak, and even included seafood. Ominously, it listed no prices.

"I don't know what to order," Kat said after a quick glance down the menu.

"Let me order for you," Gus answered.

Kat did not appreciate men who assumed that reading complicated menus was beyond a woman's shallow grasp. "I know what the menu says, Gus, but the Colonel had us turn in our credit cards," she didn't quite lie. "I'm just not sure I can cover the bill."

"I was told that local credit cards were showing up on the black-market. Your Colonel is a wise man." Gus agreed. "This is my treat today." Since their individual fortunes were probably both within a few million of each other, Kat decided it would be nice to be pampered by someone of her own age for a change. After the decisions she'd made yesterday, why not let him puzzle over the choice of salads?

"So," Kat said, starting the dinner conversation, "your father took you into the family business immediately after university?"

"Hardly. My father isn't one to waste time on purely academic study, hands-on experience is also required. I started in this business when I was thirteen. If you can believe it, he had me spend my summer holidays working in the mail room! I have advanced slightly since those days," he said with a grin.

"No university?"

"No, well actually, my father brought in top professors from Nu Paris, Rhinestadt or wherever, to do it 'on the job.' My high school graduation project was setting up a pharmaceutical manufacturing plant, shadowing one of my father's best people, learning all he knew, then writing it up for my father and Professor Jelique. I think that was his name. Jelique gave me an A. Father went through the paper point by point, showing me why it deserved no better than a B. I never saw that professor again."

The wine waiter arrived with a cabinet-sauvignon whose label Kat knew would have been expensive in Nu New England or San Angeles. Gus expertly went through the ritual of sampling the vintage. "Very good," he nodded after the obligatory sip. "You'll enjoy this," he assured her.

Kat waited while her glass was half-filled, then preformed the mandatory sampling, praised it extravagantly, then set it down next to her carbonated water and promised herself not to touch it again. After last night, she wasn't going down that road twice.

"It doesn't sound like there've been a lot of permanent fixtures in your life?" Kat said, deliberately trying to move the focus away from the wine.

Gus thought on that one. "No," he finally grinned. "Haven't you heard, the only permanent thing in life is change?"

"I did read it somewhere," Kat agreed with a wry smirk. "I could usually count on a few things though. Monty was always there to take me to hockey practice or a match, and to cheer me on. And his wife always had something good as a treat in the kitchen when we returned. There was always extended family too, aunts, uncles, cousins."

"My uncle Christian died in a power-boat accident when I was about seven. Aunt Stephanie had one of her numerous love affairs go sour in a rather major way. If she hadn't insisted in gallivanting off to the most remote places, she might still be alive. By the way, the vehicle outside is equipped with a full emergency medical station. The driver isn't certified for brain surgery, but I know he'd love to try."

Kat put her elbows on the table, rested her chin on her hands, and batted her eyelashes dramatically. "Listening to you makes my childhood sound rather, well, delightful on reflection."

"Oh come now, it couldn't have been all that great. Nobody has a good childhood. All the professional authorities and child-psychologists tell you how bad it is."

And so the lunch went on, each of them cheerfully trying to better the worst element the other claimed about their upbringing. It was a game that Kat had never played before; it was hard to get a fair hearing when even those closest to you were envious. At university, Kat had quickly learned that even those she let down her guard around could not believe a Severn ever had any reason to complain.

The meal went surprisingly quickly, and when Kat

excused herself to the little girls' room, she was startled to find two hours had passed. Washing her hands, she stared at herself in the mirror. No, her nose hadn't gotten any smaller, and what the local climate was doing to her skin would have Mother running for the nearest spa for a facial. Her hair was cut shoulder length, just long enough to be put-up in the regulation manner the Fleet prescribed. *Gus is undeniably excellent company, so could this develop into something more? Do I even want it to?* He was one of the few men who wouldn't be after her money if Aunty Dee's financial searches could be trusted. Of course, Aunty Dee was sure Gus, or at least his father, wanted her dead for some unknown reason.

She dried her hands and threw the used hand-towel into the basket provided. Eying up the sprays, lotions, perfumes and other personal necessities offered for use beside the sinks, she briefly considered attempting a makeover to appear more glamorous, but quickly realised she had absolutely no idea where to start, so returned to the table. Gus was talking into his comm-link. "Unload them as quickly as you can," he said, then stood up to greet Kat. "If you can take time for a dessert, I think you will find some very nice gifts waiting for you when you return to your warehouses."

"What would you suggest?"

The waiter had already brought over a trolley festooned with chocolate, fruit and baked confections to make the soul water as much as the mouth. A sniff told Kat these were not artificial stand-ins but the real thing. The 'imp bit her,' as Monty's wife Beth would say. "Thank you, just leave the trolley here. Come back in an hour to pick up the crumbs," she laughed.

"You heard the lady," Gus said, waving the man away.

"No, no really, I wasn't serious," Kat said. "I'm really too full to be worth much back at work this afternoon. Do you have any sorbet?"

"Cranberry and raspberry, peach and mango or lemon and lime." The waiter said.

"Lemon and lime," Kat said.

"The same for me," said Gus, though he looked longingly at the cart as it was rolled away.

"Just because I'm passing, doesn't mean a growing boy

like you has to," Kat pointed out.

"Discipline, my father says: Discipline yourself, because nobody else can, or will." Gus quoted. "But I suspect you have already discovered that when rebelling against successful parents, one must always be selective. Not all of what they have given us should be ignored."

"Oh, yes," Kat answered sincerely, "But separating the good stuff from all the crap can be the challenge of a life-time."

"Is that why you joined the Navy, or Fleet, or whatever you call it?"

"Is that why you're in Anchorage?"

"I'm here to see for myself what needed doing."

"Yes, but why are you doing it in the first place? Your father can't be too happy that you're taking a detour on your way to that new construction project in Russia," Kat said, turning all the generalities they'd tossed about over lunch into a very specific *'What are you doing here?'* that would make Aunty Dee so proud.

"Yes, but the straight route across the Pacific would be pleasing my father just that bit too much. I have to get a little of what I want too. The route through the Panama Scar is a little bit shorter and much less hazardous, even with all the contamination, than going via Suez. So, I flew down from Nu New England, joined the ship off San Salvador de Americas and diverted her in here, then we'll go on to Magadan."

"But why do you want to do this?"

"Ah, now that would be revealing a bit too much for a first date, don't you think?"

Maybe, but then again, it would be nice to know what was really going on behind that perfect smile, those hooded eyes. *He's undeniably the most charming company. Too charming?* But before Kat could come up with further probes, her comm-link went off. "Ensign Severn," she snapped.

Her stomach went into free fall, and the fine steak she had just eaten started demanding re-visitation rights to her mouth. "Any casualties?"

"Don't know yet," Jack shot back.

How very typical of Jack. "I'll be right there," Kat said standing and almost knocking over the waiter bringing their sorbet. Gus rose just as quickly and went through the formalities of covering the bill. His bodyguards assured the way to the vehicle was clear, as Gus signed off on a bill that made even Kat gulp. Outside, it was only lightly snowing, yet there was no one else on the street, on the roof, or at any window. The locals had learned long ago to hide when things went boom in the middle of the day.

ONE : FOURTEEN

In a brief fifteen minutes Kat was back at the warehouse complex. A gaping hole showed in the south side of her office-block cum watchtower. Smoke billowed from her office.

"I'm going to have to leave you here," Gus said. "There is only so much stretch in my father's instructions before Heinrich and Gerhard get me into a straight-jacket," he said with a grin, nodding towards his bodyguards. "Look out for the trucks and the bridge-boat units, they're still being unloaded. I really wanted to be here when they arrived."

"Wanted to see what I looked like when I'm excited, maybe steal a kiss?"

"The thought had occurred to me."

He's flirting at last, Kat briefly thought, *it's only taken him two hours!* She gave him a peck on the cheek. "I've got to go. See you next time I see you."

He laughed, maybe a bit startled by her kiss. "Yes, I definitely will see you again." And then he was gone.

Kat didn't look back; it was time to switch back into 'Fleet' mode again. *Where were the casualties? Where were the attackers? How safe is this place?* She tapped her comm-unit. "Jack, I'm back at the warehouse complex, any update on the casualties?"

"We've collected all three of the wounded inside Warehouse Two." That was where Kat's office was. "All other personnel are present or accounted for. We were lucky. No one was killed." Jack reported.

That was good to hear. Kat double timed it over to Warehouse Two. Ellen Tutt was wrapping a bandage around one civilian's arm. Leading Crewman Leonard, Kat's accountant, was lying down, his uniform torn and bloody. A medic had already arrived from the main base and was checking him over.

"Ouch," Leonard said as a bloody section of shirt got lifted up.

"Can't be too bad if you can still complain," the medic chided.

"Bad enough. Damn it, why didn't my dad ever have a day like this at his office?"

"Probably because your dad never pissed-off the bad guys like we did yesterday?" Kat shrugged.

"I doubt it, my dad always runs with the bad guys, respectable ones, not like the ones we took on yesterday, but just as nasty. Good to see you back, ma'am."

"Sorry I wasn't here for all the fun." Kat said, kicking herself for taking a two hour lunch.

"No, ma'am, it's good that you weren't. You think I look bad, that rocket took your desk apart. Now you'll have to spend *all* your time walking around the yard."

"Guess I will," Kat agreed. "Is he going to be okay?" Kat asked the medic.

"He will be, on the assumption that I don't slit his throat to shut him up," the medic grinned.

"I could entertain you with a few of my accountant jokes?" Leonard suggested.

"Where's that scalpel when I need it?"

Everything was evidently as much under control as it was likely to get given the circumstances, so Kat headed for her office. Ellen joined her. "I didn't know your people had rockets?" Kat said.

"Our government had a small arsenal: they were not considered appropriate personal property. I think they were intended for use against pirate shipping, should it have ever entered the docks."

"So why are they not still in the arsenal?"

"It burned down about three months after the snow started."

"Let me guess. There was no big explosion."

The older woman nodded. "The fire was surprisingly low energy for what the building was supposed to be holding."

"Has anyone used rockets since then?"

"No."

"So there's potentially more where this came from."

"I would imagine so, but you must take note of what has actually been done here. Only two rockets have been fired, both at these offices. One targeted your office, the other the observation-post on the roof. None were aimed at the warehouses where the food is stored, or at the yards where the people work."

"Selective shooting, and very accurate," Kat concluded.

"I believe so."

At her former office Jack was overseeing the hose-team putting out the small fire that had finished what the rocket had started. As Leonard said, nothing remained of her desk, and she now had a new window to look out of. If Kat had been here, nothing would be left of her either. *Well, Aunty Dee, Gus von Welf was the main reason I wasn't here. Does that prove anything to you?*

It did to Kat.

"Any problems at the main base?" she asked Jack.

"Not a thing. Commander Deane is still sleeping off his 'liquid lunch.'"

Kat surveyed the fire-crew, all locals. Oz detached himself from the hose team.

"Most of us did part-time service with the local fire department." Her foreman explained. "We know the drills."

"Do you have any idea who might have done this?"

"Got the same guesses as you, ma'am."

"Thank you for stepping in, Oz." Kat turned to Ellen. "If any of your people feel the warehouse has become too dangerous I'll see if I can find them work elsewhere."

Ellen turned back to the foreman. "Oz, any of your people want to take her up on that?"

"I'll ask around, but if they wanted to go, they'd have already gone. Most of us approve of what you did yesterday." He gestured at the fire gutted room. "But obviously not everyone!"

"They could have killed me," Kat pointed out.

"I know that, ma'am. And if I find out who was behind this, you'll be the first to know. But right now, I really don't know anything, so unfortunately I can't tell you anything."

"Fair enough," Kat said. "A number of new trucks are being unloaded at the docks, along with some other heavy equipment. The trucks need to be moved back here. You know any local drivers we can trust?"

"I'll send my boy into town and get a couple," Oz replied.

So Kat went about the rest of her day as if it were normal to have her work space blasted to rubble during her lunch break.

True to his promise, von Welf's ship did unload ten large all-terrain trucks, one fitted with a crane, and six sets of components that promised to assemble into various water-defeating forms. Kat gave Gus a thank you call. He seemed enchanted by her delight, but made no offer to come over and share it up close and personal. His ship had just received a schedule change, his father was cutting short Gus's trip. Apparently there was now some kind of financial irregularity that was going to delay their new construction project. *Am I being too subtle with him*, Kat thought, *should I just come straight to the point. And what point was that exactly?*

Later that afternoon, Colonel Hepburn gave a low whistle as he dismounted from the lead military vehicle; just moments after the returning convoy drove through the warehouse complex gates. "Ensign, you do insist on having all the fun, don't you."

"Sorry about the mess, sir."

"Casualties?"

"Three injured. Only one was Fleet, my accountant, Leading Crewman Leonard. My office is wrecked. The sandbags minimised the damage to the observation-post, and a local construction engineer has already confirmed there is no significant structural damage to the building, but the searchlight is scrap."

"So, are you going to put a guard up there tonight?"

"Yes, Colonel. I'll take the duty with a couple of Land Force troopers."

"The troopers will take the duty. You will not."

"Sir."

"Don't you 'sir' me, young lady. You might have forgotten, but I haven't. You are one of those Severns, and I have no intention of getting hauled in front of the High Command to explain how I got the Prime Minister's only daughter killed."

"But, you won't have got me killed, sir."

"*If* such a thing happened, it would have happened on my watch, and in case you hadn't noticed, in the Armed Forces, if it happens on your watch, you are ultimately responsible for it. I know that, believe me, I know that, Ensign. Now, how did your time go with what's his name, von Wealth?"

"Mr von Welf has been kind enough to provide us with ten trucks and six convertible boats or bridges. He also took me off base for a two-hour lunch, which explains why I wasn't at my desk when it got blown into very small pieces."

"You and him hit it off then?"

"Better than I did with the locals, it would seem, Colonel."

"Ensign, you will soon discover that it is a rare day when everyone is happy. If you have one of those days, savour it, as they are not a common occurrence."

Kat chuckled. "If I get one sir, I'll take your advice."

Colonel Hepburn stayed with her as she checked in the other two convoys. He also checked out the new trucks as they began to arrive from the docks. Local mechanics gave them the once-over and pronounced them fit for use. Kat doubled the night shift so that all available vehicles would be loaded for a 'straight after breakfast' departure. The Colonel frowned as he took in the new vehicles. "I hate to admit it, but I'm embarrassed by my riches. Until the 24th Battalion get here, I've probably got more trucks than I have qualified drivers to get them rolling."

"The 24th are due tomorrow, aren't they? I've already got a dozen local buses under hire," Kat said.

"I got a signal just before we left this morning that the contracted civilian aircraft bringing them here blew two engines in Nu New England. I'm not too sure if it's being repaired; replacement civilian aircraft are being hired, or military transports are being tasked, but the 24th won't be arriving for at least another couple of days."

"So we'll have food and transport, but no one to move it out to where it's needed." Kat didn't like the taste of that in her mouth. There were an awful lot of hungry kids out there.

"Ensign, that NGO you're funding?"

"I didn't say I was funding it, sir."

"No, you conveniently managed to overlook that rather significant piece of information when you briefed your superior officer. Didn't you think I could do a computer search too?"

"No, sir, I mean yes, sir. I mean . . . you know what I mean, sir."

"I probably do. I was a moderately rebellious Lieutenant once-upon-a-time too. Fortunately, I dodged the insubordination charges as well as I expect you will. Now, could you hustle me up ten civilians who will be able to (a) keep any NGO gunmen riding shotgun in line and (b) follow any orders given by the likes of Commander Deane and Lieutenant Harper?"

"Ellen and Oz are pretty level headed. I've met a priest, a teacher and a couple of former salesmen who I think have the respect of the locals and could also get along with capable Fleet personnel."

"I didn't say anything about capable, I said Deane and Harper."

"Maybe Ellen and Oz should be assigned to them."

"Then you'll have the base to yourself tomorrow, as I'm going to get just about everyone in uniform out on the convoys."

A quick conversation with Ellen got Kat a list of local people who could keep control of a team of civilian riflemen, as well as get along with a Fleet co-ordinator. Oz was out: he refused to carry a gun and Kat wasn't willing to put him out there without a weapon. Instead, he volunteered to work the warehouses all night to get all the trucks loaded.

A good day's work done, Kat now needed to go back to the main base. As no vehicles were available, she would have to walk, despite the Colonel's orders. As Kat headed for the gate, Ellen and her two gun-toting daughters fell in beside her.

"I can take care of myself," Kat told the older woman and patted the pistol at her hip.

"I know you can, I'm just enjoying an evening stroll."

"Ellen, it's hardly stopped snowing all day."

"I know. Maybe I'm getting used to it." After several more sallies by Kat, just as cheerfully and absurdly parried by Ellen, the women left Kat at the gates to the main base. Kat was just in time for the evening meal, which was all under control and tasting amazing, despite Cowell having had a second day out on the relief convoys. The Colonel came in for a cup of coffee just as she settled at a table. He joined her.

"Your accommodation has been moved, Ensign."

"Sir, don't you think that's taking things a bit far?"

"Blame your friend Byrne. He received a directive that the 24th Battalion want to accommodate all their Enlisted Ranks into the same block. Probably so their Senior NCOs can keep the troopers out of mischief. He therefore needed to re-organise a few things in the officers' accommodation too, and so had Amelia find you new quarters."

"I thought the 24th's arrival was delayed."

"It is, but like you, Ensign Byrne didn't get the word." *Or is he in collusion with a certain sly colonel.* "He made sure the cleaning staff knew you were moving room, but just not where to. So, a new room, and yes, all those around it are empty too, before you ask. Well, at least they're empty until the 24th arrive."

Kat couldn't argue as long as no one else would be on the receiving end of any more rockets intended for her.

Jack was in the foyer, waiting for her when she returned to the officers' accommodation block. "You've been upgraded, ma'am." He said with a grin and a bow.

"The Colonel told me what you did. Thanks."

"I didn't do anything." Jack lied. "Here's your new key-card. You've moved up a floor, that's Fleet Lieutenant's or Land Force Captain's accommodation. The only downside, Harper is on the same floor, but she's at the other end of the building."

So, despite herself, Kat had a good night's sleep.

Kat felt like an 'unregistered voter' on election-day as she gulped down her breakfast at zero five hundred the next morning, she wanted to participate, but couldn't.

Cold, pre-packed meals were handed out to all for lunch, including those not going out, which Kat discovered was less than ten, even including Leonard and the three still in the med-centre from Kat's first drive out in the country. The Colonel had also striped out the Headquarters building for the day.

Kat caught the troop transport to the warehouse

complex to resolve any last minute glitches, of which there were very few, and to wave good-bye to just about everyone she knew in Anchorage, if not all Alaska. Master Crewman Cowell was commanding her own convoy today. Jack, with local chefs would be responsible for the delivery of the evening meal when the convoys returned.

With the yard empty, Kat checked in with Oz. Her foreman assured her that he and his civilians would get the containers and drop-pods scheduled to arrive today unloaded and their contents moved into the designated warehouses, then get the next shipments made-up in readiness for tomorrow's convoys.

Together they looked out into the worst snow storm she'd seen since arriving in Anchorage and Kat told him to keep his crew safe. "That's what I've got the fire support for." Against his principles to carry a weapon it might be, but he wasn't averse to having armed men and women patrolling the warehouse complex's perimeter, despite the appalling weather.

As she headed back to the main base at little under an hour later, Kat noted that she had a tail. Ellen's daughters were with her again. They didn't follow her through the gate, which had just a single uniformed Fleet guard today, but joined the half-dozen gun carrying civilians walking the main base perimeter.

Kat checked in briefly at the med centre; the MO, with a single medic had the wounded well in hand. As she wandered the halls of the deserted Headquarters, Kat heard the echoes of her footsteps; the place was totally closed down. At the end of the first floor hall, radio static drew her attention. Even the Operations team had even been drafted into the food convoys, but their equipment still monitored the radio nets. One radio was on the military command frequency, enabling Kat to listen in on any of the convoys. That only made her feel even more left behind. She had Safi turn that one down and put a key-word watch on it for anything like *Mayday, fire, attacked* and *ambush*.

The other radio was monitoring the civilian network. Kat sent it on another scan. It went through the frequencies, hit on a line of static, and hung there. She hit the 'scan' function again, and this time it did a longer search before stopping on another band of static. Kat settled into the duty chair, put her feet up, and tapped the Scan button at regular intervals as the search function stopped on static yet again. It took a couple of minutes before she realised it was sticking on about the same frequency every time. She sat up, hit 'scan,' and watched as the search went up the band, hit the top, then began again from the bottom, before settling, once again on the same spot.

She did it again and got the same results.

"Would you like me to isolate the signal from all the background noise?" Safi asked.

"There's a signal in all that static?"

"Yes."

"Do it."

The speakers went silent, then gave out a loud burst of static. "Sorry," Safi said as it cut off. The static came back, low this time. Kat thought she heard words among the crackling: 'cold,' 'starvation.' Then again, cold and starvation were the expected norm around here. Finally Safi hit on the right algorithm, and the message came in. Weak, but clear.

"You've got to help us. We haven't asked for help before, but we need it now. Can anyone hear us?"

Kat grabbed the handset. "This is Ensign Severn. You are coming through weak but clear," she shouted. "Say again last message, over." She keyed off and waited. The static was there. Only the static. "Safi," Kat demanded.

"No signal."

She leaned back in her chair and counted slowly to ten. At ten, she changed her mind and counted to one hundred. If she tried to call them, she could miss their incoming signal. As Kat started to despair of ever hearing from them again, the radio came to life. "Batteries are low, about to die, but I'm going to keep repeating for as long as I can. This is the former Pacific Rim Energy Corporation's strip mining facility on the Chuitna River. We've got an out-break of what appears to be typhus. Two deaths so far. A dozen or more are now showing symptoms. We burned the bodies. We're sick, we're hungry. There has been a large avalanche and we are now cut off by road. We have no aircraft on the strip that can fly in these conditions."

"Safi, enlighten me about typhus."

"Epidemic typhus fever is a disease that occurs among

people living in overcrowded and unhygienic conditions, being spread by lice infected with the bacteria *Rickettsia prowazekii*. The lice excrete infectious faeces as they feed on human blood. People become infected when the faeces are rubbed into small cuts on the skin. It is the faeces, not the lice bites that spread the disease. Common symptoms include fever, headache, chills, tiredness and muscle aches. About half of people who become infected develop a red rash that begins on their back, chest and stomach and then spreads to the rest of the body except for the face, palms and soles. Other symptoms may include vomiting and sensitivity to light. In severe cases, complications may include kidney failure and brain inflammation. Symptoms usually appear between seven to fourteen days after exposure. It is currently treated with antibiotics. If untreated it will kill between thirty and seventy percent of those infected. The main . . ."

"Enough. Does our warehouse have an appropriate antibiotic to treat it?"

"Yes, approximately a thousand units."

Kat squeezed her eyes closed. A thousand units would be a drop in the ocean if this spread from the mine workers to the population of Anchorage. "Safi, show me where this mine is." If it was cut off by avalanche it meant it must be up in the hills on the western side of the Inlet.

"Overlay this map with the latest satellite imagery available."

The Chuitna was a forty kilometre long river that had its headwaters in the Alaskan mountain range and flowed through a broad expanse of forest and wetlands before draining into the western side of the upper Cook Inlet between the abandoned villages of Tyonek and Beluga, about seventy kilometres west of Anchorage. Supporting data informed Kat that the river was home to all five species of Pacific salmon and several species of trout, and the area was normally abundant with wildlife, including moose, wolves, and bears. The river was vital to the extraction of coal being strip mined along its eastern bank, some ten kilometres inland. Although some roads were marked, the majority of the two hundred and twenty-five kilometre road journey to Anchorage was along tracks and un-surfaced roads.

"This imagery is seven days old. We have had

continuous cloud cover since then," Safi told her. Continuous cloud-cover meant continuous snow-fall. If it was bad last week, it was worse now.

Kat was on her feet. At the door she remembered that she should call this in, advise the Colonel. But he was up north, and the problem was to the west. She pulled two pieces of paper from a stack next to the radios, scrawled a quick note detailing where she was going and why, left one in the Ops room and the other on the Colonel's desk, then raced downstairs to the med-centre. "We have an outbreak of typhus about seventy kilometres away, across the Inlet. Their location is now cut off by road due to an avalanche," she announced.

Commander Goodhew, the Medical Officer had his feet up on the desk, reviewing a medical journal on his data-pad. "Oh, crap," he said, feet slamming to the floor. "We could quarantine the area; the infection should die off once there is no live food source for the lice."

"There are over a two hundred people at that mine. You can't just seal them off and leave them to die."

"Better than bringing them back here and having it spread through the population in Anchorage."

"But we have the appropriate antibiotic to help them. We could treat them, feed them, and then quarantine them near here until they're given the all clear."

Goodhew thought about her proposition. "Okay, but I only have one medic."

"So, who's coming with me?" Kat asked.

"Maddox may still have internal bleeding," the medic said. "I guess that means I go and the Doc stays here." She started filling a pack. It was Leading Medic Tremblay, who had been out with Kat on the first convoy two days ago.

"If they've got typhus, Sarah, there could be all kinds of other opportunistic diseases," the MO sighed and started adding to the medic's equipment packs.

"Meet me at the docks in an hour. I'm going to pick up the antibiotics at the warehouse." Kat said and started moving for the exit. "There are around two hundred people listed for the mine. We'll take two hundred and fifty initial doses. Safi, signal Oz to get someone at the warehouse to locate them and have them ready for when I get there."

"I have located them in Warehouse Three. The foreman is having someone get them."

"Jack," Kat called him on her comm-link. "What are you up to?"

"My neck in truck parts," he answered.

"Meet me at the docks. We have a problem."

Kat picked up her armed escort as she double-timed it out of the gate. She ignored them as they trotted along about fifteen metres behind her. Oz met her in one of the oversized vans at the warehouse gates. He showed her the two pallets of emergency rations and five small boxes secured in its rear compartment. "That's two hundred and fifty initial dose units, but unless I'm reading it wrong, it expired three weeks ago."

Kat climbed into the van's cab. "To the docks if you please, Oz" she ordered, as he got back behind the wheel. She tapped her comm-link. "Commander Goodhew, our typhus antibiotics expired three weeks ago. Can we still use it?"

"Damn!" was followed by a pause. "It might do. Maybe use a slightly larger dose than normal. I can't believe I'm saying this."

"I'm taking two hundred and fifty doses for two hundred people. You might want to start processing some more."

"I can't. We don't have anything like the facilities needed to manufacture antibiotics; it'll have to be flown in."

"Understood."

The truck equipped with the crane, along with two of the bridge/boat rigs had gone, taken by the Colonel's north-bound convoy. Kat headed for the container nearest the water's edge, broke off the seal and opened the doors. She found a small keypad and tapped it awake. Component by component assembly instructions appeared, depending on the type of construct required. After reading through several screens, Kat punched '4' on the controls. As promised, the instructions for a river-going, flat bottomed dory appeared. Ten meters long and two wide, a high prow and a control pillar to the rear, not unlike the small landing-craft used in the conflicts of the mid twentieth century, except the bow was pointed and didn't drop down. Kat studied the instructions. Oz interrupted a dozen men stacking sandbags along the harbour wall against the rising water of the inlet, and between them, forty minutes later, they had a boat. Kat studied what they'd assembled and decided it looked good.

"Who's going?" Oz asked.

"Me, Ensign Byrne, Leading Medic Tremblay, both of whom should be here any minute, and I need some men, people who know these waters."

"Ellen said you weren't supposed to leave town."

"I'm not supposed to make a truck run. This is different."

"If you say so, young lady. Keep this up and you're going to get yourself killed."

"A lot of people have tried so far. I'm still here."

"Oh, so you know you're pushing your luck?"

"Oz, please just load the boat."

"I'll just load the boat," he conceded. "Matt, get your butt into town. Go to the *Willy Dall* and tell Esteban we need Hugo. This lady's going out on the inlet, so she's gonna need the best river runner in town."

"I'm on it," said a young lad of maybe fifteen, as he took off, running towards the town.

"You can have Eric, that big bear of a man over there. You might need climbers if there's been an avalanche, and you'll need local knowledge. Tuluga, Amaru, I need you over here." Two men, who looked to be of Inuit origin, started jogging towards them.

Tremblay arrived, shortly followed by Jack. He looked around, as if expecting to see fire or smoke competing with the falling snow. "What's happening?" he asked Kat. She explained. For emphasis Tremblay started giving antibiotic shots to everyone identified for the trip. "Kat, you're supposed to stay here," was Jack's reaction when she finished explaining the situation.

"Already had that conversation," said Oz as he filled the vessel's deck-mounted collapsible fuel reservoir. Eric, Tuluga and Amaru were busy transferring the emergency rations from the van into the boat, followed by the medical supplies. "I'll let Hugo review the load distribution before we secure it. Some weight might help the stability, but too much . . . well, I don't need to tell you that the inlet is a killer these days. Have you ever been out on the open water in a small boat?"

"My parents own a sailing boat. I've sailed it on the Peconic."

"This isn't going to be anything like that."

"I didn't think it would be."

Hugo arrived with Matt not far behind him. The brown skinned man of maybe thirty-five looked over the craft, hopped aboard, studied it a bit more, and then ordered, "Lash everything down real good once you've finished the loading. The inlet is going to be a bitch, and I don't need any more trouble than I've already got. Matt, get me some oars and poles." Again, Matt was off running.

The men finished loading the boat, and with cargo nets and rope began liberally lashing everything down. Hugo picked up two of the five small boxes of antibiotics. "Are these why we're doing this stupid thing?"

"Yes," Kat said. "You understand the potential problem we face if we don't try and treat these people?"

"They die, and if it spreads, we all could die. Do you think I'd be doing a thing this crazy for any other reason? I have been to the mine complex many times, and they are good people, but this is pure madness. Oz, get everyone a lifejacket. And get three back-packs. We'll have the Fleet people wear the medicine."

Kat didn't like being reduced to a pack animal. She opened her mouth, but Hugo cut her off before she got a word out. "Listen, lady, I am the captain of this boat. This is my world. Hugo knows everything there is to know about this inlet and its rivers. You want to get this stuff to those miners, you listen to me. You do what I tell you and you might just live."

He eyed the inlet in front of them with a scowl on his face. "The Cook Inlet is bad these days: clogged with snags and eddies that will spin you around, but that river is going to be a whole lot worse. Yet I think maybe, just maybe, Hugo can get you up there."

"Maybe!" Kat exclaimed.

"Hugo's 'maybe' is a lot better than the dead you'll most certainly be without me, girl."

"Do it his way, lady. Otherwise, I won't send these people out," Oz added.

"I wasn't arguing. You think it's best we wear the

antibiotics?" she asked Oz.

"If you go in the water, you'll float, and these guys will do their best to pull you out. Those boxes go in and they'll sink. I guess we could try and do something about that, but I think Hugo just did."

"Looks that way," Kat had to agree.

Ten minutes later, cargo secured, they pulled away from the dockside. "I should be back before the Colonel is, but if I'm not, tell him where I am," Kat hollered at Oz.

"Why not use that clever thing on your wrist and tell him yourself?"

"He's got a lot on today. Why worry him?" she said and then started bailing. In the time since they had assembled the craft, a good three centimetres of snow had fallen, turning to slush in the bottom of the boat; anyone not busy elsewhere bailed.

"You know the 'little people's luck' that keeps me safe?" Jack asked from where he bailed across from Kat. "Well, I just saw them waving me goodbye from the harbour wall. Even they don't have enough 'luck' for this."

"Jack, we have *got* to get up that river," Kat said, gesturing with her thumb at the pack on her back.

"No, *someone* has got to get it up-river Kat; nobody's died and left the job specifically to you. Me, I'm starting to wonder how much of the Severn stuff in the history files is there because somebody didn't know how to let someone else do their job." Kat didn't have an answer for Jack, so said nothing.

Hugo quickly brought the boat up to its full speed of about twelve knots. It handled the waves of the inlet reasonably well, breasting each one with a cloud of spray that ended, for the most part, back in the water. Things were fine right up until they hit a snag with a thud, then a bump, followed by a sudden loss of power, despite the still racing engine.

"Damn sinker," Hugo growled as he brought the boat around and idled the engine.

Off to their right, just a few centimetres below the wave trough, a log, maybe thirty centimetres in diameter and spiked with shorn-off branches, spun from their impact. Hugo pulled something the size of a large cigar from his jacket pocket and twisted the end, waited until the log settled down to a stable rocking motion, then thumbed the button that sent the mini-flare hurtling into it. It stuck, a red flare igniting at its back end. The next moment, Hugo was on his radio.

"Esteban, I've got a 'sinker' out here near the harbour wall. It's marked. You'd better come and get it."

"Spotted your flare already," a man's voice came back. "We're under way. You in trouble?"

"Maybe. I think we dinged our prop. I may need a tow."

"Can do two as well as one."

Kat was not ready to go back. She dropped her bailing bucket and headed for the control pillar. "You think you can do better?" Hugo said, his face a mixture of macho defiance and rank embarrassment.

"Maybe I can," Kat said, punching the keypad adjacent to the wheel. The small screen came to life. "On the *Berserker*, I recently had to become the resident expert on the ship's configuration when we changed from surface to sub-surface after it didn't go quite as planned. There might be a way to compensate for the prop by routing the power into the two water jets."

"You think so?"

"I won't know until I've tried." The view screen was small, and the keypad just numeric; Kat found herself keying through a complex series of screen options, diving deeper and deeper into some kind of software program. It didn't help that the screens had been written by someone for whom English was a very foreign language.

"You're not going to be dumping us in the water are you?" Jack asked with a grin. Kat took the question for serious, particularly after the nods his comments got from Amaru and Eric.

"I'll try not to, but you might want to check your lifejackets. You never can tell what a Fleet officer might do once they get out onto deep water," she said, returning his grin.

"Very funny," Jack didn't laugh. Eric still gave his lifejacket a good pull, and Amaru eyed the waves around them dolefully. Kat found something that claimed to be propulsion options, located their vessel configuration, found water jets, then hit the enter button. The screen blinked twice, before going blank.

"Did that give us back any propulsion?" Hugo asked.

"Try it," Kat shrugged, not at all sure.

Hugo eased the throttle up; the boat took on way. "Feels right," he said. "Yup, feels okay. Think you can take the dent out of the bow too?" He pointed to where the metal was pushed in.

"Don't push your luck!" Kat replied. That got a laugh from Hugo and the rest of the crew. Hugo brought the boat up to just under its full speed, posted two lookouts with long poles forward and ordered the rest back to bailing.

"You have the latest imagery of the inlet?" Hugo asked Kat.

Kat unzipped her jacket a few centimetres to enable Safi to project a pre-volcanic eruption map, before enhancing it with the latest satellite imagery of Cook Inlet, showing all the recent snowfall.

"Okay, we're about here," said Hugo, pointing at the projection. "That's Fire Island off to our left. We need to move over to the north-western bank, but I want to avoid the mouth of the Susitna River, that is one very big and very dangerous mess. Once past that, we'll go close in until Ladd's Landing, then pick up the Chuitna."

Safi added their current location with a green 'plus' appearing on the display.

"Safi will monitor our position. Let me know if you need to view this again," Kat told him, before going back to help Jack, Tremblay and Eric with the bailing.

ONE : FIFTEEN

Kat didn't have to ask when they hit the Chuitna River. Even with Hugo putting the water-jets up to full power, their speed reduced considerably as they moved against the raging current. Bare tree trunks stood starkly out of the turbulent waters, marking where the river bank had once been. Even when the snows eventually melted, this area was going to need a long time to recover.

She stood, stretched her back, and turned to Hugo. "Shouldn't we stay nearer the centre of the river to avoid the submerged trees?"

"Not if you want to get there before next week. The current out there is a good six, maybe eight knots faster than the edges, and we need to stay away from that. Hitting a tree is far from good, but out there, that's just asking for trouble. Tuluga, Amaru, stay up front, keep your eyes open. We don't want to wrap this woman's boat around another tree or a rock."

The snow picked that moment to fall even harder, and visibility dropped to hardly a boat length. Hugo cut back on the throttle a little, and their headway fell to almost nothing.

Progress remained painfully slow as the lookouts on the bow poled them away from rocks, trees, even the bloated carcass of a moose. Kat glanced a few times at the main channel, but there was no going there. Maybe this had once been categorised as a 'low-flow' river course, but now the snow swollen water fought itself, rolling up, and then crashing down in a shower of white water. Water gone mad, with the power to smash trees to matchsticks and rocks into gravel. Dangerous as it was along the flooded banks, the main stream really was suicide.

Their slow progress up-river was punctuated with moments of sheer terror. Poling off a tree, a stray current suddenly grabbed them, sending them down-river sideways and slamming them into a rock they'd just passed so carefully. Even big Eric was unable to push them back off. They all applied poles, oars and hands onto the rock, only to unbalance the boat. Freezing water poured in over the dented gunwale.

"Fleet personnel to port. The other side, left," Hugo yelled as Jack went right. Kat and Tremblay fought their way hand over hand up the cargo nets and lashings to hang as far over the left side as they dared, raising the severely dented, but fortunately un-pierced right side off the rock. Tuluga and Amaru helped Eric push the boat off and Hugo let the current carry them downstream a hundred meters while he made sure all was well before putting any power back to the water-jets and renewing their fight with the wild river.

Kat glanced at her watch; they'd be doing well if they reached the mine before dark at this rate. She considered calling the Colonel but quickly dropped the idea. She was committed; he could hang her for mutiny or insubordination later. And, there was probably very little he could do to help them now anyway. Kat focused on riding the river.

The snow blanketed everything. Jack suggested they should look for pillowcases to match. Eric answered he was ready for bed, with or without blankets. Which then raised the question from Hugo as to who would share a bed with whom. Tired, wet, cold, they could still laugh. If she had to ride a river gone mad, this was the crew to do it with.

As the hours went by, Kat grew even more fatigued. Her muscles ached in places she didn't know she had. They couldn't just ride this boat but had to work every moment to keep from being bashed against the metal sides or slammed into the stack of rations, maybe shattering the glass vials of vaccine in their back-packs. Kat stayed on her feet, stooping over to bail, flexing her knees as the boat rose up to slap her or dropped out from underneath her. This was nothing like the day she and Jack had shared sailing the *Rubicon* on the Peconic. Would she ever want to be on a body of water bigger than a bath-tub ever again?

"That's the airstrip." Hugo pointed to his right. The tattered orange wind-sock was just visible, contrasting against the white of the snow. The hanger had a huge drift of snow against its doors. "The main complex is next, about two kilometres further up river. We should be there soon."

Just as Hugo finished speaking, they rounded a bend in the river, the snow was banked to several metres on each side. Out of nowhere another eddy from the main channel caught them. Hugo held onto the wheel with both hands, his legs wrapped around the wheel's post, fighting the swirling current. The boat whirled as it rose and fell; the worst bucking they had had all day. Jack lost his hold and was half overboard before Kat got a hand to his lifejacket's rear belt. The next pitch and drop would have thrown them both over the side if Tremblay hadn't reached them, her feet entwined in the cargo lashings. Finally, Eric managed to make his way across the cargo. He grabbed Jack and Kat with his huge hands and hauled them into the bottom of the boat like a pair of drowning kittens.

Kat lay on her belly for what seemed like several minutes, gasping for breath, letting the snow settle on her, the slush soak into her. She had gotten herself and Jack into a real mess this time. *It's almost over. Just a little bit more,* she told herself as she struggled to her feet, both hands and a leg wrapped around cargo lashings.

"Thanks, Kat," Jack said.

"Thanks to all of you," Kat added peering at each of her crew through the gathering darkness.

"No, we thank you," Hugo laughed. "Think of the stories we will tell when we get back." Eric seemed to like that. Amaru just shook his head. Tuluga never looked up from his place at the bow, looking for snags.

It was getting increasingly dark. Another glance at her watch told Kat that it was a lot earlier than it should have been for darkness to fall. Part of the gloom was undoubtedly the incessant snowfall. But they were also in the shadows of snow banks, several metres deep on either side of the river. "There are rapids three or four kilometres past the mine" Hugo called through his hands. "Keep your eyes open. We'll be in deep shit if we miss the mine complex and go too far."

Kat had Safi try a scan on the radio net but got only static. "Call anyone you can get a signal with."

Safi reported another negative search. "Their batteries may be dead," Kat told Hugo and the crew. "Silence means nothing," she assured them. Why didn't it reassure her?

Amaru and Tuluga on the bow brought out hand-held flash-lights. The snow seemed to slacken slightly; although in the growing gloom it could easily have been more of a wish than a reality. They were a good hundred metres off when Tuluga's beam reflected off the glass windows in the mine's three floored office building. Hugo reduced speed, and they approached it carefully. The middle and top floor had been gutted by fire; a few of the larger timbers still showed black against the snow. Where the water and ice sloshed against the sill of a middle floor's windows, two blackened skulls eyed them through empty sockets.

"Jesus Christ," Hugo crossed himself and steered away.

"They said they'd burned the dead," Kat said. "I guess that was where they did it."

"Over there are the equipment hangars. The accommodation blocks should be up there, on the higher ground," Hugo said, pointing to his left. Slowly the boat headed in that direction. The heavy snow returned; they almost rammed the first accommodation block before they even saw it. Flood water and ice had consumed most of the ground level, leaving just the upper floor and low roof sticking out. "There's another block just along from here. Start looking for the high fence that kept the critters out." Hugo ordered.

Kat decided it was time to call the Colonel. "Colonel Hepburn, this is Ensign Severn, over." Only static. Kat repeated herself with the same results. "Safi?"

"I cannot get line-of-sight on any communications satellite from this location," Safi advised.

"It's almost dark; I am not taking us out where the current might get us." Hugo said before Kat could say a word.

"I wasn't going to ask." Kat assured him.

"We're at the fence," Eric called from the bow.

Hugo steered left. The lights picked up more flooded, iced up or snow consumed buildings. The boat bumped against things hidden in the water; again, Hugo cut the power and they poled. Another brief break in the snowfall came, giving them a quick opportunity to have a look around in the twilight. They were in the middle of an open space, perhaps a hundred metres across, surrounded by equipment sheds, a gymnasium and dining hall, all flooded and iced up. No lights showed.

"They've got to be around here somewhere," Kat frowned.

Hugo frowned too. "There's a couple more accommodation blocks, for the supervisors and managers, a bit further back, higher up the ridge." He pointed to the left, and they poled in that direction. Once past the bulk of the dining facility, the current picked up again and poling got significantly harder. Hugo reached to restart the water-jets.

"Wait a second," Kat called. "You hear that?" Although the snow fall was silent, the sound of icy flood water sloshing against the side of the boat made it hard to hear anything else. But as the silence stretched, the crew held its collective breath, the dull roar became more insistent.

"The rapids," Hugo sighed. "They must be real bad to make that much noise. But we aren't going to get anywhere against this current by poling." He turned the power up slightly, but it had little impact on their overall speed.

"There's something up ahead. Looks like a light, maybe a fire." Eric shouted from his station at the bow. Hugo cut the engine again. Eric cupped his hands to his mouth and shouted in his booming baritone, "Is anyone there."

On the third shout he got an answer. "Who are you? We're armed, don't come any closer."

"It's Hugo," their captain shouted back, "with a boat full of medicine and food. Do you want me to stop or keep going?"

"We can probably find you a place to tie up for the night, if you've got a rope."

"I've got a rope if you've got a tree?"

"No tree, but if you've got food, I'll hold the damn rope all night." Six figures slowly materialised out of the falling snow. One held up a hand, and Eric tossed him a rope. The six pulled with a will, and the boat slid up to an icy halt.

"Dear God, are we glad to see you. Are there any more boats?"

"Only this one. Where is everyone?" Kat asked as she dropped over the side into snow up to her knees.

"About half left before it got too bad. The rest are sleeping cheek to jowl in the two blocks that aren't flooded. You heard our message?"

"We know about the typhus. I have a medic here to start antibiotic treatment." Kat pointed as Tremblay clambered out of the boat, her two stuffed kit bags emblazoned with the 'snake entwined sword' emblem of the medical branch. Kat held out her hand to the man who'd been doing the talking. "I'm Ensign Kat Severn of the ABCANZ Fleet, at your service."

The handshake and smile that greeted her was friendly enough. "Glad for anything you got," said a man lowering his hood to reveal his face and hairless head. His clothes hung on him, suggesting that there had probably been a lot more to him several months ago. "I'm Lance Eastman, I'm the Assistant Manager here. How many can you get out in that boat? We've got about twenty-five sick, and two newborn babies. We need to try and climb out over the flow of the avalanche and reach the road. From there we could walk the ten klicks down to Ladd's Landing. The flood waters are rising fast, they'll be up to these buildings by dawn. It would be nice to get the weakest out by boat, if it's at all possible."

The five miners with Lance began assisting Jack, Eric, Tuluga and Amaru in unlashing the rations aboard the boat and transferring them into the snow at the edge of the floodwaters.

"How many people do you have here?" Kat asked, climbing back into the quickly emptying hull.

"Less the five that died today, ninety one. Why?"

"Because this vessel is a bit different than your average boat and can be reconfigured for different applications." She activated the control screen, scrolling through the menu. "There's an option here for a river ferry. Suitable for moving a truck of up to ten tonnes. A hundred people ought to fit. Twelve metres long by four wide. Thirty centimetres of free clearance at full load. Hugo, you willing to take that out on the river?"

"Tomorrow. Not in the dark, but you should do the conversion now, just in case the flooding gets too high during the night."

"Good idea." Lance said, as began Kat punching in the numbers to access the deconstruction, and then the reassembly sequence required to turn their river dory into a ferry. In a spectacular display of arcing electric energy, the superconducting electro-magnetic shoot-bolts that held the construct together all failed simultaneously, causing the entire vessel to come apart. The rear components were immediately grabbed by the current and dragged away. Kat only just managed to run forward and stand on what had been one of the bow components a few seconds before.

"What the hell?" she gasped, along with other similar expletives from those around her. She looked around for a small piece of panel that still had the smoking remnants of the shoot-bolt attached. She picked it up and began looking for another.

"What are you doing?" Jack asked.

"Evidence," Kat replied, "I want to know what just happened."

"If we live that long," one of the miners added sourly.

Kat and Jack got two samples of the failed shoot-bolts into a back-pack. One was completely fried, but the other might tell the right people what had just happened. Kat looked back at where the boat had been; already more than two-thirds of the panels had been taken by the rising waters.

"Let's get the supplies inside," Lance suggested. "If we're going to drown before morning, we might as well do it on a full stomach."

"I never took you for such an optimist, Lance" Hugo said.

"Almost a year of constant snow, waterlogged mine, management and tech's leaving, then the typhus, that would make even you throw in the towel."

"Maybe. You heard the man, let's get the food up to these people. Hungry folk don't make rational decisions, and the water is still rising." The boat's crew loaded up, helped by more miners that had joined them out of the ever increasing darkness. The miners returned to an interrupted conversation.

"I say we build some rafts. We've still got two timber framed buildings we could use. Tear them down and use them to float downriver."

"The timbers aren't substantial enough, they wouldn't last an hour on the river. Besides, out there is no place for anything less than a full boat. What do you think, Hugo?"

"It's real bad out there. I wouldn't say you couldn't make it, but . . . who knows miracles happen."

"I'm not trusting my life to any miracle. I say we climb out over the avalanche's flow to the road."

"It's the only option we have left, and believe me I'd rather not."

"Where is the flow?" Amaru asked quietly.

"Right behind this building," Lance said.

Amaru aimed his flash-light beam. Through the falling snow Kat could just make out a huge, cliff-like jumble of snow, ice and boulders, with the occasional broken tree jutting from it. Snow continued to settle on it, concealing many hidden dangers.

"Bitch of a climb," came from Tuluga.

"We have some rope, do you have any more?" Amaru asked.

"Yes, we have rope."

They reached the two accommodation blocks. "Almost everyone is asleep upstairs." Lance explained. "Let's see if we can get some food warming before we wake anybody up."

Another twenty lay asleep on the ground floor. At the far end three miners lay on beds sheened with a fevered sweat, while two others tended them. Tremblay headed that way, while Kat followed Lance into a small kitchen area and began heating emergency rations. The smell of coffee brought people in. They quietly received what was offered, then withdrew.

Once things were moving along, Lance tapped Kat on the arm. "We need to talk."

She followed him to the kitchen table. Lance, a female miner he introduced as Linda, and a big man who introduced himself as Harris and then tried to crush Kat's hand, took three of the chairs, leaving a fourth for Kat.

"So what do we do?" Harris asked.

Kat paused, waiting for Lance or Linda to say something, but they were all looking at her. "My medic is starting the treatment for your typhus cases as best she can. In a few minutes she'll start treating all of you too, just in case. After that . . ." Kat left that hanging.

"After that, we die," Harris snapped.

"No," Linda insisted.

"Yes we do," Harris shot back. Around the small room others stood against the wall or settled onto the floor. Everyone awake in the block was watching the four at the table, waiting to see what their fate would be. "Get real," Harris said, turning to face the listeners, not those at the table. "The water's rising about five centimetres every hour. By dawn it's gonna be in here and up to your ankles. There ain't no cavalry coming to the rescue. The damn Fleet's already here, and you can see she's now in the same mess we are. That was a really cute trick making the boat fall apart, even for a damn Severn."

"As you said, I'm in the same boat, or lack of it, that you are," Kat put in. "But I'm not going to be dead by morning."

Harris snorted derisively. "Is a helicopter gonna come and fly you away, little lady. Didn't anyone tell you? With all the acid in the snow, the corporation sold off both our helicopters. Has your Fleet brought some back?"

"No," Kat said, unwilling to lie to any of the people watching her. She looked around at them, hoping to see in their eyes that they were counting on her, no matter how heavy the burden, to get them out of this mess. All she saw was blank hopelessness, as if they already saw themselves as dead. Kat gulped; these people weren't looking to her for hope, only her approval to allow them to die.

"So, here we are in the twenty-second century, and we have nothing but our own two hands to save us, and little lady, we've worked those down to the bone already, and we still ain't saved ourselves. If we're gonna die, why should I care who else gets this typhus thing."

That absurd statement didn't even elicit a shuffling of feet among the onlookers. Kat glanced at Lance, then Linda. They were looking at the table, eyes as dead as the drowned moose they had pushed off from the side of the boat on the way up here. How could anyone become so hopeless? Helpless?

"Why shouldn't we take this shit-hole down with us?" Harris continued. "They didn't do anything for us. You know about the share offer we had, and then the corporation selling the mine without any consultation? Does little Miss Severn know about that? Maybe it's your rich grandpa who's bought this operation for almost nothing."

"I know very little about my Grandpa George's businesses, and in case you hadn't noticed, I'm an Ensign in the ABCANZ Fleet and up the very same, very turbulent, shit creek as you right now, and I'm without any paddles either." *Come on people, laugh, smile, show some emotion.*

The people around Kat just stared at the floor.

"We did a deal a few years ago and took shares options in the corporation rather than have pay rises," Harris said. "But the CEO sold the mine without any minor shareholder consultation to some European Energy consortium for one cent per dollar. All our efforts have been for nothing."

So that was it. Kat swallowed hard; they'd worked hard all their lives and now they were losing it. They'd asked for nothing, and got nothing, and now all that guys like Harris had was their anger as the river rose and took everything else they'd worked for away. The typhus was just giving Harris something to focus his anger at. Kat slowly turned in her chair, studying the people standing along the walls, slumped onto the floor. They were beat, at the end of the line, and waiting for the end to come. *Okay, Ensign Severn how are you going to make them want to fight for what is left of their lives? This is some leadership challenge!*

"Do you want to die?" Kat asked a woman who made eye contact with her for the briefest of moments. The woman flinched and dropped her eyes back to the floor.

"Is that it?" Kat said to a man standing, back resting against the wall. "You just want to lie down in the snow or let the river take you?" He shrugged.

A baby, just a few months old, let out a cry. Her mother rocked her gently.

"Are you ready to drown that baby?" Kat asked, hard and unwavering.

"No," the mother answered, tears in her eyes.

"Well you had better get ready to, because that is what this man is talking about." Kat stood. "Okay, you've got it bad, probably a lot worse than anyone else in these parts right now." She turned slowly; staring hard at each face as she passed it, demanding they look at her, listen to her.

"When Pacific Rim Energy opened this mine, what thirty years ago, there were lots of banks ready to loan them the money for the start up costs. You people, and those before you, worked hard, made this mine profitable, enabling the corporation to pay back the loans, probably even paid it back sooner than the terms stipulated?" Apparently she was right, as she got a nod from Lance and a scowl from Harris.

"And now they've sold it off, because it's not making them money, and hasn't done so for the last year. That's business I'm afraid. I really do sympathise with your position, but I can't change it. But I'm sure that once this mess is over, the new owners will be there for you and this mine will become profitable again."

"You gonna buy the mine, Severn?" Harris spat.

"Harris has your hearing gone bad. Didn't I just say I'm Fleet?" She pointed at the single yellow rank bar on her upper right arm. "You know the Fleet doesn't purchase commercial businesses, never has. We're here to get as many of you out of this mess alive as we possibly can. But Harris, you aren't thinking straight. You want to get typhus? You want it to spread? You want everyone to catch it? Think this one through with me." Kat continued her slow turn.

Eyes were up now. She had their attention.

"If we don't treat you, and the typhus spreads, then anyone who is already sick and hungry is going to die. A lot of them will be people like me, who came here to help the likes of you. Is that the thanks we get?"

A few shook their heads. *Finally, they were reacting.*

"Everyone in the Mat-Su Valley is starving. We're shipping them food just as fast as we can, but if we spread the typhus to them too . . . look, typhus normally kills about half the people who get it. So, maybe you get it, so does your wife, one of you will die. Your son, your daughter, one of them will die. But these folks are already sick and starving. Three out of every four are going to die. Your family gets it; maybe you'll be the one who lives. Maybe just your daughter. Who's going to take care of your orphaned child? There are worse ways to die than in a fever."

Eyes that had started back at her empty now showed emotions, fear, terror, anger. Now she had their attention.

"But you want to know the really sick part of this idea of Harris's? After the typhus has wiped out just about every living person in Alaska, there will still be empty houses, empty farmsteads, empty mines, that dead people worked all their lives to build. They'll all be purchased for ten percent of their actual worth, perhaps even less. And when the global corporations send out their people to make money for them, before they arrive, they'll give them a course of the appropriate antibiotics, just like the one my medic wants to give you right now, and it won't matter that the typhus bacteria might still be about. The medication will keep them healthy so they can work their life away for the corporations. Ain't that funny," Kat sneered.

Nobody laughed.

Taking her cue, Tremblay pulled out her immunisation gun, screwed a vial of antibiotics in, checked the dosage by the single lantern still burning in the kitchen and looked around. "Who wants a shot?"

The woman with the baby removed her coat and offered a bared shoulder. The medic placed the gun against her skin; it went off with a small click. She pulled the baby's makeshift nappy down to offer its rump. There was a second click. Lance had his coat off, Linda too. A line began to form.

Kat turned to Lance. "I've got climbers ready to go up and over that avalanche flow." She looked slowly around the room. "Who wants to help my crew climb the flow and get us out of here?"

"So, Kat, which one of us climbs the avalanche flow with them and who's staying here?" Jack asked in a tight lipped whisper out of earshot of the miners. A whisper that didn't hide the tremble in his voice.

"You don't have to go if you don't want to," Kat said, ready to admit she'd volunteered Jack enough for one day.

"You're so full of crap, Severn," he snapped. "One of us has to stay here. Somebody's got to give them a kick in the butt if that Harris character tries to start something up again. You're probably the best for that. A 'damn Severn' stays here and shows them they haven't been abandoned." Jack gave a resigned shrug at his own logic. "I'm going to climb that flow. If we can't make it out, then someone has to let you guys back here know. And, if we do get out, I can try to get a signal back to Elmendorf and get us some assistance," he finished.

"Sounds logical," Kat nodded, keeping her voice even.

"Yes, it's logical, but why don't I like it?"

Kat could think of a dozen reasons. "No idea," was what she said.

"I should have run the first time I saw you. Yet I keep hanging around. I'm either going to end up with a medal or end up dead, probably both. Last words my ma told me, 'Don't you go getting any medals, Jack, just you come back safe.'"

"Why don't you see if any of the 'little people' are under the avalanche flow, maybe they can help you find a way over it?"

"Don't you know your fey, Kat? You'd only get a pooka living under that mess."

"My father read me to sleep with ministerial briefings and political analysis. We never read any fairy tales."

"What do you mean, fairy tales? They're as real as any political analysis." Jack had his lop-sided grin back.

"I can't argue with you on that one. So, you'll go over the flow, and I'll keep the home fires burning." *Until the river floods the fireplace*, Kat left unsaid. They shared a laugh at nothing in particular. The people around them seemed to take heart at that. Together, Kat and Jack stepped out into the falling snow.

Lance, Eric, Amaru and Tuluga had collected a dozen men and women together. Linda brought out two flasks of coffee for them. As the climbers hefted rope, hammers and other climbing gear, Lance explained the general plan. "We've probably got enough tackle for two rope runs, cum pulley mechanisms. We should have used them days ago, but I didn't believe it would ever get this bad. I'm truly sorry," he said.

"None of us saw that avalanche coming, Lance. We're lucky we weren't all killed by it, don't blame yourself." Linda said.

"Anyway," continued Lance, changing the subject. "We'll tie off a couple of ropes here; you let it out as you climb up and over the flow. Once you've found a way out to the road, tie it off at that end. We can then clip people onto it and then those who can walk can follow the line. Those who can't, we'll just have to drag or carry out. I can't think of a better way of doing it." Lance finished lamely.

"How will we know if you found a way through?" a miner asked. Kat tapped her wrist. "Ensign Byrne will climb with you. He'll call me when you find a way through, and he'll put in a call to Elmendorf for help."

"They can't help us," Hugo pointed out. "I doubt you'll

get line-of-sight to any satellites until they reach Ladd's Landing, and even if you do get through, it's then a long drive around the Inlet, over two hundred kilometres on rough roads, and that's before the snows came. Isn't that why we came up here by boat?"

"If you do get through to Elmendorf, tell the Colonel not to use the bridge kits in any of the boat formats." Kat said.

"The boats?" Tom repeated, not comprehending.

"Yes, our one worked at the initial construct, and still held together when I re-routed the power from the prop to the water-jets, but tell Hepburn not to reconfigure them for a third time."

"If you say so" Jack looked none too sure. Kat was pretty sure Hepburn would do just about anything to give them assistance, well her anyway; after all, she was one of *those* Severns.

"Maybe that particular boat just didn't like me," Kat said, "or perhaps there's a fundamental design defect, but until we know which . . ." She didn't finish the sentence, and was trying hard to ignore the underlying question of whether its philanthropic provider wanted a certain Severn dead. That could wait for later.

Jack and the other members of the first climbing group moved off towards the avalanche flow. Kat followed, trying to work out in the darkness and falling snow where the highest ground might be, should she need it for a 'last stand' against the constantly rising water. OTA(F) had included an hour of treading water and a two kilometre swim. She'd managed that without any issues, but she hadn't had almost a hundred sick and half starved civilians to keep afloat as well, not to mention sub-zero water temperatures!

ONE : SIXTEEN

The jumble of snow, ice, rocks and trees that made up the avalanche flow started within a few metres of the rear of the accommodation buildings. The group shared out the equipment they were carrying. Amaru and Tuluga went first, Eric next, then the miners. Jack was last. Kat surprised him with a hug. "Stay safe, Jack, your ma doesn't want any medals, remember."

"It's a little late for you to start thinking about that." He grumbled but softened it with a smile. Kat had dragged a boy up the river. It looked like she was sending a man to climb the avalanche. "See you in the morning," he said and turned to follow the others. The ends of the two thin lines were tied off against two of the biggest trees available. The climbers all carried coils of the rope to let-out as they went. Hopefully it would be enough.

Kat didn't wait for them to disappear from sight but turned back to her own work.

She had spent three days preparing for the mission on Cayman Brac. For that, she'd had intel, plenty of intel, intel overload, except, as it turned out, not the right intel. Here she had nothing. There, she'd had experienced Land Force troops. Now her command consisted of everything from two tiny babies, both less than a year old, to a sixty-three year old. She had the sick, the depressed, and most of all, the tired and hungry. The tired she let sleep. At least with the rations they'd boated in, the hungry got their first half-decent meal in many months. Hopefully enough to give them strength for the climb without over-filling their half-starved stomachs. As the sleepers awoke, they were fed. Some managed to go back to sleep. Others, feeling almost good for the first time in a while, hung around, ready to do something, but unsure what. Kat started a list of people she was ready to send up the flow in the second climbing group. Harris, who'd somehow missed joining the first group, was at the top of her list.

"Aren't you going to do something?" he insisted for what seemed like the eighty-seventh time.

"No," Kat answered. They had already moved the remaining rope and limited number of karabiners to where the climb started; along with any picks and shovels the first group hadn't taken. What Kat needed to know was how high the water was and how fast it was rising, but that was one job she'd never ask Harris to do. Kat glanced at her wrist. Three hours until dawn. Probably nearer four before they got any real light. All they could do now was wait.

Turning her back on Harris, she headed for the door. Outside, she ran into Lance heading in.

"What's the flooding like?" she asked as he backed up.

"Rising fast. The other block now has water on the ground floor, and there's about twenty centimetres around the back of the building near the avalanche flow, but that's icing over fast. We're pulling the perimeter fence down. We're going to use its mesh to reinforce the ground where the climb starts."

"Sounds like a good idea."

"Could you call your colleague, ask him how things are going?"

"I could, but would you want to answer your phone if you were climbing over that flow?"

"No, I see your point, but it's the uncertainty that's making everyone edgy."

"Lance, they could get three quarters of the way through, and get stuck on the last bit." Kat didn't like to think about that, but it was the truth.

"Lance, Lance, you'd better come quick." A runner shouted as she splashed to a halt next to them.

"What's wrong?"

"Franco's fallen,"

Kat didn't ask for more explanation; she started running. The messenger did a quick reverse and led the way; Lance stayed on her heels. As advised, the flood water was over the top of Kat's boots for a short stretch, but the fencing was being laid as a carpet to aid grip through the icy waters. Kat cleared the back of the recently flooded accommodation block, spotted a light and cut towards it.

Half-a-dozen miners stood around a prone body. Even a quick glance told her all she needed to know. The arms, back and legs went in far too many different directions. Gashes on the man's face showed where he had bounced off rocks as he fell. A section of spruce tree lay across him. The climbing team had been alternating the lead. The lead climber would cover the next stretch, and then pull the rest up by a rope, a rope secured to the rocks, trees, whatever was at hand. What had gone wrong here? Had the rope broken? Had more of the team fallen and lay out there in the darkness? Kat ground her teeth as she eyed her comm-link. But before she called Jack, she'd make this dead man tell her everything he could. She knelt by the body, found the loop of rope and followed it. That required moving the body. She rolled it over with a firm shove.

"Hey, careful lady, that's Franco."

"She knows what she's doing." Lance cut in as Kat followed the rope. There was blood on it, now blood on her hands, but she followed the rope until she found the end under Franco's lopsided skull.

"The rope's been cut," she said. "Did Franco have a knife?"

"Of course he does, we all do."

"You see it?" The body was moved again, this time gingerly by men who knew and respected the man. Franco's knife was missing.

Kat stood, still holding the end of the rope, she swallowed hard at the message she read into it. "He cut himself loose when the tree he'd anchored onto came away." She had tasted the courage it took to lead a mission into hostile territory, and she'd drunk deep from the courage that let you charge into battle, guns blazing, but she had to wonder if she could have eaten from the same plate that fate had set before Franco. Could she have cut herself loose, given herself the long fall, to make sure she didn't take her people down?

"Kat, are you there?" Jack shouted from her comm-link.

"Yes, Jack. How is it?"

"Pretty bad for a while, the lead climber fell."

"We know, I'm here with Franco now."

"Was that his name?" The link choked to silence.

"May God have mercy on him," commented one of the

miners beside Kat as he knelt to close the dead man's eyes.

"We were in a bad place, but we're all through it now. The next hundred metres or so look pretty easy, but we still can't see an obvious way to where the road should be. We're all tied back together again now. I'll call you later."

"Understood."

They left Franco where he fell, his body would go back up and over the flow if they had time. Like all the climbers, Franco had been given an antibiotic shot, but Kat had no way of knowing if he was infected with typhus. If he was, she doubted the medication could have done any good in the few hours since it was administered.

The icy water was half way up her calf as Kat waded back across the low spot to the only un-flooded accommodation block. That settled it for her; with two hours until dawn, she'd get everyone dressed in whatever might keep them warm and get them relocated to where the climb started. "How are the sick doing?" she asked Tremblay as she came into the block.

The medic shook her head. "Give me a medi-vac flight, and I'll bet my last dollar that they'd all live. But taking them out into the cold, the snow . . . I just don't know, ma'am."

"I need to move them out there now. If we stay here much longer, I can't be sure they'll even get to where the climb starts."

Tremblay closed her eyes and breathed out a long, hurting sigh. "And we've got to take them, or their bodies, up the avalanche flow too. I know my duty to the wider public health takes priority over my obligation to these individual patients. Damn, I know it, but it doesn't mean I have to like it."

"Not much to like about today is there?" Kat said, putting a hand on Tremblay's shoulder. "I'll get some tarps moved up there so we can wrap the dead, unless you brought body bags with you?"

"A few, but not enough, ma'am."

Kat sent the miners out into the snow in groups of five or six. An hour later she and Linda were nearly alone. An older women, perhaps in her late fifties remained, she'd been fussing about getting everybody else ready and had somehow missed going with an earlier group. One of the two women with babies had also held back. "He's got a bad cough," she offered by way of explanation.

Kat took a last look around the abandoned room. It was strewn with empty ration cartons, antibiotic vials, the general refuse of a hasty exit. The beds were stripped of all blankets and sheets, used when the sick were carried out. If it stank, her nose was past noticing. Picking up the lantern from the kitchen table, Kat turned to the mother and child. The water was ankle deep as she escorted them outside. Kat followed Linda and the older woman; they knew the way. By the time they got to the torn-down fence that now acted as a walkway through the flooded area, the ice-cold water was up to Kat's knees and had a current to it. Kat put one arm around the mother's shoulders, the other, with the lantern, out to balance them. The woman hugged her baby close with both arms.

When they reached the low spot, it was clear the older woman had a problem. Short to start with, the water was at her waist. "You stay here," Kat told the mother, then moved up to help Linda. Holding the older woman between them, they got her across the five or six metres of what could now only be described as a running river. As a gawky teenager, Kat doubted there was any reason for a girl to be one-point-eight-three metres tall, but tonight she would have gladly added another ten centimetres to her height.

Once across, Kat handed the lantern to Linda and immediately turned back. "I'll go with you," Linda offered.

"No, you two get up to where the climb starts. There's still a small patch of dry ground there. Get yourselves dried off."

"In this snow?" the older woman laughed, "you're dreaming." But Linda got the woman moving. Kat took it slowly going back, refusing to believe the current had got even faster, the water even deeper, the temperature even colder, in the short time since she'd made the last trip.

Again, Kat put one arm around the mother's shoulders, the other out for balance. "Watch your step," she told the mother with her child. They went slowly, planting each step firmly before removing weight from the back leg. Kat was lifting her back foot when the woman beside her went down.

In a second, Kat knew she was losing her. She grabbed

for whatever she could and got a fistful of coat collar, but was dragged under by the burdened mother. Kat threw her other hand down to find the wire fence, to stop them all from being dragged away by the current. Razor wire sliced into her palm.

The fence had been meant as a guide, not as a support. As Kat and her charge hit it, it came loose. Kat fought to gain a foothold, to get her head above water, to get a breath, to hold onto the wire, to hold onto the woman. Somehow she managed them all.

By the time Kat managed to get one foot to hold they were another twenty metres downstream. Holding on to the wire and the mother, Kat knew a single foot would not hold them, but it was enough to enable her to get her head above the freezing water and air back into her screaming lungs.

Now she concentrated on getting her second leg firmly down. She slid another few metres before managing to get both feet down and solid. Still, the pull of the current on her and the mother was too much, and she was dragged another few metres further before she got her stance right above the power of the water. Now firmly in-place, her own head above the surface, she pulled the mother towards her, raising her up into the cold night air.

"Can you breathe?" Kat yelled into the woman's ear.

"Yes."

Despite their wild ride the woman was still holding her baby above the water. "The baby?"

"He's coughing."

"Good." Kat turned to face into the raging water. Feet firmly planted and leaning into the current at nearly forty-five degrees and still holding the woman with one hand, she eventually freed the razor ribbon from her bleeding palm. Then she risked a side step of a few centimetres. Then another, until she could feel the mesh of the fence under her feet again. Checking her grip on the woman, she moved forward, against the current of the water.

The water was so cold. Kat's bleeding hand stopped hurting as she lost all sensation in both her hands and feet. Now her problem was making sure her numb flesh was holding fast to the woman's collar. She moved forward again. *Careful, careful. Ignore the cramping in my calves, the ache in my thighs, the numbness spreading throughout my body.*

Time stopped as Kat made her way, step by slow step through the raging current. Despite the passing of eons, the sun still did not rise to throw even palest light on her struggle.

Only when the water was down below her waist did Kat risk settling the woman onto her own feet. "Thank you," the woman said breathlessly. The baby sneezed. That was enough thanks for this whole damned mission.

Eventually they made it back into knee-deep water. Linda and Lance were waiting for them. "I was worried when you didn't show," Linda shouted in Kat's ear. "Are you all right?"

"I think so." Kat answered, and was grateful for the arm from Lance. The miner took a look at Kat's gashed and bleeding hand. "Looks like we'll be using some of those medical supplies you brought in."

Tremblay came over and began examining Kat's palm, like a bleary-eyed gypsy fortune-teller. Then she gave Kat a tetanus booster shot, cleaned it out, and bandaged it. "That's going to give you a problem going hand over hand on the rope, ma'am" Tremblay said.

"This little thing?" Kat said, making a fist. "Ouch." It hurt like hell and didn't get very tight.

"Take it easy on the climb, no heroics," the medic advised before turning back to her typhus cases.

An improvised shelter using tarpaulins and timber that had been part of a building until very recently had been rigged-up. Eighty or so people milled about in the tiny space behind the back of the accommodation building, the avalanche flow and the ever rising flood water.

Kat looked around for what to do next.

Off to her left there was a sudden rattle as several rocks, bounced down the flow. Her comm-link came to life. "Kat, we've lost another. It's Amaru. We're only about a hundred and fifty metres from where the track should be, but there's not a good way down to it. Amaru, Tuluga and Eric are each trying a different route."

"Amaru's didn't work?" Kat finished for him as she turned to face the miners. Several women and a couple of men knelt in the snow, praying. Kat hoped their god was listening.

Sunday around the Prime Minister's residence was a day for providing a church based photo opportunity to the media. That was all her Father expected and all Kat understood of religion. Jack was out there, probably hanging onto a rock and praying for his life. Kat hoped someone was listening to all these prayers.

"No, he's fallen, but he's not injured, we can get to him." Jack went on. "Tuluga and Eric are still going forward. They didn't even stop when Amaru slipped."

"Keep me updated," Kat told him and cut the link.

"We'll know in a few minutes," she shouted to all the interested parties.

"Kat, Kat," came fast from the comm-link. "I think Tuluga's in trouble. Stay there, don't move," Jack shouted down the open link. "Let Eric move across to you, for God's sake man, don't do it."

Kat tried to picture the struggle taking place on the other side of the avalanche flow. *When you delegate a job, you have to live with the results*, she reminded herself. She ordered herself to silence. The last thing Jack or any of the other climbers needed right now was someone hassling them from the other side of the flow.

"Damn you, Tuluga," came from the comm-link. Kat looked up, ready to dodge more falling rocks, trees or compacted snow and ice. "He made it," Jack continued, his voice half awe, and half laughter. "The son-of-a-bitch made it!" That coming from the usually soft-spoken Jack got an eye raised from Kat as she tapped her wrist unit.

"Made what?" she asked softly.

"He's not down to the track," Jack quickly corrected, "but he was hanging on by a hand and a foot and it looked like he was slipping. He's back to climbing down now."

"He's safe," Kat shouted to the miners. A number of them crossed themselves.

"Kat," came excitedly from Jack almost an hour later.

"Yes, Jack."

"Kat, I can see lights, vehicles on the road, trucks, our trucks, it looks like . . ."

"Ensign Severn, can you hear me?" came an all-too-familiar and none-too-happy voice, cutting over Jack's.

"Thank God you're here, Colonel," Kat screamed. "The Fleet's here," she yelled to the miners. "They're here!"

"We're on the road on the other side of this avalanche, and the situation better not be out of hand. We've driven all night in the shittiest conditions on the shittiest roads to get here, but we're here and we're alive. I can see Ensign Byrne and some others climbing down. How many people do have there?"

"About ninety, sir. And sir," she said into the comm-link, "we can't trust those boats cum bridge constructs."

"So I found out. One went pop on me as I was pulling it back to move on. Another left a convoy on the wrong side of another angry river. Third time is not good with these jokers. Left me with a part-loaded convoy, so I came back to base early to find one of my Ensigns had gone off half-cocked."

"Yes, sir. Sorry about that, sir."

"You almost sound like you are."

"It's been a rough day, sir. Full of learning experiences."

"Ensign, I want you out of there as soon as is practically possible."

"Sir, we've got some very sick people," was Kat's answer.

Lance had come to stand beside her. "She'll be in the next group," he shouted over Kat.

"At least somebody over there has some sense. To whom am I speaking?"

"Lance Eastman, I'm the Assistant Manager of the mine."

"I'm Colonel Hepburn. I own that Ensign. Ship her back to me."

So Kat found herself in the first group that clipped karabiners onto the secured rope and made their way up and over the avalanche flow, half climbing, half hiking. There was applause as she started up the flow. She put it down to the joy of the rescue starting. It couldn't possibly be for the little she'd done.

The climb was long; some sections were snow, others ice, others over boulders and across snapped-off trees. She slid and stumbled her way down the other side, but still remained connected to the guide rope.

As expected, the Colonel was waiting for her. Oz was there too, with a good chunk of the warehouse staff. Everything seemed to be in-hand, and Hepburn didn't seem too inclined to over-supervise them. "My truck," was all he said to Kat, but he handed her a blanket.

Kat found Jack in the back of the truck the Colonel had indicated, huddled in a blanket, sipping on a cup of coffee with a big, satisfied grin on his face. He pointed at the flask and Kat poured one for herself, took a sip, and almost choked. Someone had been quite liberal with the whisky.

"No wonder you like it," she coughed.

"Good coffee, but not worth what I went through." He held out his hands, raw and bleeding. "I'm never going to even climb a flight of stairs for the rest of my life."

"Tremblay is in the next group. She can look at your hands." Kat held up her bandaged one. "Razor wire makes a lousy life-line." Jack sipped the whisky-laced coffee in silence. Kat held the cup in numb hands, letting the warmth seep into her. The whisky she could do without.

Ninety minutes later, Jack's hands cleaned and dressed, the Colonel settled into the back seat as Kat and Jack made room for him. Two of the civilian warehouse staff piled into the front seats. The driver revved up the engine from its idling state, slipped the rig into gear, then headed into the driving snow. The wipers struggled to keep the front-screen snow free. Maybe up front they had a better view, but nothing was visible to Kat from the rear seats.

"Is that fear I see in your eyes, Ensign Severn?" the Colonel chided her. Kat leaned back in her seat, concentrating on her coffee. It wouldn't do to have Hepburn think that after all she'd been through she was afraid of a little early morning drive in the country . . . even if the driver was charging blindly into a white-out. "We've got the worst cases and the medic in the back, so don't get too unwound," the Colonel advised the team up front. They both leaned forward, noses almost touching the windshield.

"Yes, boss. We'll get you back as fast as we can, maybe even alive, and for no extra charge."

"Damn civi's," Hepburn growled. "Almost as stupid as

some Ensigns I know. Just what did you think you were doing Severn?"

Kat had been expecting this. "Sir, the mine had a medical emergency that involved a threat to the public health of the wider region. Exercising independent judgement and within calculated risks, sir, I led a boat expedition to their relief. Our efforts were hampered by what I can only assume at this time is a design flaw in the electro-magnetic shoot-bolts that hold the constructs together. We were in the process of rescuing the miners when you arrived, sir." There, she'd made her report, and every word of it was true . . . sort of.

Hepburn just shook his head. "So you didn't have time to call me, to run your approach through your Commanding Officer?"

"You were committed to a convoy, sir. There were no roads to the mine. A boat was the only way to reach it." Kat said, knowing full well the truck she was riding in raised certain questions about her evaluation of the situation. "Until the shoot bolts failed it wasn't going too badly, sir. The boat went together like it was supposed to. I even repaired it, diverting the power to the water jets when the prop got bent on a log. Sir, we didn't have another choice."

Colonel Hepburn's face remained a hard mask as Kat tried to justify her actions. If anything the tightness around his eyes got tighter. "You'd accessed the boat's construct sequence twice already?"

"Yes, sir. But I didn't know it was a problem."

"If you'd touched that keypad one more time on the way up, it would have dumped you and your entire party into the river."

"Yes, sir." Kat agreed lamely.

"I found out the damn system was a piece-of-crap whilst using it as a bridge. At least it failed when no one was on it. By midday I already knew we had a problem, but no lives were put at risk. None but yours, because you didn't have any choice."

Kat didn't have an answer for that.

"Ensign Byrne, Jack isn't it."

Kat was grateful to have the Colonel's full attention shift away from her, then felt guilty all the same. Jack hadn't done anything she hadn't asked. No, this was the Fleet. She'd ordered him to do what he did. She was the senior. She was responsible.

"Yes, Colonel."

"Did you have any other choices?"

"Yes, sir. I had other choices."

The Colonel already had his mouth open. He closed it and eyed Jack for a moment. "And what makes you say that?"

"We always have choices, sir. At least, that's what my old grandma always says. No matter how bad it looks, there are always choices."

"What choices did you have today that Ensign *Severn* didn't seem to notice." *The sarcasm was thick.*

"We could have called you, sir. Asked your advice, or at least kept you informed of what we were doing. We didn't fully consider driving out here like you did, sir, but we didn't know if we'd need bridges on-route, couldn't get satellite imagery of the area because of cloud cover, and you had the only truck with a crane unit, so the boat seemed like the best option."

"So you did think about it?"

"No, sir."

"Why?"

"Kat said to take the boat, sir, and I followed her lead."

"You followed her without question."

"Yes, sir." Jack said.

Kat knew that wasn't quite true. Jack had bitched, questioned, complained, but she'd just ignored him. Ignored him, just like she always did.

"You'd follow her, even if she led you through the gates of hell?"

"Yes, sir."

"Or off a cliff?"

"Or over an avalanche, sir." Jack actually managed his trademark lopsided grin.

"Are you listening to this, Ensign?" Kat had the focus of the Colonel's attention again, but was busy digesting what Jack had said.

"Yes, Colonel."

"But are you hearing it?"

Kat took a moment before she answered. "I think so, sir."

"You are a leader. Probably the best damn leader this lash-up has. You filled a vacuum I let happen. For that I bear a great degree of responsibility. However, young lady, you can never underestimate the responsibility for the leadership *you* provide. From the moment you set foot in Anchorage, you've been leading. People who were bitter or lost, or struggling on their own, found they could trust you to lead them. That's the way it's supposed to be, but damn it woman, you are in way over your head. You are an Ensign in the ABCANZ Fleet. That means a lot, but it doesn't mean anywhere near what you, *Ensign* Severn are making it mean."

Kat had done her best to follow the Colonel, but somewhere she'd lost what he was getting at. "Sir, I don't think I understand."

"You're a *Severn*. You don't have a choice. What did your Grandpa, George Lennox say after he killed President Kwashaka? 'There was no alternative.' And that's exactly what your other grandpa, James Severn said after he took his command up Table Mountain and kicked an entrenched enemy Division off it. Just like Jack here learned from his grandmother that there are *always choices, you* learned at both your grandfather's knees that there are *no choices.*"

"That's not true, Colonel. I can count on one hand the number of days I spent with my Grandpa Jim when I was a child. He's my mother's least favourite person on the entire planet. One of the main reasons I'm in the Fleet is to get away from being one of '*those damn Severns,*' sir." He wasn't being fair to her. He didn't know anything about her. And he probably didn't care either. Kat put down her hardly touched mug of coffee, folded her arms across her chest, and prepared to ignore the rest of whatever Colonel Hepburn, he of machine-gun crowd-control fame, had to say.

But instead the Colonel said nothing.

Outside, the snow was still coming down. The driver and his mate carried on a conversation of mainly "There's a big rock." "Watch out for that tree!" "That drift looks deep, go right."

Kat was tired . . . exhausted by the day and drained by the Colonel's critique. She just wanted Hepburn to finish his reprimand and let her get some sleep.

Then the Colonel smiled.

"Family is a strange thing. I remember visiting my old dad when my son was seven or eight. I can count on one hand the number of days my dad had spent with my son. But I kept having to swallow a smile that weekend. You see, my son had mannerisms just like my dad. Now, on a seven-year-old they were cute, kind of rough, jerky, but looking at my dad push his hair back just so, or tug at his ear just the way my son did tickled me. Funny thing was that, as I said, my son and dad hardly ever saw each other, so I kept wondering how they got the same mannerisms," Hepburn said, brushing his hair back with his right hand, and then tugging his ear. Kat almost smiled.

"Your son got your dad's mannerisms from you," Jack said.

"Yes, and of course, I don't live in front of a mirror, so there was no way I could notice what I did. But my son did. And I guess I noticed what my dad did."

"But not consciously," Kat said.

"Never consciously."

Kat unfolded her arms, ran a nervous hand through her own hair, and started thinking out loud. "I remember my father telling Parliament they had no choice but to keep capital punishment on the statute books until Louis's killers had been caught and executed. I can't count the number of times I heard him say, 'There *are* no other options.' That was the way he'd send me off to a hockey match. 'Win. There is nothing else.'"

"You couldn't lose?" Jack asked, incredulously.

"Not as far as my father was concerned," Kat assured him. Then she frowned at Hepburn. "But sir, when I first saw the Base, it was in disarray. I knew I had to do something about it. I knew I had to clean up the Mess Hall, improve the food. The alternative was to just wade about in all the crap."

"Yes, and you did a good job. Thank God you did what you did. It gave me new impetus. You've got my command moving up, rather than lying on its back looking up. You've fed a lot of people. You chose right that time." The Colonel held Kat with his eyes. They were just as demanding, but somehow not as hard as when he had climbed into the cab.

"But this time, I chose wrong," she said

"Yes."

"But how do I know when I'm going to be right and when I'm heading off a cliff?" Kat demanded.

Colonel Hepburn leaned back in his seat and laughed. "Ha, that's the question every Ensign wants answered."

"And . . ." Kat insisted.

"With luck, you'll have a pretty good handle on it by the time you become a Lieutenant. You had better know it damn good by the time they pin these on," he said touching the twin yellow triangles of a Land Forces Colonel or Fleet Captain on his upper right sleeve.

That only added to Kat's confusion. "Sir, that doesn't really answer the question, does it?"

"No. You've got to answer it yourself. Better yet, the *answers,* not just a single answer. There are a lot of answers you think you have, but you actually don't."

"Sir?" That one really puzzled her.

"Who killed President Kwashaka?" the Colonel asked softly.

Kat blinked and said the first thing that came to mind. "My Grandpa George."

"Right, it was in all the media, and not a single historical data-record disagrees. How much have you read about that operation?"

"All the records, I think. The central reference library in Nu New England had a significant amount of unpublished material on the African Cape Campaign. I went through them all when I was about fourteen." *And drying out.*

"But you've never read the *confidential* after-action-review that Military Intelligence compiled, have you?"

"If it wasn't held by the central library then I guess not."

"You're cleared for it. It's old news now. Next time you get close to a secure access workstation, I suggest you call it up."

Kat didn't want to know later; she needed to know now. She was about to have Safi get it any way she could, when Jack leaned around her. "Colonel, what does it say?"

Hepburn chuckled at the unexpected source of the question, but went on. "It says that Colonel George Lennox and his wife Alexandra have got to be two of the gutsiest people on the planet. They flew halfway around the world, on a civilian airline, with a concealed bomb. Then, they carried it through the tightest security. And they did it as calm and as cool as you please, never giving anyone a hint of what they were doing. Not the crew of the aircraft carrying them and not all the security people that they walked past. Damn, that takes guts."

"So they did kill President Kwashaka," Kat said.

"It would seem so. But there are a few questions the intelligence slime writing the report didn't ever fully answer. As a visitor, Colonel Lennox was seated about as far from the podium where Kwashaka was presiding as the security guards could get him. Yet the autopsy report says the bomb went off in the President's face. There was shrapnel that went in the front of his skull that was halfway out the back."

"How do you get a bomb into someone's face?" Jack asked.

"A good question," Colonel Hepburn chuckled. "A better question perhaps, is how do you get a bomb into close proximity with someone's face and live to let people know about it?"

"But Grandpa's given hundreds of interviews about the assassination. Are you saying he lied to all those reporters?"

"I've read a lot of those interviews, young lady, and I'll bet you money that your grandfather has not told a single lie to any of those media boneheads. If you've never closed with the enemy, Katarina, you have no idea how it really is. Those reporters ask the questions their idiot editors think the average joe on the streets wants to hear. Working out the facts of what actually happened is as far from them as" he snorted, "as this place is from thawing out. No, reporters may understand garden parties, and they think they understand political campaigns, but understand what it is that the military really do, no chance!"

The Colonel turned, his full concentration on Kat. "But you know what it's like. You've closed with the enemy two or three times now, and if you're going to keep putting those expectations onto poor boys like Jack here, and those boatmen, and your warehouse staff, then you had better have a damn sight better understanding of just what the people who made 'those damn Severns' into a single word, actually did. Anyway, that's enough from me; get some sleep, both of you. We have good people taking care of things around here and the 24th Battalion, the 'Black Watch' no-less, will be arriving at some point during tomorrow. I can then turn most of this over to them." Colonel Hepburn had a strange smile on his face. "Perhaps I can talk their Commander Officer into having a 'Dining In' before I ship you two back to civilization."

Kat really didn't like the look on Colonel Hepburn's face. There was going to be something about the Black Watch or the 'Dining In' that held a surprise for her. It couldn't be the Dining In; that was just a meal. "The Black Watch, sir?" she coaxed.

"Nu Alba's finest, the 24th Infantry Battalion, the Black Watch, also once known as the Royal Highlanders. I think Sergeant Major Grant is still with them. His father was with the 24th, when they, alongside an amphibious assault company from the 81st, both under the overall command of your other grandfather, James Severn, then a Brigadier, went up Table Mountain. A Battalion and a Company out to evict a dug-in enemy Division. Not just any division either, but one whose officers were indicted for war crimes and whose sergeants and soldiers knew they were potentially going to prison if the newly elected government in Cape Town wasn't eradicated fast . . . you know the rest of the story."

Kat nodded; of course she knew the story. At least, she knew the story the way it was in the public-access historical data-records.

"Well, Sergeant Major Grant's father was one of the very few in the 24th to walk off that mountain on his own two feet. It gives him an almost unique perspective on how the Battalion won that particular battle honour."

With that, the Colonel turned towards the window, and icy, snow covered track or not, almost instantly went to sleep.

Kat was maybe ten seconds behind him.

ONE : SEVENTEEN

Kat knew she wouldn't hear the approach of the incoming transport aircraft as she sat inside the leading bus, sheltering from the incessant snow, so she kept her eyes on the end of the runway; sooner or later they'd have to break from the clouds. As usual, the met-data promised nothing but more snow. Kat wore her Number Two Dress uniform, less 'leather and metal.'

Despite the advice of the Sergeant Major back in Nu New England who'd given part of the pre-deployment briefing for this operation, she'd brought along both this uniform and her Number One Dress uniform too.

Upon returning from her 'river excursion,' Colonel Hepburn had ordered her, effective immediately, only to wear these two uniforms for the remainder of her stay in Elmendorf. "Maybe you'll get into less trouble if you don't dress for it." He might be right; for the last thirty hours she hadn't caused or gotten into anything the Colonel didn't approve of.

Of course, the Colonel hadn't gone off Base, and Kat was restricted to it as well. When her parents had 'grounded' her, it didn't mean she could skip hockey practice or ballet classes, or any of their stuff, it was just her own activities that she was prevented from attending or doing. It was the same with Colonel Hepburn. She could still run the warehouses. Indeed, she was expected to get them into shape, ready to transfer over to the 24th Infantry Battalion. Jack was still running the MT operation, and he too was clearing up any loose ends to ensure a smooth transition. It was just that neither of them was supposed to take a step out of the main base or the warehouse complex, nor deviate from the direct route between them. The Colonel had also taken to dropping by at odd times to make sure they were compliant. Five or six times a day!

It was as if he didn't trust Kat any more than her mother or father had when she was sixteen. But perhaps the

Colonel had a better cause for that lack of trust.

Accompanying the hired-in buses and their attached convoy of vans onto the runway apron had been her first trip beyond her short leash. Kat had asked Jack if he wanted to help greet the 24th Battalion; he'd jumped at the chance. Kat had also asked the Colonel if he'd like to be present too. "Who's riding shotgun?" he asked without looking up from the report he was reading.

"Every van will have an armed driver and passenger, NGO employees from the soup kitchens." Once again, just about all the military personnel were out on convoy duties, delivering food.

"You're not going to start a war or do anything else that might increase the quantity of paperwork on my desk, are you?"

"No, Colonel. Definitely not. Just simple, standard Fleet Ensign stuff. No *Ensign Severn* stuff either, sir." She grinned.

"Get out," he grumbled, then thought again, "make sure you're back here for lunch."

"Yes, sir." She saluted with her still bandaged hand. He nodded back in acknowledgement.

Both military transport aircraft broke from of the cloud at about the same time in a tight formation. Kat shook her head. The transport aircraft were trying to land side by side. This would have been virtually impossible even before the snow, but on the collection of pot-holes Elmendorf now called a 'duty runway' this was suicide.

Thankfully, the pilot of the second transport took one look at the runway and quickly came to the same conclusion. He added power and climbed into the overcast sky for a go-around. The first aircraft adjusted, went long, missing the majority of the largest holes, and did a reasonably smooth run out. It was taxiing towards the apron when the second transport touched down.

Unwilling to get out into the cold and still falling snow, Kat waited in the bus to see what would happen next. Only when the second aircraft was at a full stop did both transports lower their rear loading ramps, in perfect synchronisation.

Four men in kilts of Royal Stewart tartan marched smartly out, two from each ramp. The four men all halted as one, and then the pipes began.

"What's with the skirts, and the noise?" Jack asked on his open comm-link.

"Be careful, Byrne" growled Colonel Hepburn, apparently monitoring the net.

"That 'noise,' Jack, is the pipes, bagpipes," Kat enlightened him.

"I thought you had bagpipes in Ireland too?" the Colonel added.

"I don't think they survived the war," Jack answered in the thickest brogue Kat had ever heard from him. "And don't we thank the baby Jesus and his good Virgin Mother for that small mercy."

"And I thought I was shipping you home because you were too tied-up with Miss Severn. Ensign Byrne you are not going to survive the next few days."

"Am I supposed to be afraid of men in skirts?"

"Ladies from Hell, actually." Kat knew her military history. "Now Jack, you can either start walking back to the Base," the snow picked that very moment to fall even harder, "or you can move your six buses around to the second aircraft." Kat nodded to her driver, and he shifted into gear. "I'm bringing my six up to aircraft one. Don't worry Colonel; we'll manage this by the book."

"And why have I come to doubt a Severn's definition of 'by the book?'" the Colonel asked. "Hepburn out."

Kat ignored his last comment; her driver led the other five buses in her group onto the apron, followed by the vans for the baggage, and parked well behind the first aircraft.

Troops began filing off both aircraft, M37 assault rifles slung across their chests. Under the influence of the pipers, they quickly fell into step, taking their places in formation under the watchful eye of their Troop Staff Sergeants and Company Sergeant Majors. Their uniform was that of a standard Land Forces Infantry Battalion, webbing, chameleon body-armour, bristling with weapons and munitions, and adorned with the unique distinctions of the Battalion. Their left upper sleeve showed the single 12mm wide vertical dark green "branch of service" coloured stripe of enlisted ranks within the infantry, over which was the small ABCANZ Federation's red, white and blue flag worn by all military personnel. Below that was a dark green edged black diamond with XXIV across its centre in white, denoting the 24th Battalion. The upper right sleeve was for rank insignia only, for those that had any. Helmets were clipped to their belts on the left hip. Headdress consisted of the traditional dark olive tam-o-shanter, with cap badge and red hackle over the left ear.

As far as the Black Watch were concerned this could have been a balmy summer's day back on their parade ground in Nu Alba. Their heads were high, their steps were sure. They were on parade, and the devil could take the wind and the snow.

The Battalion's officers dismounted from the forward hatch of the first aircraft. They were smartly dressed in the same uniform as Kat, only in Land Force dark olive, rather that the Fleet's dark grey, and they too wore the red hackle and tam-o-shanter like their men. Once again, no concession was made for the snow. Kat stood and opened the door of the bus. A gust of snow promptly smothered her uniform, but she marched towards the rapidly forming command group. A short, dark haired man came forward to meet her. Kat saluted as they met. "I'm Ensign Katarina Severn, your liaison with Elmendorf Base."

"I'm Captain Kyle Ramsey, the Battalion Adjutant," the other said, returning her salute. He then proceeded to introduce Kat to Colonel Urquhart, the Battalion's Commanding Officer. Kat had already checked; Urquhart was four years junior to Hepburn in rank seniority. Urquhart seemed jovial and content to be in Alaska. Kat suspected he'd never been anywhere he wasn't happy to be.

"Captain Ramsey, let's get the troops out of the snow and aboard the buses this good Ensign has been kind enough to provide us with." He turned to Kat, "A week ago when I got our deployment orders, I feared we might have to march into town, bayonets fixed," he said with a broad smile.

Kat brought the Colonel's briefing up to date while the Adjutant passed orders to the Battalion Sergeant Major who then shouted orders to subordinate senior NCOs in each Company. It was a thing of beauty to watch the workings of a chain-of-command that had been honed to perfection over several hundred years.

"I understand that you require an Officers' Mess," Kat said as the troops moved in files to their assigned buses. Hepburn had informed Kat that the current arrangement of the senior ranks dining in the same facility as the officers would not meet the 24th Battalion's high standards or traditions.

"Quite right, Ensign," Colonel Urquhart nodded. "Mixing Officers with the Enlisted Ranks will simply not do."

"We've re-opened Elmendorf's original Officers' Club. It's not too far away. About a kilometre, from the current main-base facilities," Kat assured him.

"Good. It will be the anniversary of one of our proudest, more recent battle honours in just a few days time. Table Mountain of the African Cape, when General, then Brigadier, Severn led us up that piece of real estate."

"I have the honour of being General Severn's grand-daughter," Kat informed him.

"Then the Battalion will be honoured to have you as our guest at our Dining-In, Ensign."

Kat nodded at the offer, and then decided she'd better get it off her chest. "Colonel Lennox is my other grandfather," she added.

"Good God, ma'am, Jimmy Severn and Georgie Lennox in your family tree."

"Quite an honour, I can assure you," she responded.

"If it isn't a curse," he chuckled, leaving Kat to wonder if there hadn't already been some collusion between the two Colonels.

Once Kat got the Battalion back to the main base she took Colonel Urquhart up to Hepburn's office, where the two quickly made it quite clear that they had old-time Land Force infantry stuff to talk about, most unsuitable for a young Fleet Ensign's delicate ears, and so Kat headed back to her office at the warehouse complex.

Oz met her at the gate with Lance Eastman. "Would you mind adding a couple more foremen to the staff? The nights are getting kind of long for me."

"Lance, you want to work for me?"

"It's real hard to strip coal from a flooded mine that's over two hundred klicks away. The people here have found accommodation for me and my people, well those of us not infected anyway, but we have to work, even if the food is free."

"The pay's pretty poor," Kat pointed out. "Only ten ABCANZ dollars a week."

"Better than nothing, and after that miracle, we reckon we owe you something."

"It wasn't my miracle," Kat shook her head. "You all worked hard to climb that avalanche flow."

"I didn't mean the climb out. The miracle was you even knowing we were in trouble. That radio I was hollering into, it was good for talking around the mine complex, from the strip back to the offices, out to the airfield, maybe as far as Ladd's Landing but never much further, never more that fifteen, maybe twenty klicks. We had a re-broadcast mast and receiving dish set up on Lone Ridge but that got taken down in another avalanche three, maybe four months ago."

"Satellites?" Kat asked. Her father always said 'miracles' were what simple folk used to explain perfectly understandable happenings . . . once you applied logic or science to them.

"Limited coverage, twice a day, but the positioning was real low on the horizon. The re-bro overcame that, but once we lost it, it became very limited and of poor quality. Then the corporation sold the mine and the satellite access was no longer available. Can't tell you how surprised we all were that you even heard my call for help."

Not as surprised as Kat was rapidly becoming. She hired Lance and one of his foremen to work with Oz overseeing the warehouse. Several of Lance's people were joining a road-building crew that would work with the Black Watch's assault pioneer troop, putting things like the runway into better shape, constructing permanent bridges for the road convoys and, in general, starting to put the regions infrastructure back into better order. Ellen and Oz saw real growth opportunities for the Alexander Langdon-Lennox Fund for Displaced Farmers. Kat would certainly have to structure the fund on a more formal basis before leaving Anchorage.

There were a lot of things to think about as Kat settled down behind her new desk, in her new office, on the other side of the building from her fire and rocket damaged original one. Leading Crewman Leonard was back at work again, analysing the accounts and keeping her legal.

Why did her mind keep gnawing at the question of a radio signal that took a few extra bounces? *No doubt the atmospheric conditions in this region have to be way outside of what was generally considered 'normal.' So, no one has ever succeeded in getting a direct message out from the mine facility before, only with a re-bro. Probably, no one had ever been so desperate, as unrelenting in their efforts, as Lance has been. Okay, so a 'miracle,' made possible by his diligence and a volcanically scrambled E layer or F layer or whatever it is that radio waves bounce off. Easy explanation.*

"Safi, when did the von Welf cargo ship clear Cook Inlet?" Might as well eliminate the first question Aunty Dee would ask.

"The ocean freighter *Argent Stallion* cleared the mouth of Cook Inlet on Tuesday at 12:54 local."

"When did you intercept the message from the mining facility?"

"Tuesday, 09:42 local." Okay, so Aunty Dee would get a second question.

"What time did I first activate the boat-bridge construction kit?"

"Tuesday, 10:47 local."

Kat gnawed her lower lip. There was one more question Dee would ask. "Safi, did the *Argent Stallion* ever have line-of-sight down the Chuitna River valley?"

"The *Argent Stallion* cleared the docks in Anchorage on a non-standard transit route the previous afternoon. After an overnight stop near Fire Island, she moved off at 08:27 the following morning. Her routing gave her a one-hundred-percent probability of line of sight up the lower reaches of the Chuitna River valley, for approximately twelve minutes, just over an hour after starting out."

No point beating around the bush with her own computer. "And those twelve minutes just happen to correspond to the exact same time period that we were intercepting the message from the miners."

"Yes."

So there it was. That 'miracle' could well have been someone on the von Welf ship, maybe Gus, maybe not, sending her up a deadly river in a boat with a big potential hole in it. But just because Gus had the *potential* for killing her, it didn't necessarily mean that he *wanted* to kill her. Their first date couldn't have been that bad, surely. Kat tried and failed to laugh at her own joke. It made no sense. Why would Gus von Welf or his father, want Katarina Severn dead?

One thing was clear: her mother and father wouldn't consider that question. "Safi, search the net for similar occurrences of bridge-boat constructs failing in the way our one did."

"I have already conducted that search. There are no other instances of any similar failures in any of the 12,395 kits manufactured to date. Likewise, there have been no reports of similar failures in other constructs using the same specification of metal composition or electro-magnetic shoot-bolt design, either during manufacture or subsequent operation."

"Thank you, Safi, and thank you for thinking ahead of me," Kat told her HI. Dee must have passed along some very interesting upgrades last time.

"You are welcome. I will endeavour to do similar searches in the future."

Kat leaned back for a moment and stared at the ceiling. *Once was chance. Twice was coincidence . . . maybe. But, three times? That has to be 'enemy action.' Question is, who is the enemy?* Kat really didn't want to think a nice young man like Gus already had a hit-list. Of course, Kat considered herself to be a nice young lady, but she was certainly on someone's hit-list!

"Kat," Safi said tentatively.

"Yes."

"Are you aware that a half million ABCANZ dollar donation has been made to the Langdon-Lennox Fund?"

"No, Safi. I've been leaving the money side of it to you. Who made the donation?"

"It is anonymous, but since it came in, I have been back-tracking the money transfer. It is highly likely that it came from Gus von Welf."

"Before or after his ship left Cook Inlet?"

"I cannot be completely certain, but it appears to be afterwards."

Kat mulled that over. *Would Gus really be putting funds into the bank account of a dead person. Not likely. Anchorage has the potential to be major trade nexus for the north Pacific, just like it had been before the war. If Gus knew anything about what his father was scheming, would he really be giving me money? Was he trying to compensate?*

Kat was surprised at how much better she felt, deciding that Gus was not out to kill her, then again, it was Gus who had flown down to join the ship and diverted it into Anchorage. And, if Ernst August senior wanted Anchorage's trade potential, how far would he go, with or without his son's collusion? What more should she do before she left town?

Kat stared out of the window at the swirling snow. It melted against the glass of her heated office window and ran down to the sill. About ten centimetres of snow clung to the sill, but beneath the snow, only visible through the window glass was a good caking of dirt. Not dirt, ash. Volcanic ash. "Safi, has anyone recently visited the volcano that blew up and caused all this mess?"

"No, Mount Spurr technically remains active, and has not been visited since the initial eruption. Access by both air and foot remains impossible."

Why visit a volcano when it was visiting you? "Has anyone done any analysis on the ash?"

"There is no report in any public records of such a study."

Kat spotted an empty jar amongst the coffee making facilities. Maybe she was crazy, but maybe it was time to get a bit paranoid.

Outside, coffee jar in hand, she looked around for the building's climate control unit that heated or cooled the offices as required. Rising steam gave away its location as falling snow evaporated against the hot pipes. There was some discharge into a culvert that ran the length of the back edge of the building. Most of it remained frozen over but a short section was visible and snow free, adjacent to the steaming pipes. Oz came up as Kat was staring into the ditch's murky depths.

"Can I help you?"

"How much volcanic ash was in the rain after the initial eruption?"

"A lot. So much the sun didn't cut through the ash laden clouds, screwed the weather system good. Then the snow came, and never went away. Maybe when the usual thaw comes next spring things might start to get back to some kind of normal."

"Do you think any of that original ash might be down at the bottom of that ditch?"

"I wouldn't be surprised if there was some. You want a souvenir?"

"Ought to have something. Might have it made into a vase or a ceramic pot, you know?"

Oz studied her for a long moment, and then got the attention of a boy, probably no more than twelve. "This lady wants some of the ash from our volcano. Do you mind getting a bit dirty?"

The kid looked like he'd just been asked if he wanted to go to heaven. In no time he was up past his knees in the water and using the coffee jar to collect from the lowest part of the culvert.

"This what you want, ma'am?" he said, presenting Kat with a brimming jar as proud as any suitor handing a diamond ring to his girlfriend.

"Certainly is," Kat said, screwing the top back on. From her pocket, she pulled a dollar coin. "For you, thanks."

"My mum would never let me take it," the boy said, bobbing his head and not touching the money. "You've been feeding us. She'll slap me silly if I take it."

Kat pulled out a second coin. "This is for your mother for raising such a polite boy. Now take them both, and run along."

The lad did not look convinced, but a nod from Oz did the trick. He grabbed both coins and ran for the gate, dripping mud and ash laden water all the way. "The least I could do for messing up his clothes," Kat chuckled.

"And for humouring a woman who's got to be crazy," Oz said.

Kat looked down at the coffee jar, wiped some of the sludge from it, and turned back to her office. "We'll see who's crazy," she muttered.

*   *   *

Two evenings later, Kat followed Colonel Hepburn into the Officers' Mess of the 24th Infantry Battalion, The Royal Highlanders, or Black Watch. Their invitation was as much due to what Kat and Jack had done for the Battalion in the last seventy-two hours as for who she was. With the help of Ellen and Oz's contacts amongst local craftsmen, the disused Officers' Club of the original Elmendorf Base was reopened for business, in the full and true traditions of a very Scottish 'Officers' Mess'. Overstuffed chairs were scattered around the room in tasteful conversational groupings. The walls now displayed portraits of past Battalion Commanders and depictions of battles from the 24th's illustrious history, from Guadeloupe and Passchendaele, to Al Basrah and Table Mountain. The place was heated nicely, newly carpeted, and smelling of fresh paint, and Kat could hardly believe it was the abandoned dump they had started with. Or that such a haven could exist in the cold and misery of Anchorage. The historical data-records Kat had studied told of how a bit of England had been transplanted to India in the eighteenth and nineteenth centuries, and she'd wondered how that could have been so. Now she saw how . . . and why . . . as Scotland came to Alaska.

A new wall, pierced by double-width French doors, separated the bar and seating area from the dining room. As Colonel Urquhart met Colonel Hepburn, a young Trooper hovered at his Commanding Officer's elbow, ready to take drink orders to the bar.

Commander Deane, Hepburn's XO, and Commander Goodhew, the MO, were already in a corner, deep in overstuffed chairs, both with a whisky and immersed in a conversation with the Battalion's Medical Officer and Quartermaster about what was the best single-malt whisky available. Lieutenant Harper had passed on the invitation to attend with a sniff, exclaiming loudly to the operations team about 'drunken debauchers.' Colonel Hepburn, in Harper's presence at the time, had chosen to ignore the comment. Both of the other Ensigns drew the duties that evening, leaving Kat and Jack, the Colonel and all the officers of the 24th free to drink and, or 'debauch,' so long as they were correctly dressed for the occasion.

Colonel Hepburn, with Kat and Jack as escort, were the last to arrive. Kat's ceremonial dress uniform, modified for mess occasions, had been a most interesting fashion statement at the medal ceremony in Nu New England a few weeks ago. Especially against all the corsets and skirts the other women wore; but here she was dressed as per the regulations. Although she and the other Fleet officers wore a dark grey tunic and everyone else present was in the dark green tunic of Land Forces, the rest of their uniforms, the white breeches, tall black boots and crimson waist sash were identical, regardless of service. Colonel Urquhart made sure that the visiting Colonel and his four Fleet officers were made to feel most welcome. The newest addition to Kat's uniform, the miniature of her Meritorious Service Medal, was pinned proudly onto her tunic over her heart.

"What will you have?" Colonel Urquhart asked, greeting them jovially, then turning to the Trooper at his elbow. "Pass the word to all Mess staff: these Officers' money is not good at the bar tonight. This lady's grandfather went up Table Mountain with the Battalion. He was a good fighting man."

"Yes, sir," the Trooper said, looking at Kat as though she was some kind of goddess.

"And make sure their glasses never go dry."

"Yes, sir. What can I get you, ma'am?"

Kat had become totally comfortable ordering non-alcoholic drinks, but clearly, a soft drink would not be appropriate for this kind of occasion. The Colonel's whisky hadn't dragged her back into the bottle. Grandpa Jim might be right, maybe she wasn't an alcoholic. With a swallow and a smile, Kat said, "A white wine with soda, please."

Jack ordered a neat whisky, and Colonel Hepburn ordered whatever Colonel Urquhart was drinking, and the Trooper turned away to the bar.

Urquhart turned to Hepburn, "You said she had guts in a fight; let's see if she can be just as stalwart in the Mess. Now, I've a mind to show you a few things." And with that, the two senior officers left Kat and Jack standing alone in the Mess.

Kat stood there alone for all of two seconds before a young female officer approached her. "I'm Captain Grant. I understand we share the same good fortune."

"Hi, I'm Kat Severn. What fortune might that be?" Kat asked.

"Both your grandfather and mine are amongst the few who walked off of Table Mountain. Had they not, we wouldn't be here. I'm Antonia," she said holding out her hand, "but everyone here calls me Toni."

Kat shook the offered hand. "This is Jack. He's from the Emerald City, but don't hold that against him."

"Ah, a fellow Celt then. You liked our pipes?"

"Loved them, a wee bit of home, so far away from Emerald shores."

Kat almost choked on the first sip of her newly arrived drink.

"It can't be that strong," Toni said.

"Exactly the way I ordered it," Kat assured Toni and the young Trooper who'd brought it, while eyeing Jack like the rat he was.

"We always have choices," Jack reminded her.

"Social coward," Kat whispered back.

"Politically astute. I would have thought, being a politician's daughter and all that, you'd have a better appreciation of the subject?" Jack responded.

"Am I walking into the middle of something?" Toni asked.

"Only something that started at OTA(F) when someone sprained his ankle on an obstacle course," Kat said, nudging Jack in the ribs.

Toni studied them for a second longer, then smiled and shrugged as much as the 'lancer pattern' tunic ever permitted. "Let me introduce you to some of the Battalion's other junior officers."

Kat found herself trying to remember a long list of names, but made easier by a Land Force tendency to give most people a nickname. 'Smokey' was Lieutenant Coals. 'Tiny' was, of course, a huge bear of a man. The junior end of the Officers' Mess seemed comfortable and at ease, and delighted to meet Kat.

It was when Toni passed Kat to Captain Ramsey for introduction to the more senior members of the Mess that things got complicated. The corner with Commander Deane and Commander Goodhew had acquired several more officers by the time Kat was pointed in its direction. Kat wasn't sure, but it seemed that the Troopers waiting-on had already made quite a few trips to this group to refill empty glasses. The Battalion's MO looked unlikely to be vertical by the time dinner was called. After the obligatory round of names, Kat was prepared to bow out and return to the junior officers when the Battalion's Quartermaster blurted out, "And what does a Severn think about the potential breakup of NATO, the continental Europeans going their own way?"

A bit surprised, still, Kat found that an easy one. "I'm a serving Fleet Officer, sir, I stand behind my Commanding Officer and in front of my crew," she said, deflecting the question.

"So you'll just do whatever you're told," the Battalion's MO said, leaning forward in his chair and almost falling out.

"I'm kind of new to this, just an Ensign, but I understand that we're supposed to follow orders." Kat smiled and took a step back. It wasn't enough to get her clear of the conversation circle, however.

"But what if a greater good is involved?" put in a Major with the winged dagger insignia of Special Operations high on his right arm. "If some idiot orders me to charge a heavily defended bunker, it's usually understood that mission-command enables me to use smoke and seek out his flank." That got nods from his mess colleagues. "So what's our duty to the greater good? When Colonel Lennox killed President Kwashaka, was *he* following orders?"

"Yes, but not prescriptive orders."

"So, when evil is rampant, the soldier, for the greater good, may have to act independently?"

"All the data-records I've looked at indicate that Kwashaka was pretty evil." Kat pointed out. "I don't see anybody around at this present time that comes even close to him. Do you?" Kat wanted out of this discussion. It didn't look like anyone was taking notes, but you could never tell if someone had their own HI or personnel computer set to record. "Safi," Kat whispered through clenched teeth, "start recording." At least she'd have a transcript of this conversation if it did hit the media.

"Yes, evil as blatant as Kwashaka's makes it easy to know a soldier's duty. But what if it's insipid, tepid evil, wearing away the soul and psyche of humanity a little at a time? Evil that seeks to turn virtue into vice and pass vice off as virtue, a bit today, a bit more tomorrow?" That didn't require an answer from Kat; she'd learned long ago to keep her mouth shut. No reporter ever got a sound-bite from silence.

"Yes," another officer filled the pause. "When did you ever hear a civilian even comprehend the concept of 'duty?' They have no values, no standards. I don't think *honour* is even in their vocabulary. My daughter is going to university, so we got her a new data-pad and 'honour' wasn't in the spell-checker's database!" That got snorts all around. Kat didn't believe that was true, but it made a good story.

"Strange, it was in mine," Kat said before she realised her mouth was open. *Damn, my psychotherapist was right, I've far too much fight in me. I need to think before I open my mouth.*

"Your father is at the pinnacle of our government. Your grandfather is the CEO of the Lennox Group. Some might see you . . ." He faltered as if searching for words.

"As part of the evil," Kat supplied.

"More like allied with its sensibilities," the Major countered. "Listen, we in the military all know the score. The game is rigged from the top. When the common people don't like it, we're the ones who get called in to maintain stability. Look at your Colonel Hepburn. Some agri-farmers in New Zealand didn't like the hand they'd been dealt, so he and his Battalion get tasked with restoring order. Dumb agri-farmers and terra-formers don't know when to call it quits, so a lot of them die. Hepburn did what he was told to do, and look where it got him. He had all the power on South Island. When they ordered him to face a Court Marshal, he should have marched his Battalion up to the government buildings in Nu Auckland and sent them all scurrying down their rat holes. Then the media would have made him the agri-farmers hero rather than their murderer."

Kat couldn't say she was shocked. Back in university there had always been that hard right-wing element, ready to call for 'war' as the solution to virtually every situation.

"What people need is a good war and a sense of duty to cleanse them of their dirty money and low moral standards."

The veterans back in Nu New England had said pretty much the same thing. Why was hearing it from a serving officer sending chills down her spine?

Because these are the people that are supposed to stand between civilisation and all-out war, not the ones to instigate it. The real question was, was this man serious, or was it just the alcohol talking? Was he just pissed-off that his Battalion was stuck in the frozen-over, backside-of-beyond on a humanitarian tasking, or might he really want to march into town and take over Anchorage's government? Kat suppressed a smile. He'd have a hard time finding any government to take over! With a government that met only once every three years, they had wasted no money on a fancy parliament building. When it was time to convene they used the same building that the weekly cattle auctions were normally conducted in.

Even if this guy was for real, he wasn't her problem. Colonel Hepburn would have the job of facing him down. And if it was only talk, whether drink fuelled or anger inspired, it still wasn't Kat's problem. She'd faced kidnappers' guns and roving bands of heavily armed, hungry bandits. She'd shown she had the stomach for a real fight. This kind of bull session seemed all a bit tame now.

"Please excuse me. Nature calls," she said and wound her way out of the group to head for the ladies room.

Facing the mirror, back to the stalls, she briefly considered a transfer to a Land Forces unit as she straightened up her uniform. It might be a good idea, except these guys charged with machine guns when they went into battle, and the Fleet was smart enough to take a decent bunk and good food when they went to a fight. Kat splashed some water on to her face, told Safi to stop recording, and prepared to go public again. Captain Grant was waiting for her.

"Ignore him," Toni assured her. "You did well not to bite."

Kat laughed. "I kept wondering if someone was recording it all. I learned long ago to be careful what I say."

"It can't have been easy, growing up a politician's daughter," Toni said.

"Not many realise just how hard it actually was," Kat agreed. "Any chance I could dodge his company for the remainder of the evening?"

"That shouldn't be too difficult," the Captain assured her. "We have a skiff team. One of the best in Nu Alba. The coach and team are dying to talk to you."

"Then let's talk skiff riding!" And that provided plenty to fill the time until dinner was called.

ONE : EIGHTEEN

One of the waiting-on staff stopped to whisper to the Battalion's Second-in-Command. He rose, adjusted his tunic, and faced the mess. "Colonels, Honoured Guests, Mess Members . . . dinner is served."

The Officers began moving, some none to steadily, to form a parade line. Those Majors not seated on the top table led off, including Commander Deane and Commander Goodhew, then came the Battalion's Adjutant and other Captains. Kat figured that as mere Ensigns, she and Jack would bring up the rear with any of the Battalion's Lieutenants, but Toni gently took Kat's elbow and led them to join the Captains.

And thus they walked into the dining room, resplendent with linen and crystal, china and silver. The smell of roasted beef almost knocked Kat off her feet. In pride-of- place, stood the Battalion's flag or 'colours,' richly embroidered with their greatest Battle Honours. The ABCANZ Federation's flag stood with it, crossed behind the top table. Other flags, those of their vanquished enemies, captured in battle hung along the walls.

Kat took the place Toni pointed her to, but did not sit down. Then the pipes started. Accompanied by two drummers, all in kilts of Royal Stewart tartan, the Pipe Major led the Battalion's Commanding Officer, his guest Colonel Hepburn and the more senior Majors of the Battalion to their places on the top table. In the confines of the Mess the noise was tremendous. Kat almost had Safi do a second check on the structural integrity of the building, but she was having too much fun watching Jack.

His mouth hung open, his eyes were larger than dinner plates, and his ears were hanging on by a thread. She could have shouted to Safi and still no one would have heard her.

The pipes stopped. Colonel Urquhart graciously thanked the Pipe Major, who then, along with his drummers in escort, marched from the room.

The Padre then recited the Battalion's collect: *"O God, whose strength setteth fast the mountains, Lord of the hills to whom we lift our eyes: grant us grace that we, of The Black Watch, once chosen to watch the mountains of an earthly kingdom, may stand fast in the faith and be strong, until we come to the heavenly Kingdom of Him, who has bidden us watch and pray. Thy Son, our Saviour and Lord. Amen."* This was then followed by *grace*, before they then sat, and the soup was duly served.

"I understand you've had an exciting time of it." One of the other Captains said to Kat. With that opening, Kat gave any listening a quick overview of what she'd done and discovered about the local situation.

"So the fighting is pretty much over and done with," another Captain summarised the most salient points of Kat's briefing.

"Perhaps. Some of the farmsteads still wouldn't give the indentured workers the dregs from their septic tanks. Too much has happened between them, too much blood has been spilt. You can spot those farmsteads, the size of the farmstead and the workforce required to run it is far, far greater than the numbers who queue up for the food. Others are the exact opposite. Great long lines of hungry and you can't work out were they could possibly all sleep. And of course, there's still your primary mission to support the Apprehension Squads coming from MaxSec Florence. I believe they'll be here the day after tomorrow. They said there was no point in them coming in until the supporting Battalion was in place."

"How do you think it will all shake out when all this is over?" a different Captain asked.

"Your guess is as good as mine. I'm just glad it's not part of my mission. If you don't mind some advice, I'd suggest you don't let it become part of yours either. There are some very nasty things at work here that you're not going to solve with a rifle."

That drew nods. "No real surprise there," Toni added, "considering the trade and strategic value of this location. The business potential in the north Pacific region is huge."

"I came across that when I was researching this place, it

does have great potential as a trade nexus. It was before the war, so why shouldn't it be so again?"

"What about the military, strategic value?" another Captain added.

"Military value is nice, but it only really pays off when you're at war," Kat pointed out.

"You haven't been paying much attention to the media then, have you?"

"When you're up to your neck in shit and snakes, it doesn't leave much spare time," Kat replied.

"You might want to reacquaint yourself with current events before your trip back to civilisation," Toni suggested.

"Why? What's happening?"

"There are a lot of unhappy people, right across the World. Europe, Russia, Latin American Confed, even the Arab League," another Captain commented.

"And getting unhappier each day," another Officer added.

"Any number of places could rise up against their respective elected governments. It's more than a little odd that it's happening in so many places at the same time."

"And you know that little girl you rescued in Cayman City?" Toni said. Kat nodded. "Hardly a day goes by that she or the criminals that grabbed her aren't in the news."

"I thought that would have blown over, surely its old news by now?"

"Believe me, it's not blowing over," Toni assured Kat.

"Or isn't being allowed to blow over," Kat's comment was greeted by shrugs from the other Officers.

The young troopers waiting-on cleared the soup away and a second course of fish arrived. Then Toni continued. "Several nations have already set up travel restrictions. We have. Anyone not an ABCANZ Federation citizen now needs a visa to visit any of our member states or dependencies. No visa, no entry. Some foreign business types are screaming it's just another way to restrict trade, cut them out of lucrative business."

"Let me guess," Kat cut in. "Anyone serious about business applies for a visa. The 'one world, one market' types or those more interested in media attention don't."

"Got it in one," a Captain grinned. "I always said that the Severn's must have something between their ears."

Kat flashed a toothy smile at her supporter.

"The European Union has formally withdrawn all its assets from NATO taskings," Toni said.

"Have we withdrawn ours?" Kat asked

"No, not yet. Your father has dodged the issue so far, but it's being reported as primarily being a financial issue. Europe claims she can't fund NATO taskings in addition to their own operations at the present time." It was back to that same old issue, *money*. In her studies at university Kat had discovered that in most nations, certainly those in continental Europe, taxation was about the same as that of the ABCANZ Federation, but much more of Europe's money went on social services. European governments usually spent on health, schools and policing the streets. ABCANZ spent a higher percentage of its central taxes on scientific research and the military, expecting individuals to make some personal provision for health and education. That very same military had then almost always been used, operating under a NATO flag, to prevent rogue states starting another war like that which had almost destroyed the entire planet thirty odd years before. If Europe was now having to spend even more financial resources on its social deficiencies, then something had to give, and in peace-time that cut was always taken by the military.

The states within the ABCANZ Federation, despite the thirty years of peace, still had some very different ideology and values about what was important compared to other nations. The big question was: could world politicians manage the transition undoubtedly coming without it all falling apart with a very big bang? Different Officers along the table had different opinions. Kat kept hers to herself.

The main course arrived to special honours. Two chefs carried a full roasted carcass of Angus beef in, suspended from a pole. A slice was cut and offered to their Commanding Officer, he deferred to his guest, Colonel Hepburn, who accepted it, cut off a large portion, and with his fork still in his left hand, bit into it. Only after he declared it perfect did the servers begin to cut and distribute the choice cuts to the remainder of the Mess.

"You have an interesting way of doing things," Kat told

Toni.

"We don't always do that, it's really all for show as we've guests in the Mess tonight, but it is a Battalion tradition."

"When you've finished your meal, I have a question about your traditions," Kat said as a thick slab of beef was set before her.

Finally, over an hour later, when cheese and biscuits were being placed in front of them, Kat turned to Toni.

"Was it tradition that took this Battalion up Table Mountain?" That got nods from all in hearing. "Colonel Hepburn suggested I hear from Battalion Sergeant Major Grant the story of Table Mountain, the way his father told it to him, and the way he told it to you, both before and after you put on that uniform. The Colonel suggested he might tell me about it during this Dining In."

"Oh no," Toni shook her head. "The Battalion Sergeant Major would never enter the Officers' Mess, well certainly not during a Dining-In." Kat was beginning to suspect that there was a right way and a wrong way, the Fleet way, and the Land Forces way.

One of the other captains turned to Toni. "Why don't you tell her the story. I've heard you enlighten new Lieutenants when they join the Battalion. And it wasn't just the new Officers that were spellbound in the Mess that night."

It took a bit more coaxing, but soon Toni turned from her selection of cheese. She patted her lips with an immaculate white linen napkin, laid it down, then started. "If you paid attention in your 'current affairs' classes, you'd know that the situation in southern Africa was bad. The old government of President Kwashaka had used the military to beat the population into submission. His troops spent more time on rape and murder than on foot-drill. More hours roaming the streets with knives and clubs than on the rifle range." She paused.

"The population that had descended from European settlers had started migrating west long before the war, but these events galvanised their resolve, and all provinces and cities except the Western Cape were effectively abandoned by them. Many of the big players ran for the airports, taking their numbered Swiss bank accounts with them, but the ordinary people just migrated west into Western Cape Province. The Western Cape eventually declared itself independent of the government of Pretoria. This was obviously declared illegal and the army, such as it was, moved against Cape Town, taking up positions in the mountains above the city. The newly formed Western Cape government had very few troops of its own and knew it couldn't move against them, so had no option but to let them stay up there. Unfortunately the man in command of the besieging troops knew about the hydro-electric plant on the Palmiet River and moved troops across to take it, thereby cutting-off the power to the city. With no electrical power the city couldn't hold out for very long. Western Cape asked the fledgling ABCANZ Federation for emergency assistance. Although newly promoted to Brigadier, James Severn had very few troops tasked to his new command, as most of our forces were committed elsewhere. A company of amphibious assault infantry were landed within a few days and they 'held the fort' until the resident Battalion on the Falkland Islands could be transferred across the southern Atlantic. A few supporting arms arrived in due course, gunners, engineers and alike, but it was only ever a Battalion sized battle-group. That Battalion was the 24th, The Royal Highlanders, The Black Watch."

"Hear! Hear!" rang out up and down the table, and Kat discovered that the Mess had grown very quiet. Glasses were raised in toast. Embarrassed to share this sacrament of her hosts with a white wine soda, Kat followed their lead, and flagged down one of the Trooper's waiting-on. "A whisky, if you please." She'd be ready for next time.

"There are a lot of gadgets in modern warfare. All sorts of technology that can make a man think he is a soldier even when he's not. The enemy division on Table Mountain didn't have that many gadgets, and certainly the majority of them were probably not that certain how to use them, but they could hold guns to the heads of the technicians who did know exactly how to operate them. There would be a bloody butcher's bill for anyone who tried to take their position."

"So, that said, never trust the enemy to play fair, and never trust a Severn, period." Toni said with a smile for Kat. "If he couldn't beat them with new soldiering, he figured to take them down the hard, old-fashioned way. So he came to the

'Ladies from Hell' and that amphibious assault company who held the line next to us. He offered us a black night, as black as the devil's own heart, full of rain, thunder and lightning. Then he added in an Electro-Magnetic-Pulse that fried several hundred years of technological advancements from every soldier within fifty kilometres. Radar, radios, even night-vision goggles became just more dead weight for the poor foot soldiers to carry. With a will, the 24th Battalion, and the company from the 81st, stripped their rifles of range-finding and image-enhancing technology. It was iron-sights and cold bayonet steel for the rest of that night. Almost six hundred Black Watch and a hundred or so amphibious assault infanteers went out for an evening stroll in Satan's garden."

"Hear! Hear!" again rang out. Kat's drink had just arrived. Glasses were raised all around.

Before the glasses were down, Colonel Urquhart was on his feet. "To the 81st. The only ones man enough to take the Ladies from Hell to that dance!"

"The 81st" rang through the Mess.

"In the teeth of the storm, the Battalion went up Table Mountain. The first line of defences hardly knew we were coming until we were upon them. They had only two options: fight and die, or surrender and take their chance with a jury. The second line knew we were coming, warned by the flash of our weapons as we took the first positions. With surprise gone, the pipers started to play. Machine guns spat and mortars belched. Artillery fired . . . all blind. Men lived and died by the throw of a demon's dice. Here a troop, there a squad, moved forward across the killing ground. They fought their way into the fox holes and the trenches. Men fought and men died until the second line of enemy defences fell to us."

"Hear! Hear!" again was answered with a toast. Kat drank, but the warmth in her stomach could not dispel the chill that made her shiver. Toni's words had transported her, the entire Mess. They were there, in the lightning-streaked darkness, in the shell-shattered rain. The troopers of the Battalion that dark distant night weren't men, but had taken on legendary personas.

"Our own artillery, after shelling the second line of defences, rolled back to start on the third. Not a man of rifle and steel that night could help but bless the gunners who made the enemy cower and cry, then throw up their hands at the sight of cold steel and sound of the pipes."

"But as we closed on that third line, the gunners did not lift their fire. Our Colonel fired the agreed-upon flare, but the enemy masked the pre-agreed signalling colour in every hue of the rainbow. The gunners looked on in despair, unable to fathom what was happening up at the bayonet's point. Runners were sent, but feet could not out-run bullets. Three men ran with the Colonel's orders. Three men died."

"Then up stepped Staff Sergeant Foster, a soldier of twenty years gallant service. 'I'll carry the message, Colonel. If a sly old fox like me can't get across this ground, no angel in heaven can either.' Staff Foster slipped out of the trench like a ghost. Like the dawn mist on a Loch, he flitted from shell hole to shell hole. When flares turned the stormy night into a tempest-torn day, he froze like a rock. Shells flew at him . . . and missed. No minion from hell could touch that messenger."

"But fortune is not mocked, and the devil must be paid. At but a stone's-throw from the first taken trench-line, a rocket caught the brave Staff Sergeant, picked him up, and flung him broken into the trench. With his dying breath, he passed the Colonel's message to a young Trooper Urquhart." Toni glanced briefly towards her Colonel. "Now the torch was his. Without a backward glance, that trooper raced. Like a fearless stag, he crossed the shattered land to where the gunners plied their trade."

"On the word of a Trooper, the guns stood silent. On the word of a Trooper, Table Mountain seemed split by quiet. And with a roar we rose up, each man, each woman still able to move forward and close with the enemy. The enemy in the third trench who did not run, died where they stood. We, the 24th Battalion, The Royal Highlanders, The Black Watch, with a handful of brother infantry from the 81st, took down a Division that storm racked night."

Once more the cry of "Hear! Hear!" was raised, and the glasses were held high and drunk deeply. Toni seemed exhausted, as if she'd climbed Table Mountain herself. She certainly had taken the Mess there. When she began again, she was subdued.

"In the morning, when the Generals and politicians who led the enemy saw the flag of the ABCANZ Federation atop Table Mountain, they despaired. It is said that you could walk from one end of the defences to the other without touching the ground, for the uniforms discarded by the enemy as they deserted were so thick." She paused. "So, when you gather for a drink, raise your glass with a thought to those fine 'Ladies from Hell,' who went dancing that night up Table Mountain."

The glasses were up and drained. "The Ladies from Hell."

Colonel Hepburn cleared his throat in the following silence. "When did you first hear that tale, Captain Grant?"

"At my grandfather's knee, Colonel," she smiled. "I couldn't have been as tall as his stick, for he was the Battalion Sergeant Major, as my father is now."

"Yet you took a commission?"

"Yes, sir. Both my father and grandfather agreed the family had worked for a living long enough. This time they wanted an Officer." That brought the odd snigger from the more junior Officers and the table, finding humour in the thought that they did not work for their pay. As silence returned, Colonel Hepburn continued.

"The day you pinned on the single bar of a Land Forces Lieutenant, I suspect your father had some advice for you. As misfortune would have it, there was no one there to perform that sacred duty for Ensign Severn. Would you be kind enough to share with her what your father or grandfather gave to you?"

"Colonel, without consultation with my father, I would rather not. He may not forgive me, and he is not a man to cross, as well you know!"

The sober looks exchanged amongst the Officers at the table showed agreement. It was never wise to cross the Battalion Sergeant Major!

Colonel Urquhart stood. "I think I can arrange suitable absolution for you from Sergeant Major Grant." He said, his face showing no emotion. The Mess broke into laughter, but quickly fell back to silence when he did not join in, but just stood, his demeanour quite serious. "If the Ensign who bears the name of Severn has neither the blessing nor the advice appropriate to her calling, I can think of no better words than those the Battalion Sergeant Major shared with you."

Toni nodded solemnly. She slowly stood and turned to face Kat with a look so sombre it brought a tear to Kat's eye and an emotional tremble that she had not felt at either her university graduation or her commissioning on completing OTA(F), or for that matter being under fire. Kat found that to be the centre of such intense attention made her skin burn. But that was not what made her tremble, it was the look in Toni's eyes.

There is nothing so frightening in the world as the face of absolute truth.

"These are the words of the Battalion Sergeant Major," Toni began softy. "The stories are true, I have not lied to you. You will now take command of people. Men and women who are cold, wet, tired, hungry, maybe scared, maybe hurt, just like those in the stories. The difference between these people behaving as civilians, or as soldiers in such circumstances is *you*, their leader. It is now your duty to help them to dig deep within themselves, to find the moral courage and the drive to go on, to do what you have determined must be done."

"When the moment they have trained and lived for comes, you may hold the power of life or death for your people. Therefore, you must become their servant. Are their feet dry? Is their food decent? Do they have somewhere to sleep? You must provide for them, always putting them before yourself. You have been given authority over them, but do not abuse or waste it in any way or for anything that doesn't prepare them for that critical day when death may be at their side."

"You or they may live, you or they may die. Despite all the care that you put into your training, chance may call the tune when the moment comes, but that is no excuse to leave anything more to the element of chance than the circumstances dictate."

"Despite all you have heard in the stories, there is no place for heroes. You do not make yourself a hero. If you chase after glory, you are wasting your time, and worse still, their lives. Glory will find you on its own. If you must spend time thinking of future glory, pray that you and yours will be ready for this heavy burden if it falls upon you in the heat of battle."

"And finally, remember, we tell these stories not to

entertain or bask in the glory of others. We tell them because we must. We tell them to keep the faith with the faces that haunt our nights and shadow our days. They gave their tomorrows so that we might have a today. They gave up all that they might ever have – love, children, and sunsets – not for a medal, but for a faith; not for a nation, but for comrades; not because they were ordered to, but because they chose to."

"If you choose this uniform, you enter into that faith, a faith lived and died by so many before you. Break that faith, and though you still breathe, there will be no life within you."

Finished, Toni collapsed back into her chair, as if some spirit was leaving her body. Kat sat in silence, feeling more sacred than she had ever felt before. Somewhere Colonel Urquhart called for the pipes and the top table moved back into the bar area. Despite the noise, it did not break the silence in Kat's heart. She had gone through her university graduation dwelling on the anger of the words that had passed between her and her parents over her decision to join the Fleet. She had gone through her OTA(F) commissioning parade mad that neither of her parents could find time in their so busy schedules to come and see her Passing Out. Her thoughts on both occasions had not been on what she was doing but rather on where she was from. Moments when she'd been wrapped up in being one of *those* Severns.

But here, these strangers, with their traditions had kept something alive that brought her closer to what it meant to be a Severn that she had ever been before. Yet, rather than making it smaller for her, it had grown her into something much more. Something was growing inside her, something she could not even begin to explain. Understanding would come in time, and time she had plenty of.

No longer hungry, Kat sat, hands folded into her lap. Around her most of the Mess had left the table and returned to the bar. She could hear the pipes playing in the other room. They left her alone, in her silent little bubble, like a child swimming in its mother's womb. And as with such a child, sounds, feelings, actions, all impinged on her and were taken into account, not so much by the eyes and ears and fingers but somehow grasped whole.

When all was done and her bubble finally burst, Toni

was still at her side. "Thank you for sharing with me what you've treasured in your heart." Kat said.

"And I will keep it there until it is time to pass them along to my own children," Toni replied

"I hope they won't mind the loan of them to me?"

"There's something very magical about them. Even when shared out, they're just as strong."

Colonel Hepburn personally drove Kat and Jack out to the runway, late the following day. "Not exactly the way I arrived, Colonel" Kat said, when he offered, thinking *he really wants us gone.*

"And this place isn't anything like what it was when you arrived," Hepburn said. "Is it always this way with Severns? Their Commanding Officer either wants to charge them with insubordination, or give them high praise and medals; perhaps even both?"

"You tell me, Colonel. I'm somewhat new at this Severn business," Kat said, and realised it was true. At twenty two years old, she was only just discovering what she was really about.

The newly contracted civilian transport aircraft played the usual game of 'dodge the pot-holes' on its run-out along the runway. As several dozen Fleet enlisted personnel along with two new Officers found their way from the aircraft and onto the bus Kat had hired in, Colonel Hepburn turned to her. "Give my compliments to Commander Ellis. If he's anything like the man he was at Staff College, he'll be happy to know he has a fighter like you aboard his boat."

"He hasn't shown much appreciation so far," Kat laughed. If what the *Berserker's* commander had been passing her so far was his idea of appreciation, he was a very strange man indeed.

"You have to remember that men like your Commander put on that uniform to be war heroes, and there hasn't been much call for that recently. I tried to talk him into transferring to Land Forces, but he so wanted to command his own ship. I wonder if he now regrets that?"

"I'm not about to ask him," Kat said.

"No, don't. It would ruin the effect of the Insert Report

I'll be forwarding for your OJAR. I suspect it may change the way he looks at you now that he knows he's got a lioness and not some debutante pussycat."

Kat could hope.

The trip back to Nu New England was long, as it went via the San Angeles Conurbation, just as it had on the way out. This time the stopover was four hours rather than two, but it was good for a bit of airport shopping, half-decent eating, catching up on recent news . . . and what Kat had been putting off. She and Jack studied the media feeds with ever-growing scowls. As far as the media was concerned, what they had been doing in Alaska didn't exist.

"And we could have been killed," Jack snorted.

"Not a happy thought," Kat said, knowing that someone had been killed. How could she tell Crewman Joel Collin's parents that their son had died fighting for something important when the media were completely ignoring it? Kat had Safi research all the bereavement letters sent home in recent literature. Feeling guilty, Kat cobbled together a letter based on some of the better ones and sent it off, telling herself it was better for the parents to have a good letter now than something better later.

Despite the lack of media coverage on Alaska, nothing else reported in the media prepared Kat for what happened as she walked through the crowded arrival hall at Union airport back in Nu New England early the following morning. A young woman walked up to Kat and Jack, looked up and down at their uniforms, shouted something about them being a total waste of time and money, spat at them both, then dodged back into the crowd before a stunned Kat could grab her arm.

As Kat stood shaking with unspent rage, Monty appeared.

"Sorry, I should have messaged you to change out of uniform. There's a lot of bad blood around," he said, hugging her close.

"And if I get my hands on that bitch, it will be flowing out of her nose," Jack growled.

Kat, surprised, gave Jack a silent raised eyebrow.

"I mean it. I didn't go through losing your signal on that insertion and chasing round in Alaska's snow with people shooting at me for that kind of treatment."

Unbidden, Kat again saw Crewman Collins lying in the snow. Snow that was rapidly turning red with his blood. Choking, she tried to find something profound to say. Maybe a poet or a politician could; she couldn't. "How bad is it?" she asked Monty, willing him to talk, fill her head with anything but what was coursing through it.

"Your father's just about keeping a lid on things here, but tensions are high all over the world. The only thing I'm certain about is that I don't even begin to understand it all. There are riots everywhere, but particularly in the European states, over health, education, employment, law enforcement, you name it. Their governments, who are already spending a fortune in these areas, have pledged to spend even more, but something has to give. As of two days ago, the European Union withdrew all its assets from NATO operations, and the Kalmar Union and the Nu Habsburg Reich have withdrawn from the Alliance completely, citing current budgetary and economic pressures as the reasoning. The limited assets of the Lublin Union and Southern European Alliance are still in, but only just, so that only really leaves the ABCANZ Fed's states that remain committed. It won't be long before nations re-ignite their old hatreds for one neighbour, or no longer tolerate the religious zealots of another. What good could another war possibly bring? For me, the big question has to be; who, or what, is inciting the people to riot and protest, it's far too wide-spread to just be coincidence, and to what ends, what can all this possibly achieve?"

"Lots of questions, but not many answers," observed Kat.

"Sounds real confusing," Jack put in.

"Like juggling with eggs!" suggested Monty.

"Not eggs," Kat countered, remembering that one of the most prominent players in European politics was Ernst-August von Welf, senior. "Try grenades, and why do I suspect the pins are out on more than a few of them?"

"You're starting to sound like me," Jack grinned.

"Only on a bad day. Monty, I need to run some errands,

are you busy?"

"What do you have in mind?"

"I need to see Dee."

"That might be a problem. And speaking of eggs." The car was waiting where Kat expected. There was a new security agent riding shotgun. Kat remembered him from trailing her brother Edward at the reception a month ago. The agent was out, peeling a large sticker from the rear window. The windscreen was spattered with eggs.

"A group of kids ran by," the agent explained as he slowly pulled off something declaring 'One world – One Market.'

Kat tried her hand at another sticker, 'Less public spending, yet more public taxation.' Jack pulled off one announcing 'Beans and blankets, not bullets and bombs - Cut military spending.'

"Do I hear some jingoism jangling?" Jack asked.

It wasn't a joke to Kat. "Looks like the opposition has discovered its slogans. Professor Barrett always said a good slogan could be more dangerous than an assassin in starting a war."

"If you say so," Monty shrugged, as he manoeuvred the car into the early morning traffic, the wipers struggling to clean the congealing egg from the screen.

So now there were liabilities to having a car registered to the Prime Minister's household. As the car moved slowly through the Nu New England commuter traffic, she leaned forward. "I take it the problem meeting up with Dee isn't just because my father doesn't want me to."

"Right. Tensions are high, daily protests against this and that, it's nothing like as bad as Europe, but it's still very real. Then there are the media hounds looking for any scrap of trash, gossip or scandal to headline the tabloid websites. They must get paid by the second! Anyway, The Residency is surrounded by them, as is Bagshot. I had a convoy of them behind me when I left to come and pick you up."

"They're still there," the Agent said, turning around in his seat. "By the way, ma'am. I'm Mike. I'll be going with you whenever you leave the grounds."

"Not bloody likely," Kat snapped, pushing herself back

into her seat.

"You might find me useful to have around."

"There have been three attempts to kill me in the last five weeks. So far the score is me three, them nil. I don't need help."

"They only have to get lucky once to make it them one, you nil, nothing, dead," Mike pointed out softly.

"Are you snooping for the Prime Minister?"

"I take it your father doesn't want you meeting this Dee person, but you intend to, come hell or high water, and you consider meeting him or her more important than me keeping you safe."

"I consider meeting her a damn sight more likely to keep me safe than *you* hanging around, and *you* telling the PM what I get up to."

"I'm a big girl now, so buzz off and leave me alone," Mike translated for her.

"Good grief, they actually assigned me one that understands plain English," Kat marvelled in pure sarcasm.

"Listen, my report only has to say you went out, you came back, I was with you. That's a Fleet Officer's uniform you're wearing. You give orders and you expect compliance. Just how much trouble do you want to make for me and the boss man who issues my orders?"

Jack snorted at that, "Nice try, Mike, but you haven't been around Severns long have you? They don't give a shit about the problems they cause for us lesser mortals."

Kat shot Jack a scowl. Then again, she guessed she did deserve it. With a sigh she gave in. "I'll see what I can do to help your boss stay content, Mike. What would you call it, Jack, 'penance', for how I treated Colonel Hepburn?"

"More like how you treated me. And I'll believe it when I see it," he said, settling back into his seat and folding his arms across his chest.

Ten minutes later, Kat conceded, "Okay, I may need a little help breaking out," as the car drove into Bagshot. Fully armed Land Force Troopers stood at the gate checking IDent cards; others patrolled the perimeter wall. They had to. There were five media trucks parked across the street. All were fitted with satellite transmitters, dish-up and sending live feed from around the house. Kat spotted at least six news reporters, their camera teams tracking the approach of the car.

"They've got airborne cameras too," Mike said before Kat asked. "But if you really want out of here unseen, I might be able to lend you a hand. You scratch my back, etcetera."

"I'll think I'll take you up on the etcetera. Have you got any running clothes?" she replied.

"I do, but only if you're willing to wear the NNE University sweatshirt I give you," Mike said with a conspiratorial smile at Monty.

"Monty, have you been telling tales?"

"If it will get you into a sweatshirt that will stop a five-point-five-six round at fifty meters, you're damn right I tell tales."

"You wouldn't happen to have an extra one, now would you?" asked Jack.

"What a green one with Emerald City University on it?" Mike smiled.

ONE : NINETEEN

An hour later, Kat was wearing lycra gym shorts and a sweatshirt with a Kevlar and titanium interwoven lining. She, Jack and Mike were jogging their second lap of the ivy-covered perimeter wall, approaching Kat's 'special section,' when Mike muttered into his comm-link, "Close them down," and led Kat through her own private escape hole.

"How long have you known?" she demanded a minute later as they walked nonchalantly away from the wall.

"Probably since your grandmother paid to have it installed."

"But the Severns weren't a political family back then," Kat shot back.

"No, they were descended from British royalty, and they had money, lots of money, and there is no such thing as having money and not being in politics," Mike reminded her, sounding very much like her old political history professor. Kat knew a losing argument when she stepped in one.

"Safi, get us a taxi."

Within a few minutes, they were heading for the Common Room, the one place Kat had been able to tell Dee to meet them without actually saying the name. Dee seemed as reluctant to trust the public comm-net as Kat was. Mike directed them into a dimly lit corner, usually reserved for the young, restless and in-love types, but as it was still only mid-morning, it remained mostly unoccupied. Kat and Mike got their backs to the wall. Jack scowled and settled into a chair between Kat and the door. "You have a problem with this?" she asked.

"I don't like having my back to whoever might be shooting at you," Jack said with a glance over his shoulder.

"Don't fidget, and don't look around," Mike told Jack

313

sharply. "Don't worry, I'll keep lookout. Our biggest worry is a media type getting her on camera, although heaven knows why?"

"I'll settle for cameras over guns any day," Kat commented.

"I doubt you'll have to worry about a shooter today. The Prime Minister's politics are not that divisive," Mike told her, apparently unaware that Kat had not been joking about the three attempts on her life. Well, the Prime Minster had no doubt overseen Mike's briefing. Kat decided it was time to bring Mike up-to-speed, but he was still providing background information to the current situation. *He's bright, as well as handsome, good body, interesting to listen to, good analytical mind*, Kat mused.

"Right now, people aren't sure what is going to happen. And big players with lots of money in a high-stakes game don't particularly like the unknown, the uncertainty. They want to know which way to jump well before the time comes, but you learnt that at your father's knee."

"And some of them like to get a thumb on the scales that decide which way we all will jump," Kat finished the statement.

"You're the expert on these things," the security agent shrugged.

She ordered soft drinks all around when the waiter came. It was the same one who had served them before, but with them being in attire that wasn't out-of-place, he paid them little attention this time. Dee arrived just as their drinks did, and after the obligatory embrace of true, unconditional affection, she slipped into a vacant chair, moving it so Mike's view remained unhindered. In trousers and a sweatshirt that bore a logo of one of the pre-war 'ivy league' universities that had combined together post-war to form the NNE University, she looked the perfect 'old professor.' "Good to see you," she said. "Are you having an interesting break?"

"Travel is such a character building experience," Kat offered, "but it's certainly good to be back where the sun shines."

"I've been rather busy with local matters to keep my eye on what you've been up to, Kat. Why do we need to meet?"

Kat wanted to scream at Dee that Anchorage and

Collins's death and all the renegade prisoners she'd killed were worth people's time. Still, the fair part of her had to admit her personal struggle on that frozen piece of real-estate hardly held a candle to all humanity choosing sides and deciding whether to go to war. Kat pulled the two charred and twisted shoot-bolts from her back-pack and passed them across the table. Dee took them, held the up to the light, turned them over, and frowned.

"Enlighten me." Dee said.

"Over twelve thousand constructs have been made that utilise these superconducting electro-magnetic shoot-bolts. The six units that ended up in my little sideshow are the only ones to-date that have a peculiar tendency to fail, quite spectacularly, the third time you re-configure the construct into another form. Those two are samples of what had been holding together a perfectly sea-worthy boat one moment, that became a pile of scrap metal the next."

"Kind of leaves you up the river without a paddle, or a boat," Dee said, unashamed at not passing up the opening.

"In the worst possible way at the worst possible time," Kat agreed dryly.

"Assassination attempt number two?" Dee asked, and Mike's head jerked around to look at Kat. Yes, her dear father had only told him what met the Prime Minister's elevated interpretation of 'proof.'

"No, probably number three. A rocket attack took apart my desk the day before. I wasn't there, being at lunch with a friend of yours, Ernst August von Welf, the Eighth of that name. He saved my life, Dee."

Dee raised a doubting eyebrow at that. "Any idea what earned you the rocket?"

"I took down some wannabe warlords the day before."

"So the rocket was probably a local response to local stimulus from you." Kat nodded. "And what was *he* doing in Anchorage?"

"Delivering aid. Food supplies we needed. Ten trucks we were desperate for."

"Any boat or bridge kits in the delivery?" Dee asked, turning a shoot-bolt over in her hands.

"Six of them. Three went pop. The other three will spend their lives permanently as bridges."

Dee placed the shoot-bolts back into the discarded back-pack. "'Quenching,' is I believe, the technical term for what happened, but most labs probably couldn't tell you anything from these. I know a few that might. It would be nice to get a look at one that still thinks it's part of a bridge."

"Safi," Kat said out loud, "purchase six boat/bridge constructs, each from different retailer within the Federation. Deliver them with my compliments to Colonel Hepburn at Elmendorf. Ask him to accept them as a trade for the three he still has, explain we want them for further analysis," she paused for a moment. "Anyone want to bet that somehow they get activated for a third time before we can get them into a lab?"

"Hire a security team to escort the new ones out, and be certain the old ones come back. I'll have Max give Safi the details of a reputable one."

"What I can't understand is, why?" Kat allowed herself to muse out loud on this attack for the first time. "I mean, trying to kill me while rescuing that little girl in Cayman City . . . I suppose that just might have got the Latin American Confed up in arms at what they could perceive as military intervention in their back yard . . . highly unlikely, but not impossible . . . but me drowning while on an emergency medical run? What political purpose could that possibly serve?"

Dee just shook her head. "Sometimes I wonder what you Severn's have between your ears! Honey, your dad, your Grandpa Jim, even your Grandpa George, are all up to their receding hairlines trying to prevent society collapsing and catapulting us into another war. You add grief onto the load they're already carrying, and they are bound to start making mistakes, sooner or later, it just adds to the considerable pressure they're already under."

Kat listened to Dee, tried to picture her father broken down with grief over her demise. It just didn't fit. Then she thought of all the changes in the family after Louis's death. It has cost both her parents dear. Would her death cost them as much?

Maybe. Maybe not.

"I'll have to think about that," she told Dee. "What's the latest? Are we really going to war?"

Dee blinked at the sudden change in topic. She took a

moment to rub her eyes with both fists. For the first time in Kat's life, she realised that her aunty was old. She knew Dee was older than her mother, but by how much? "I do hope not," Dee finally whispered. "I do hope not, it would do very few any good."

"Who thinks it would be good?" Kat asked incredulously.

"Old farts who've fought in one major war but have now forgotten just how dreadful it actually was. Fresh-faced heroes that are tired of doing a great job of nothing and have no idea what the true face of war is really like." Kat winced, remembering her '127mm marksman.' *But he was just a kid . . . and now would never grow up to learn any different.*

Dee eyed Kat, seemed to measure the wince against some unknown scale, and shared a smile with her niece.

"You've grown up since I last saw you."

"Aged," Kat offered as an alternative.

Dee nodded. "Then, of course, there's the nutters who want to rule the world, for reasons comprehendible only to shrinks. Included amongst them must be your friend Gus's father and late grandfather. He's currently busy trying to form a new European focused alliance. Almost all have signed up, Kalmar, Nu Habsburg, Balkan Alliance, European Union. We're being portrayed as the bad guys, again. Lublin and the Southern Alliance are still sitting on the fence, probably trying to figure out who they should join, better join or have to join."

"Have to?" Kat asked.

"Von Welf's commercial operations have mortgages on lots of overseas developments and are squeezing them damn hard. The European Union has a reasonable military, and they were the first to haul their units out of NATO commitments. People are looking at geography differently. Short trade routes might be fast invasion routes. Take your disaster in Anchorage, the whole north Pacific is within easy reach. Do we need to consider repositioning our Fleet assets up there? Why do you think we sent the military in to assist when it started to go wrong, even though many of them aren't ABCANZ Fed citizens? We needed to help them fast before someone else got in before us."

"The milk of human kindness and compassion?" Jack

offered.

"Hardly. Do you want to speculate as to who has brought up the Alaskan farmsteads that have 'all of a sudden' become available for sale?" Dee asked.

"No. Safi, instigate *actual* search to that effect." Kat instructed. Safi responded within a seconds. "Companies owned by the Von Welf corporation, concealed behind various associate companies and trading shells have purchased the majority of the farmsteads."

"Anything else new regarding the von Welf's?"

Safi continued "One of their ships paid a visit to Anchorage eighteen months ago. According to the data records it left a week later. However, there's no record of that ship turning up anywhere else for almost another year."

"What kind of volcanic explosion was it that wrecked the local eco-structure?" Dee asked.

"Ah, could you check that out too, please?" Kat asked. "There's a small jar of volcanic ash in there for analysis," she said tapping the back-pack.

"Young woman, you are paranoid." Dee beamed.

"I contracted it from the people around me," said Kat, getting to her feet. "Safi, order a taxi. I want to go and see my Grandpa George."

Dee shook her head. "He's even harder to see than your dad. I can't get in to see him, my own father!"

"I thought that might be the situation, but I need some answers, and Grandpa George is the only one who can even guess at them. Mike, are you ready to protect me from his over-zealous private security guards?"

He made a face. "Over-paid in my book."

"Can I walk back to Bagshot from here?" Jack squeaked. "Remember, I don't do guns, I don't do power lunches. I'm just a simple lad from the Emerald City."

"Come on, Ensign Byrne, move out," Kat started, then froze in-place, remembering Colonel Hepburn's little talk in the truck. "Jack, if you really want to sit this one out, it's okay by me."

Jack reached for her forehead, felt it. "Are you sick?"

"No, just remembering what Colonel Hepburn said. Sometimes I do think too quickly about what I want, and give no consideration to what others might need."

"Good God," Dee drew herself up to her full height, turned her head to first stare at Kat with her right eye, then her left, like some monstrous bird of prey. "You really are growing up, Kat. You're actually starting to sound mature. Be careful about that. You can never follow in your father's footsteps if you start considering other people's needs. Come to think of it, I'm not sure any of your recent ancestors suffered from that affliction, although some of them did have the saving grace of putting their necks out a few millimetres more than the ones they were pushing."

Kat shrugged off the theatrics. "Maybe I acquired a little humility amongst the snow in Alaska."

"No," Dee shook her head dourly. "More like wisdom. A horrible weight to bear for one of your disadvantaged upbringing. However . . ." Dee grinned, all teeth . . . "since you're heading off to meet your old grandpa, I don't think you've acquired too much of it to dampen your fun. Now, please, if you'll excuse me," she said, getting to her feet, "I've got a couple of gaps to fill in on a very big jigsaw puzzle."

"The taxi is waiting outside," Safi advised.

"Well, Mike, just you and me then."

"And me," Jack added.

"I thought you wanted out?"

"Hey, a boy's got the right to at least say what the sensible thing would be to do, even if he then doesn't actually do it!"

Just over an hour later Kat paid off the taxi driver at the entrance to Lennox Towers. They'd already had to pass through three checkpoints to get that far. Their IDent cards had gotten them past the first two, but only Kat's holdings in the Lennox Groups' preferred stock had gotten them past the last.

The complex was huge, with food courts, shopping malls, fitness-suites and apartments for those who lived and worked there, clustered around the base of the needle. It was much speculated that her grandfather had not been 'off-campus' in several years. Kat knew for a fact that wasn't true, as Grandpa regularly inspected his various business ventures. That said, he did move about at strange hours and kept his whereabouts as hard to follow as any spy's. Kat had previously put his eccentricity down to old-age, but of late, she suspected that it might actually be one of the contributing factors to his continuing longevity.

Under an 'information' sign was a guard station with camera monitors and half a dozen men in matching grey suits. One rose and smiled a "may I help you," as Kat led Mike and Jack through the automatic door.

Kat ignored both the smile and the offered help and marched for the bank of elevators. Several were open; Kat picked one. Marching in, she took station in the middle of it, leaving Jack and Mike to arrange themselves to either side of her. "Floor two-twelve," she ordered.

"Thank you, two-twelve," the elevator responded.

Two guards were now running to get into the closing elevator. The doors stopped closing.

"Your request has been overridden," Safi advised.

"Override their override," Kat ordered. The doors finished closing a second before the rather startled guards would have lost arms or worse. Kat turned to check how Mike and Jack were taking matters. Jack's eyes were not quite as large as when he'd been introduced to bagpipes close up, and Mike seemed nonplussed as he removed his IDent Card and Security Service warrant badge from the pocket of his running shorts and palmed it ready for use. Good.

The elevator opened on the two hundred and twelfth floor. Kat marched out, followed by Jack and Mike, one on each side. Sweatshirt and gym shorts had helped them blend in on the university campus, but among the suits the effect was quite the opposite. Talk stopped, people eyed them, but the upside was that people got out of their way, fast. Kat led them through double glass doors into a large waiting area, furnished with chairs, sofas and small conference rooms off to each side. The receptionist's head came up as they entered. Eyes locked on each other as Kat marched towards her desk. "May I help you?" the woman asked, a professional smile on her face.

"I'm Katarina Severn, here to see my grandfather, George Lennox," Kat said without slowing.

"Do you have an appointment?" came right back.

"No," Kat said, and changed course from the desk to the

double, highly polished walnut veneered doors beside it.

"You can't go through there," the woman shouted, getting to her feet, but she'd been outflanked on this one. Kat was at the door before the receptionist could get away from her desk.

"Yes I can," Kat said and pushed through the doors into yet another foyer. The receptionist here was big, male, and already on his feet.

"I require verification of who you say you are."

That was reasonable. Kat marched to his desk, placed both hands onto a glass plate and glared at the camera mounted on the wall. Finger-print and retina IDent's confirmed, she sidestepped to allow Jack and Mike to do the same. With all three of the intruders stopped on the waiting side of the desk, the man settled back into his chair.

Kat took that moment to lead her small assault team around the desk and through the door it guarded. "You can't go in there until I process your IDent checks," the man shouted.

"And probably not for a month after that," Kat said as she ushered Jack and Mike through and closed the door behind her.

The next room was small compared to the two that had preceded it, but the carpet was almost as deep as the snow in Anchorage. The walls were panelled in more polished walnut. Off to one side were a few chairs grouped around a spectacular view over a formal garden on the terrace a dozen floors below. The room stank of wealth and power. Directly ahead of Kat sat an older woman seated behind a desk made from a slab of thick marble or granite. At either end of the desk stood two more men in matching grey suits. Each held a pistol out in the standard two-hand stance, aimed at Kat.

"Don't take another step," the gunman on the right said. Kat decided that, just this once, she would comply with the people holding the guns. She halted.

"I'm going to raise my left hand," Mike said slowly. His words were soft and hard in the way hired killers had that manner of saying the nastiest things in the nicest way. "It has my warrant badge and IDent Card in it."

"Do it slow," the left gunman said. Kat tried to act unconcerned as her stomach went into somersaults. It was a whole lot easier to face armed men when she had her M37. But she wasn't here to shoot her way in. She waited, hoping she'd find the right words when this macho ritual was complete.

"I am Mike Stieger of the ABCANZ Security Service, assigned to the Prime Minister's family. This is Katarina Severn, his daughter. You are in violation of section 108 of the 2065 Security Act in that you are armed in the presence of a person designated as being under Security Service protection. I will ask you only once to put down your weapons."

"I am Senior Private Security Agent Valentine Parks, of Clearwater Security's, Nu New England Bureau. You are in violation of Public Offence 62-1045, in that you are trespassing on personal property. It has been legally posted that this property is protected with lethal force, in compliance with subsection 54a of the aforementioned offence. You have been warned; now remove yourselves."

"I guess this is why you're not big on family reunions," Jack said.

"Yep," Kat agreed. "By the time all our security details have finished citing their legal authority, the food's gone cold and it's time to go home."

"You should drop in on the Byrne's next time you're in the Emerald City. We'll show you how this is supposed to work."

"I may take you up on that," Kat noted that she and Jack's effort at humour hadn't got even a flicker of a smile from the gunmen nor the secretary. *There is such a thing as being too professional. Enough.*

"Grandpa George," Kat announced loudly, "This is your granddaughter. You know it's me, and if you're not sure, your man at the last desk has had enough time to process our biometrics. How long are you going to make me wait out here?"

"And why do you suddenly have a need to talk to your grandfather, young woman?" the secretary asked in a cold, clipped voice.

"Grandpa, I really don't think you want me shouting for all to hear just why a twenty-two-year-old woman suddenly feels the need to know a few things about what's going on in her family. Aren't there a few skeletons that you want kept in the closet?"

A door to the right of the secretary opened. A white

haired man in a dark blue suit stepped out. He was almost two meters tall, explaining where Kat got her height from. "Gentlemen, I think you can put down your guns." The guards quickly did. The man then turned around, back towards the open door. "We can finish this later," he told a man and woman who quickly stepped around him and left by a door to Kat's right. "All right, young lady, you've interrupted my day. Come in and tell me what is so urgent."

"Sir," Mike said politely, "I should scan any room she's going to be in alone with another individual."

"I believe I have the appropriate security clearance, young man. I can assure you that my office is the safest place on Earth."

"For you, sir, yes, but for her . . .?" Mike left the question hanging.

"You government types! I see nothing's changed. Just get on with whatever it is you have to do!" Grandpa George spat.

Mike moved to the door, gadgets appearing in his hands that Kat had never suspected could be hidden in shorts and a bulletproof sweatshirt. The senior Clearwater officer did a good imitation of joining him at the hip as Mike went by. A few minutes later both reappeared. "You have a personal workstation in your desk, as well as a recording device in all four corners of the room," he told Grandpa George, but the report was really for Kat.

"Shall I have my HI make a full transcript of our meeting?" Kat asked.

Grandpa George scowled. "All security and recordings off, Password: Eta, Iota, Nine Two. Happy now, young lady?"

"You know Severn's need far more than that to make them happy, Grandpa," Kat smiled as she entered the room alone. It was vast. Double height with glass on two sides, offering a magnificent view of the city and out across the bay, even better that Dee's penthouse apartment's vista. The room was cream, cream carpet, cream walls, creamy brown marble desk. The sofa and chairs around the matching coffee table were all cream leather. The room even smelled cream if that were possible. Grandpa George headed for the desk and only seemed to relax when he had it between him and Kat. *Nice way to treat family.*

"So, what is it you want to talk about so urgently?"

"Grandpa, aren't you going to ask me how I am?"

"Goodwood, how is Katarina Severn?" he growled at his own HI.

"Katarina Severn is no longer in psychotherapy. Her last doctor's visit involved a full physical check-up while applying to the Fleet for a commission, which she passed. Her last medical issue involved an infected blister while at Officer Training Academy."

"I know how you are, so we don't need to do the small talk. What do you want, Kat, and please, don't waste my time."

You don't know the half of me, Kat wanted to say. Instead, she opened with. "Who's trying to kill me?"

Grandpa George actually blinked twice on that one. "Goodwood, have there been any attempts on Katarina Severn's life?"

"None, sir."

"Three, sir," Kat corrected his HI. "I have a pretty good idea on one of them, a local issue in Alaska, but the other two puzzle me. Why would someone want to kill me?"

Grandpa swivelled in his chair to look out over the city. "You seem to have the matter under better control than I. What do the Justice Department think?"

Kat stood, stepped up to the desk, then rested both hands on the cold marble. It could have been cut from Grandpa George's heart for all the reaction she was getting from him. "The Justice Department are not involved."

That got his attention. He swung round to face her. "Why not?"

"Because there's no evidence that any of them took place. My father says if there is no evidence, they didn't happen."

"Your father's an utter fool."

"I believe he has a similar opinion of you, sir."

Grandpa George snorted at that, but he looked up at Kat with pale blue eyes, intense and demanding. "What makes you think someone is trying to kill you, despite the lack of evidence?"

Kat settled back into her chair and quickly described the Cayman rescue mission. As she talked, Grandpa's frown deepened. "So, it was only a defective piece of equipment prevented you from walking right into their trap."

"Yes. I keep meaning to talk to Father about the low grade equipment on Fleet issue, but since the only sub-spec item I'm intimately familiar actually saved my life, I'm on rather weak ground."

Grandpa George barked a laugh at that, but was straight back to 'business' the next second. "So what makes you so sure you were the target of that minefield?"

"I captured the ringleader's computer. Dee took it apart. She found a message saying the ship they wanted had been given the mission and to prepare the 'welcome.'"

"How could they know where to put this 'welcome'?"

"I did a check on the last seven rescue missions the Fleet has undertaken. All involved a night insertion into the bad-guys back yard. My commander was out to set some kind of record for the shortest time from drop-off to last shot fired. I think our doctrine has gotten a bit predictable, and someone set me up."

"Reasonable conclusion. And the second murder attempt?"

Kat described her trip up to the mining facility and the boat falling apart. "Dee has the fried shoot-bolt samples I salvaged from the boat. She's sending them to a lab she trusts for analysis."

"It could have just been an accident. Superconducting electro-magnetic fixings are pretty new. My yards have only been using them for the last two or three years. Boats and bridges, what a waste of clever technology!"

"Of the twelve thousand plus constructs that have been made to date, the six assigned to me appear to be the only ones with this little defect."

That got Grandpa George sitting on the edge of his seat. "So, who provided you with the boats?"

"Von Welf."

"Von Welf!" Grandpa exclaimed loudly.

"Von Welf," Kat repeated. "The mining facility was out of radio contact with everyone. A von Welf vessel happened to be leaving the inlet when I mysteriously received the miners' distress call. It didn't leave the inlet until I was out in the boat and had already modified the configuration twice."

"And the next time you changed the composition of the boat's components?"

"It would go pop," Kat snapped her fingers.

"Von Welfs." George Lennox roared as he shot from his chair.

"Who did you go to, to get the money when Louis was taken?"

Kat's question stopped Grandpa in his tracks. He retreated back to his chair. With a wave of his hand that took in everything out of the window, he said, "Why would I have to go to anyone for money?"

"Wealth is one thing, liquid assets are quite another. I've been through the archived accounts. My father came to you, but most of your money was in trust funds. Your brother Charles had the company pretty heavily invested in post war development and expansion projects. I don't think either of you could have provided my father with the money he needed."

"Didn't matter. Poor little Louis was dead before we received the ransom note."

"But neither you, nor my father knew that. I don't think the people who set up Louis's abductors had any idea they'd employed 'dumber' and 'dumbest' for the undertaking"

"Set up, not hired?"

"Grandpa, they wouldn't have gone to their deaths if they'd known anything significant. Louis's abductors didn't receive any up-front money, and neither did the punks in Cayman City. There are far too many similarities between the two incidents. Only the head honcho knew anything of consequence about the Cayman events, and he's conveniently died from a heart attack before he could start singing."

"Heart attack," Grandpa said slowly.

"Just like the truck driver that killed Lizzy Hervey-Severn," Kat threw across the desk.

Her grandfather looked like he'd been hit by a truck. Or more likely, was again seeing again the truck that hit him. "It was an accident," he whispered. "I saw the truck coming, but I couldn't get out of its way. I tried. Twenty years I've been seeing that truck in my dreams. I always think I can get out of the way. I never do." He shook his head. "I walked away, so did

Alexandra and Jim, but not Lizzy. They did an autopsy. There was nothing, no drugs, no alcohol, nothing in the truck driver's blood."

"Grandpa, they didn't take a blood sample until two hours after the crash. Even back then, they had illegal drugs that could be fully metabolised in that time, oxymetakaolin perhaps, or something similar."

"And von Welfs have always known their way around the drug underworld," Grandpa sighed. "Ernst-August the Sixth just happened to be visiting Nu New England when your brother was kidnapped. You know his son went to university here with your dad, even dated your mother once or twice."

"She never lets us forget. Insists I get to know his son."

He winced. "Von Welf offered me the money. Said we could work out the details later. Then the police located the farmstead and the manure pile with the broken breather unit protruding from it. I didn't need the money after all." He sighed again. "That's when I quit politics. You're too big a target out there. I quit the government and made sure I'd always have enough money to do what I needed to do, and fast. Enough money to build a wall around me so no one could get through. I told your father to quit too, but the fool runs for my old job instead."

"So you think the von Welfs *are* behind it all?"

"There's enough bad blood between them and both the Lennox and the Severn families. Jim was a great soldier, but every time he turned around during the post-war clean-up he was stepping on von Welfs. He closed down a couple of unauthorised operations in central Asia, Samarkand, I think it was, where the von Welfs had supposedly made significant investments. He also closed down part of their alleged drug running network, if you believe the rumours. They denied any involvement, of course!"

"What do you believe?"

"Jim believed he was closing in on the von Welfs, but he wasn't targeting or persecuting them specifically, they just happened to keep crossing his path over and over again. Go and see him too, ask him about it. But, as your father would no doubt point out, you couldn't prove any of it in a court of law, so some would say it never happened."

"I'm getting a bit tired of almost getting killed in circumstances that can't be proven in a court of law, Grandpa."

"Then steer well clear of the von Welfs!"

"Kind of hard to. I go wherever the Fleet sends me."

"Resign. Come and work for me here, in this tower. Nothing moves within fifteen kilometres that I don't know about and authorise. I've made myself a fortress of people who believe in what I'm doing, are well paid, and would die for me. What have you got?"

"Jack and Mike out there, until I go back on duty."

"You'd be safe here. We don't even send our school children out except on non-scheduled tours and with an armed escort. No better place to raise a child."

"Sounds good, but I don't have any children just now. When I do, I'll think about it."

"You should live so long."

"Grandpa, I intend on doing just that."

Goodwood, the HI sitting on Grandpa George's desk began to buzz.

"Kat," Safi announced softly in her ear, "I hope you will excuse my interruption, but Europe just announced that it is sending a large naval expeditionary force into the north Atlantic."

"What?" came from both sides of the desk. "Looks like it's a bit late to resign my commission," Kat swallowed.

"Good God, have the Europeans taken leave of their senses? A large and unauthorised formation in the north Atlantic is highly provocative, if not actual justification for war."

"I thought industry and commerce wanted a war, or at least a break-up of the old order," Kat goaded her grandfather, wondering what he'd say.

Grandpa George glared at Kat like she'd just failed the first grade. "Europe is Lennox Group's biggest trading partner. Why would I want to lose a very lucrative market? A war just messes up all my business plans. No businessman in his right mind could possibly want war."

Safi interrupted again. "The official line from Europe is that their fleet is moving to Flores, in the Azores. It's symbolic, the nearest piece of dry land to the mid-point between the two continents, to participate with the ABCANZ Federation in officially dissolving NATO."

"You don't need an expeditionary battle fleet to haul down a flag." He shook his head. "I really don't understand what this is all about. We've been allies and trading partners with Europe for hundreds of years. This fleet must be what they say it is, they can't want a war any more than we do, so why behave so provocatively?" He shook his head again. "Whatever Europe is trying to say, they're saying it all wrong."

"Excuse me for interrupting," Safi cut in, "All Fleet personnel have been recalled for duty." Kat had only stepped off the aircraft from Elmendorf six hours before. One day she might actually get more that forty-eight hours into her leave before being recalled to duty!

"Thank you, Safi." Kat looked at her grandfather, but said nothing. He just smiled, a sad smile, and offered her his hand. "Good luck," he said softly.

ONE : TWENTY

Three hours after leaving Lennox Tower Kat had repacked her kit and led Jack down the central stairs at Bagshot. A hastily contracted ocean liner was scheduled to depart Nu New England later that afternoon for the seven hundred nautical mile, thirty-four hour run to the Fleet's facility in Bermuda. It was apparently more cost effective to contract a single ocean liner for a few days than the multiple aircraft needed to return all the crews of the 1st Fleet's Fast-Attack and Hunter-Killer squadrons to their offshore base. If they pushed it, they could be back aboard the *Berserker* by early morning the day after tomorrow.

As Kat crossed the entrance hall, she found Land Force Troopers still positioned either side of the doors to the library, but the doors were now thrown wide open to facilitate a constant flow of Officers and messengers. She paused for a second. Yes, Grandpa Jim was in there, surrounded by Brigadiers and Commodores and civilians who must have ranked just as high. It looked like Aunty Dee at a workstation towards the back of the room, but Kat wasn't sure. The 'old guard' had assembled, so the situation must be serious. Trusting that the fate of humanity was in good hands, Kat continued towards for the main doors.

"Wait a minute there, Ensign," came from inside the library, in General James Severn's official 'command' voice. Kat kept walking; she wasn't in his chain-of-command. Pity the poor officer that was, and made the old general shout.

"I mean you, Ensign Severn. Halt."

Kat halted, then put down her kit bag. "I'll tell Monty to wait for you," said Jack and quickly left.

"Where are you heading?" Grandpa Jim asked as he came into range of his normal voice.

"Back to my ship," Kat answered; then because she

couldn't suppress the question, she said what every serving sailor or soldier was asking, "Is there really going to be a war?"

"Your dad has me, and a lot of other good people doing our damndest to see that there isn't," he said. They stood there, each measuring the hopes and fears in that statement; then Jim started gnawing on his lower lip.

"Listen, Kat, we're putting together an operational staff here. The Fleet's also re-commissioning just about anything that can float. Hang around here for a week or so, we might be able to get you an XO's slot on a frigate or something."

Kat forced her breathing to stay even. Was Grandpa trying to get her out of harm's way? Was the situation really that bad? "Is the European formation really expeditionary rather than just a ceremonial or political statement?"

The old General gave her one of his patented shrugs, "God only knows. Their politicians aren't talking to us, at least not to the likes of me anyway. We have all the usual intel and surveillance sources working overtime, not to mention hum-int being fed from our Nu Britannia based assets. And we still don't know which European state is calling the shots. Probably the European Union, if you want me to speculate, but we have no official confirmation. In fact, we don't know much more than what you hear from the talking heads on the news broadcasts. I'm beginning to think that 'intelligence' is just a grand word for *glorified guess work!*" He scowled at the lack of real information amongst all the noise.

Kat took a deep breath and shook her head. "General, Grandpa, the *Berserker* might be small, but she's one of the best we have. When you send her where you need her most, you're going to need her to be the best she can. I might be new, but I'm a hell of a lot better prepared than any 'just commissioned' Ensign could ever be." Then she shrugged. "Besides, it's my turn."

"Be careful, kid."

"You mean don't do anything you wouldn't do?"

Grandpa Jim swallowed hard on that. "Don't do anything stupid. Our family have all the medals gathering dust that we need. Remember, half of what you read about us in the historical data-records isn't true."

"Maybe poorly researched," Kat answered, "but not lies.

Next time I'm home, why don't you and Grandpa George talk me through the details on a few of the more interesting stories?"

"It's a deal, Ensign. You come home, and we'll have a long talk." And Kat discovered that Ensigns could hug Generals, and if the Troopers standing guard or anyone thought any different, well, they could just drop and give the old General fifty press-ups.

Kat and Jack got onto the last of several lined-up civilian buses that took the assembled military personnel from the cruise-liner terminal along to the dock-side for departure. It was standing room only on the short ride, but Kat managed to grab the last empty seat, only to then give it up when Captain Duvall, her Squadron Commander, climbed on at the very last moment. Standing in a very full aisle, Kat remembered reading that it was illegal to move people in this kind of vehicle with more than six standing. Today there were more like twenty six standing, crammed into any available space. Rules were forgotten today. That was when it hit her. All safe bets were off; someone really expected a war . . . and soon.

The contracted *Carnival Adventure* had been hastily converted from civilian cruise-liner into troopship. Kat was lucky; although she was allocated to a tiny cabin, it did at least have a single-bed. The two Ensigns across the hall were none too happy to be sharing a double. Nevertheless, there was also a camp bed in the corner of Kat's tiny space. Thankfully it was only going to be for a couple of nights. She waited to see who her room-mate was going to be and couldn't suppress a grin when Chief Petty Officer Martinez showed up at her door.

"I didn't know home was Nu New England for you too?"

"It isn't," Martinez said, dropping her kit bag. "I'm a Texas City girl, but I was visiting my brother and his family." The Chief glanced around, her nose twitching like she was smelling something most unpleasant. "Hardly what I expected for a luxury cruise-liner."

"Crew quarters I guess. Probably just happy to keep boys and girls apart. This is a bit of a rush job."

"Yeah, suppose it is," the Chief shrugged, then frowned at the cot, "Which bed do you want, ma'am?"

"I'll take the camp bed. This is a twenty-two knot run all

the way; a younger back will handle it better."

The Chief gave Kat a canted scowl but didn't argue. As she stowed her gear, the Chief asked over her shoulder, "What you hearing about us going to war, ma'am?"

"Some good people are doing their best to see it doesn't come to that. What are you hearing?"

"I didn't have to pay for my beers last night. Lots of loudmouths saying it's time we showed those continental Europeans a thing or two. Of course, none of them are on this ship."

"But they're flocking to the recruiting offices?"

"I doubt it, most wouldn't pass the initial evaluation, either too old, too stupid, or not tall enough for their tonnage," Martinez chuckled, but then got serious. "I saw General Severn was back in town. He one of the good people you were talking about?"

"Wouldn't deny it to a friend, but wouldn't confirm it to an enemy," Kat dodged. She also didn't mention his offer of finding her a job on the staff.

"Your old man is doing the political two-step. I listened to him for five or six minutes last night, but couldn't work out if he was for or against us blasting the European fleet out of the water. Politicians!" Martinez said, shaking her head.

"He's just trying to build a consensus," Kat explained.

"He'd better do it quick. That European fleet is on its way."

Kat sat on the side of the bed. "This is crazy. Yes, Europe has a lot of big ships, some with very capable weapon-fits, but none of them have deployed in all-out-war since the big showdown thirty odd years ago. Back in university, I knew a kid from Nya Svealand. His dad ran a large timber logging operation. Once a year he and his workers would man two or three old warships, them and a thousand others, doing their annual bit of active duty. He said they would go aboard, make sure the engines still turned over, and check that all the weapon systems still lit green. God only knows what they'd do if any of it was red. Chief, this kid's dad was a reserve Commodore! Most of his factory's managers were Captains or Commanders. It's all a big show. If it came to a fight, the *Berserker* could probably slag three of four of those ships without breaking into a sweat."

"But ships just like those sat offshore and slagged whole cities in the last war, remember what we did to Shanghai? I don't want them sitting off Nu New England, not with my brother and his family on the receiving end."

"Your attention please. Please prepare for departure. We will be achieving speeds in excess of twenty knots in approximately thirty minutes. You are reminded that all external deck areas are off-limits whilst the ship is moving in excess of twenty knots for your safety," echoed down the contracted cruise-liner's corridors from the public address system.

"I'll help you get that camp-bed made up," Martinez offered. "Not a lot to do for the next day or so. I'd try and get as much sleep as you can, ma'am. I know Commander Ellis only too well. He'll push us all real hard when we get back aboard."

Kat followed the Chief's lead, catching up on her sleep, following the news, and reviewing the technical manuals on her bridge station. It had been a two hour flight going back from Bermuda to Nu New England, yet it took thirty-four hours to return by boat. And that wasn't going to be nearly fast enough for their skipper.

"What took you so long?" was Commander Ellis's predictable greeting as Kat and Jack reported to the *Berserker*'s bridge five minutes after coming aboard.

"Contracted liner could only make twenty-two knots," Kat offered, while taking her position at 'warfare systems.' "You know how slow these civilian vessels are, sir."

"So why didn't you two get out and push?" the XO asked. Kat suppressed a shake of the head. There were hard cases, and then there were nut cases.

Commander Ellis eyed Kat as she activated her station. "I'm a bit surprised you even bothered to join us, Ensign Severn. I figured you for a nice safe staff job somewhere."

Kat turned. "I was offered one, sir, but I declined."

The skipper raised an eyebrow a fraction and glanced at the XO. "So, you wanted to be on the best ship in the Fleet when the shooting starts."

"I told the General that he'd want the best ship to be the best it could possibly be when he needed it, sir."

"Acknowledged," the Commander said with a nod. He actually seemed to be enjoying himself in Kat's presence for a change. "I liked the Insert Report I got from Elmendorf."

"Colonel Hepburn sends his compliments, sir."

"Good man. Got a bad rap. He reports that you handled yourself well in some pretty tough fire-fights."

"I did my best, sir."

"You're ready to smash those European warships heading across the north Atlantic then?"

Kat took a deep breath. "Yes, sir," she said, giving the short, crisp answer the skipper wanted. Any comment to avoid war was out of place on a fighting ship's bridge, and especially under this Commander!

"To your stations then, if you please." Ellis ordered.

Kat was already at the warfare systems station, next to the helm, both just in front of the Commander. Jack took post at his bridge station, monitoring the ships reactor and other electrical and mechanical systems.

Commander Ellis brought together offensive, defensive, navigation and damage control into a series of simulations; hostiles appeared just within the extremes of the *Berserker*'s sensors. When Kat asked how they got there, the Commander snapped, "It's my job to present you the targets. It's your job to neutralise, or better still, destroy them!" So Kat, Jack and a new Ensign at the helm, Morgan, went through each simulation Ellis presented them with. Twisting and turning, dodging and charging until all the hostiles were sent to the bottom or got blasted into atoms. Kat's hands danced over the controls.

"And now we do it all over again."

And so they did. Away from the bridge, Kat knew the rest of the crew would be going through every possible drill, from a hull breach to reactor containment failure. Only once did she hear 'abandon ship'; that one obviously wasn't very popular with the skipper. On the bridge, Kat went through problem after problem, ascertaining which targets had hostile intentions and getting their missiles or torpedoes away first to thwart them.

It was very late by the ship's clock when Kat went looking for her cabin.

*   *   *

Reveille was at zero-five early the next morning. Kat showered, dressed, gulped down breakfast and was on the bridge by zero-six-hundred. And the simulations began again. "You're taking too long to engage them. I want them neutralised within fifteen minutes of them first appearing on our long range sensors. Morgan, be more aggressive. Severn, you're waiting for the computer to present firing solutions, use more initiative, anticipate."

Easier said than done, Kat could have said. Was the target closing or opening the range? But she kept her mouth shut and spent a bit more time evaluating the targets' behaviour in the next simulation. Yes, the skipper had the targets tactics programmed to be just as gung-ho as he was. The next two sims both had the enemy closing fast. Kat was right on target with her first shot next time.

"Good shooting, Ensign. You have to think like they do."

"If you assume they're always going for your throat sir." Kat risked.

"If they aren't, Ensign, then it's their funeral. There's only one rule in war, hit them first, hit them hard, anything else just makes for more widows on our side."

"Yes, sir," Kat answered again, the only answer she knew Ellis would ever accept.

"When are we going to intercept the European fleet, sir?" Morgan asked.

"As soon as we get orders to do so, Ensign," the skipper assured him.

"I hear their older ships are taking it real slow." Morgan added.

"Probably because their maintenance isn't what it could be," the XO grinned. "They had to cut speed down to five knots just to stop them falling apart!"

"But it only needs one or two to find their way across to Nu New England and start shooting," the Commander pointed out.

Of course, Kat thought, Europe could have ordered her ships down to five knots to give the politicians more time to sort this whole mess out. She kept that thought to herself; she was on a warship, and its job was to defend all Federation territory in the North Atlantic. The skipper was making sure that the tip of this spear was as sharp as he could possibly get it. Kat wasn't about to do anything to blunt it.

At noon, while the crew was at lunch, Ellis ordered Jack to begin the conversion to sub-surface configuration by raising the nacelles on both sides until they were on the same plane as the main hull. "Severn, look over his shoulder. I want this right first time." Jack worked slowly and methodically as Kat joined him at his station. He went down the check list without a word from Kat. This reconfiguration was a standard procedure; it had been done often enough that it should go flawlessly. Preparation done, Jack reported. "Ready, sir."

The skipper nodded to the Chief at the comms station. "All hands, stand-by for hull reconfiguration," he announced. "All departments report in once reconfiguration complete."

"Execute hull reconfiguration on my mark," Ellis ordered. "Mark." Jack started tapping away at his bridge-station. With most of the crew at lunch, there was little risk. The *Warrior* class fast attack corvettes were the first to employ moveable outer nacelles in their design, and although there had been issues initially, reconfiguration was, in theory, a standard procedure. The two outer hulls or nacelles, apart from providing extra stability at high surface speeds, housed the water-jet propulsion units when silent sub-surface running was required. In their highest position, in the same plane as the main hull, the main hull sat lower into the water when still on the surface and this reduced their speed considerably, but once submerged, and if combined with the main engines, they provided unequalled underwater speed. Lower the nacelles to their mid point and the main hull sat higher in the water when on the surface, causing less drag and higher speeds, and finally there was a little used 'low' setting that raised the front of the main hull right out of the water. This configuration, combined with all engines and propulsion units gave them a surface speed in excess of 45 knots.

"Now the *Berserker's* a real warship," the Commander growled happily. "Chief, have all departments reported in that reconfiguration was successful?"

"Yes, sir, the board is green."

Ellis stood. "Bridge team, take thirty minutes, get some

lunch. You've handled those easy problems fairly well. Now let's see how you get on with a few more complicated ones."

Wondering how the simulations could possibly get any harder, Kat went to check her cabin. With most of the crew at lunch she passed quickly through the narrow passageways. She stopped briefly to check how bad the upheaval her cabin always seemed to endure during a hull reconfiguration was, then took a quick walk through the enlisted women's quarters. There were no major problems, although a couple of the girls seemed a little apprehensive, like they knew that this time it was for real.

Kat arrived late for lunch. A ship as small as the *Berserker* had no wardroom; the Officers shared their meals with everyone else. Most of the crew had already eaten, the exceptions being the bridge crew and, apparently, the engineering team. The XO had commandeered one table, as far away from the hot-plates as was physically possible. The ship's Engineering Officer, Lieutenant Carlin, surrounded by his Chiefs and team was at a table about as far away from the XO as the compartment permitted. Jack had joined the engineering staff and was undoubtedly into some deep technical discussion. Suppressing a sigh, Kat headed for an empty space next to the XO. With the Executive Officer at one elbow, she soon had the ship's Communications Officer at the other. The XO, Communications and the Engineering Officer all held the same rank, but the XO held the senior post, with all three normally working an eight hour shift on the bridge, seven days a week, every week, as the Duty Officer. Kat and the other ensigns would also be standing watches, supposedly shadowing the Duty Officer. That was how it was meant to be if the *Berserker* had had her full wartime establishment of fifteen officers, instead of the nine currently aboard, as per her peacetime complement. *Right!* On their last routine patrol Kat had stood watch as the Duty Officer and had on occasion been relieved by Chiefs. She wondered if it would change this time out.

"So, things got exciting in Anchorage?" the XO started as soon as Kat sat down.

"They had a bandit problem," Kat said simply.

"And they don't have one anymore?" the Communications Officer asked as he joined them.

Kat measured her response carefully as she sampled the

meal before her. "We took out a few bad elements. Fed a lot more hungry elements. Problem solved."

"That's putting a fine twist on what I hear was a major fire-fight," the Executive Officer insisted.

"It got plenty hot for a while, despite all the snow," Kat agreed.

"So, are you looking forward to it getting hot here?" the Comms Officer leered.

"I'd like to hope cooler heads prevail," she said to her food.

"God save us from cooler heads!" the Comms Officer snapped back.

"This has been coming for years," the XO said. "Bureaucrats in continental Europe have been leading us around for far too long, always us doing their dirty work. It's time we did what we want to do, not what suits their agendas."

Kat didn't need to answer that, so she concentrated on eating. The XO filled the silence with every familiar argument for war. Rationally, to Kat, they added up to nothing. But hadn't Professor Barrett warned her class that it was a rare war that had a solid basis in reality? "Emotions, watch for the emotions that inflame," he'd said. Kat had dutifully taken notes, but she hadn't been one of the believers that day. Just now, it was starting to look like the old prof did actually know what he was talking about. Lunch finished, she stood and picked up her tray.

"Ready to sink those European warships?" the XO demanded.

"I'll shoot whatever the skipper puts in range," Kat said.

"Good, Ensign, Very good," the XO said with a broad grin.

Commander Ellis was still on the bridge when Kat returned, having taken a equally brief lunch in his adjacent day-cabin. He had simulations waiting that made those of the morning seem decidedly easy. It was a long afternoon that extended well into the evening.

When the Commander finally released them, Kat quickly found her cabin. Chief Martinez was already snoring, reminding Kat how much she hated sharing a room; the *Berserker* was a cramped ship even in peacetime.

*   *   *

At zero-six-hundred the next morning Kat was back at her bridge station. The skipper was already there, hunched over his own station, apparently oblivious to his bridge team as they arrived, powering up their positions, and awaiting his 'pleasure.'

Ellis punched his ship-wide comm-link. "This is Commander Ellis. The Fast-Attack Squadron of the 1st Fleet has been ordered to the Azores. Once there, we will rendezvous with other assets from the ABCANZ Fed's 1st, 3rd and 5th Fleets and move to counter this threat from the European states. As of now, I consider this ship to be on a war footing. Ellis out."

"Safi," Kat whispered, "Update. What's going on?"

"Media reports suggest that the combined fleet of the European nations is just under one hundred major surface vessels in composition. They intend to meet in the Azores to officially mark the dissolving of NATO. The islands of the Azores are almost uninhabited, although the Southern European Alliance's military does maintain a small maritime surveillance facility on Flores, the most westerly of the island group. An unusually high number of internationally recognised safe-transit-routings start and terminate in the area, making it one of the busiest shipping nexuses in the north Atlantic."

"Cut the standard data babble, Safi. Tell me something I don't already know!" Kat ordered, her gut knotting. "This is supposed to be a peaceful meeting, right?"

"Commentaries and news reports run the full spectrum, from war to peace, to high-stakes gamble, usually reflecting established editorial positions and past commentaries."

"And what does our Prime Minister say?"

"He hails it as peace in our time."

Kat remembered that quote from somewhere, searched her own memory, found it, and didn't like it.

"Helm," the Commander announced, breaking Kat's train of thought, "move us from within the harbour, get us into open water. Let's start you three on some more demanding simulations." So Kat got down to business and it stayed that way through the rest of the day. Arms, hands and head all aching, she stumbled to her bunk and slept, fully clothed where she fell.

*   *   *

Next morning, Chief Martinez was brushing her teeth as Kat awoke. "You slept right through reveille," the Chief advised through the foam in her mouth. "I thought you could use a few more minutes. You know your hands were moving in your sleep?"

"I was dreaming battle scenarios," Kat admitted.

"Well, you were at it full bore."

Kat stripped, removed Safi and stumbled to the shower and was under the spray for several minutes before she noticed the change in the ship. Grabbing a towel, she asked the Chief, "Do you recall us diving, or entering a Safe-Transit-Routing?"

"No, and I'd know if we had during the night, No matter how tired I am the change in air-pressure always wakes me up."

"Safi, did the bridge announce us diving or entering a STR during the night, or did I miss one yesterday?"

"It was not formally announced as per SOP's, but the ship dived and entered an STR at zero-eight-seventeen yesterday morning. We are now one hundred and twelve nautical miles off the Avalon Peninsula, Newfoundland."

Kat lifted her hand, estimating the vibration. "Twenty-five knots, maybe a bit more."

"Twenty-eight, ma'am. I thought you bridge types could sense it."

"Skipper must have done this when I was deep in a sim. No announcement either."

"I heard there's supposed to be a war on or something," the Chief said dryly. "Might account for Fleet Command ordering something a bit less predictable, and peacetime SOP's being disregarded."

"Must be," Kat agreed. The skipper had put them on a war footing, she had to stop thinking peacetime drills. They'd packed them into the buses to take them to the dockside, and then into the *Carnival Adventure* to get them back to Bermuda. So why not stop using Standard-Operating-Procedures? Nothing about this was even close to 'standard.'

Kat's day vanished, again lost in battle simulations. Targets were moving faster, jinking and zigzagging. There were friendly ships now as well to keep track of. The simulated ocean became far more cluttered as coastlines, rocks and sandbanks entered into the exercises, altering their attack approach vectors due to shallow seas. "Damn it, Morgan, you just accelerated us into a sand-bank. We'll be a sitting duck if we get jammed onto one."

"Sorry, sir. I identified the designated target, and I went straight for it."

"That's the right stuff when we're in deep water, but battles, real battles take place where there's something worth fighting for. Nine out of ten sea battles in the last war were within a hundred kilometres of dry land. Get used to working in the shallows Ensign, or I'll get someone who can."

"Yes, sir."

"And, Severn, why'd you miss them as they went by?"

"Rate of closure for a firing solution needed to be re-calculated following the simulated sandbank collision, and exceeded the capacity of the system, sir."

"I didn't ask why the computer didn't give you a shot; I asked why you didn't take a shot."

Because she didn't want to waste their limited resource of very expensive Marlin torpedoes or Harlequin missiles, but that wasn't the answer the skipper wanted. "No excuse, sir."

"That answer may keep me from chewing your tail, Ensign, but it won't keep the enemy from blasting this ship open and spilling your shipmates into the ocean. You see a shot, you take a shot. Let me worry about our armament expenditure. Do you understand?"

"Yes, sir." Kat also noticed there were no euphemisms now. European ships were referred to as *enemy*, pure and simple. It was getting harder in her fatigue-fogged brain to remember that Grandpa Jim said he was doing his upmost to keep this all from happening. Kat's hands were trained. They were operating the ships weapon and warfare systems all day; no wonder they remained animated as she slept. Like a well trained automaton, she was reacting with little or no thought. That was what Ellis wanted; that was what Kat gave him. The quick smiles he rationed her were worth it.

She didn't get many smiles for the rest of the afternoon as shallow water and sandbanks swung the simulated *Berserker* here and there, giving her damn poor shots. Kat was a zombie as she made her way to her cabin that night. Surprisingly Martinez was still up.

"Crew's a bit edgy," the Chief said as Kat peeled off her sweat-soaked uniform. Martinez took the dark grey one-piece ship-suit from her and ran it through the washer-dryer unit. "The skipper hasn't posted the ships routing on the mess-hall screen."

"Once again Chief, that's a peacetime practice," Kat said as she removed Safi, placing her HI onto her bunk-side locker. "We're on a war footing."

"I know, but isn't that pushing it a bit far, I mean, who are we going to tell?"

"You know Ellis far better than I do Chief, but from where I'm standing, I wouldn't put anything past him at the moment."

"Safi, can you establish what routing are we using?"

"We are approximately halfway along Safe-Transit-Routing BM Nine."

"Nine!" Kat was fully awake. The first five STRs out of Bermuda were the ones most frequently used, and were all flagged green. Nine was never used. "What's Nine flagged as?"

"Black" Safi responded.

Safe Transit Routings had been re-established about five years after the war ended. Internationally recognised, they kept shipping away from areas of known danger, such as wrecks, pollution, radioactive or chemical contamination, and excessive weed growth. Civilian vessels only ever used green flagged routes at speed, and amber at slower rates. The military was a bit more daring and would traverse amber flagged routings at speed and red routes at a slower rate. Both stayed away from black. Black routes were without doubt a contradiction-in-terms, there was nothing safe about a black route and extreme caution was always advised, and therefore they were never used. Never used in normal circumstances, but 'war' certainly didn't constitute 'normal circumstances.'

"BM Nine is flagged as black!" Kat exclaimed.

"We are on a war footing," Chief Martinez whispered.

"Safi, project the shortest course, leaving via Bermuda's STR designated BM Nine to the Azores. Display"

A three-dimensional projection shot from Safi to dance

mid way between Kat and Martinez. BM Nine would take them on a course away from Bermuda towards Iceland. About two-thirds along they would have to change onto another STR to bring them back towards the Azores.

"The ship will arrive in the Azores on STR AZ Fourteen. That too has not been recently used and is also flagged black." Safi advised.

"What's the shortest STR between these two points? Kat asked. "BM One," said Safi, enhancing the projection with a green line.

"And from the Azores to Nu New England?"

"AZ Four, also flagged green." Another green line joined the first.

"Show our projected route," ordered Kat.

A black line added this extra detail to the display.

"Assuming we arrive submerged, we are most likely going to come-in right behind the European fleet's position." Martinez frowned.

"And well away from our own assets, with little chance of mutual support," Kat finished. "But we're assuming that we'll use STRs. We could just go 'off-piste' and do our own thing. Safi, estimate times and speeds required to meet these course predictions. Alert me of any further changes in our current course, speed or depth."

"Good thinking, ma'am. But even if this is our intended route, what does it all actually mean?" asked the Chief.

"I have absolutely no idea," Kat admitted with a shrug. She also had to admit she was tired, wasn't going to get much sleep, and desperately wanted a lot more than she was likely to get. She would think about this further in any down-time she got tomorrow. Right, like she'd been getting a lot of that lately.

Kat drifted off into a deep sleep within seconds of hitting the pillow. Her dreams were vivid. No matter how she fought, the European ships were always first with their salvos. No matter how fast she got her torpedoes away, the enemy's weapons were always quicker, tearing apart the *Berserker*. Time after time she watched Jack, Martinez and the rest of the crew as they drowned in the churning inky black waters of the Atlantic.

ONE : TWENTY-ONE

Next morning, breakfast wolfed down, she was heading for the bridge when Corporal Torres found her. "Excuse me ma'am, the skipper hasn't posted our course. This route doesn't fit with any of our previous trips out. Some of the lads are kind of worried."

"Trust me," Kat told the Corporal who'd inserted with her to rescue the little girl only six weeks before. *Six weeks*. It felt like a lifetime had passed since then. "This ship is heading for the Azores. The skipper is just taking a different route. You've just got to stop thinking like it's still a peacetime operation."

"Is it really going to be war then, ma'am?" The Corporal's face was a mixture of emotions, hard to read, leaving Kat to guess what answer he wanted.

"The Prime Minister and a lot of good people are doing everything they can to see that this ends peacefully. But you know our Commander. If it comes to a fight, he wants the *Berserker* to be the best there is in the Fleet."

"Yes, that's the skipper. Thank you, ma'am." He saluted, and was gone, and Kat was late for the bridge, but she suspected what she had just said would be half way around the ship before lunchtime.

"So glad you could join us," Commander Ellis said as Kat slipped into her seat at zero-six-hundred exactly. "Ensign Byrne, you've been getting off too easy. Morgan and Severn haven't let the ship take enough hits. I'm putting you on your own set of sims. Morgan, you're still not using the shorelines and shallows to our advantage," he paused. "We operate independently, forget about staying in formation with the rest of the Squadron. Push it. Work it through. Severn, you're still waiting too long for the computer to offer you a firing solution. Think ahead of the damn machine. I know you've got the killer instinct, use it."

Ellis drove them hard all day. He was not pleased when Kat missed two shots; one when the *Berserker* made an actual course adjustment and not a simulated one. Safi's whispered notification distracted Kat just long enough for her to miss the shot, despite having 'target lock.' "Ensign, you took three minutes to set our weapon systems up for that shot, then you went and missed the optimum. Damn it Severn, that should never have happened."

"Sorry, sir. Our change of course distracted me for a second. It won't happen in battle."

"You bet it won't. Take a break, all of you. XO, Comms, my day cabin, now."

"Yes, sirs" answered him.

Kat and Morgan dropped down a deck and aft to the Mess area. Kat wrapped her hands around a hot mug, willing the warmth to soften the knots in her fingers and palms of her hands.

"Bet you can't wait to get some real European ships in our sights. I'm sick of these simulations, not feeling the ship responding to the helm. Let's get this on for real!" Morgan crowed.

"We're not at war yet," Kat pointed out.

"What's the matter, you like those continental Europeans? They've been pushing us around for far too long. Before the war it was bureaucrats in Brussels; since the war it's been more of the same from Rhinestadt and Nu Paris. It's about time we followed our own agendas and not theirs."

"So we show them the door and take off on our own. You don't need to go to war for that, I can assure you."

"You think they'll let us just walk away? We're the biggest contributor; they'd be screwed without us."

"But a war with Europe is going to leave a lot of ordinary people dead."

"What's the matter, Severn, you afraid?"

"Morgan, have you ever had a loaded weapon pointed at you?"

"No." That let some air out of him.

"Well, when you have, two or three times, I'll buy you a beer and we can compare notes. Until then, shut the hell up." Kat terminated any further debate, putting down her rapidly cooling coffee. "We need to get back," she snapped.

The skipper cut them loose early that evening. "Have some down time, get a good meal, take a long shower. Get some rest. We'll be arriving at the Azores at zero-nine-hundred tomorrow. Life might get somewhat interesting after that."

Kat headed for her cabin. "Safi, what transit-routing will effect a zero-nine-hundred arrival in the Azores?"

"As predicted, STR AZ Fourteen," the computer answered.

"Have you picked up any news?"

"No, we have been submerged for the last three-and-a-half days at our maximum operating depth. I have been unable to obtain any updates."

The entire squadron was following one another, at speed, and submerged down the STR. Thankfully, using a black flagged routing meant there would be almost no risk of running into any other shipping coming in the opposite direction.

"Kat," Safi said, "you asked me to conduct my own searches and let you know if I find anything that does not match a pattern I am familiar with."

"Yes."

"Immediately after the Comms Officer met with Commander Ellis, he loaded some new routines, that although currently dormant, I am unable to discern their purpose."

"Something that will put us on a war footing?" Kat asked.

"I have a list of all systems and routines to be loaded when a state of war is declared. These are not part of that sequence. I am unable to effect any interface with this software."

"But it's not active?"

"It is currently inactive," Safi confirmed.

"Let me know as soon as it starts doing something."

"I certainly will."

Kat rubbed her eyes; trying to rub away the exhaustion. Her brain felt half dead. All this had to mean something. Why would her father or Grandpa Jim order a Fast-Attack Squadron to take this roundabout way to the Azores? Why would they want their best ships arriving behind the European Fleet?

Assuming the European ships had already arrived, they should have cruised over to greet the ABCANZ fleet and undertaken whatever symbolic ceremonial activity they intended to do. Kat had a mental image of Admirals, Generals, even a politician or two, saluting as flags got hauled down.

A shower didn't help. She even forgot to remove Safi. Like a high-value watch, her HI was manufacturer guaranteed to be immersion proof to a depth of two hundred metres; however Kat didn't routinely tempt fate with her most valuable asset. She stumbled, naked and exhausted onto her bunk and promptly found sleep.

"Ma'am, are you still awake?" Martinez asked her a few seconds later when she entered the cabin.

"Only just. Is something wrong?"

"Nothing, I guess. What you told Corporal Torres, good words. I think it dumped about ten tonnes of fear off this boat."

"Thanks," Kat said, pulling the covers over herself.

"Word is, we're going to get there early tomorrow."

"Yes, that's correct." Kat didn't want to wake up any further.

"You know which STR we're using?"

"Looks like the one my HI predicted, AZ Fourteen."

"So we're going to arrive right in the middle, if not behind the European fleet. How do you think they're going to take that?"

"How should I know?" Kat barely kept her growing irritation out of her voice.

"I sure hope there aren't any overzealous weapon's operators on their ships. Some of their ships might be old, but they have guns that are good out past 30 klicks not to mention anti-ship missiles and torpedoes, and we're almost certainly going to be well within range of all of it."

Kat blinked and turned over. "We certainly will be."

"I know our Marlin torpedoes are good for twenty-five klicks at top speed, as is the 127mm gun and the Harlequin's can take out a ship at a hundred, so we must be able give as good as we get?"

"Chief, stop worrying. They won't be hanging around an STR exit that hasn't been used in God knows how long, on the off chance we might have used it. The European ships will have probably sailed over to meet our big ships. Some smart Quartermaster will have brought along a couple of barges of beer, and sailors from both fleets will be having a few drinks while Admirals and politicians stand around making polite small-talk."

"I sure hope so ma'am."

"I thought you were up for a live shoot?"

"Be nice to know all these years of training were actually for some practical purpose, but ma'am, a war between us and Europe, that isn't going to be good for anyone."

"Get some sleep, Chief. We all have to be at our best tomorrow." Kat rolled back over and tried to go back to sleep, but tomorrow's tactical situation kept floating around in her head. *What if some twitchy weapons operator in the European fleet launched something at the ABCANZ 1st Fleet's Fast-Attack Squadron? Well, this was what the* Warrior *class were designed for, was it not?* "The rapid movement of a vessel into a position of greatest advantage, to enable the exploitation of any enemy weakness, whilst avoiding enemy threats," was how Kat roughly remembered the official Fleet doctrine, although she preferred the analogy of the boxer; "being fast enough on his feet to avoid the opponents blows until the opportunity presented itself to deliver the all important knock-out punch." But this was all way above her pay grade. Captain Duvall and Commander Ellis could sort it all out; this was nothing for a lowly Ensign to worry about.

"Twenty seconds until we surface," Ensign Morgan announced.

"Severn, I want a full tactical display with ranges and bearings fifteen seconds after we surface," Ellis ordered.

"Yes, sir" Kat said and checked her board. All range-finders were on-line: laser, optical, radar and sonar. They showed the rest of the squadron in-line ahead of them. *Templar*, Captain Duvall's ship, led *Spartan, Samurai, Ranger, Praetorian, Highlander* and *Gladiator*. Commander Ellis was far from pleased that the *Berserker* now occupied the rear position.

"Are we in formation?" he asked Morgan.

"Within 150 metres, sir," the Helm reported back.

"Good, keep us there."

Kat watched the seconds until surfacing . . . three, two, one. There was the usual disorientation in her inner ear as the air pressure balanced. Parts of her board blinked red for a fraction of a second before returning to green, as receivers got no response to the various search signals they had emitted only micro-seconds earlier.

Her board showed more real targets than Kat had ever seen in any simulation.

The Squadron quickly formed into a wedge-shaped deployment. The *Templar*, in command, took point, with three corvettes echeloned out to the right, the flank nearest to the European fleet, while another three made up the left side. *Berserker* remained back, in a key, central position, ready to fill any gaps or exploit any opportunities. Kat took that all in at-a-glance, but it was the combined fleet of the European states that made her fight to keep her mouth closed and her bowels and bladder under control.

Huge capital ships, heavily armoured against torpedoes and anti-ship missiles, were arranged in eight rows, each twelve ships long, gleaming in the early morning sunshine. The eight European Nations, the European Union, Southern European Alliance, The Balkan Alliance, The Nu Habsburg Reich, Turkey, the Ukraine, the Kalmar Union and the Lublin Union had all sent their twelve most capable ships to participate. Without a moment's hesitation, Kat's hands went through the drills, establishing range and bearing, correlating that with her own ship's movement and began seeking firing solutions. The European ships remained at a steady five knots; they did not manoeuvre, did not stray from line ahead. In ten seconds Kat had it all displayed.

When orders came from the *Templar*, assigning the *Berserker* four specific targets, it took Kat less than twenty additional seconds to identify them, establish distance, and assign one to each of the *Berserker's* already loaded torpedo tubes. No more simulations. This time it was for real.

The Mk 67 'Marlin' was an underwater missile of unparalleled ability. Still referred to as a 'torpedo' throughout the Fleet, it was pre-programmed before launch. Technological advances in smart internal guidance systems and target seeking software, combined with high speeds provided the Marlin with a one-hundred-percent kill probability if ever used against non-military shipping. However, the similar advances in torpedo counter-measure technology used by most modern warships, such as guidance jamming, Over-Pressure-Pulsing, electro-acoustic decoy signatures and alike had virtually negated all the Marlin's clever technology.

Behind Kat, the bridge hatch opened, and the nine-man Land Force's detachment filed in, taking up positions against the bridge's rear bulkhead. In full chameleon body armour, they looked as out of place as Kat had been at Lennox Tower in sweatshirt and shorts. Commander Ellis nodded at the Sergeant, then tapped his comm-link.

"All hands, this is Commander Ellis. Today, we show continental Europe what the ABCANZ Federation is made of. For too long they have called the shots, but here, today, we throw that aside. I have been informed that a state of war now exists between the ABCANZ Federation and all European states. You have your orders. The *Berserker* is the best in the Fleet. Let's show them what we can do. Ellis, out."

With a tight, proud grin, Ellis turned to Morgan. "Close with our assigned targets." Now it was Kat's turn to get the full intensity of Commander Ellis's attention. "Severn, you may engage with Marlin torpedoes when the enemy is at twenty-five kilometres."

"Yes, sir," came automatically from both the Helm and Kat.

Without thought, her hands went into motion, checking targets, verifying the speed and vector of closure. The European ships didn't alter speed or course in reaction to the arrival of the fast-attack squadron. They were making it easy.

Easy? Too easy!

As Kat's fingers raced over the board, her mind raced as well. *War! We are going to war! What had changed the Prime Minister's mind? What could make Grandpa Jim give up on a peaceful solution to this mess? Where was a media update when you needed it?* "Safi, get me a news feed, now" she whispered. With all these ships here, there had to be at least a dozen media groups broadcasting these events in real-time.

"All channels are jammed," Safi reported in her earpiece.

"Jammed! Who's jamming?"

"*Templar* is jamming all traffic to and from the Squadron."

"Even on the command net?" That certainly wasn't Standard-Operating-Procedure, even in war-time!

"On all channels," Safi confirmed. Kat bit her lower lip. She was about to go to war. About to attack Europe's combined fleet! And for the first time in her life, she knew virtually nothing about what has happening. No, she knew the most important data there was. She knew her father, and her grandfather. Would they do this?

"Safi, tap into the ship's message traffic, there's got to be some explanation to these orders." Kat had never been one to do what she was told, at least not until the 'bigger picture' was explained. And this certainly needed explaining!

"Attempting."

"Sir," the Comms Officer's high pitched voice got the skipper's attention immediately. "Someone is trying to gain unauthorised access into our communications log."

"From where?"

"From within this ship, sir."

"Isolate the source," Ellis ordered. "I want to know who it is."

"Safi, stop," Kat whispered through tight lips.

"Sergeant Jones," Ellis ordered.

"Yes, sir," the big Australian sergeant acknowledged, snapping to attention.

"Prepare to dispatch a team to locate this saboteur. You may shoot on sight, and shoot to kill," the skipper growled.

"Yes, sir. Corporal Torres, you and two others,"

Torres signalled two troopers, who moved with him towards the hatch, ready to respond.

"Comm, update," Ellis demanded.

"Access was repelled, sir. Whoever it was has dropped out again."

"Let me know the second it comes back."

"Safi, what happened?" Kat whispered. "I thought Dee gave you everything you needed to hack into almost anything."

"She did." Safi almost sounded hurt by the rebuff. "But the *Berserker*'s net is being monitored by Checkpoint Security. I think it's the software I told you about last night."

"Never heard of them."

"They're a small company based in Rhinestadt that don't normally retail outside the European Union and Russia."

Rhinestadt, von Welf's home city. What was non-standard European software doing on an ABCANZ ship about to go to war?

"Range to targets?" enquired Ellis.

"Forty-five klicks, sir" Kat reported with the part of her that was still the *Berserker's* Warfare Systems Officer. The other ships in their formation began to spread out. Kat checked her assigned targets. She had a column lead . . . that would be the nation's flagship . . . and the fourth, seventh and ninth ships behind it.

"Warfare Officer, status," the Commander demanded.

"All four tubes are loaded with Mk 67 Marlin acoustic homing torpedoes, sir. Torpedoes are set to high speed, with proximity and contact detonation, and maximum yield warheads. Both Harlequin racks are deployed awaiting targeting data as back-up," her mouth was almost too dry to talk.

"Immediate reload once torpedoes are away. Target the twelfth ship in the same line. We'll show the rest of the squadron how the *Berserker* can hit five targets with four tubes."

"Yes, sir" said Kat, her fingers moving to comply with the orders.

Something is wrong here! A voice yelled in her head. Those warships aren't expecting an attack. Is my father really ordering a surprise attack? Would Grandpa Jim do this? Kat couldn't answer that. Did Grandpa George give President Kwashaka any chance at all? No. But these ships held sailors and troopers just like them.

"Safi, can you pick up any external communications?"

"Nothing."

Would Grandpa Jim, who went up Table Mountain, fight like this? Would her father? They were Severn's. They would *never* give orders like these. *So what are you going to do, kid?*

Jack says there are always choices. She glanced over her shoulder; he was looking wide-eyed at her. *Colonel Hepburn,*

I'm not seeing a lot of choices here! She checked the range, coming up on forty kilometres. Not much time to make a choice. So Katarina Sophie Louisa Severn, what are you going to do? We're here to keep this European fleet from reducing Nu New England to smoking ruins. This fleet is a threat. A threat? They're here, not doing anything threatening at all, just cruising at a low speed in review formation.

"Sir," she said softly, "there's something wrong."

"What?" Commander Ellis snapped.

Kat stood, fingers still resting lightly on her station. "This situation, sir."

"What situation?" Puzzle only slightly marred the Commander's confidence.

"This is a surprise attack, sir."

"Of course it is. You want to give that massed firepower a chance to open up on Nu New England? Sit down, Ensign, you have your orders."

"Yes, sir. But from whom? The Prime Minister doesn't have an underhand bone in his body. I know. He's my father. If he fights you, he does it up front and in your face. And these ships, sir. They're not making any effort to threaten our ships. Our nation."

"Targets at forty kilometres," the Helm said. Each passing second put them closer to releasing those torpedoes, closer to a massacre.

"What's the matter, Severn, don't you have the backbone for a fight? I should have known. Sergeant Jones, remove this coward from my bridge."

You just made a big mistake, Commander. You just made this personal. Kat turned to the Land Force detachment; not one of them had moved from the bulkhead. "Am I a coward? I inserted on a rescue mission with you all. Without me, half of you would have drowned on the initial insertion. Without me, all of you would have died in that minefield. I was the first in the door, and the first to the girl. Was that the act of a coward? Is standing here the act of a coward? Commander Ellis, these orders did not come from the Prime Minister, or the High Command. Where did they come from?"

"From the only people who have a right to give them, you spoilt brat," the Commander snarled, letting his temper give her the chance of legitimacy she hoped for. "Those orders came from people with enough guts to take what you money-grabbing types have wasted for too long. You have no honour, no duty. You and your kind have power, yet you don't use it. Well some of us know how to use power too. There's European power, sitting out there fat and stupid, and in a few minutes we're going to annihilate it. How's that for power?" Ellis raised his fist. "And then we'll blast them again. We've had enough of being boot-licking dogs, Severn. We're going to do what is right. Sergeant, shoot her."

Sergeant Jones stood against the bulkhead. He watched Ellis with widening eyes. Slowly, his M37 came up, into his shoulder. Kat found herself facing a loaded weapon . . . again. *Well, Toni, my Black Watch friend, I guess this is where family tradition leads a Severn.*

"Is this what you want to be, Sergeant Jones?" she said, strength rising from within her with each word. *Is this the inner strength that took Grandpa Jim and the Ladies from Hell up Table Mountain?*

She pointed at Commander Ellis. "That man suggests that you've been the boot-licking dogs of the rich and lazy. Are you ready to become the boot-licking dog of the power-mad and crazy? Because that, Sergeant Jones, is where you're heading. You might not like my father's politics, but ordinary citizens elected him. Do you think the Commander and his associates can do a better job? The same people that didn't spot the minefield before we inserted? You would think an Officer so keen to set a new record for the fastest rescue mission would mention a little thing like mines, wouldn't you. So what else isn't he telling us? Is this really what you want?" She moved her gaze from the inactive Sergeant to those around her. "Do you want to follow the orders of whoever just happens to be the biggest, baddest bastard around? Is this what you want for your children, your grandchildren? A world ripped apart by whatever warlord can pull together enough muscle to silence the opposition? There's no discussion here, these are men drunk on power. So drunk, they couldn't even run a good insertion, yet you're prepared to consider them running a government? I'll ask again, who gave the orders we're following? Comms, you've been in on this from the beginning, who's calling the shots?"

The Lieutenant at the communication station turned red. He nodded towards Commander Ellis, "Sir?"

"None of your damn business, Severn. People like you have been calling the shots for far too long. You can't even conceive that others might know what our nation needs better than you and your kin. Your kind have kept us suppressed for far too long, paying us a few bucks to risk our lives while you make millions in your sleep. Your time is up. Sergeant Jones, shoot her, shoot her now."

"Ma'am, I'm sorry," Sergeant Jones said, taking aim.

"Don't move a muscle," Corporal Torres cut in, his weapon level. "You so much as twitch, Sarge, and I'll stitch you into the bulkhead."

The XO was out of his seat. As he turned on the Land Force Troopers, a pistol appeared in his hand. Trooper Chang was already bringing up his rifle. "Put it down, sir, or so help me, you'll be dead before you can bring it to bear."

The Executive Officer sensibly froze.

"Drop that weapon, sir," Corporal Torres said. "I mean it XO, you too Sarge."

"You'll hang for this," Ellis screamed.

"Ma'am, I'm just a simple grunt, but I'd really like to know if I'm on the right side here?" Torres asked.

"Comms, open all standard ABCANZ frequencies." Kat ordered.

The Commander shook his head.

"Screw you," the Comms Officer said.

"Safi, slave the comms station to Jack's board. Then hack it. Fast."

"Comm station slaved. Hacking in progress."

"Jack?" she asked, knowing once more she was assuming he'd follow her, demanding he follow her, give her the proof that would prove to the crew that they should follow her. Would he back her once more?

His hands were already flying across his board. "I'm working on it," he snapped. "Damn, the *Templar* is putting out significant jamming on all frequencies." He glanced around the bridge crew. "Someone onboard that ship really doesn't want us getting anyone else's viewpoint."

"Push it," Kat ordered. "Narrow the frequencies to just

the emergency command net. Tight beam it along STR AZ Four, that's the shortest route back to Nu New England from here. She had to contact Fleet Command or higher. If the European fleet hadn't reached the island of Flores yet, it was a good bet that the ABCANZ Fleet hadn't reached it either.

Five seconds later, Jack shook his head. "I need more power. I can't burn through all this jamming."

"Divert power from the weapon systems," Kat ordered. Jack tapped at his board. She almost forgot how to breathe as his readouts continued to show red. These people needed proof; she had to provide it.

"Thirty klicks," Morgan announced, to anyone still listening.

Then Jack got his grin back. "Done it, I'm getting something."

". . . hell do you think you're doing. 1st Fleet's Fast-Attack Squadron, answer me, Goddamn it, what do you think you're doing?"

"That's my Grandpa Jim," Kat breathed. "When I last saw him, almost a week ago, he was working with the Prime Minister to find a peaceful way out of this crisis. Anyone still think we're supposed to be doing this?" Kat said, turning to face the bridge crew. Faces went from pale to determined as she stared at them. In the background, Grandpa Jim tried, rather emphatically, and using expletive filled language she'd never heard him ever use before, to raise Captain Duvall.

"Shall I acknowledge him?" Jack asked.

"No," Kat swallowed. "The Squadron's too spread out. If this attack is going to be stopped, we've got to do it ourselves. And it needs to be a surprise, to stop them trying to counter it."

"You can't do this," Ellis screamed. "Don't you see you're blowing our only chance? You're giving rich bitches like her all the aces."

But no one was listening to him anymore. Eyes were concentrated on displays, fingers tapped boards, the bridge crew was with Kat. "Sergeant Jones, are you with us now?" she asked.

"Yes, ma'am. I've got two children, and I know which world I want them to live in."

"Sergeant Jones, Corporal Torres, get these men off the

bridge. We've got a battle to fight and a war to stop."

"Yes, ma'am. You heard the lady," Corporal Torres ordered.

"When you first came aboard," Ellis spat, "I thought you had all the makings of a fighter. Now I see you're just as full of crap as all the others."

"Sir," Sergeant Jones growled, "you either shut up and start walking or, I'll shut you up and have the XO and Comms Officer carry you out." He raised his rifle butt.

Kat let the Sergeant handle Ellis; she had other problems. "Morgan, you all right with this?" she asked as the skipper finally fell silent and sullen, and was escorted from the bridge.

"I guess so, er, ma'am, but this isn't quite the Fleet my family talked about."

"Or mine," Kat agreed with a raised eyebrow. On her board the other corvettes in the squadron were still spreading out. The *Gladiator* was nearest, at just over a kilometre from the *Berserker*. "Okay, here's what we're going to do. The Squadron needs a wake-up call that lets them know they've got big problems. Morgan, prepare for evasive manoeuvres on my signal."

"Yes, ma'am," the helmsman said through a hard swallow. Kat settled into her seat, flexed her fingers, diverted the power Jack had used to break the jamming back to the weapon systems, and reprogrammed a single torpedo, still at fast speed, contact detonation, but with a low yield warhead. She'd worked the warfare systems on the *Berserker* long enough to know this class of ship's most vulnerable spot. Hit a fast-attack corvette three-quarters along her length, and you'd damage the main drive, but not the reactor itself. It would then go on a highly erratic course until they cut the power, but at least her crew would live to tell people about it.

Kat took a deep breath, waited for her hands to settle on the controls, then set the crosshairs of the targeting computer carefully onto the *Gladiator*. A glance at her systems: laser, optical, sonar and radar. All gave slightly different ranges. She entered a good compromise, re-checked the warhead was on its lowest setting, waited for the computer to give 'weapons lock,' then fired.

Her display showed the progress of the torpedo as it quickly spanned the short distance between the two corvettes. Weapon Systems confirmed the impact as her torpedo smashed into the targeted point on the hull. It all happened too fast for the *Gladiator*'s crew to comprehend what was occurring and deploy any countermeasures against it. The *Gladiator*, as predicted, promptly took on a wild, gyrating course, then cut power and fell back, behind the rest of the formation as it lost speed.

"That certainly got their attention," Jack chuckled.

"Yep, sure did."

"Ellis, what's happening?" came over the Squadron's command net.

Kat hit her comm-link. "This is Ensign Severn, now commanding the *Berserker*. Your attack orders are illegal. You are ordered by ABCANZ High Command to break off your attack run. If you do not, I will engage you."

"Severn? Where's Ellis? Oh, shit. *Highlander* and *Templar*, you will attack the *Berserker*. All other ships, continue your attack on the European fleet."

"You wanted their attention," Jack said, raising an eyebrow in resignation as to the new mess Kat had gotten him into.

"Morgan, get us into position to engage the left echelon."

"Yes ma'am," he answered. Kat hit her comm-link again. "All hands, this is Ensign Severn speaking. I have relieved Commander Ellis. Our attack orders are illegal. ABCANZ High Command have ordered us to prevent this attack on the European fleet. I have just damaged *Gladiator*, and we will shortly begin attacking the remainder of the squadron. Whether you were part of this attack conspiracy or stand with the ABCANZ High Command, right now I suggest we all need to stand with the *Berserker*, because if we don't, we're going to be dead, real quick. Severn out."

"Oh, stirring words," said Jack, sarcastically.

"Not now, Jack. They'll just have to do. Morgan, evasive manoeuvres. Jink this ship about like you've never jinked her before."

"It will ruin any firing solutions," Morgan pointed out.

"Don't worry, just do it. I'm more interested in us dodging their weapons than us hitting them."

"*Highlander* and *Templar* are coming around, ma'am," Jack advised her. "Weapons are hot, they'll have weapons-lock in less than ten seconds."

As well as the armour thickness shielding the main drive, the fast-attack corvette had another design issue. Most major surface ships had their weapon systems in turrets or mounted on launchers that enabled them to engage targets from almost any angle. However, the fast-attack corvette's four torpedo tubes were fixed within the hull and the twin Harlequin launchers had a limited traverse of just sixty degrees either side of the bow's centre-line, mainly due to the mechanisms required to retract the launcher rails when the ship dived. Their only exception was their turret mounted 127mm gun, and although capable of direct-fire ship-on-ship engagement, the majority of its numerous munitions types weren't 'smart' so could not be controlled once fired.

Kat used the short time remaining before the attackers could engage the *Berserker* to send three low yield torpedoes at the three ships of the left echelon. She missed them all, except perhaps the *Ranger*. It didn't matter; getting their attention was more important. What was more interesting was the behaviour of the *Spartan* and the *Samurai*. Both slowed, turned out of line away from the European fleet. *I bet there are some interesting discussions taking place on their bridges.*

Kat's breakfast nearly jumped back into her throat as Morgan threw the *Berserker* about. "Missed us," he crowed.

"Turn us, bow on to the *Templar*," Kat ordered.

"Bow on, aye ma'am," he answered.

Kat tried to line up a shot at the Squadron Commander's ship, but every time she was about to get 'weapon lock,' Morgan jinked the ship. Tubes reloaded, and warhead yield configured to its lowest possible setting, she snapped off a few more near-misses.

"Sorry if I'm messing up your shots, ma'am," Morgan said.

"Keep it up. If I can't hit them, they can't hit me."

Highlander and *Templar* shot past the *Berserker*, and Morgan swung the bow back around to engage them, but they had gone. Both ships had lowered their nacelles and were heading at a high surface speed back towards the STR they had recently arrived from. "He's running!" Jack shouted.

"Jack, get me a channel to the rest of the Squadron," Kat ordered.

"Go, channel open." Jack advised.

Kat accessed her comm-link. "*Berserker* to the 1st Fleet's Fast Attack Squadron. Please note that the Squadron Commander is now running back to the STR we arrived here along. I suggest you too consider your options."

"*Spartan* here. Lieutenant Ryan acting commander. We're with you, Severn."

"*Samurai* here, Ensign Dune doing the temporary honours. Where do you want us?"

"Engage *Praetorian* and *Ranger*. Keep them away from the European fleet. I'll chase the Squadron Commander."

The *Templar,* having dropped her nacelles and gone to forty plus knots, began a zigzagging course. Thankfully, the speed quickly stripped away her proximity to the European fleet, but it got her moving rapidly towards a transit route that if entered could provided a potential safe haven, enabling them to evade pursuit. The zigzagging also prevented Kat from taking an effective shot at the *Templar*'s vulnerable main engines. For reasons known only to Commander Ellis, he had not lowered the *Berserker*'s outer nacelles when they had surfaced, making it impossible for them to match the *Templar*'s current surface speed. All Kat could do was maintain the *Berserker*'s present speed and observe the evolving situation.

A couple of European warships had began to train their weapon systems onto the *Ranger* and *Praetoria*n, and the two ships soon got the message that they weren't just getting attention from their sister ships. The multiple 'weapons lock' sounding in their respective bridges must have finally got the message across and both ships broke off their attack and raced for the STR, *Samurai* and *Spartan* right behind them.

"I guess this might be a good time to report in," Kat said, tapping her comm-link. "This is Ensign Katarina Severn, acting Commander the ABCANZ Corvette *Berserker,* Pennant kilo-one-zero-one, calling any Fleet Commands." The main screen split as two faces appeared, one familiar, the other one very familiar.

"This is Admiral Lefebvre, commanding the combined European Fleet. Do you want to tell me what I just saw?"

"This is General James Severn."

"Bonjour, Jim. I trust you are well."

"I've been better Jean, I've been better. I'm working with General Hanna, on this one. It looks to me like you've just had your arse saved once again, and by another Severn, but my eyes aren't what they used to be, so I could be mistaken."

"No, It looked that way from here too, Jim," the Admiral responded with a chuckle.

"Now Jean, you can either sit there and wait for another bunch of idiots to do something stupid, maybe this time directed at the ABCANZ Fleet, or you can go over to Flores and do what we both know must be done."

"Jim, my orders state I am to wait for General Hanna to reach Flores before proceeding."

"And Jean, General Hanna's orders are to meet you at Flores. Now, just between two old warhorses, I'm thinking of suggesting to Hanna that he repositions our Fleet around Corvo until you arrive." Kat checked her board. Corvo was another island of the Azores, twenty kilometres to the north-east of Flores.

"I think we've wasted enough time and resources already," Admiral Lefebvre said, looking off screen. "Corvo looks like a good enough location as any for a temporary fleet concentration."

"Pure coincidence, of course." Grandpa Jim grinned.

"Pure coincidence," the European Admiral agreed and his half of the screen went black as the link terminated.

"Now that we have that settled, Ensign Severn, do you have any issues?" Grandpa Jim said, turning his attention to Kat.

"Just the normal ones of a mutineer, like what to do with the old Commander, and are the crew with me?" She shrugged. "Do you want more captives to interrogate?"

Grandpa Jim pursed his lips at the hot potato she'd just dropped into his lap. Was the battle only half over, or could she let the running dogs escape and order beers all round. Was the 'fat lady' warming up her vocal chords? "Kat, as much as I hate to say it, I think the European fleet needs to see us in hot pursuit. Also, I want to talk to the bastards who set this all up. What the hell did they think they were doing?"

"I have the Commander, XO and Comms Officer of the *Berserker* under guard. I'll see what I can do about getting you Captain Duvall. If you'll excuse me General, I'm going to be a little busy."

"Understood, Severn out."

"Severn out," Kat repeated, liked the feeling, then switched track immediately. "Jack, lower our nacelles. Helm, as soon as reconfiguration is complete, accelerate us smartly to thirty-five knots. Lay in an intercept course for STR AZ Fourteen."

"Aye, ma'am. Thirty-five knots, to STR AZ Fourteen."

Kat tapped her comm-link again. "Chief Martinez."

"Yes, ma'am," came back instantly.

"Could you please conduct a walk-about of the ship? Reassure all of the crew that they are on the right side. Let me know if there's any trouble. You know, the sort of thing I'd be doing if I wasn't a bit preoccupied up here."

"Understood, skipper, happy to oblige."

Skipper. That was a title Kat hadn't expected to earn for a good few years. Well, she hadn't finished earning it today. She studied her board. At forty plus knots the symbols for the *Templar* and *Highlander* were making good progress back towards STR AZ Fourteen. The *Berserker*, despite now accelerating, was still significantly behind. However, Kat didn't need to catch them, only disable their engines, and as long as the two ships continued to run, she had their undefended sterns for targets.

She set the warheads on the torpedoes to their lowest level and started shooting at *Templar*'s and *Highlander*'s sterns as their zigzagging route presented opportunities. Her first shot was off to the left of *Templar*, her second to the right. The third torpedo detonated mid-point, with *Highlander* to the right and *Templar* to the left. Kat tapped her comm-link. "Captain Duvall, I can keep this up all day. Sooner or later, I'll get you. If not now, I'll get you when you slow down to enter the Transit Routing. It's a losing proposition."

Two salvos later, both *Templar* and *Highlander*,

instead of continuing their zigzagging towards STR AZ Fourteen, took off along a long tacking arc round to the right that quickly took them away from that STR. "Where are they heading?" Jack asked.

"I think they've just picked another STR, one they can outrun us to. Morgan, any suggestions?"

A map of the Azores appeared on half of the main screen, detailing all fifteen of the STR's that started or finished within the region.

"They could be making for any of those, ma'am."

Kat rubbed her eyes, trying to remember what a ship's Commander was supposed to think about at a time like this. She thumbed her comm-link. "Engineering, how's the engines and reactor?"

"We're good. All your shooting, and running at this speed is making everything work hard, but the reactor's only at about eighty-five percent."

"Captain Duvall is trying to get away, but the High Command would like a few words with him. Any suggestions?"

"We've got an inexperienced crew aboard, skipper," that word again, and coming from a lieutenant who might have been in on the conspiracy, was good to hear. "You might not have noticed, the way Ellis was keeping you all deep in simulations, but we never drilled at anything greater than twenty-eight knots. I would suggest, that you give the crew at least half-an-hour at thirty-five knots before going up past forty. If we don't find any problems, then take us towards fifty. I know it's probably slower than you'd like, but we've got a lot of new people onboard who've never been on a big boat doing this kind of speed."

Which sounded good, but could be an excuse to let the *Templar* escape? But the Engineering Officer and his Chiefs tended to keep to their own company. Hell, if he wanted to stop this pursuit, all he had to do was flood the reactor. "Thanks, Engineering, we'll follow that. Lieutenant Carlin, in case you haven't noticed, you're the Senior Officer aboard now, therefore there's a vacant chair here on the bridge if you want it."

"If you will excuse me, Miss Severn, I expect I'll be needed here if you intend to put any more loading onto the reactor and engines. I know the manufacturer claims these boats are supposed to be good at forty-five plus with no pain, but I'd rather keep an eye on things here. You've fought us fine so far, Ensign. Until you can get me a relief that I trust like I trust myself, who's going to keep these systems from blowing us all into little pieces, I'll stay back here."

Which was the first Kat had heard about Engineering having a potential problem with the ship doing over forty-five knots. "How bad is it, Lieutenant?"

"Nothing I can't handle. If I get any real problems, I'll be the first to shout."

Kat was rapidly discovering a Commander's job was no 'walk in the park.' So much to be continually thinking about, considering, evaluating, selecting.

"Comms Chief, announce to all hands we will be going to forty knots in thirty minutes and to speeds in excess of that as soon as we can; if all is well."

It took the *Berserker* almost an hour to work up to a forty-eight knot running speed. Among other things, the ship's tiny brig had bare metal fixtures and furnishings. Tempting as it was to let Ellis and his co-conspirators take this speed the hard way, Kat had Corporal Torres find mattresses for them. By the time the *Berserker* had safely achieved this faster running speed, both the *Templar* and the *Highlander* were well out of effective torpedo range.

Far behind them, the other ships of the Squadron fought their own battle. Two experienced Commanders against two jumped-up junior Officers who were getting their first taste of command in the middle of an offensive action. However, the decisions made by the designers of the fast-attack corvettes came home to haunt the two rebel Commanders. Running, their weapons were pointed in the wrong direction, their engines fatally open to damage. It took the *Spartan* and the *Samurai* a while, but time was on their side and luck was against *Praetorian* and *Ranger*. Long before they made it to the STR, their engines were successfully targeted and their skippers replaced by subordinates who were not all that interested in fighting for a small group of rogue Officers who hadn't told them who, or what, they were actually fighting for.

That gave Fleet Command plenty of new recipients for

interrogation, but Kat wasn't about to bet that even Ellis knew the whole story. If the 1st Fleet's Fast-Attack Squadron had managed to neutralise the European fleet, what did it intend to do next? The ships might be nuclear and could go on forever, but the crews needed to be resupplied, and what about repairs and refits. *Templar* was running, but where to?

Now that the *Berserker* was up to, and maintaining a more effective pursuing speed, Kat got all the ships loyal officers and chiefs on the same comms channel. "Engineering, how are we doing?"

"Lost power to number two torpedo tube. Don't know why. If it's alright with you, I'd prefer not to send a repair team nosing around it while we're at this kind of speed, and I've already got my best people on the engines and monitoring the reactor."

"Lieutenant, Engineering is your domain. You run it your way. Is our acceleration causing you any problems?"

"No, not the way we did it, cranking it up gradually, but if I were the skipper of the *Templar*, I'd be real worried about how fast Captain Duvall went to full speed. Us, we're under control. It's them I'm worried about."

This gave Kat a negotiating option. Why not make a friendly call to the Squadron Commander and suggest he review his engineering boards? That brought a dry chuckle to her. "What else do I need to know?"

"Chief Martinez, here, skipper. The galley crew have never cooked a meal at this kind of speed. I suggest cold cuts until we slow down."

"Good call, Chief. Any other issues?"

"No, ma'am. You've got a good crew here, and we're all with you." That was good to hear.

The principle problem with a 'stern chase' is that it takes time, even at forty-eight knots. The peacetime establishment for a fast-attack corvette didn't make allowances for a battle running over normal working hours. Lieutenant Carlin kept his entire watch and maintenance team on duty. On the bridge, there was no way Kat was leaving the offensive weapons board or relieving Jack from his station. Morgan was just as reluctant to go below. "Who knows if or when they're going to turn and fight. I'm here as long as you are . . . ma'am"

So, Kat scheduled Jack, then Morgan, then herself for a thirty minute doze at their stations and had the ship's officers and chiefs do the same for the entire crew, two thirds alert at their posts, one third resting.

By the time Kat awoke from her little nap, it was a much clearer what the *Templar* was attempting.

"Looks like their heading for STR Ten, Eleven or Thirteen." Morgan commented.

"Safi, what's your analysis?" Kat asked aloud.

"AZ Ten is a red flagged route that would take them directly to the Fleet's facility at Georgetown on Ascension Island. It is not impossible, but I consider it most unlikely they would run to one of the Fleet's own bases. AZ Eleven is flagged red and goes to Cuidad Guarico in the Latin American Confed, and Thirteen is black and in-theory goes to the Triangulo de Caribbean Centrale. However, I have no data to confirm if it has been successfully navigated in recent years. These routes are also intersected by at least four other STR's that could take them to five other locations in the Atlantic."

"They've got to slow down soon, or . . ," Jack swallowed the rest of that thought.

"They'd be mad to enter a red or black route at that kind of speed," Morgan finished.

"Whatever they do, let me make it quite clear, we will not be following them into any STR at anything like this kind of speed. Any questions? Any discussions?"

"Fine by me," Jack said.

"Engineering, what's your situation."

"No change. Three tubes are operational. Reactor is holding just outside the red. Everything looks stable."

"We're back within torpedo range again, ma'am." Morgan reported.

Kat resisted the temptation to start firing; preferring to see what Duvall's next move would be. She ordered another sleep rotation, and was just about to take her own thirty minute nap, when Morgan frowned. "I'm getting activity along STR AZ Ten."

Ten minutes later, six blips appeared on Kat's radar

screen as they exited the STR.

"This is the ABCANZ's corvette *Berserker*, Pennant kilo-one-zero-one, to the ships that have just exited STR AZ Ten. Identify yourselves," Kat demanded, and waited to see if Captain Duvall had friends arriving.

"This is the ABCANZ's destroyer *Yukon, Pennant delta-three-zero-six,* and escorts," said a female voice. Kat exhaled the breath she was holding. "I hope the party isn't over, and you haven't drunk all the beer. We're 3rd Fleet's northern patrol formation out of Georgetown, Ascension."

"*Yukon*, this is Ensign Severn, acting Commander of the *Berserker*. 1st Fleet's Fast-Attack Squadron launched an unauthorised attack on the European fleet. We are in pursuit of *Templar* and *Highlander*."

"I'll say you are. You're not going into an STR at that speed are you?"

"I'm not, but I'm not too sure about them. Can you prevent them from using STR AZ Ten or Eleven?"

"Not a problem, *Berserker*, happy to help, but why don't you use a Harlequin?"

"High Command wants the Squadron Commander for questioning, and their crews may not have been complicit with recent activity. We need to stop them, not blast them out of the water."

"Roger that, *Berserker*. *Yukon*, out"

Kat checked the tactical overlay on her board. With *Yukon* now effectively blockading AZ Ten, and her escorting assets denying AZ Eleven within the next hour, Duvall's options were fast running out. With her course locked onto AZ Thirteen, and its high speed, the *Templar* was potentially in very serious trouble.

After another twenty minutes had passed that impeding 'trouble' was further highlighted by a message intercept. "General Hannah to Commander 1st Fleet's Fast-Attack Squadron. Your situation is hopeless. You will be intercepted long before you can enter any STR. If you enter a black routing at your current speed, you will almost certainly be committing suicide, and killing your crew. Cease all acceleration and prepare to be boarded."

"Holy mother of God," Jack half prayed. "The *Templar*'s accelerating: fifty, fifty-five knots."

"She's going to come apart," Morgan shook his head. "Ma'am do you want me to match their speed?"

"Engineering, Duvall's just gone to fifty-five knots. Any suggestions?"

"No Ensign. Just a fact. You go to fifty-five knots I *will* come up to the bridge and relieve you of command. Do you want to spend the rest of the day in the brig with Ellis?"

"No Lieutenant, I just wanted your opinion. I have no intention of arguing with you." Kat opened her comm-link again. "*Templar, Highlander*, this is Ensign Severn. Be advised, the engines on these boats cannot hold fifty-five knots for prolonged periods. You are risking catastrophic failure. If you enter a black flagged STR at that kind of velocity you are potentially signing a death warrant for your crews. Do those of you not in on this conspiracy really want people like Captain Duvall deciding whether you live or die?"

"Do you think anyone was listening?" Jack asked.

"We'll know soon enough."

A minute later the *Highlander* cut all power. "*Templar*, stand down," Kat called. "Don't let Duvall kill you all. Somebody over there put a stop to this madness before the ship blows-up around you."

No answer. Kat studied the course of the *Templar* on her screen.

"*Templar*, you have missed the safe trajectory for STR AZ Thirteen. It's now to your port-side. I repeat, *Templar*, you have missed the STR entry and are on course for the weed banks of the Sargasso. Cut all acceleration and prepare to be boarded."

"She's zigzagging to the right," Morgan said.

"And waving just a bit too much of her engines at me," Kat muttered. She configured her three operational torpedo tubes into a firing pattern, set them for a high-speed and entered the best estimate she had for a long range shot, reduced their warheads to minimum yield, then fired. The three torpedo salvo had a good spread. All missed, but Number Four missed the least. Quickly, Kat tightened the pattern and realigned it around the firing data used for Number Four. Again, she racked up three more misses, but this time Number One was closest.

Reworking her firing solution, she tightened the salvo spread even further, Kat moved her fingers over her station's board as quickly as their forty-eight knots allowed. She only had 6 more Marlins, enough for two more salvos.

Again, Number Four was close, very close, causing the *Templar* to briefly shudder, before resuming her course, and speed. Kat adjusted her firing solution for the final salvo as she listened to Jack mumbling a prayer for the lives of the *Templar's* crew. She paused for a minute, her fingers poised on the fire controls. The *Templar* began to shudder again, enabling Kat to make a final adjustment. Achieving positive 'weapon's lock,' she fired.

For a long second she waited. She'd shot the *Berserker* dry of Marlin torpedoes trying to stop the *Templar*, now only Harlequin's or the 127mm remained. She had to slow the *Templar* down somehow, make her unstable, and just maybe give some sane person on-board the chance to take control of the situation.

Somewhere on the *Berserker*, radar and sonar pulses went out and came back. Somewhere laser and optical systems did their measuring. Somewhere a computer assessed all the data feedback and reported it to Kat's station. It seemed like ages that the blip on the screen continued, unaffected. It wavered for a brief second, then began a series of wild, erratic loops.

"You got them, you got 'em!" Morgan shouted.

Kat let her hand fall on the comm-link. "*Templar*, you are out of control. You cannot make it back to the STR. For God's sake, cut all engines before they explode. Don't let that bastard kill you all," Kat pleaded. "Damn it, if I can replace a ship's Commander, so can you."

The *Templar* seemed to momentarily settle back on its original course. Then all acceleration died.

"This is Commander Wade, Commanding Officer of the *Templar*. I am surrendering the ship to a junior officer. Captain Duvall is unconscious. What do you want me to do?"

"Reduce your speed by twenty knots and come about." Kat ordered. "And see that Duvall gets some medical attention. There are a number of senior Officers that would like to have a word or two with him."

"They can have him," came back from the *Templar*. "Mad bastard nearly killed us all."

And so, the strange tale of 1st Fleet's Fast Attack Squadron came to a close. The ceremonies at Flores and Corvo were long finished and the respective fleets on-route back to their home bases before Kat got the *Berserker*, *Templar* and *Highlander* down to a more manageable manoeuvring speed.

"Coded message coming in," the Comms Chief advised.

Kat viewed the encrypted message at her station. It didn't seem at all secret to her. She tapped her comm-link once again. "This is Ensign Severn. Fleet Command has ordered *Berserker*, *Templar* and *Highlander* to rendezvous with the carrier *Vindictive*, still at anchor off Flores. All personnel suspected of being involved in the attack conspiracy will be transferred to the *Vindictive* and flown back to Nu New England in the custody of Fleet Law Enforcement. All other Officers are ordered to the *Vindictive* for initial debriefing and are now on temporary assignment to Fleet Command as material witnesses. All three corvettes will draw new officers on temporary assignment from the *Vindictive*'s crew to get them back to the Fleet's facilities on Bermuda. Severn out"

That left the crew in an up-beat mood. Jack eyed Kat when she didn't join in the smiles. "Anything in there about you?"

"Yes. Ensign Katarina Severn is detached from the *Berserker*, with orders to report immediately to Fleet Command in The Capital."

"Detached?"

Kat knew they weren't about to make her the Commander of the *Berserker*, but to remove her from post? Not like this, surely? She tried to look on the bright side. "At least I'm not under Law Enforcement escort."

ONE : TWENTY-TWO

The aircraft carrier *Vindictive* docked in Nu New England's Hampton Roads Fleet facility late the following evening; Kat and Jack were two of the very few permitted to leave her. As expected, Monty was waiting for Kat at the dockyard gates as she exited. Surprisingly, two messages came in quickly via Safi. "Glad you made it back in one piece, regards George," was Grandpa George's brief response, but signalled that Kat was included amongst the elite few that were permitted to call him just George. The message from Mother was simple. "We are expecting you for supper at The Residency tomorrow evening." So at least the family wasn't distancing itself from their mutineer. Not yet, anyway.

Kat paused at the top of the stairs. It was early morning: the dawn rays shone through the crystal chandeliers in the entrance hall of Bagshot sending tiny rainbows dancing on the black and white tiles below. On mornings such as this, a much younger Kat and Louis had tried to catch the rainbows, hoping for the fabled crock of gold to come their way. Was she any closer to finding the end of the rainbow now, all these years later?

Just like that morning of her first skiff ride, ten years before, Grandpa Jim, dressed in civilian clothes, stood at the bottom of the stairs. He was talking with Grandpa George. George had his back to Kat and his voice was low, but his hands flew wildly as he remonstrated with his old friend. Jim shook his head. He'd been shaking it since Kat had first spotted him; he kept right on shaking it. Then he noticed her coming down the stairs, stiff in her immaculately pressed Number Two Dress Uniform.

His eyes took on a sparkle, and his mouth went from frown to smile in the second it took for him to notice her and look up. George paused his discussion in mid-hand wave, and turned to see what Jim was beaming at, and did his own version of 'proud grandfather.' "Have we told you lately what a fine young woman you've turned out to be, Ensign?" Grandpa Jim smiled.

Kat stopped at the foot of the stairs, "What brings you out of Lennox Tower, Grandpa George? And why are you both up so early?" she asked in a soft voice.

"Meetings in The Capital with this old duffer," George spat. "You?"

"Another session with my inquisitor. He's been asking me the exact same questions ever since we left the Azores. He asks the same questions, and I give him the same answers. He obviously likes zero-eight-thirty meetings."

"I was subjected to the inquisitors a few times," George commented. "I survived. You will too."

Kat nodded; she'd faced rifle fire and ship mounted weapon systems. Why worry about another little talk with some nobody from Fleet Intelligence? Or supper with Mother and Father, for that matter. Somehow, tonight didn't hold nearly the terror it once had.

"What are you two doing for lunch?"

They exchanged a look. "I am not going to lunch with Olivia and William. Absolutely, categorically, no way!" George snorted.

"Before Kat shipped out to the Azores," Jim said, "she wanted to ask us both a few questions."

"I know, she came to see me," George said raising an eyebrow.

"One of my COs, not Ellis, said that if I intended to be another one of those damn Severns, I had better get a good understanding of just what those Severn's, and the Lennox's for that matter, *really* did, and how they managed to survive doing it. Like the autopsy that confirmed the bomb went off in someone's face, yet the bomber walked away?"

"Oh that," said George, glancing at Jim, who just grinned. George shook his head ruefully. "I should have known you'd be asking me about that one day. Okay, Kat, tell you what, assuming you survive your little chat with the 'grey slime,' and if we don't get lynched by the mob that Jim and I are about to go and see, we'll meet you, just you mind, about eleven o'clock for an early lunch."

"Eleven o'clock!" Jim protested. "That bunch of old wind-bags will only just be getting started!"

George gave Jim a wide-mouthed, full toothed grin. "Who do you want to spend the time with General, the politicians or your granddaughter?"

Grandpa Jim laughed. "Her."

The three of them turned for the door. Outside, Monty had brought Kat's car around, but Grandpa George's gigantic limo was ahead of him. A Land Force Trooper, also in Number Two Dress saluted and held the door as the two men climbed inside. Grandpa Jim boarded the dreadnought as if it was carrying him to a funeral . . . his own.

Kat headed towards her car. Monty was behind the wheel; Mike was in the front passenger seat. Neither had any intention of getting out and opening the door for her. With a shrug, Kat opened her own door and slid onto the backseat. She waved a hand at the leviathan ahead of them. "What has a girl got to do to get service like that?"

"Save the world a couple of dozen times," Mike grinned. "Until then, the exercise will do you good," Monty added.

Kat licked her finger, then drew three lines in the air. "Three down, how many to go?"

"Too many," Monty mumbled as the car moved off. "You know, an old timer like me was getting used to a world that was nice and quiet. Maybe even boring, but safe. Old farts like me like to have their family come home at night."

Kat frowned a silent *What's he talking about?* at Mike.

"His eldest grandson has an appointment at a Recruiting Office for his Oath of Allegiance this afternoon," the security agent explained.

Kat opened her mouth to say something to her old friend, then closed it. He'd cheered her when she joined up, but your 'adopted' child was one thing, your own flesh and blood, quite another. She searched for words . . . and discarded *I'm sorry, I'm pleased for you, and I'm sure he'll become a great soldier. I hope he'll come home after three very boring, but safe years,* almost made it out of her mouth. "I'm sure he was raised right," was all Kat could finally manage.

"Yeah, maybe too damn right." Monty checked his onboard computer, then half-turned towards Kat. "Is all this political posturing going to be worth it to us simple folk who just want to do our jobs and come home at night to enjoy our children and grandchildren?"

"I really don't know. What did you hear about the situation in the Azores?"

"Not much," Mike interrupted. "The media feed was cut-off rather suddenly," he said, leaving Kat to suspect that her security agent knew a bit more than her driver. Once upon a time she thought Monty knew everything. Times were changing, leaving Kat all the sadder for it.

"Yeah," Monty said, turning back to the road ahead. "We spent a whole day without news. Longest blackout since the war. When the cameras finally came back on the Generals, Admirals and politicians are all smiles, and the sailors are happily knocking-back the beer. So just why is your father asking the Senate to double defence appropriation?"

Kat leaned back in her seat. She'd been a bit busy on the trip in; the endless debriefings hadn't left much time for news updates. She rejected the temptation to have Safi give her a quick summary. If the truth, the real truth, as to what was actually happening was as confused as Monty seemed to be, even Safi might be hard pushed to separate the genuine signal from all the background static.

"I really, truly, don't know," Kat finally said.

Monty continued to watch the road. Mike gave Kat what might have been the slightest nod of approval, but then again, it might have been a bump in the road, and he too turned to face front again.

When Kat got out in front of Fleet Command's imposing facade, Mike joined her. "Are you coming to my meeting?" she asked.

"I understand your last trip out got a bit exciting."

Kat smiled. "People *were* pointing guns at me. Again! Are you volunteering for ship duty?"

"Maybe you ought to avoid any duty where I can't provide my services."

"And what kind of services might they be?"

"I take your bullet," he said simply, eyeing the hallway

ahead of them. "Any other grief you earn along the way is your problem."

"I'm sorry," Kat said and found that she did actually mean it. She'd been so consumed by her own job, she'd forgotten that others had jobs to do too. How could she have forgotten that, especially after the rifting that Colonel Hepburn had given her!

Mike paused by the doors signed 'F2-Inteligence.' "Ensign, you have your job. I understand you're getting rather good at it. I have my job. You concentrate on yours, and I'll take care of mine."

Kat identified herself to a civilian receptionist who directed her towards the adjacent conference room. Its door was closed; a sign beside it flashed 'IN USE - TOP SECRET.' Mike raised an eyebrow as he settled into a chair and picked up an out-of-date magazine extolling the virtues of pre-war countryside living.

Inside Kat found the Lieutenant who had questioned her twice a day aboard the *Vindictive*, as well as a Commander she hadn't met before. Forty-something, brown hair, just starting to grey. He wore nothing other than rank insignia on his uniform, no name, no branch-of-service identification, nothing. The Lieutenant began with his usual list of questions. What was Kat's job on the *Berserker*? What did she know of the voyage? What happened on the bridge that morning?

Kat gave her usual answers. That took the usual hour. Then the Commander leaned forward. "Who helped you plan your mutiny, Ensign Severn?"

"What?" Kat bridled at this new line of questioning. "No one."

"So, how long had you been planning your mutiny?" he shot back.

"I didn't plan it." But the rapid fire questions just kept on coming. After five minutes of who, what, when, where and why questions, all ending in that nasty word 'mutiny,' Kat's temper snapped. "Commander, sorry, I don't know your name, but I can assure you that Captain Duvall's and Commander Ellis's actions didn't leave me a lot of options. What would you have rather I did? Follow orders and opened fire on the European fleet?"

"No, no, Kat," the Lieutenant jumped in. "But you must admit that the smooth way you took over the ship leaves people wondering if you hadn't planned something on your own and just got lucky when their illegal actions gave a fiction of legality to your previously planned course of action."

"Absolute crap," Kat spat back at him. Then she spent the next hour explaining to this nameless Commander why the Land Force Troopers had chosen to follow her rather than obey the orders of the *Berserker*'s Commander. That she'd been right didn't seem to matter one little bit.

Kat was drained by the time they let her go. Leaving Mike to follow along in her steaming wake, she stomped for the nearest exit. Outside, she found a day far too beautiful for how she felt. Spotting a pair of curved stone benches overlooking the Anacostia river, she collapsed onto one.

"How'd it go?" Mike asked, taking up position behind her.

"They haven't hung me from the yard-arm yet," she growled. Kat was mad; she wanted to hang a few people herself. Starting with that nameless Commander. What did he expect her to do? Follow orders, open-fire on the European fleet, and when the war was over, tell the media from the winning side, "Well, I was just following my orders?" *No way!*

She took a deep breath; she could smell the faint pine of a nearby evergreen tree.

Mike maintained his silent surveillance as Kat attempted to compose herself for what was left of a miserable day. Several deep breaths did nothing. She ought to do something. What was on her schedule? Oh yes, the lunch appointment with her grandpas. *Wouldn't that look good! They accuse me of mutiny, and I run off and tell my Grandpa.* Have to cancel that.

Why? They are so wrong about the mutiny, and they're wrong about my relationship with my grandpas too! I'm only just getting to really know them, and I'll be damned if I'll let that 'grey slime' Commander stop me! Still angry, Kat stood. She'd planned to include Jack in her meeting with her grandpas, let him get an insight into what 'those damn Severns,' were really like. No way was she going to change that either. "Safi, call Jack."

"How'd your meeting go?" asked Jack's voice a few second later.

"Not too bad. Had better, had worse," she lied. "Want to meet up for lunch?"

"I'm not scheduled for another torture session with my inquisitor until fourteen hundred," Jack laughed. "Where do you want to meet?"

"I'll have Safi call you back in a minute with the venue," Kat said and ended the call. "Safi, get hold of either Grandpa Jim or Grandpa George."

"How'd it go?" came back Grandpa Jim's voice moments later.

"Nothing I couldn't survive. How is yours going?"

"Oh, I think we've done just about all the damage we can here," was followed by a laugh that from anyone else would have sounded decidedly evil. *Grandpa Jim didn't have an evil bone in his body. Or did he?*

"Where are you?" Kat asked.

Grandpa Jim rattled off the address; Safi projected a map for Kat. "I'm not too far away. Do you know the coffee shop in Garfield Park?"

"Yes, I think we can evade the media circus. You want to meet there?"

"It should be quiet, it's still a bit early for lunch."

"See you there as soon as we close this down, say in about twenty, twenty-five minutes," was Grandpa Jim's closing remark.

That didn't go too badly. Kat smiled to herself. "Safi, flash over a map to Jack so he can meet us at the coffee shop in Garfield Park."

Mike coughed. "You're not going to warn him who's going to be there?"

"Why ruin his morning?" Kat laughed, feeling a big chunk of the morning's misery lift from her.

Despite the park only being a kilometre or two from the Fleet Command complex, Mike insisted they take the car. Monty didn't have any trouble finding a place to park.

Mike preceded Kat into the coffee shop, did a visual security assessment before ushering Kat and Monty into a suitable corner.

"How can I help you? What would you like today?" a waitress asked, taking in Kat's uniform without so much as a blink. Apparently Fleet personnel were no strangers to this watering-hole.

"Coffee, regular" Kat ordered.

"Same," Mike and Monty repeated.

As the girl turned for the drinks, Jack arrived. He slid into the chair next to Kat. She considered warning him about the nameless commander and what might lay ahead, but decided she wanted to be able to say under oath the she had not colluded any of her testimony with Jack.

The waitress returned with a large pot of coffee and three mugs. Grandpas George and Jim came through the door as the coffee was being poured. As they stopped across from Kat, the waitress took them in with a brief nod. "Good morning, gentlemen, what can I get for you today?"

Grandpa Jim glanced around the table and ordered. "Beer, draught if you have it, one," he said pointing at himself. "Two?" he pointed at George. "Three," as his moving finger took in Monty and got a negative shake. "Three," was Jack. Mike and Kat also declined the offer. "Three then, if you please." As the waitress headed for the counter, Grandpa Jim took the last empty chair.

In a second, Mike was up and offering his chair to Grandpa George.

"No, stay seated," George said.

Grandpa Jim turned to Kat. "Who are these two gentlemen?" he asked.

"I believe you met Ensign Jack Byrne at my medal presentation, when he wasn't too busy hiding." Jack tried to nod at both the older men and glare at Kat, all at the same time. "He was also my right hand-man when the *Berserker* took on the rest of the squadron in the Azores."

"Well done, son," came from both Jim and George. Jack's face blushed.

Kat figured Jack had had about enough attention as he could survive. "And this is Mike Stieger, my new Security Service agent. Mike, meet my Grandpa Jim. He's my mother's least favourite person in the whole world," she said with a grin.

"Still, after all these years?"

"Oh yes. She still hasn't forgiven you for introducing me to skiff riding."

"That woman has too long a memory," said Jim, trying hard to keep the conversation light about his old friend's middle daughter.

"You've already met my Grandpa George. The father of my mother, another war-time legend, former Prime Minister and the current CEO of the Lennox Group."

"Gentlemen, if you'll excuse me, I'll be over by the door," Mike said, backing away while still trying to keep his attention focused on the people talking to him as well as do the required search sweeps. Kat almost laughed, but then remembered whose job it was to take her bullet.

Grandpa George took the agents elbow. "No way, young man. If you're going to hang around with the likes of us, you need to know the seedy-side too. Warts and all. Anyway, my people have us covered from outside, and this old duffer needs special, close protection," he said, indicating Grandpa Jim.

Mike eyed the old general. "From whom, sir?"

"Himself," Grandpa George laughed.

"I may slit my own throat," Grandpa Jim grumbled.

"Don't let him fool you," George cut in, grabbing a chair from the next table. "Despite what he might say, he's actually really quite chuffed."

"It's a stupid idea," Jim spat. "It's half-baked. They don't know what they want, and this is a poor solution to fix whatever problem it is they want solved."

Still unrelenting, he paused briefly as the beer arrived. Grandpa George then stood and raised his glass. Automatically, the others followed suit with either beer or coffee. "To his Majesty, King James of the ABCANZ Federation," George Lennox said in a most serious and solemn manner.

Kat clanked her coffee mug with the rest, mainly because Grandpa George was busy making sure there was a loud enough clink to drown out Grandpa Jim's obscene response to the toast. "King who of what?" Kat said, sitting down after the sip from her coffee.

Glowering at George, Grandpa Jim explained. "Some jokers in the Senate, who are old enough to know better, think we'd punch more weight in the newly emerging order of international politics if the Federation had a King sitting above all the petty politicking. By this time tomorrow, they'll have thought-it-through and realised just what a crap idea it really is." Jim raised his glass, "To peace and quiet in a well-earned old age."

"Hear, hear!" Monty said, joining the toast. Kat raised her mug with a heartfelt, "Hear, Hear!" of her own.

Ignoring them, Grandpa George leaned back and took a long drink from his beer. "In your dreams," he muttered.

"They want a non-political ombudsman," Jim snapped. "Well, I can be a non-political ombudsman. I don't need some stupid crown on my head to listen to a lot of whinging politicians."

"Without a crown, you won't last a week. You'll tell them to stuff their bitching where the sun doesn't shine and take-off for some South Pacific Federation Dependency," George chuckled.

"Well, at least there, I'd be doing something worthwhile."

George just shook his head. "Not like you'd be doing that here? Jim, everything we fought for thirty odd years ago is starting to come apart. They want you to help keep our piece of it together." Kat nodded; glancing around the coffee shop, she saw people whose lives were being orchestrated for them by the old men and women elected to the Senate. Her own life amongst them. Yet, she and all these people would undoubtedly be a lot better off with the likes of Grandpa Jim having some influence in the proceedings.

"Damn it, George, we've served our time. It won't be long before I'm pushing up the daisies. It should be kids like Kat here that are shaping the future, not the likes of you and me."

Without realising it, Kat had leaned back in her chair, counting the different emotions racing through her. She was glad her grandfathers were still around for her to get to know. Yes, it was for the likes of her to shape the future, but she didn't mind sharing it with them too.

Kat knew from her university studies that when the ABCANZ Federation had formed, the top political job had been titled 'Prime Minister' rather than 'President' as four of the five constituent nations had 'Prime Minsters' and had forced the issue with the United States. So why not make Grandpa Jim the 'President,' why resurrect the monarchy? That had been done away with when the Federation was formed, driven primarily by factions in Australia. Grandpa Jim's second or third cousin back in Nu Britannia still technically held the title, but must have agreed to relinquish it to him to see the institution of 'Monarchy' restored.

"Am I missing something here, Grandpa? Why 'King.' Why not 'President.' She asked.

It was Grandpa George who chose to respond. "Many nations now have a Prime Minister and a President, but the 'President' is usually a former Prime Minister and typically carries 'baggage' from his or her time in that office, and often still has a political affiliation. The Senate, for once agreed that, that was not the message we want to send other countries. Jim has no political allegiances and needs to be seen as being above all their petty manoeuvring and scheming."

"But this really should be Kat's generation's time," said Grandpa Jim, trying to steer the conversation back to its original subject.

Kat leaned forward to touch the arm of the man who was more of an icon to her than an actual person. "Grandpa, it is my world, but that doesn't mean there isn't room for you too. It belongs to me, and all the other people here too, including you. It looks like we might be in trouble, and if we need someone that we all remember as a good guy to have around to hold it all together, well, what did they say back in your day, 'Shape up, or ship out?'"

"Probably a lot more often than they do today," George grumbled, "but don't give him a choice, because I know which one he'll take."

"I still think this 'King' idea hasn't been thought through. Traditionally, nobody from the King's family can sit in the Lower House of Parliament. I can't see your father voting for that somehow. And, I'm not even the most senior candidate; I'm seventeenth or eighteenth in-line to the old British, or Commonwealth throne, having descended from Viscount Severn. My distant cousins back in Nu Britannia are far more eligible than me."

"How many times have we been over this?" George interrupted. "None of the others have your record of doing what was morally right, even when it wasn't necessarily the most popular course of action. You're a decorated war hero, of the right lineage, and a known public figure who has never put individual gain before his public duty. You are the right person for this, and you know it, even if you don't particularly like it or want to admit it."

"I just keep thinking of Sir Arthur Wellesley," Grandpa Jim replied. "History remembers him for being an outstanding general. A memory thankfully not sullied for his pretty poor showing as Prime Minister some thirty years later. I hope I can be more of an Eisenhower."

"No one is asking you to become a politician, in fact it's because you're considered to be above those very same squabbling politicians, and I should know, that you've been approached. You're perfect for a non-political head-of-state, Jim"

Kat, the political history student sat up straight. She and her university friends had come up with some fairly radical ideas during their debates in the Common Room, but this was a new one. "What is the Senate really trying to achieve?" she asked.

"Who knows? They certainly want to cut down on the money in politics," George explained. "For the duration of the time Jim is King, none of his direct family can donate money to a political party. They think that will help keep big money out of politics. But your father isn't going to agree to all this without a fight."

Kat knew that money was the fuel, and the bane of politics. This approach had the advantage, if nothing else, of not being tried in recent history. However, the mention of her father meant this scheme-of-manoeuvre was potentially going to stretch out to Kat as well.

"The Federation's economy has grown significantly during my father's tenure as Prime Minister, why would we want to end it?"

No answer was forthcoming. The opposition would no doubt push for him not to remain in office, but removing one Severn to replace him with another? It just didn't make sense.

Kat continued to think through the ramifications of what she was being told.

This didn't fit, it really didn't make any sense to Kat at all. Despite growing up in a family that had breathed politics for every day of her short life, despite studying recent political history at university, she couldn't even begin to fathom the reasoning or the implications of what this actually, really meant. The official line being verbalised by her grandfathers certainly didn't cut-it with her and posed many more questions than it answered. She knew a game was being played out here, and she also knew it was way above her pay-grade, but still she couldn't even begin to fathom out what the 'bigger picture' was that this somehow fitted into. But right now she had enough problems of her own. She was going to have to park this one up and hope that as future events began to evolve, something would happen that enabled her to fathom-out the reality of this quite bizarre new development.

"Grandpa, I think you would make a great King, I really do, and I sort-of see the logic behind what the Senate is trying to achieve, but that doesn't mean you're going to make me a Princess, does it? Because I've got to tell you, I've have all the problems a growing girl can handle just being the Prime Minister's brat."

Grandpa George laughed, but Grandpa Jim just stared across the table at Kat. Then an evil smile spread across his face. Kat had a feeling that many had died during the war after seeing such a smile. "What do you think, George?"

"There wasn't any discussion about any additional royalty, just you."

"There's a lot of things that there wasn't any discussion about."

Kat shook her head. "Why do I so wish I had kept my big mouth shut?"

"No, Princess," Jim said with that same evil grin, and Kat winced, "that's just the sort of talk your old grandpas like. It gives us old farts good ideas."

"No, bad ideas, very bad ideas," Kat insisted to a grinning table.

Grandpa Jim sat there eyeing her with his tight smile for a brief moment, looking very much like Kat thought a King should. *Perhaps the Federation could use a King just now*. Before she finished the thought, Grandpa Jim got to his feet. All followed him. He raised his beer, and five rose with him. "To us, and those like us. May there always be enough of the few to keep this world turning for the many."

Kat shivered and answered, "Hear! Hear!" with the rest. So this is what it felt like to be the 'us' to the likes of Jim Severn and George Lennox. Was this what it meant to be among 'the few?' She took a long drink from her coffee.

Safi gave her the computer equivalent of a cough. "Kat, you are ordered to report immediately to General Hanna's office in the High Command," her HI announced.

"Oh, oh," Grandpa George said with a grin. "One of those Friday afternoon talks with the boss. I guess our little chat about the true facts, rather than the official line, of our illustrious past deeds will have to wait for another day."

"Do you want me to put in a good word with Hanna for you?" Grandpa Jim offered.

Kat straightened her shoulders. "No, sir. This is my problem, and I'll handle it." *It's my career, so I'd better be able to handle it.*

"Wouldn't have expected any other answer," Grandpa Jim said. "What a Severn gets into, we get ourselves out of."

"Probably because no one else could get themselves in to so much crap so fast and so deep," Grandpa George mumbled through his smile.

Kat laughed with them, realising that they were giving her all that they had to give. A joke and a laugh and a light-hearted confidence that she could handle her own problems.

With that she took leave of them.

Time was against them and Monty quickly drove the five kilometres across The Capital to the other side of the Potomac River and the ABCANZ Federation's military High Command. Once through the gates and inside the main complex, they had covered several corridors and an elevator before Mike announced unnecessarily, "Here's General Hanna's office."

The doors parted, and Kat presented herself to the General's secretary. "Ensign Severn reporting as ordered for a meeting with General Hanna."

"The General is waiting for you. Go straight in"

Kat squared her shoulders and marched forward. How hard could this be? She'd rescued a little girl . . . and got shipped off to the frozen-over, backside-of-beyond. She'd fed a lot of people . . . and damn near drowned for the privilege. She'd gone hell-for-leather into her first fire-fight. . . only to discover she needed to refine her targeting for her second. Now she had led a mutiny and fought a small maritime engagement to prevent a much bigger one. Explaining to the Chief of her father's military just how and why she'd mutinied shouldn't be too painful.

The double-doors into the General's inner office slid open. General Hanna sat behind his desk, deep in reports, but he glanced up as she entered. She marched to the proper place in front of his desk, but as she did so, he was already out of his chair. He moved with quick, smooth steps around his desk. She ended up saluting a moving target. He didn't return the compliment as he wore no headdress, instead he offered his hand. As she shook it, he said, "Well done, Ensign. Very well done."

Good start.

"Might as well get comfortable," he motioned her in the direction of a sofa. She settled into one end as he took one of the pair of chairs opposite. Just as Grandpa George's office was cream, this one was grey: pale grey walls, dark grey carpet, gun metal furnishings. The general looked out of place in his dark olive uniform. Kat crossed her ankles, folded her hands in her lap, and prepared for whatever was to come.

The general cleared his throat. "I guess that I should start by thanking you for saving my neck. All I could think about as 1st Fleet's Fast Attack Squadron spread out was that after they'd made their attack run, they'd then lead the very angry remnants of the combined European fleet back towards the main bulk of our fleet, guns a-blazing."

"Was that what Captain Duvall intended?"

"Yes, but that is not public knowledge and will remain so. The politicians on both sides are still trying to find a way to smooth this over."

"Rather them than me," Kat said. "Where was Duvall planning on running to? Who was his pay-master?"

"We've checked his bank records. I don't think anyone

was paying him," the General said wearily. "I think he was doing something he believed in."

Kat considered all the talk she'd heard from those in uniform and decided that just might be true. But then she remembered him in the company of Ernst-August von Welf the Seventh at the medal ceremony a month or so ago. "But, he'd have to take our ships somewhere. This wasn't the start of an internal revolt by the Federation's military, was it?"

"No, he apparently acted alone. He refused to tell us what he had planned for the squadron."

"Refused?" Kat didn't like the finality of that word.

"Captain Duvall died of a heart attack last night."

That knocked Kat back. "A real one or . . ."

"One of the other type," the General scowled. "We were able to follow the money on that one. The civilian contractor who brought him his evening meal had a strangely excessive bank account."

"You wouldn't be willing to tell me where the money led, would you, General?"

"No, but I suspect that if I don't tell you, Dee Lennox will no doubt hack it out of our database soon enough." He almost smiled. "A small business in Rhinestadt. A software firm."

"Checkpoint Security?" Kat finished.

"Yes. We already noticed their unauthorized software on our ships, so this provides us with no new leads," the General said, settling deeper into his seat. "There is one bit of information that you might have a personal interest in. Captain Duvall deliberately selected the *Berserker* for that little girl's rescue. He was most angry that you scuppered his entire plan by surviving what he'd set up for you during the abduction." General Hanna looked puzzled. "What exactly did he do?"

"I and my squad of Land Force troopers were ordered to do a night insertion . . . into the middle of a minefield," Kat said, both glad to have one mystery answered, and frustrated that Duvall wasn't around to answer more about it. *But . . . he could never have financed that kidnapping on a Fleet Captain's salary, but there's no use following that one further, not now anyway.* "Are you getting anything out of the other Officers, like Ellis?"

"Painfully little. They claim that Captain Duvall hadn't told them what his full battle plan was. They were just following orders." The General made a sour face at that.

"And what will you do with them?" The answer to that would pretty much tell her what her own fate might be.

"Hang them from the highest yard-arm, even if I have to build it myself, is, I believe, the terminology you Fleet types would use, and it's most certainly what I'd like to do. But in reality, nothing is probably what I'll settle for."

"Nothing?" was out of Kat's mouth before she knew it. *Damn it, you have got to do something about opening your mouth first and thinking second.*

"Nothing," Hanna repeated. "Oh, their careers will be over, although most of them are eligible for retirement anyway. But a court-martial would only give them the public platform they want. And I'll be damned if I want any of my Officers wondering if they can trust their superiors' orders, or the citizens of the Federation wondering if they can trust my Officers." It was hard to disagree with that. It also told Kat what awaited her.

General Hanna remained seated, but turned and reached over to his desk, picking up two small boxes. Opening one, he handed it across to Kat. She eyed its contents: the Order of Merit. *Nice medal.* The second one contained the Cross of Valour. *Very nice medal.* She held them in her lap for a moment, then closed the boxes and handed them back. She'd learned at her father's knee to let silence grow until the other person filled it. General Hanna took back the medals, placing them on the low table between them.

"I've read Colonel Hepburn's full report. You did well in Anchorage. Very good for a *junior* Officer." The emphasis was on *junior*. Kat ignored that and said, "Thank you," softly so as not to interrupt or let the General off the hook for filling the silence.

"You earned the Order of Merit in Alaska," Hanna said. Kat nodded but refused to ask why the Cross of Valour was also on the table. Hanna eyed her as the silence stretched. "You, Ensign, are a problem," he finally growled. This time from his desk he pulled a clear plastic wallet and handed it across the table to her. Within was a single piece of paper. Her resignation from the Fleet. Already completed with today's date.

Kat locked her face down even as her stomach went into free-fall. This was just another fight. Unlike the last one, the incoming salvo was only paper and couldn't kill her. She finished reading it and looked up. "You want me to sign this, General?"

"Resign from the Fleet today, and I'll give you the Cross of Valour for your part of whatever didn't happen in the Azores."

Why the Cross of Valour? It was a civilian decoration. The highest civilian decoration, although military personnel could also receive it. Awarded for 'acts of great heroism or most conspicuous courage under circumstances of extreme peril,' but nevertheless, a civilian decoration. Then she made the connection, the penny dropped, it was back to the same technicality as before. What had transpired in the Azores couldn't be considered combat. Open hostility hadn't been declared, and even if it had, she'd engaged her own side, well sort of, and hence the Cross of Valour.

The General is playing politics. "This is my father's doing, isn't it?"

He snorted. "If your father even whispered publically that he wanted this, I'd fight him tooth and nail to keep you, and just as publically. The High Command would have my head if I did anything less."

Kat considered herself politically astute; this clearly was a political hot potato in her hand. She glanced again at the resignation. "So why are you asking me to resign?"

"Ensign Severn, just where exactly shall I post you next? You relieved your last Commanding Officer, and his superior was trying to kill you."

Kat could certainly see the situation from the General's perspective. *Colonel Hepburn would have her back. Or would he? It had been a learning experience . . . for both of them. But it was not an experience either of them needed to repeat. Another ship-duty would be her first choice, but what skipper would want her on his bridge? "Hello, sir, I'm the Prime Minister's brat, maybe even a Princess. I hope we'll get along fine, and by the way, I relieved my last CO." Right. No way would they give her, her own command. Ensigns do not command, and besides, even command positions are subordinate to someone. Even General Hanna, senior man in the ABCANZ Federation's military, reported to her father,* and Kat knew too well that her father considered every citizen eligible to vote right across the Federation to be his boss.

"I understand, sir. I don't know who would take me. But there has to be some place in the Fleet for me?" she said, placing the resignation on the table between them. "I won't resign, sir."

"Why not?" Now it was the General who seemed content to wait for her answer.

"Because I want to stay in the Fleet, sir."

"Why?" he shot right back.

Kat paused for a moment; Chief Martinez's late night counselling session came to mind. "General, an old Chief once asked me why I joined the Fleet. She wasn't very impressed with my answer." General Hanna smiled, leaving Kat wondering if he'd also had a similar counselling session as a junior Officer. "A captain in the 24th Infantry shared her family story of how her grandfather, and mine, survived Table Mountain, and what it means now, to be an Officer in their shadow." That seemed to surprise the General. Kat leaned forward; her answer must be short. She poured all the passion she could into its few words. "General, I am Fleet. This is my home." She passed back her unsigned resignation. "I will not walk away."

General Hanna glanced at the unsigned resignation, sighed, removed it from the plastic wallet and tore it in two. "That settles that then. A word of advice to you, young lady. Half the Officers in the Fleet are applauding what you did. The other half think you're a mutineer who should be cashiered with the others. Good luck telling the two apart."

He reached for the medals on the coffee table. First he picked up the Order of Merit. "You earned this one in Alaska. Wear it in good health." He tossed it to her. "There will be no formal ceremony." Kat looked at the box; this wasn't the way it was meant to be. Her team in Elmendorf, people like Crewman Collins, they deserved better. But because of her, there would be no official recognition. Would all her joys be so mixed?

The General picked up the Cross of Valour, opened the box, studied it thoughtfully, then closed it again. Standing he muttered, "We'll think about this one for a while. Let's see how successful the politicians are in making the whole incident disappear. We'll see what the Europeans want to do about your role in the Azores before we do anything we can't undo."

Kat followed the General's lead, sensing this meeting was over. She stood, then saluted; he nodded in acknowledgement. She marched slowly from his office, the doors closing behind her.

Mike fell into step beside her as she silently headed for the main exit. When she'd arrived, Kat had expected to be leaving as a civilian. Instead, she was still an Ensign in the Fleet. For the first time in her life, she knew what she wanted. She'd demanded it. She'd refused to give it up . . . and it was still hers.

She smiled as she came into the bright daylight. The deep blue of the sky held no rainbow, but Kat was a little bit closer to finding what lay at the end of one.

"I see they didn't hang you," Mike said with a grin.

Looking around at the iconic buildings of The Capital, sky-lined across the Potomac, she smiled. "No they missed their chance. The Fleet still has a damn Severn!"

"So why do I feel like saying, God help us all?" Mike said.

"Because it just might be true," Kat said and waved for Monty to bring the car.

END OF PART ONE

PART TWO

TWO : ONE

"Engineering, let's see if we can finish the test run this time," Commander Anderson announced.

"And let's try not to blow up the ship," Ensign Kat Severn added under her breath. Still, she nodded agreement with the Commander of the *Comanche*, the first of the new batch of *Warrior*-class fast-attack corvettes, as did the others on the bridge around her. The reduced crew attended to their duties, faces professionally bland in the reflected reds, ambers, blues and greens of their respective bridge stations. The cool, processed air didn't actually smell of fear, not quite.

The Commander turned his attention to Kat. "Ensign Severn, match your board to Engineering. Inform me if you see anything wrong, and this time, only use Fleet-issue equipment."

"Aye, sir," Kat tapped her station, converting it from offensive weapons into the ship's engineering station. Everything was green. Question was, would the board show anything red before the *Comanche* was nothing but radioactive scrap?

The second batch of *Warrior*-class corvettes would take the best features from the existing class and incorporate the very latest technological developments. Foremost of these was 'super-cavitation' on a scale not yet tried. Super-cavitation essentially created a large bubble of gas that wholly enveloped the hull, enabling the ship, when submerged, to travel at a far greater speed by reducing the drag on the hull. The concept wasn't new, but until now only torpedoes had ever successfully worked, never a ship of this size.

So the *Comanche* had spent much of the last two months inside Lennox Group's 'Development Dock' within Nu New England's Hampton Roads Fleet facility, converting herself from surface to sub-surface configuration and then activating the systems that generated the gas bubble around the hull.

Trying to iron out what did, and what didn't quite work. Solve that problem and another forty-eight of the class were planned for production.

"Engineering, I show all areas are green," Kat said.

"Aye. All systems are green," the Engineering Officer confirmed from his location over fifty meters further aft. Kat had just under a year's service since leaving Officer Training Academy (Fleet) and was yet to meet an Engineering Officer who valued any viewpoint that originated outside his domain of reactors, generators and the maze of superconductors that connected them together.

Nevertheless, it had been Kat who had terminated two of the last five tests.

"Safi," Kat whispered through her teeth, "are the engines stable?" Her pet personal computer around her right shoulder might weigh less than three hundred grams, but it was a hundred times more capable than all the other computers on the *Comanche* combined, not to mention fifty times more expensive.

"All engineering readouts are nominal," Safi confirmed, into Kat's earpiece, verifying her visual assessment.

"Watch them. If you see anything developing that threatens the ship, tell me. If time's too short, act on it yourself."

"Commander Anderson does not like it when I do that."

"That's my problem. I just want to be alive to have it," Kat whispered, noting that the latest upgrade had inadvertently added something to Safi's personality, *backchat!*

"Helm," the Commander ordered, "Reconfigure the hull to sub-surface mode, then take us down to fifty meters. Hold her steady on course at a speed of fifteen knots."

"Aye, sir. Dive to fifty meters. Fifteen knots, steady as she goes." The Ensign at the helm wore the relaxed expression expected, but one eyebrow lifted towards Kat. He was counting on her to save them all, no matter what the skipper said.

"Engineering, give me eighty percent on the reactor."

"Reactor coming up to eighty percent . . . at eighty percent now, sir."

"Helm, increase speed to thirty knots. Steady on course."

As the helm answered, Kat did a full review of her

board. Safi was doing the same review many times a second, but Kat did not trust any man-made device with her life, not even Safi. All was green. Around Kat, the ship groaned as the hull-pressure and speed increased.

"All hands, this is Commander Anderson. Prepare for high speed submerged sea-trials, Anderson out." Kat and the rest of the bridge crew clicked home their newly installed restraint harnesses.

"Engineering. One hundred percent on the reactor if you please." No sooner had the Engineering Officer reported that the reactor was at one hundred percent than the skipper ordered the helm up to forty-five knots. Kat held her breath and eyed her board. The *Comanche's* first test cruise had ended at this point; the Engineer himself flooding the reactor.

Ten seconds into forty-five knots, Kat let out her breath . . . and everyone on the bridge seemed to breathe easier. The Commander held the course and speed for a long five minutes as every station reported in, not just Engineering. No problems. Nor should there be. The *Warrior*-Class ship had been capable of this kind of speed before all the recent enhancements.

"Ensign Severn, do we have clear ocean ahead of us?" the skipper asked.

As quickly as Kat could at forty-five knots, she converted half of her board's display back to its normal offensive weapons systems, and did a search. All range-finders came back negative: laser, optical, radar and sonar all showed clear. "Nothing ahead for two hundred and fifty nautical miles, sir."

"Load and fire all four torpedo tubes, in your own time, if you please."

"Yes, sir," Kat answered and walked her fingers over her board. Four Marlin torpedoes leapt from their respective tubes, two on each side of the main hull. Lethal up to twenty five kilometres at a speed of sixty plus knots. "All tubes loaded and fired, sir."

"Remote-detonate warheads at ten kilometres," the Commander ordered.

"Aye, sir," Kat acknowledged.

"Reload all tubes," the skipper continued.

The energy flow from the reactor to the capacitors that

discharged the torpedoes out of their tubes and clear of the hull when the order was given to 'fire' remained optimal. Kat checked: there was still plenty of power to keep the fusion containment field up and direct the flow of super-conducted plasma to the twin engines, maintaining the *Comanche's* speed at forty-five knots.

"No problems," Safi reported unnecessarily, but Kat was not about to stifle a good report.

"No problems," Kat announced to the Commander after a thorough check of her board.

"All systems working well within their safety margins," the Engineering Officer reported in.

Commander Anderson cracked a tiny smile; test runs two and three had not got this far. "Helm, activate Cavitation Envelope. Once the envelope is established, take us up to sixty knots. Steady on course. Engineering, put us in the red, let's see what this ship can really do." "Aye, sir," answered him back. Kat locked her eyes on her board, now back to mimicking engineering. The 'reactor flood' button was right under her thumb.

"Power flow to torpedo tubes isolated. All tubes now disabled," she told the skipper.

"No problems," he muttered, his eyes intently studying on his own board.

"Steady at sixty knots, sir," the helm answered through gritted teeth.

Again Anderson went down the department list. Every station reported itself nominal. That put them past test four's failure point.

"Seventy-five knots, if you please, Helm. Keep her steady on this course."

"Reactor stable at one hundred and eleven percent overload," Engineering reported. "One hundred and twelve percent . . . no problems. One hundred and thirteen percent . . . all stations steady. One hundred and fifteen percent and everything is still looking good."

"Very good, Engineering. We will hold the reactor there. Let me know if anything changes," the Commander said.

"Safi, update" Kat whispered.

"There are some interesting anomalies in certain

systems, Kat, but none should be any threat to the ship."

Interesting choice of words for a computer. "I show all green," Kat said after checking her board to verify Safi's report.

"So does mine," the Commander confirmed.

"We are at seventy-five knots," the helmsman announced. Kat watched the seconds tick away on her board for a full minute before the skipper spoke, and then it was to the entire crew. "All hands, this is Captain Anderson. The *Comanche* has now done what no other *Warrior*-class ship has done before; held seventy-five knots for a full minute. We will have completed all of the scheduled qualifying requirements of these sea-trials after two more tests. Anderson out." He paused briefly. "Helm, turn to starboard, forty five degrees, on my mark . . . mark."

The helm responded as ordered. Kat did not feel the ship bank onto its new course. "On new course," the helm confirmed.

Everyone breathed a sigh. One more test to go.

"Helm, execute evasive manoeuvre pattern Alpha."

"Evasive manoeuvre pattern Alpha, sir. Executing now."

The ship rose suddenly, it jinked right, then left, then left some more, dodging imaginary incoming hostile torpedoes.

"Problems are developing in the . . ." Safi began. Kat's board still showed green. Sucking in air, Kat's gaze raced from green light to green light, reaching for any sign of something going wrong. Nothing!

"Flooding reactor!" Safi shouted in Kat's earpiece.

Kat was thrown forward in her harness as the ship went dark and dead around her.

"Where are those damn auxiliaries?" the Commander snapped. Ventilation hummed as Engineering corrected the problem with the backup power generator. The bridge took on light as boards came back to life. Emergency lights cast long shadows. Systematically, Kat studied her board; nothing told her why Safi had shut down the test.

"Engineering, are you back on-line yet?" Anderson asked into his comm-link.

"Yes, sir. We lost no test data. I'm organising it while my team initiates a reactor purge and re-start."

"Am I to understand that you did not initiate that

flooding of the reactor?"

"No, sir. We didn't hit the button down here."

"Thank you, Engineering. As soon as you have a rough idea of what happened, report to my day-cabin."

"Aye, sir."

"XO, you have the bridge. As soon as we get propulsion systems back on-line, set a fifteen knot course back to the shipyard. They should have our usual berth waiting for us."

"Yes, sir."

"Severn, you're with me."

"Yes, sir." Kat replied. "Safi, what happened?" she demanded through gritted teeth as she stood and followed the skipper to his day-cabin, just off the bridge.

Commander Anderson settled into his chair at the head of the table, as the XO announced the ship would shortly be getting under way. Kat closed the door, about turned and stood to attention.

"Have I missed something about my ship, Ensign? Last time I checked, there were three 'Reactor Flood' buttons on this boat. Mine and the Engineering Officer's, like every ship of this class. I am fully aware the *Comanche* has a third, authorised to you because of your position as the coordinator of these sea-trials, and I suspect, because of your unique relationship with the shipyard." That was a rather original way of saying her Grandpa George owned the shipyards that manufactured the *Warrior*-class fast-attack corvettes.

"Yes, sir," Kat agreed, stalling, praying the Engineering Officer would show up with whatever reason Safi had for stopping the test only moments before the Commander could have declared them done and over.

"The Engineer informs me that he did not flood the reactor. And I know I did not use my button. Therefore, that only leaves you, Ensign."

Kat's board would show no contact between her and the red button. No point in claiming that she had. "No, sir. I did not flood the reactor." *Stall, stall.*

"Then who did?"

Kat stood straight, dreading the answer but unwilling to lie to her skipper, and certainly not about to tell a lie that could be disproved almost as fast as she said it.

"Whoever flooded the reactor saved our butts," the Engineering Officer said, opening the door . . . and saving Kat's. "Excuse me, Commander; am I interrupting a private interview, of the 'without coffee' variety?"

"No, Pete, take a seat. You too, Severn," the skipper said wearily. Lieutenant Peter Kurkowski, the *Comanche's* Engineering Officer, with two oversized technical data-pads under his arm, settled into a chair. Kat took the one opposite him.

"Enlighten me, what went wrong this time, Pete?" the Commander asked despondently.

"Specifically? The superconductors on the containment coil for the plasma heading into our starboard engine were point four of a second from no longer being conductors, however the reactor was thankfully flooded, and thus prevented the containment coils from overloading and reducing us into scrap metal." The Engineer ran a hand through his short hair. "I assume it's that fine computer around your neck, or wherever you locate it, that we have to thank for saving our lives?"

Kat nodded. "My HI spotted the developing problem. It tried to advise me, but the problem came on too fast for me to react."

"It!" Safi spat in Kat's ear-piece.

"Your pet computer was working faster than the ones in my engine room," the Engineer finished, not missing the skipper's scowl. "Commander, I understand, and fully appreciate that you don't like the concept of having non-standard, non-issue software roaming around the innards of your ship. And, I can't pretend that I much like it either, but rather than look a gift-horse in the mouth, why don't we tell the shipyard that we need a computer like she's got. Hell, if Ensign Severn was posted off this ship tomorrow, I swear I'd go out and buy one for myself. What would a Heuristic Intellect like yours set me back?"

Kat told him the cost of Safi's last upgrade. He let out a low whistle. "Guess we keep you around for a bit longer then."

The Commander's scowl got even deeper. "Pete, what exactly went wrong with the systems to cause that kind of failure?"

"This is just a personal hunch, but I think the system

that prevents the containment coils from overloading needs to be up-scaled, it needs to be a lot more robust. It uses a series of electromagnets, but they can't cope with the extra power they're being asked to handle during the cavitation process. In addition, the engine spaces have been considerably re-arranged. There's the extra armour over the more vulnerable areas, as well as the compressors and generators that manufacture and maintain the cavitation bubble that have also been squeezed in. The reactor has got smaller, much more compact, but we're asking it to power even more equipment."

"Are we asking too much?"

"Perhaps, but we're nearly there."

"Are the new Engineering Spaces really too small? Quart into a pint pot and all that."

"Almost certainly. I can't get easy access to a lot of the equipment to maintain it. Whoever designed it must think we have a crew of midgets or children aboard, and I wouldn't send anyone near it at the kind of speeds we've been reaching. But we don't want to upset the ergonomics of the ship. The power-to-weight-ratio of this design is second to none. We need a space that is small enough for a fast fighting ship, but still realistic to work in."

"How much bigger?" the Commander asked.

The Engineer plugged one of the data-pads into the day-cabin's projector and a highly detailed three dimensional model of the ship's skeletal structure appeared in the centre of the table. It quickly sequenced through the modifications so far undertaken from the existing *Warrior* class design through to the current evolution of this ship. Tapping away at the keypad, the Engineer enlarged the engineering spaces. "There. That's about what I think we need."

"Calculate the structural requirements required to achieve this alteration. Add it to the display." Kat ordered. A second later Safi had added a list of weights to the graphic. Again, the Engineer whistled.

"An extra one hundred and thirty-two tonnes of weight! You need that much just to give me enough room to swing the proverbial cat. No offence or pun intended," he said with a grin towards Kat.

She ignored the Engineer's quip, "After the damage the

Gladiator sustained in the Azores," Kat said, *damage I did the targeting for*, "the shipyard wants the Engineering spaces to be better protected on these new ships."

"How much does a hundred and thirty-two extra tonnes of ship cost?" Pete asked.

Safi gave Kat an estimate in her earpiece, and Kat told him. He didn't bother whistling at that one; he just looked at the Commander and groaned. "I guess that explains why we're out here trying to find a solution." The Engineer leaned back in his chair, stared at the ceiling of the day-cabin and took several slow breaths. "Could we relocate any of the new super-cavitation equipment into other areas of the ship?"

Commander Anderson raised an eyebrow in Kat's direction. She shook her head. "The shipyard did extensive pre-build modelling simulations and testing. The extra equipment needs to be where it is to achieve the optimum power-to-weight distribution. They couldn't find better locations without a significant redesign, and there isn't the budget for a new class, this is just a mid-life upgrade."

"Why am I not surprised?" Pete snorted. "Why does it always come down to money?" Both Officers carefully avoided looking at Kat. That her Grandpa George was the CEO of Lennox Group who part-owned the shipyards, and Kat's personal portfolio contained several hundred million dollars of Lennox Groups' preferred stock did not prevent them from holding the universal low opinion that Fleet Officers had of the private sector and industry.

Kat saw no reason to be anything other than candid with them. "The shipyard is currently developing something new that might help. Could we upgrade the electro-magnets that control the containment coils to superconducting electromagnets?"

The Engineer chuckled, and the Commander rolled his eyes at the ceiling. "They did warn me that neither restraint nor common sense has ever been mentioned in any of your Appraisal Report's, Ensign. Just where exactly would you suggest we find the space to locate the liquid helium and nitrogen tanks required to keep the magnets in their superconductive state amongst our already highly restricted Engineering Spaces?"

"Sir, Lennox Group's technical people are currently working on something new. They're small, and have self-contained jackets for the helium and nitrogen, so they wouldn't need any more space than the existing equipment. However, they do have a habit of quenching, and quite spectacularly, when activated for a third time, so they'd need to be permanently powered."

"So the reactor will have to power even more equipment?" the Commander presumed.

"No, once energized, the magnets can then be short-circuited, effectively becoming a closed loop that will run independently for several months, even if the reactor was intentionally flooded like today," a nodding Kurkowski confirmed, as he took on and assimilated what Kat was suggesting.

The Engineer sat up. "Have the technical people got a working prototype of this available yet?"

Kat shook her head. "They're not that far along."

"You both know full-well that we're not authorised to install untested hardware anywhere onboard this ship. Having your HI roaming about is bad enough, even if it is proving to be somewhat advantageous for our continued longevity."

Kurkowski disconnected the data-pad and got to his feet. "If you'll excuse me, sir. I want to find out if my people have got anything new regarding that last test run."

"Keep me updated, Pete."

Kat stood to follow the Engineer. "A moment, Ensign." A knowing smile crossed the Engineering Officer's face as he closed the door behind him. She turned to face Commander Anderson, going back into a position that would have made her Drill Instructor at OTA(F) proud.

"Once again, Ensign Severn," the Commander began, "you have succeeded in turning insubordination into a virtue."

Kat had no answer for that, so kept her mouth shut.

"One of these days, it will not be a virtue. One of these days, you will discover why we do things the Fleet way. I only hope that I will be there when you discover that . . . and that no good sailors die alongside you."

Again, Kat had no answer for the *Comanche's* Commander, so she used the Fleet's all purpose response: "Yes, sir."

"Dismissed."

Kat marched out of the day-cabin. Once more, she'd been raked over the coals for doing the right thing, but the wrong way. Still, the Commander hadn't been as hard as he could have been. At least he had rifted her as "Ensign," and not "Princess!"

By thirteen-hundred, the *Comanche* was in her usual place, tied up and secured in Development Dock Three, with the crew quickly settling back into their 'alongside' routine.

Kat followed the *Comanche*'s Commander and Engineering Officer into the shipyard for their usual post sea-trial debriefing with the usual shipyard managers, in the usual conference room. After almost two months of ongoing trials, far too much of this job was becoming 'usual.'

Today, Lennox Group's 'usual' team had been supplemented with a number of new faces. "We followed this morning's activity," the civilian Project Manager said, "and thought it might be beneficial to add a few scientists to today's debriefing."

"Then you are aware that Ensign Severn has informed us about some new super-conducting electro-magnets?" Commander Anderson began, taking in the four new attendees. "So, am I correct to assume that you're the team working on that particular project?"

A man leaned forward in his seat. "Yes Commander, my team has been evaluating new applications that might be suitable for this technology," he paused briefly. "Following Princess Katarina's success in obtaining us a number of un-quenched samples for further analysis." Kat winced as the use of 'Princess.'

"And . . ." Kurkowski said, not letting anyone 'off-the-hook' as soon as the lead scientist had stopped talking. "I think the containment coils on the *Comanche*'s reactor might be good candidates for this technology, provided you can prevent them from involuntarily quenching themselves. Obviously, you understand my Commander's reluctance to even consider proceeding down this route if this technology is not currently robust enough for a shipboard application."

"Our testing hasn't progressed that far," the man admitted with a sour frown directed at one of his subordinates. "But we're close. The technology is certainly robust enough, and we had already considered this a highly viable application, but we don't have a working model available to install just yet."

"When might a working model be available?" Commander Anderson asked.

"Six weeks, sir, absolute minimum," a subordinate scientist replied. "Two weeks to finish our current test program, then another month working with you to design and manufacture something that could be installed onboard. Six weeks total, and that's pushing it hard, no contingency."

"Five weeks," the Chief Engineer shot back. "You and I can begin working on a potential design whilst the testing is being completed. Maybe less if you can get a prototype unit manufactured quicker."

"There are a lot of potential problems," the Project Manager said, glancing at his palm-top computer. "There's also the little matter of the funding. These trials have already exhausted their allocated budgets. Who's going to provide the extra money required?"

Commander Anderson shook his head. "I'll have to check on that. Who's paying for this super-conducting EM development?"

"Lennox Group," the Project Manager said, and Kat nodded. Grandpa George was footing the bill for the work on the electro-magnets because he was still hoping to identify who had tried to kill Kat in Alaska several months before. In addition, if Lennox Group paid for *all* the research and development, then Lennox Group got *all* the profits. Grandpa George was such a warm hearted man!

"Okay," the *Comanche*'s skipper continued. "That gives me about a week to get approval for additional Fleet funding. I'll get back to you by the end of this week with an update."

"I'll look forward to your call," the Project Manager said with a smile that had the proper blend of predator and supplicant that all government contractors required.

Meeting over, they started back to the ship. "Pete, you have any further questions?" got a quick negative from the Engineer. "Severn, we might as well stand the crew down.

Anyone who wants leave, who has entitlement, can have it. That includes you, Ensign."

"I'll stay here, sir, keep an eye on the shipyard staff."

"I'd much rather you didn't. They don't know if they're talking to a Fleet ensign, a Princess, or a major share-holder of the Lennox Group. Until I get additional funding approval for these new developments, I can't risk someone taking one of your nods as a works order or authorisation to proceed."

"You've never expressed that concern before, sir."

"I've never heard anyone in the shipyard call you 'Princess' before. I don't know who that scientist is, but I don't want any problems."

Kat didn't know how to answer that. "I don't need any leave, sir," she finally concluded.

"We will almost certainly need your 'special relationship' with the shipyard over the next few weeks, but for now, keep your distance, stay away from the boffins until I get the extra funding authorized. Now, I do believe you have a social commitment this evening?"

"A State Reception, sir," Kat scowled again. She'd hoped the *Comanche*'s latest sea-trial would have taken slightly longer, and given her a good excuse to be absent.

"Right, so why don't you head on up to The Capital."

"Sir, did my mother . . ."

"No, the Prime Minister's wife has not taken to issuing me with orders for you . . . not yet anyway, but my wife did notice the less than complimentary gossip on the red-top media sites following your absence at last week's charity ball. So my HI, obviously nowhere near as smart as yours, is now searching the resurrected "Court Circular" and other official engagement sites for what I suspect might be your social responsibilities. Ensign, we all have our duties. And as long as you insist in juggling your Fleet duties with those of a Princess . . . I don't ever expect you to short-change the Fleet, but I also can't afford to report to the Prime Minster, or even his good lady, every time you short-change the other."

"Sir, I *joined* the Fleet, I got press-ganged into this Princess stuff," Kat spat.

Anderson actually smiled. "We must all bear our burdens, Ensign. The METS station, I believe, is that way," the

Commander said, pointing Kat towards the shipyard gates and the Municipal-Express-Transit-System station just outside. The city-wide transport network would take her west, then north, away from the shipyards, and towards The Capital.

Kat glanced at her watch, which was faster than asking *'Safi, what's the time.'* "My mother will be delighted to know that I have five and a half hours to get transformed. I'll tell her my Commander now shares her concerns for my social calendar."

"Or at least his wife does," Anderson added as he turned back towards the *Comanche.*

Kat had made no arrangements with Monty or Mike to be picked-up, and even if Safi called them now, it would take over ninety minutes for them to drive down to the shipyards from The Capital, and other ninety minutes to drive back. And that was assuming they were currently in The Capital. It would take more than three hours for them to get here if they were currently at Nu Bagshot, and that was making the assumption the traffic was kind and there were no hold-ups, and it never was, and there always were. There was no way they could pick her up and get back to The Capital in time for her to change and be ready for the Reception start time. No, calling them to arrange to be picked-up was not a viable option, so she ordered Safi to purchase the required tickets for the METS service.

Despite the obvious security risk, limited alternatives dictated that she take the next train that stopped.

She plopped herself down into a vacant seat. She could spend the short journey to the connecting main-line station in the city district of Richmond reflecting about the mess this Ship's Duty was rapidly becoming. General Hanna, the Chief of the ABCANZ Federation's military, had said he didn't know where to dump his least favourite multi-millionaire junior Officer, Prime Minister's brat, and now Princess, and, oh yes, mutineer. *But I didn't pick my parents! And I didn't have much more choice in relieving my last skipper!*

But, Kat had asked for a ship-duty. Like every other junior Officer in the Fleet, she wanted it in the worst possible way. And she'd gotten just about the worst ship-duty anyone could possibly get!

With the *Comanche* tied up in 'Dev-Dock Three' going

through endless sea-trials, the enlisted crew slept in the transit accommodation within the shipyard. The Officers had all been allocated rooms within the Hampton Road's Officers' Mess, but on a Friday evening everyone that could, went home. For Kat, that meant going back to Bagshot for the weekend.

Even at university she'd shared an apartment with another girl. Here, she was a grown woman, spending her weekends sleeping in the same room she had as a child. *And for all this I went to university and joined the Fleet! It could be worse; at least Mother and Father are at The Residency and not at Bagshot too!*

"Kat, would you like to review today's mail?" Safi asked, bringing her out of her moody reflections.

"Might as well, anything good?"

"I have deleted most of the junk mail. Financial reports have been archived. I can give you a synopsis of them as usual on Monday morning. There is a recorded vid-message from Jack Byrne from earlier this morning. I have not accessed it."

"Thanks, Safi," Kat said with a smile. Jack was the one real friend she'd made in the Fleet. Problem was, he was still on the *Berserker*, and she was now on the *Comanche*, but that was the way the Fleet did business. She flipped up the small screen on her wrist's comm-unit to enable Safi to begin transmitting the vid-message.

"Hi Kat," Jack started, a laugh in his voice. "I've got some leave to burn." Kat knew where she'd like him to burn it too!

"Turns out, you're not the only one with a military heritage. My grandmother's brother died a few months back, whilst we were at Elmendorf. Anyway, he had lots of stuff that the rest of the family hadn't seen in years, if ever. Turns out, my great, great, oh I don't know how many greats, grandfather was a sergeant in the 8th Light Dragoons, out in India during the early nineteenth century. He fought at Laswaree in 1803 and was apparently wounded during that battle. They sent him back home to Ireland to recover, and he ended up marrying the very nurse who tended him. I really do want to see Laswaree, Kat. I've got myself a real cheap seat on a positioning flight for a Russian transport aircraft, you know the big, heavy-lift ones, and then a scheduled flight from Nu Piter down to Nay Dilli, so

I'm heading out there for a couple of weeks." *Maybe I will take some leave. It might be fun doing a Battlefield Study . . . with Jack.* "This leave," Jack continued, "I'm not going anywhere near a Severn. With a bit of luck, no one will come close to almost killing me, and I can actually relax," he said softening his words with one of his trademark lopsided grins. Despite his grin, Kat felt like she had just been punched in the stomach. It wasn't her fault Jack had been so close during the three attempts to kill her. He'd only been at risk for two of them. Still, she couldn't really blame him for wanting to distance himself from the Severns, and her in particular!

"Hope we can catch up for a few days when I get back. Bye." Jack's face disappeared.

"I'm sorry Jack feels that way," Safi offered into her ear. Her HI's last upgrade was supposed to make Safi a better, more compassionate companion. Kat really wasn't convinced.

She shrugged. She hadn't exactly told him. "Hey Jack, I really want to spend some time with you." *So, what could she expect?*

The METS service was reasonably fast, and after crossing high over the waters of the Hampton Roads it stopped only twice in the city districts of Hampton and then Williamsburg before gliding silently into the main-line, multi-platformed Richmond District station.

The express service to The Capital was in the final stages of boarding. Kat headed for the first-class passenger carriage and settled into a window position of the three-across bank of aircraft-like seats. She buckled in; this was the express service, covering the two hundred kilometres back to the capitol in around forty minutes.

As she got comfortable, a uniformed man with Commodore's rank sat down in the aisle seat, leaving the one between them still unoccupied. Kat concentrated on staying out of his face by looking out of the window. No view just yet, they were still in the station. The panoramic window reflected Kat's face . . . and the Commodore's. He was watching her. *He looks familiar. Where?*

Right. Scowling, Kat turned to face him. "I know tensions are a little high in the international arena right now, sir, but a few months ago you were a Commander. Rather rapid promotion?" She took in his uniform, and as before, it told her absolutely nothing, "Even for Fleet Intelligence?"

The man shrugged. "A Commodore interrogating a mutinous Ensign, even an Ensign whose father is the Prime Minister, might get people talking. I figured a Commander was about the right rank. What do you think?"

Kat thought she'd had enough of this man's 'games' the first time they had met and let the angry Prime Minister's daughter and multi-millionaire speak. "I didn't much like the topic of conversation, no matter who was pushing it at me. I didn't plan the mutiny. It just happened."

"We know that now," the Commodore said, leaning back in his seat as the carriages pulled away from the platform and gathered speed. "Once we'd finished debriefing those who took your side against Commander Ellis, and it was clear you did nothing illegal beforehand. In fact, some damn good leadership in some tough situations. Very few officers could have earned that kind of trust and respect, and in such a short space of time."

"Is that flattery from Fleet Intelligence?"

"I like to think that truth is my business,"

"Ha, humour too," Kat shot back.

"Would you care to make it your business?"

Kat let her eyes rove across the city-scape outside the window. She picked out the ruin of the old Virginia State Capital buildings and surrounding parkland below them, then the line banked over to the right and followed the passage of the James River.

"Is this a formal job offer?" Kat asked.

"General Hanna doesn't know where to assign you. You're just one of several 'hot-potatoes,' he currently has. He offered me the chance to solve one of his problems, and one of mine. I can certainly use someone with your skills and unique opportunities. Unlike Anderson, I don't mind you using your own computer."

"For what? Does the Chief of the Defence Staff expect me to spy on my own father?"

The Commodore rubbed his eyes. "Tact is obviously not one of your strong points."

"I'm not a spy," Kat said. "And certainly not on my own father."

"I don't want you to be. General Hanna doesn't want that either."

Kat took that with a large pinch of salt. "So, just what kind of job are you offering me?"

The Commodore swept a hand out at the panorama passing outside the window. "The world is both a challenging and changing place right now. It is inhabited by the most dangerous of species . . . man. There are people who want this or that and frequently don't want other people to have this or that. Latest intel updates suggest the Horn of Africa is about to rip itself apart yet again in another civil war," he said. "As a 'Princess,' and yes, I know you hate that word, you can go lots of places an ABCANZ Fleet Officer can't or shouldn't. You can learn and do things the Federation needs to know and get done. And I could help you as much as you could help me."

Kat turned back to staring out of the window. The line that the carriages now moved rapidly along was running alongside the river, then passed under one of the illuminated legs of the gigantic red spider sitting atop the local gridiron stadium.

When she had passed out from the OTA(F), her first posting had taken her away from the city to the ABCANZ Federation's 1st Fleet's off-shore base on Bermuda. At that point she'd been glad to leave the city, but right now, as it stretched out as far as she could see and any direction, it all looked mighty fine.

Did she want to protect it?

Wasn't that why she had put on this uniform? Wasn't that why she hadn't resigned when General Hanna had requested she do so a few months before? That, and a wish to get away from a father and mother who left their daughter very little air of her own to breath. That, and a desire to save a bit of 'this,' see and do a bit of 'that,' as well as sample whatever 'the other' might throw at her along the way too.

Exactly what she'd so far done.

Did she really want to let this man call the shots from now on?

It has to be better than the Comanche, she reminded

herself.

But the *Comanche* was a job for Ensign Katarina Sophie Louisa Severn. Not the Prime Minister's brat, or a Princess, or a rich kid. This Commodore, if that was what he really was, wanted her for all the things about her that she wanted to escape from.

Was his comment *"you can go lots of places an ABCANZ Fleet Officer can't or shouldn't. You can learn and do things the Federation needs to know and get done,"* another small part of true reasoning behind making her Grandpa Jim into a King?

She shook her head. "I'm very sorry, Commodore, but I've got this job. A ship depending on me. I wouldn't want to disappoint my Commander."

"I doubt he'd shed a single tear if you got new orders."

"Yes, but the Engineering Officer loves what Safi and I do."

"My budget could get Pete Kurkowski a very good computer."

This bastard even knew the Engineer's first name!

"What is it about *no* that you don't understand, sir?" Kat asked.

"I just wanted to make sure *no* was really *no*," the Commodore said, undoing his breast pocket and handing Kat an old fashioned, printed business card.

'Claude Finkelmeyer, Project Planning and Systems Management. 0101-202-6345-459.'

Kat eyed the card for only a few seconds. "Safi, you have the details?" Kat whispered.

"Yes."

She then tore the card in half, then each half into half again, before handing the four pieces back to the man. "Not interested."

He gave her a crack of a smile. "Wouldn't have expected anything less from you, but General Hanna wanted me to try. Have a good evening. Maybe I'll see you at the reception this evening."

"What rank should I look for?" Kat asked to his back, despite the sign flashing for all passengers to remain seated. The man continued, making his way into another carriage. *And they say I don't follow the rules!*

Part Two continues in:

THE KAT SEVERN CHRONICLES

CLANDESTINE WARRIOR

GLOSSARY OF TERMS

1st Fleet	The ABCANZ Fleet that operates in the waters of the North Atlantic, including the Caribbean.
3rd Fleet	The ABCANZ Fleet that operates in the waters of the South Atlantic.
5th Fleet	The ABCANZ Fleet that operates in the 'European' waters of the Baltic, Black, Mediterranean, North and Norwegian Seas.
24th Infantry Battalion	A light infantry battalion of the ABCANZ Land Forces. Recruited predominantly from Nu Alba, the battalion has inherited the battle-honours and traditions of the Royal Highlanders, or Black Watch.
74th Infantry Battalion	A mechanised infantry battalion of the ABCANZ Land Forces. Recruited from both islands of New Zealand, the battalion has inherited the battle-honours and traditions of the Royal New Zealand Infantry.
81st Infantry Battalion	An amphibious infantry battalion of the ABCANZ Land Forces. Recruited from San Angeles, the battalion has inherited the battle-honours and traditions of the 1st Battalion, 4th Regiment USMC.
127mm	The standard calibre of the guns mounted on most ABCANZ Fleet vessels, usually turret mounted, firing a 21kg shell over 25 kilometres.
ABCANZ Federation	The Federal alliance formed by the United States, Britain, Canada, Australia and New Zealand in the latter years of the war.
ABCANZ Fleet	The Maritime (Navy) component of the ABCANZ military.
ABCANZ Land Forces	The Land (Army) component of the ABCANZ military.
Agri-farmers	Agricultural (crop growing) farms and their associated work force.
airport apron	the area where aircraft are parked, unloaded or loaded, re-fuelled or boarded.

Al Basrah	Principal city of southern Iraq. Scene of heavy fighting in March and April 2003 during the Liberation of Iraq.
Alberta City	Smallest of the five ABCANZ cities in North America, situated in the former Canadian province of Alberta. Within it are the pre-war cities of Edmonton and Calgary.
Amy Johnson	Pioneering English female aviator of the 1920s and 1930s.
Arab League	Also known as LAS, or the League of Arab States. A large, post war Muslim state extending across North Africa and the Middle East. From the former countries of Morocco in the west, to Oman in the East. Remains heavily contaminated in the Suez, Palestine and Kuwait Bay regions.
Avalon Peninsula	Large peninsula in the southeast of the island of Newfoundland, Canada.
Badlands	Vast radioactive and chemically contaminated wasteland of North America. Reaching from Nu New England on the east coast, right across to San Angeles on the west. Infested with many mutated life forms, both animal and human.
Bagshot	Home of the Severn dynasty. Situated in the Suffolk district of Long Island, Nu New England. Named after their original family residence, Bagshot Park in Surrey, England.
Barstow Logistics Base	Large military logistic and storage facility in the San Bernardino district of San Angeles.
Battalion	Land Forces formation consisting of 4 'fighting' companies with a command/support company. Approximately 600 men, commanded by a Colonel.
Bermuda	The 'off-shore' base used by some elements of the ABCANZ's 1st (North Atlantic) Fleet.
Berserker	A Viking warrior. The name of a Fast-Attack Corvette (K101) in the ABCANZ 1st (North Atlantic) Fleet.
Branch-of-Service	Both Fleet and Land Forces are broken down into 15 separate departments or branches.
Camp Richardson	Former US Army base in Anchorage, Alaska. Abandoned after the war.
Category D Prisoners	Low risk, non-violent prisoners. Usually incarcerated for crimes such as embezzlement, fraud, money laundering, tax evasion, public office abuse and other similar offences.

Cayman City	A small, wealthy city in the Caribbean situated over the North Sound on Grand Cayman, an ABCANZ Federation Dependency.
CEO	Chief Executive Officer.
Charlotte	The only city in the ABCANZ Federation Dependency of the Virgin Islands in the Caribbean. The city is crescent shaped, linking the islands of St Thomas, St John and Tortola.
Chief	Chief Petty Officer (see Enlisted Ranks).
Chief of the Defence Staff	The senior person in the ABCANZ Military. A five year post, rotated between a Land Force General and a Fleet Admiral.
Chuitna River	From its headwaters at the base of the Alaska Mountain Range, this 40 kilometre river cuts through a broad expanse of forest and wetlands, to its mouth on the western shore of upper Cook Inlet between the remote villages of Tyonek and Beluga, west of Anchorage.
civis	Military slang for 'civilians' and for wearing civilian clothing instead of uniform.
clip	Slang term for a weapon's magazine.
CO	Commanding Officer.
Comanche	A fierce Native American tribe of the Southern Plains of the United States. The first 'upgraded' Fast Attack Corvette being developed for the ABCANZ Fleet.
Command and Staff College	An academic facility that Land Force Officers attend at various stages to advance their careers through promotion. Located in the Quantico district of Nu New England.
Common Room	An on-campus cafe-bar, cum fast-food dining establishment used by the students of NNE University, located in the Mercer District of Nu New England.
Company	A Land Forces formation consisting of 3 'fighting' Troops with a command/support Troop. Approximately 120 men, commanded by a Major.
confidential	A level of Security Classification. Above 'restricted,' below 'secret.'
Cook Inlet	A 290km inlet stretching from the Gulf of Alaska to Anchorage on the southern coast of Alaska.
Cook Straits	The largest ABCANZ City in New Zealand. Located on both the North and South islands and the 23 kilometre span between them.

cordite	A smokeless, now obsolete, propellant that replaced gunpowder in the early 20th century.
Corvette	A warship, smaller than a Frigate, but larger than a Patrol ship.
Corvo	An island in the Azores, twenty kilometres north-east of Flores.
Cross of Valour	The ABCANZ Federation's highest civilian decoration, awarded for acts of great heroism or most conspicuous courage in circumstances of extreme peril.
Cuidad Guárico	A large city of the Latin American Confederation encompassing all of the former Venezuelan state of Guárico.
cyalume stick	A plastic tube containing chemicals that when mixed emit a glow. Used in night operations for visual signalling or identification.
det-cord	Detonation Cord. An explosive filled cord used for detonating the main explosive charge. Can be used on its own to clear a passage or fell a small tree.
DSM	Distinguished Service Medal. Awarded to members of the ABCANZ Armed Forces for distinguished leadership, bravery and/or resourcefulness in a combat environment.
Division	A large military formation used by most nations ground forces. Consisting of multiple Brigades, usually three but can be more if required.
Double-time	Military slang for moving at a pace faster that walking, or marching. Usually jogging or running.
Elmendorf Base	The small ABCANZ Federation military base in Anchorage, Alaska. A former USAF facility.
Electro-Magnetic-Pulse	EMP. Second generation, non-nuclear device that produces a short, but high intensity electromagnetic shock-wave inflicting irreversible damage to electronic equipment, particularly computers, radio and radar.
Emerald City	A small city of the European Union, and the only city in Ireland. Located on the east coast in former province of Leinster.

Enlisted Ranks	Fleet	Land Forces
	Fleet Chief Petty Officer	Sergeant Major
	Chief Petty Officer	Staff Sergeant
	Petty Officer	Sergeant
	Master Crewman	Corporal
	Leading Crewman	Lance Corporal

Crewman................................. Trooper

EOD — Explosive Ordnance Disposal. Military terminology for the process by which hazardous explosive devices are rendered safe.

ERB — Emergency Ration Bar.

European Union — The most powerful of the post-war European states. Much smaller than the original 'EU' but consisting of the former states of Germany, France, Belgium, The Netherlands, Luxembourg, and Ireland with the northern, industrial regions of both Spain and Italy. Joint Capital cities: Nu Paris and Rhinestadt.

F2 Intelligence — One of the principal departments within Fleet Command. (F1 Personnel, F3 Operations, F4 Logistics etc). Land Command departments are prefixed 'G'(General) instead of 'F' (Flag) and High Command departments 'J' (Joint).

Falkland Islands — The ABCANZ Federation Dependency in the South Atlantic. There is only one city, Fitzroy, which encompasses the former habitations of Stanley and Mount Pleasant and is the main operating base of the ABCANZ's 3rd (South Atlantic) Fleet.

FDO — Fleet Daily Orders. A document published daily by all Fleet establishments on behalf of the Commanding Officer detailing daily routine and any supplementary announcements.

fey — Irish term for fairy folk or spirit.

Field Rank — Land Force officers holding the rank of Major or Colonel are considered to be of 'Field Rank.'

Fleet Command — The overall authority on all matters appertaining to the ABCANZ Fleet (Navy)

Fleet Support Facility — An ABCANZ Fleet base that had no ships permanently based from it, but provides re-supply to any Fleet assets that require replenishment.

Florence — See Maximum Security Florence.

Flores — The most westerly of the islands in the Azores.

Fort Greely — Former US Army launch site for anti-ballistic missile defence system in Alaska. Targeted during the war and completely destroyed.

Fort Lee — A large ABCANZ military facility in the Prince George District of Nu New England. One of the many units located there is the ABCANZ Fleet's School of Electrical and Mechanical Engineering.

Gardiners Island	A 10km x 5km island in Gardiners Bay, at the eastern end of Long Island, Nu New England.
Georgetown	The only settlement on Ascension Island, and the 'off-shore' base used by some elements of the ABCANZ's 3rd (South Atlantic) Fleet.
Gladiator	The professional arena fighter of Ancient Rome. The name of a Fast-Attack Corvette (K102) in the ABCANZ's 1st (North Atlantic) Fleet.
(to) go off at half-cock	An expression used to describe taking a premature or ill-considered action, originating from the days of 'flintlock' muskets where the 'half-cock' position was the position for priming the pan, with 'full-cock' for actual firing.
grey slime	The derogatory term used within the military for Fleet Intelligence. 'Green slime' is Land Force equivalent.
Guadeloupe	Caribbean island taken from the French by British forces in 1759. Returned in 1763 after France agreed to renounce claims on all territory in Canada.
hackle	A small plume of coloured feathers attached to the ceremonial headdress of some ABCANZ Land Force Regiments.
Hampton Roads	The largest ABCANZ Fleet Base. Home of 1st Fleet as well as many other Fleet and Land Force training, educational, research, evaluation and intelligence facilities.
Harlequin	A highly effective short range, ship or aircraft mounted anti-shipping missile used by the ABCANZ Fleet.
headdress	Military terminology for any kind of cap, beret, or helmet.
head-up-display	A transparent display that presents data without requiring users to look away from their usual viewpoint. Originally used by pilots, enabling them to view information with heads "up" and looking forward, rather than looking down at instrumentation. Now used in many military and non-military applications.
HI	Heuristic Intellect. A personal computer that modifies itself as it learns.
High Command	The supreme military headquarters that sits above Fleet Command and Land Command.
Highlander	The medieval warrior of the Scottish Highlands.

The name of a Fast-Attack Corvette (K103) in the ABCANZ's 1st (North Atlantic) Fleet.

HSM — Humanitarian Service Medal. Awarded to any member of the ABCANZ military who distinguish themselves in specified military assistance of a humanitarian nature.

hum-int — Human Intelligence. Usually a network of covertly placed informants and/or agents.

Insert Report — A report written on an individual for insertion into their OJAR if on temporary assignment outside their normal chain-of-command.

Inuit — A group of culturally similar indigenous people inhabiting the Arctic region. Formerly referred to as 'Eskimo.'

IVeNS — Integrated Vehicle Navigation System. A combination of historic mapping, satellite updates, GPS and ground penetrating radar that ensures vehicles remain 'on-route' regardless of weather or terrain conditions.

Kalmar Union — The post-war European state that encompasses the former nations of Denmark, Norway, Sweden, Finland, Iceland, Greenland and their former territories in and around the Norwegian Sea. Capital City: Kalmar City. The name is taken from the previous union of these nations between 1397 and 1523.

klicks — A slang term for kilometres.

knot — A unit of speed used by shipping and aircraft, equal to one nautical mile (1.852 km) per hour.

Land Command — The overall authority on all matters appertaining to the ABCANZ Land Forces (Army).

LatCon — Latin American Confederation. A post war nation that includes all of Central and South America, less Brazil and a few islands in the Caribbean.

Lennox Group — An ABCANZ Federation engineering conglomerate. Global headquarters located in Nu New England. The company has four main business sectors: Industrial, Energy, Military and Healthcare.

Lennox Tower — Located at the tip of Manhattan in Nu New England, a needle-like tower that is the corporate headquarters of a global industrial conglomerate, the Lennox Group.

LEO — Law Enforcement Officer

less leather and metal — An unofficial expression used with Number 1 or

Number 2 Dress uniforms to indicate that swords, scabbards, sword belts, full size medals and headdress are not to be worn (usually because it is a social event), in which case a waist sash and miniature medals can worn in lieu.

Lublin Union — Also known as the Union of Lublin. A post-war eastern European nation comprising of the former states of Lithuania, Latvia, Estonia, Poland and Belarus. Capital city is Novi Lublin on the former Polish-Belarus boarder. The name is taken from a previous union of these states between 1569 and 1791.

M37 Assault Rifle — Standard issue, 5.56mm assault rifle of the ABCANZ Military. 40 round magazine. Effective range of 400 metres.

M49 Mines — Land mines that use chameleon circuitry and heat exchangers to mimic the surrounding terrain. Designed to neutralize foot soldiers in body armour or un-armoured utility vehicles.

MACC — Military Aid to the Civilian Community.

Magadan — The most easterly city in Russia on the Pacific coast. Became the home of the Russian Pacific Fleet, following the loss of Vladivostok to China during the war, despite being frozen up for four months each year.

Make Ready — The order given to change the 'state' of a weapon from 'loaded,' (magazine fitted, but no round in the chamber), to 'ready' by cocking the weapon and thereby chambering the first round.

Maori — The native, warrior race of New Zealand. The name of a Fast-Attack Corvette in the ABCANZ's 2nd Fleet.

Marlin torpedo — Mk67 Marlin. The standard sub-surface anti-ship missile used by the ships of the ABCANZ Fleet.

Mat-Su Valley — The farmable land between the Matanuska and Susitna rivers in southern Alaska.

Max Sec Florence — The ABCANZ Maximum Security Prison built in the Rocky Mountains at Florence, in the former state of Colorado. Thousands of kilometres to the nearest city and surrounded by the inhospitable, heavily contaminated and radioactive terrain of the mutant infested 'Badlands.'

Max Sec Narvassa — A former underground ABCANZ Maximum Security Prison built onto the tiny Caribbean island of Narvassa. Abandoned after a seismic shift caused extensive flooding.

Med Centre	Medical Centre.
medi-vac	Medical Evacuation.
Mercer	A district of Nu New England. Located within this district is one of the eight Ivy League educational institutions that combined post-war to form NNE University.
met-data	meteorological data (Weather conditions and forward forecasting).
MO	Medical Officer.
Mount Spurr	Highest volcano in the Aleutian Volcanic Arc of Alaska, 130km west of Anchorage. Last significant eruption was in 1992.
MSM	Meritorious Service Medal. Awarded to members of the ABCANZ Armed Forces for outstanding meritorious achievement, in a non-combat environment.
MQ-22 Griffin	An older, but combat proven Unmanned Ariel Vehicle (UAV) designed for long-range, high-altitude surveillance missions. Able to fly in any weather conditions.
MSZ	Manoeuvring Safety Zone
MT	Motor Transport. All Land Force units have some type of MT department. Responsible for the allocation of vehicles, drivers, their training, and the routine maintenance of vehicles within the unit.
mutant	Any life-form (including human) where it, or their parent's DNA sequence has been modified as a result of exposure to radiation, viruses or mutagenic chemicals.
nacelle	Usually a pod, separate from the main hull or fuselage, that holds engines, fuel, or equipment on an aircraft or a ship.
nano-techs	Tiny programmable robots capable of performing simple repetitive technical functions.
net	Slang term for a Radio Network.
NATO	North Atlantic Treaty Organisation. A collective defence treaty, formed in 1949. Responsibly expanded beyond military remit when United Nations disbanded in late 21st Century.
NGO	Non-Governmental-Organisation. Providers of specialized technical products, knowledge or services to support development or relief activities implemented on the ground by other

organizations.

nominal role
A list detailing the name, rank and service number of all assigned personnel.

Nu Alba
A small ABCANZ city located in the Lowlands of Scotland, running right across from the east coast to the west. The only city in Scotland.

Nu Auckland
The principal ABCANZ city in New Zealand. On North Island, this was the first region decontaminated after the war.

Nu Bohemia
The second largest city within the Nu Habsburg Reich, encompassing a large part of the former region of Bohemia.

Nu Britannia
The large ABCANZ city in England. Covers almost all the land of the south-east, or 'Home Counties' as far north and west as the former town of Northampton. Sometimes referred to as Brit-City.

Nu Canterbury
A small ABCANZ city on the east coast of South Island, New Zealand. The central part of the former region of Canterbury, it includes Banks Peninsula, Christchurch, Waipara and Ashburton.

Nu Habsburg Reich
A far-right post-war nation in central Europe, encompassing the former nations of Austria, Czech and Slovak Republics, Hungary, Slovenia and Croatia. Capital City: Nu Vienna. A large city within which are the former cities of Vienna and Bratislava to the south and Brno to the north.

Nu Hawaii
A small ABCANZ city in the Pacific Ocean spread around the apron of the three still active volcanoes on Big Island, Hawaii.

Number One Dress
The reference given to the uniform worn for formal Ceremonial and Mess occasions by the ABCANZ Military. The same tunic, breeches and boots are worn for both, but the 'accessories' are tailored to suit. (See 'less leather and metal.')

Number Two Dress
The reference given to the uniform worn for parades and when in barracks by the ABCANZ Military. The same tunic, shirt, boots and cap are worn for both, but the tunic and tie are omitted for everyday wear when in barracks. Usually only worn by officers when in barracks, and not the enlisted ranks.

Number Eight Dress
The reference given to the camouflaged combat uniform worn for everyday 'in-barrack' use by enlisted ranks and by all personnel when operationally deployed. This is standard 'temperate climate 'splinter' pattern' camouflage

on general issue to all personnel. Specific, non-standard camouflage patterns, such as those for desert, tropical or arctic environments are only issued as required and also have their own reference numbers.

Nu New England
: The vast, principal metropolis of the ABCANZ Federation, encompassing most of the original 13 States of the USA, the states south of the Great Lakes, as well as parts of southern Ontario and Quebec Provinces of Canada.

Nu Paris
: The joint capital city of the European Union. Built post-war, slightly further south than the old city of Paris, covering significant parts of the former regions of Bourgogne, Centre and northern Auvergne.

Oath of Allegiance
: The oath undertaken by all personnel at the beginning of their military training/careers.

Officer Ranks

Fleet	Land Forces
Admiral..................................	General
Commodore..........................	Brigadier
Captain.................................	Colonel
Commander.........................	Major
Lieutenant...........................	Captain
Ensign..................................	Lieutenant

Officers' Mess
: A military establishment, in which commissioned officers eat, socialise and are accommodated in isolation from the enlisted ranks.

OJAR
: Officers' Joint (Fleet and Land Force) Appraisal Report. An annual report written on all military officers.

ops-room
: Operations Room. A facility, manned 24 hours a day, where all incoming communications, reports and information are received, logged, analysed and processed.

Order of Merit
: An ABCANZ Federation decoration awarded to both civilian and military personnel for exceptionally meritorious conduct in the performance of outstanding services and achievements.

Orders Group
: Or 'O Group.' A prescriptive format of meeting in which commanders inform subordinates of their intentions.

OTA(F)
: Officer Training Academy (Fleet)

Pac-Rim En-Corp.
: Pacific Rim Energy Corporation. Original owners of the strip mining operation on the Chuitna River, Alaska.

Panama Scar — The location of the Panama Canal in Central America. Despite being 'nuked' during the war because of its strategic importance, it remains navigable, although the radioactive contamination in the area is still considerable.

Passchendaele — A series of battles fought between July and November 1917 for control of the ridge and village of Passchendaele near the Belgium city of Ypres.

Passing Out — A parade held at the end of the Commissioning Course for officers, Basic Training for the enlisted ranks, to mark their successful 'passing' from the civilian world into that of the military.

Peconic — The bay of water between the North Fork and South Fork at the tip of Long Island, in Nu New England. Popular for sailing.

Pennant — Abbreviated reference to 'Pennant Number,' the visual flag referencing system originally used to identify warships in 18th and 19th century. Duly replaced by numbers painted onto the hull in the 20th and later centuries.

p-file — Personnel File. The individual career records of each member of the military.

pooka — The most feared of the Irish fairy folk. Nocturnal, always creating harm and mischief.

Port Salish — An ABCANZ city on the Pacific coast of North America, encompassing parts of the former Washington state around Seattle and the parts of British Columbia around Vancouver and Victoria.

Poteen — A traditional and very strong Irish 'moonshine' whiskey, illicitly distilled from malted barley.

Praetorian — The elite Guards of the Emperor of Ancient Rome. The name of a Fast-Attack Corvette (K104) in the ABCANZ's 1st (North Atlantic) Fleet.

Quartermaster's Dept — A logistics facility on all military bases responsible for the storing, maintenance and issue of military equipment to base personnel.

Ranger — The elite US Army unit formed during World War II. The name of a Fast-Attack Corvette (K105) in the ABCANZ's 1st (North Atlantic) Fleet.

re-bro — Re-broadcast. The relaying of a radio transmission via another formation or vehicle.

Rhinestadt — The joint capital city of the European Union, situated to the east of the River Rhine encompassing the entire former German region of North Rhine-Westphalia.

RIB	Rigid Inflatable Boat
ROTL	Low risk, non-violent prisoners who are 'Released-On-Temporary-Licence' to work in the community prior to their release from incarceration.
rounds	Military terminology for ammunition. From bullets in a rifle, to shells in an artillery system, all are referred to as 'rounds.'
Rubicon	A river in north-eastern Italy. The idiom "Crossing the Rubicon" is to pass a point-of-no-return, and refers to Caesar's crossing of the river in 49BC, which was considered an act of war. The name of the sailing ship owned by the Severn family on Peconic Bay, Nu New England.
Samarkand	Second largest city in Uzbekistan. Major nexus of central Asian drug trade for many decades.
Samurai	The elite warrior class of medieval Japan. The name of a Fast-Attack Corvette (k106) in the ABCANZ's 1st (North Atlantic) Fleet.
San Angeles	The second largest city in the North American territory of the ABCANZ Federation. Encompasses most of the former state of California.
San Salvador de Americas	A large city of the Latin American Confederation situated on the Pacific coast of Central America. Includes all of the former nation of El Salvador and western districts of Nicaragua, Guatemala and Honduras. North of the contaminated region known as the Panama Scar.
sAPPHIre	s-ADVANCED PERSONAL PROCESSING HEURISTIC INTELECT-re. Shortened to 'Safi.'
Section	An ABCANZ Land Forces formation of four men, sometimes referred to as a 'fire team.'
Senior NCO	Senior Non-Commissioned-Officer. The group of ranks above 'Junior Ranks' and below 'Commissioned Officers.'
SCIF	A small, sub-surface craft used by the military for covert beach insertions from larger vessels. The abbreviated form of Scuba Craft Insertion – Fast.
Shinnecock	The location of numerous waterside marinas within the Suffolk district of Nu New England, at the far end of Long Island.
sit-rep	Situation Report. An update on the current situation.

skiff — A civilian corruption of <u>SCIF</u>. The smaller, faster, civilian version of the military Scuba Craft Insertion - Fast.

smart — Guided or programmable munitions intended to precisely hit a specific target, thereby minimizing damage to surrounding infrastructure. Opposite of 'dumb' or unguided munitions.

SOP — Standard-Operating-Procedure. A set of rules, instructions and guidelines that define routine procedures.

Southern European Alliance — A post-war European nation, also known as 'The Pigs.' (Portugal, Italy (southern half), Greece and Spain (southern half). The original 'break-away' states of the old <u>European Union</u> with less robust economies. Also included are the islands of Malta, Cyprus, Sardinia, Sicily and the Balearics for geographic, economic and historic ties. Capital city: Barcelona. Many of these regions had previous been united under the 'Crown of Aragon' from 1344 to 1713.

Spartan — The elite warrior culture of Ancient Greece. The name of a Fast-Attack Corvette (k107) in the ABCANZ's 1st (North Atlantic) Fleet.

Special Ops — Special Operations. An elite, Special Force unit within the ABCANZ Land Force infantry.

Speedbird Imperial Airways — Originally formed by the merging of the "One World" carriers: American Airlines, British Airways and Qantas. Subsequently merging with Air Canada, Air New Zealand, and US Airways of the "Star Alliance" to form a Federation wide carrier.

Squad — An ANCANZ Land Forces formation of eight men, usually in two sections or 'fire-teams,' each of four men.

Squadron — In the <u>ABCANZ Fleet</u> a formation of several ships. In the <u>ABCANZ Land Forces</u>, the title used by some <u>Branch-of-Service</u>'s for a formation the same size as a <u>Company</u>.

Standing Orders — A set of procedures for the everyday routine of a military facility.

Stern Chase — When the pursuing craft follows directly in the wake of the vessel being chased.

STR — Safe-Transit-Routing. A navigational route used by shipping to avoid wrecks and contamination. Categorised Green, Amber, Red and Black, depending on how 'safe' the route is.

Susitna River	A 500km river in central southern Alaska. Stretching from the Susitna Glacier to <u>Cook Inlet</u>.
Suez	The canal linking the Mediterranean with the Red Sea. Due to strategic location it was extensively bombed with Atomic, Biological and Chemical munitions during the war. Returned to operational status within ten years of hostilities ending, but region remains heavily contaminated and the Red Sea is infested with pirates.
tab	Slang term for a march or run with full equipment.
Table Mountain	A flat-topped mountain forming a prominent landmark overlooking the Southern African city of Cape Town. Defining battle of the African Campaign of the late 21st Century atomic war.
tam-o-shanter	The traditional Scottish headdress worn by many <u>Nu Alba</u> Regiments.
TDT	Tactical Data Tablet. An A5 sized 'ruggedized' computer, used by military commanders. Known universally as a 'battle-board.'
Templar	The elite warrior monks of the Crusades. The name of a Fast-Attack Corvette (k108) in the ABCANZ's 1st (North Atlantic) Fleet.
Terra-formers	Highly paid teams who clean up contaminated land, returning it to a usable condition.
Texas City	The third largest of the Federation's five North American mainland conurbations. Includes the old cities of Dallas, Fort Worth, Austin, Houston and Galveston.
thermo-baric	Thermo = heat and baric = pressure. The combined effects of heat and pressure as a deliverable weapon. Also known as a Fuel-Air Weapon, whereby the ignition of the fuel uses up all available oxygen. Napalm was an early, well-known derivative.
top secret	The highest level of Security Classification.
Triangulo de Caribbean	A large city of the <u>Latin American Confed.</u> <u>Central</u> The largest area is Port-au-Prince on Haiti, with sea-spans linking it to Kingston on Jamaica and Santiago on Cuba.
Troop	A Land Forces formation comprising of 3 'fighting' Squads and a command/support Squad. Usually 32 men strong, commanded by a Lieutenant.
Turkey	A nation located in both Europe (3%) and Asia

(97%). Its biggest city, Istanbul, was heavily contaminated with biological and chemical weapons during the war, but largely untouched by conventional blast or nuclear munitions. Decontaminated and now known as Nu Constantia, it replaced Ankara as the nation's post-war capital. Land remains heavily contaminated in the south-eastern regions along the border with the former countries of Iran, Syria and Iraq.

UAV — Unmanned Aerial Vehicle.

Ukraine — An eastern European state to the north of the Black Sea. Heavy contamination to the east of the country after the war following the extensive bombing of the River Don & Volga link to the Caspian. Principal city: Kiev. Second city: Sebastopol.

Uzbekistan — A poor, land locked nation in central Asia that was largely unaffected by the war.

Ville d'Azur — A large city of the European Union situated on the Mediterranean coast, in the area that was Provence and the Cote d'Azur of France before the war.

Vindictive — 'To seek revenge.' The name of an Aircraft Carrier in the ABCANZ's 1st (North Atlantic) Fleet.

Weapons Free — The least restrictive weapon control state. Weapon systems can fire at any target not positively identified as friendly.

Weapons Hold — The most restrictive weapon control state. Weapon systems may only be fired in self-defence or in response to a formal order.

webbing — The pouches worn around the waist by military personnel.

Western Cape — Originally a province in the south-west of South Africa. It broke away from being ruled from Pretoria during the war. Now an independent nation thanks to ABCANZ Federation intervention. Principal city: Cape Town. Closely allied to, but not a member of the ABCANZ Federation.

Whale Island — Fleet Gunnery School located on the southern coast of Nu Britannia, in the Portsmouth district of the city.

Willy Dall — A bar/diner in Anchorage, Alaska, frequented by the staff of the adjacent Port Authority, the Harbour Masters and by local dock workers.

Named after William Healey Dall a prominent naturalist and scientific explorer of Alaska in the late nineteenth century.

<u>wiring diagram</u> Military slang for an Organisational Chart, as it resembles an electrical wiring schematic.

<u>XO</u> Executive Officer. The appointment of 'second-in-command' on an ABCANZ Fleet ship or shore facility.

<u>Yukon</u> A former federal territory of Canada. The name of a Destroyer (D306) in the ABCANZ's 3rd (South Atlantic) Fleet.

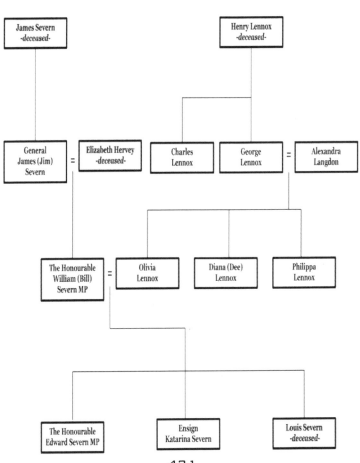

MENTIONED IN DESPATCHES

To Mike Shepherd and Kris Longknife, without whom this work would have never existed. Elements of this story are, undeniably, theirs.

A significant 'thank you' must also go to John Wagner, Carlos Ezquerra and Pat Mills, who captured the imagination of a ten year old boy and never released it. Elements of Kat Severn's world are an embellished adaptation taken from their numerous post nuclear conflict societies.

The inspired creations of the late Gerry Anderson and the influence they had on that same boy must also not go without special mention, as must those of the legendary George Lucas.

To John Welfare, a colleague from the military and a friend for over twenty years. A proof-reader and a 'sounding-board' for concepts in technology and plot, his corrections, council and sanity-checks were always greatly appreciated.

Dr Andrew Stewart of the Defence Studies Department of King's College London and the Royal College for Defence Studies at Shrivenham who provided ideas and insight into a possible late twenty-first, early twenty-second century world in the political and economic arenas, as well as the social, religious and environmental spheres that would undoubtedly influence a future global conflict.

It would be most amiss not to acknowledge the family and friends who were dragooned into proof-reading early copies. My very own 'Aunty Dee' who provided prompt grammatical corrections, combined with adulation and encouragement cannot go without special mention. As must Ian Wright and Karen Hewitt who also gave much valued comments and several suggestions for improvements during the early stages, along with later, but no less valued input from Gina Mombelloni, Gillian Brazier and Cousin Sam.

Mara Osio, who thankfully assumed the role of editor, cannot go unacknowledged. Her enthusiasm and focus, despite a very hectic personal schedule was little short of miraculous.

Chris and Dave at Packard Stevens Photography, ably assisted in hair and makeup by Nicola Moores, who took my random conceptual ideas for the front cover and turned them into an impressive reality and to Josie Hall for personifying Kat in those images.

My sincere gratitude to Pauline Tebbutt and the team at Fast-Print Publishing for their patience, assistance and professionalism.

Finally, the management and staff of the Comsa Palace Hotel in Brno, Czech Republic, where significant parts of this work were either written or researched during the evenings of numerous business trips over many months. The Movenpick Hotel in Taba, Egypt where a partial re-write was undertaken following those initial proof-reads, and the Centralny Hotel in Kedzierzyn-Kozel, Poland where the final version was eventually realised.